Give Me a Smile

by

Richard Veit

WingSpan Press
Livermore, California

Published in the United States and the United Kingdom by WingSpan Press, Livermore, CA

The WingSpan name, logo and colophon are the trademarks of WingSpan Publishing.

First edition 2023

ISBN 978-1-63683-052-0 (pbk.)
ISBN 978-1-63683-495-5 (hardcover)
ISBN 978-1-63683-958-5 (ebook)

Give me a smile
Give me a sense of who I am
Give me a breath of vanished days
And fires that once blazed within

from "GIVE ME A SMILE"
Don Black (words)
John Barry (music)

Give Me a Smile

Jonathan Michael Swenson was a radio announcer, assigned to the morning drive-time shift for the second lowest rated station in its big-city demographic. Although a college graduate, he had secured that degree in the liberal arts instead of something marketable. Consequently, Jon's salary amounted to a pale shadow of what his wife, Nikki, routinely earned as a loan officer for GoldSpire Bank. In many households, this would have been cause for marital strife. Not so with the Swensons. Jon's male ego was still reasonably intact, fed by the assumption that his next screenplay was sure to take Hollywood by storm.

Jon Swenson was an antiquarian at heart, chronically falling prey to the seductive lure of nostalgia. His favorite films, for instance, dated mainly from the thirties through the seventies, and rarely did he watch a television channel besides Turner Classic Movies. His most idolized pop groups were The Beatles and ABBA. He still used an outdated iPod, which contained over 650 hour-long episodes of "Lux Radio Theatre." The baseball teams that most captured his fancy were three historical curios: the Boston Braves, the Philadelphia Athletics, and the St. Louis Browns.

Jon's announcing duties ran each weekday morning from six to ten, hosting a smorgasbord of oldies from artists like The Grassroots, Dusty Springfield, The Beach Boys, and Neil Diamond, with an occasional Ray Conniff or Henry Mancini thrown in for the geriatric crowd. Jon liked the tunes quite a lot, but of course this retroactive format stood no chance in the ratings war against today's heavily promoted megahits. In his off-the-air hours each afternoon, he was a passive member of the station's sales team, mostly contacting potential clients via the telephone or email.

His wife, Nikki Swenson, did not share Jon's eccentricities, but she tolerated them to some extent. After all, she had become aware of his affinity for the past a long time ago, eleven months before the couple were pronounced husband and wife. She well remembered their second date, when Jon gave her the choice of going to the local multiplex for *Jurassic Park* or attending an out-of-town Buster Keaton film festival. Sensing his preference, Nikki chose the latter, and she was prone to humor him whenever such decisions arose. Viewed objectively, by every conventional standard, theirs would be described as an exceedingly happy marriage. And yet, that outward façade of stability was soon to be shaken from within, instigated by a seemingly inconsequential happenstance at his place of employment.

Between September and May, school groups occasionally toured the radio station's modest facilities, in the mistaken belief that these field trips were of some educational benefit. Students generally shuffled past the studio with nary a glance at what was going on inside. Jon would sit there behind the soundproof glass, imparting pearls of wisdom like "A monster hit of the swinging sixties, 'Nights in White Satin' from the Moody Blues' 1967 album *Days of Future Past*," or "That was 1973's 'Touch Me in the Morning' by Motown's supremely Supreme diva, Diana Ross." Most of the youthful onlookers had never so much as heard of these artists, prompting Jon's cynical side to speculate that the visitations were actually a ruse by which teachers could seek relief from the confinement of their classrooms.

But one particular tour proved to be different from all the others, possibly even life-changing. Through the studio's window, he saw a high school class from the suburbs, about two dozen boys and girls in number. Among those filing by was a dark-haired lass who could not have been much taller than five foot four, nor older than fifteen. Her sweet face did not alter its expression whatsoever as she gazed into the announcing booth and, briefly, at the disc jockey himself. Jon was stunned and could not take his eyes off her until she passed entirely from view.

Where had he seen her before? The answer, without question, was that he had never done so. Then why did her appearance affect him in such a profound manner? He could not keep his thoughts off her for the rest of the workday, long since her class's departure from the radio station. It finally struck him that the girl closely resembled someone he had known in previous years. This unsuspecting sophomore, whom he surely would never see again, brought to his mind the half-forgotten memory of Abby Pierce.

On the ride home, Jon continued to struggle with the enchanting vision. It threatened to overwhelm his emotions— and not in an altogether unpleasant way. In fact, thinking about Abby after all these years was a nice sensation, and he wondered whatever became of her and all the others in his Darnell High School class.

Nikki Swenson, thanks to her bankers' hours, was already in the initial stages of preparing dinner when Jon walked in the door. He greeted her with a kiss and began thumbing through that day's stack from the postman.

"Any bills, Nix?"

"Of course. What a silly question."

Jon flipped through the half-inch-tall pile, immediately discarding everything that appeared to be junk mail. He tossed a blue-and-orange brochure into the trash, just like he always did whenever one arrived.

After dinner, instead of focusing on his nascent screenplay, *A Murder to Die For* (working title), his thoughts drifted to that colorful brochure, which he promptly fished out of the wastebasket. On it was an internet address for accessing the Darnell High School web page, as well as a convenient registration form for the DHS Silver Jubilee Reunion.

But life is usually not as simple as an online button might suggest. For one thing, this decision would require a fourteen-hundred-mile journey. For another, he did not have a spare thousand dollars lying around in a shoebox. Even if he were able to beg off work, there was no guarantee that Nikki could do likewise, and it seemed irresponsible to go without her.

Jon paused for a moment, his cursor hovering over SUBMIT. How hairbrained it now seemed—signing up for such a foolhardy excursion, amidst veritable strangers, halfway across the country. Nonetheless, he could always enroll and then back out later, especially if Nikki held strong objections. He would not yet be committing any money to the undertaking, and there were nearly eight months left to reconsider. This PDF registration form was little more than a show of interest, an informal pledge that was anything but legally binding.

Click.

Jon Swenson's life settled back into its normal routine, and he forgot all about that tenth-grade cutie who triggered his impulsive contact with Darnell High School's alumni committee. But the committee did not forget about him.

During the week before Thanksgiving, another blue-and-orange piece of mail arrived. It was a picture postcard, depicting a cartoon horse with a speech balloon that said, "Pay up, pardner! Don't say NEIGH!!!" The horse was wearing a blanket bearing the initials DHS, and in the background was a football stadium whose scoreboard proclaimed, "Home of the Mustangs." On the reverse side, among a selection of disclaimer statements, one of the checkboxes was already ticked: "We have received your registration information. Please remit a deposit of $40 (payable to Darnell Alumni Association), with the balance of your fee due 60 days prior to the event. Hotel discounts are available. We look forward to seeing you at the Silver Jubilee Reunion in June!" It was signed, "Barbara Essegian, Reunion Committee Chair."

Jon gave the postcard a cursory look and flipped it onto the kitchen counter.

"What's that?" his wife asked. She craned her neck to see.

"High school reunion. I get them all the time." He handed the postcard to her. "At one point, I was actually toying with the idea of going," he said, "but now I've decided not to."

"How come?"

"Too expensive, and I'm not sure if I can get off work." He cleared his throat. "Besides, I wouldn't want to go without you."

"That's sweet," she said, "but don't worry about me. I wouldn't know a soul there anyway."

"You wouldn't go ballistic if I went?"

"I've always encouraged you to attend those reunions, ever since we were married."

"Maybe so, but I—"

"And you've never wanted to go, that's all."

Jon nodded. "True enough."

"So, feel free to sign up ... assuming we can rake together the plane fare, and you can get off work."

He stared at her in disbelief. "You're really serious about this, aren't you?"

"Absolutely. Lauren and I will be fine by ourselves. You know, doing girly things."

"Bonding."

"If that's what you want to call it," Nikki said. "It might turn out to be good for us."

"For you and me ... or for you and Lauren?"

"I meant Lauren, but who knows? Maybe both." She handed the postcard back to him. "The school's twenty-five-year mark won't ever come again."

Jon rubbed his chin. "We've never taken separate vacations before."

"This wouldn't be a whole vacation, would it?"

"Just a weekend ... the third weekend in June."

"So we'd still have our regular two weeks of vacation together. And you wouldn't lose any of your accrued days."

"Only one," he said. "It's a Friday-Saturday-Sunday event."

Nikki touched him on the nose. "Go ahead and take the plunge. You'll regret it if you don't. You've never been to one of these things, and you haven't seen your old pals for a quarter-century. You deserve to have some fun."

He scowled. "Is that what this would be?"

"You had fun at my college reunion, didn't you?"

"Oh, sure, like having all thirty-two teeth extracted, one at a time."

"It wasn't that bad."

"Okay, then ... a root canal without novocaine."

So it was decided. Having received his wife's blessings, Jon proceeded to send Barbara Essegian a check for forty dollars. Try as he might, he could not remember anyone by that name in his graduating class. Maybe that was her married name. He consulted his most recent edition of the Darnell High School *Corral*, but the three Barbaras among DHS seniors rang no bells in his memory. One was kind of attractive, but she did not look like somebody who would organize a social committee. Another had moved away before graduation, so she was out of the running. Probably it was the third one, Barbara Walsh, a mousy girl with crooked teeth—administrative material for sure.

The holidays came and went, and Jon Swenson made steady progress on writing his latest unsold movie script. As April drew to a close, he felt ready to disseminate query letters among a carefully selected assortment of motion picture agents, some thirty in number. No longer was the manuscript called *A Murder to Die For*, having given way to the more suggestive title *Kiss Me Where It Hurts*. Now all he could do was sit back and wait. By this stage of his literary career, he had become adept at enduring the sting of rejection.

All of May and the first half of June went by, and the only response from prospective agents was a substantial stack of form letters, all of them in the negative. Jon knew that *Kiss Me Where It Hurts* was better than most every movie he would watch that year, but there was nothing he could do to promote his stillborn project. Without proper representation in Hollywood, he had zero chance of landing a contract.

"Who do they think they are anyway?" Nikki said. She was indignant at how shoddily the New York and Los Angeles agencies were treating her husband's masterpiece. "Those arrogant hypocrites couldn't construct a screenplay of their own if their lives depended upon it. That's why they're agents instead of writers."

Jon shrugged his shoulders. "I've learned not to take it personally. Turning people down is what agents do for a living, mostly."

"That's a pathetic existence."

He could only chuckle. "These days, I count it a moral victory to get a rejection letter that's politely worded."

●　　●　　●

On the third Friday in June, Nikki drove Jon to the airport. It was a morning flight, so the couple would be apart for nearly three whole days—one of their longest spans of separation since being united in matrimony.

"Text me as often as you can," she said.

"Okay, will do."

"And remember that you'll be two time zones earlier than I am."

"In other words, honor the sanctity of your beauty sleep."

Nikki giggled. "Please do. There's not a minute to lose."

Jon walked alongside her toward the security area and reached into his carry-on for the boarding pass. "I wonder if I made a mistake, signing up for this thing."

"You'll have a wonderful time," she said. "Anyway, it's too late to back out now, and plane tickets aren't cheap."

"I'll miss you."

"Same here." She grinned at him. "Be sure to act your age."

"No problem there. Everyone will look like they're in their sixties or seventies ... except for me, of course."

"Of course."

They kissed, and Jon strolled away with a jaunty wave of the hand. Then and there, he decided to treat this weekend as one giant adventure. He would be lonesome, sure, and no doubt bored stiff, but old curiosities might be satisfied and old regrets laid to rest.

A flight attendant smiled at him as she passed by, rolling her piece of luggage. That made him feel good. Jon visualized Cary Grant as a middle-aged man and fancied that he bore a vague resemblance. Not that he was as handsome as Cary Grant, but he did have an air of burgeoning maturity about him, and that counted for something.

He sat next to the window, slightly behind the left wing, and peered at the tarmac while an airport worker tossed baggage onto a conveyor belt. As of yet, no one had sat in the middle seat, but an obese man with bald head and walrus mustache was on the aisle. Whoever claimed the B spot might be crowded for space.

Less than five minutes before pushback—just when Jon began thinking that he might have the luxury of an empty seat beside him—a teenage girl squeezed into the vacancy, careful not to jostle the aisle passenger's belly in the process.

"Hello, sir," the girl said to her neighbor on the left.

Jon nodded his head. "Hi there." Somehow, it was always a bit off-putting when young people addressed him as "sir"—not offensive, exactly, but akin to being slapped in the face by Father Time. Could he no longer deceive anyone into thinking that he was still in the prime of life?

He forced a smile. "Headed home from college?"

"No, sir. My grandmother died, and I'm going to her funeral."

"Oh. Sorry to hear that."

The airplane began rolling backward from the gate, and that marked the end of their brief conversation. Whenever he flew, Jon enjoyed staring out the window much more than chatting with random acquaintances. He always hoped that did not cause him to appear snobbish to others. In this case, it made scant difference, as the millennial female was already busy playing some video game on her cellphone.

The flight consumed three and a quarter hours and ended with a smooth landing on a wet runway. The Los Angeles forecast called for light rain throughout the afternoon and night, giving way to mostly sunny skies for the balance of the weekend.

When the obese man stood to retrieve his carry-on bag, the way became clear for the teenager to sidestep toward the aisle. As an afterthought, she turned to the gentleman next to the window. "Nice meeting you, sir."

"Yes, likewise." Jon returned the smile, but by then she was reaching up for her backpack, ear buds reinserted. Jon chuckled, envisioning this girl as she listened to a shuffled playlist during her own grandmother's funeral.

An airport courtesy van took him and a half-dozen other travelers to the hotel, which stood fourteen stories tall and was quite elegant for its mid-range $225 charge. The only reunion activities scheduled for Friday night were "Registration/Greeting" at seven o'clock and "Cocktail Hour" at nine. The first promised to be a two-hour stretch of preparatory dullness, and the second held no interest at all for him. That being the case, he took thirty minutes or so to simply browse around the lobby, eyeing people as he ambled along. It was fun to speculate whether any of them in their lower forties were former classmates. Who could say? Wearing the camouflage of twenty-five additional years, everyone would seem like a stranger to him.

Finally, Jon reported to the hotel's front desk, received his key card to room 819, and asked where he might find the Darnell High School reunion.

"Ballroom D," the attendant told him. He indicated a corridor near the elevators.

"Anyone here yet?"

"Oh, yes, sir. Lots."

That could wait. Upstairs in the room, Jon called home on his cellphone. "Nix! What's up, Sweetie?"

"Just a typical Friday night. We finished dinner, and Lauren has a date."

"Same kid as last week?"

"Uh-huh. John Lennon glasses and all."

"What's his name?"

"Jason, I think."

"Didn't she already have a Jason?"

"This is Jason the Second." Nikki giggled at her own joke, and even Jon had to laugh, despite the frustration of rearing a teenage daughter in the family.

"Why'd you eat dinner at home?" he asked. "Is Jason the Second too cheap to invest in a meal?"

"Broke. He bought a pair of tickets to the ReFlexion Dome."

"A rock concert?"

"Seems to be. Some group called Caliper Squid. They're very popular right now, according to Lauren."

"Expensive seats?"

"All she would say was 'mosh pit.' Have you heard of that?"

"Black-and-blue territory ... pretty rough," he said. "Can you tell her not to go?"

"Too late. Jason the Second picked her up ten minutes ago."

Jon showered, put on some casual clothing—slacks, no tie, shirt open at the collar—and went down the elevator. Sitting by himself in the hotel restaurant, he paid $28.95 for an eight-ounce sirloin, garden salad, and a medley of seasonal vegetables. Then it was off to Ballroom D and a close encounter with his distant past.

Inside the immense, rectangular room was a wooden table, behind which sat two women at their computer screens. Jon approached them a bit tentatively, trying to verify that he had entered the proper venue. Then he noticed the blue-and-orange tablecloth with a small DHS logo emblazoned upon it. The women chatted with each other and sipped their cups of coffee.

"Jon?" came a male voice from behind.

He turned around to see a portly gentleman with graying hair and a pencil-thin mustache—but no nametag. Embarrassed, Jon shook his head. "Hmm, I know the face, but I can't ..."

"Tyler Bohannon. Left guard on the football team."

"Of course! How are you, T. J.?"

"Married, with four kids," Tyler said. "You?"

"Married, with one. Are some of the old gang here?"

"Not sure. I just arrived."

"Did you marry a Darnell gal?" Jon asked.

"Initially, yes, but it didn't take. Third time's the charm, so they say."

One of the registration ladies interrupted, but very politely. "Excuse me, but are you gentlemen here to sign in?"

"Yes, ma'am," Jon said. He walked up to the table.

Tyler, though, waved to him and went the opposite direction.

"Mustang or spouse?" the registrar asked. She sounded blasé, as if tired of repeating that same question, *ad infinitum.*

"Mustang," Jon said.

She typed something onto the keyboard. "And you are ..."

"Swenson ... Jonathan Michael Swenson."

Jon stole a peek at her nametag: BARBARA ESSEGIAN. She was still mousy with crooked teeth.

"And are you staying with us at the hotel?"

"Yes, ma'am."

Barbara grinned. "You don't have to keep calling me 'ma'am,' you know. I already feel old enough, as it is." She handed him a nametag and circular badge. "Wear these whenever you're at one of our functions, so people won't have to wonder who you are. A quarter-century is a long time."

"Is Essegian your married name?" He knew that it was.

"Yes, I was Barbara Walsh in my school days."

"Did we know each other?" Jon asked.

"Apparently not. I don't recognize you."

"Same here. Sorry."

"Don't apologize," Barbara said. "Believe me, there'll be a lot of mistaken identities this weekend." She pointed toward her colleague. "I didn't meet Michelle Lockerie here until a couple of hours ago ... and we attended the same high school for four years, plus two years of junior high before that."

Michelle flashed a broad smile. "Isn't that a sad commentary on our social lives as teenagers?" Looking Jon in the eye, she blushed. "I do remember you, though. But I was too shy to start talking to a wide receiver."

"Don't worry about that now," he said. "I've lost most of my blazing speed."

Michelle had a ring on her left hand. So did Barbara. So did Jon Swenson.

"Here's your ticket for tomorrow night's dance," Barbara said. "It was included in the registration fee." She double-checked her computer screen and stack of nametags. "I don't find anything for your wife. 'Nikki,' is it?"

"Yes, that's right. She's at home with our daughter."

"How old is she?" Barbara asked. "Your daughter, I mean."

"Lauren is sixteen, going on twenty-one ... and there's certainly nothing wrong with *her* social life. She's kind of boy crazy these days."

"I remember."

Jon looked confused, so Barbara explained.

"How it was to be a sixteen-year-old girl. Those Friday nights, waiting for the telephone to ring."

There was an awkward silence, and Jon thought he could see some unguarded emotion strike the woman. She was quite homely, and her lifetime of private sorrow showed.

"Listen, maybe we can get together sometime this weekend," Jon said to her. "You, too, Michelle. That is, if your husbands won't mind." He grinned at both of them, and like most people will do in such a setting, they automatically responded with an affirmative nod.

When Jon was finished registering, he wandered around the hotel's main floor for over an hour, casually browsing through many of the shops. Not being a drinker, he had no desire to attend the cocktail hour. Nor did he wear his nametag or photo badge, preferring to remain anonymous on this first night of the reunion.

The main concourse offered a dozen or more large-screen televisions, most of which were tuned to Major League Baseball. Jon seated himself at one end of a plush sofa and watched, with little interest, an inning or two of some game between expansion clubs—the Rockies and Diamondbacks perhaps.

Or was it an interleague contest between the Blue Jays and Marlins? It made little difference to him. Jon loved baseball for its history, athleticism, and strategy, but he no longer paid much attention to specific teams. He could tell you that Rogers Hornsby hit .424 in 1924, and yet he would be hard-pressed to recall who was the most recent National League batting champ.

Sitting next to him was a young man wearing Los Angeles blue. "So, you're a Dodgers fan, I take it," Jon said.

"Always have been. My great-grandfather had season tickets to Ebbets Field. Rooting for the Dodgers is part of our family's DNA."

"Do you play high school ball?"

"Yes, sir, third base," the boy said. "I'm just a sophomore, so I'm on the JVs."

"Is your team any good?"

"Not very. We lose more than we win."

Soon thereafter, the teenager's father came into the lounging area. "Ready for a movie, Sport?" he asked.

The boy stood. "Dad, I was telling this man about Grampa Wicks in Brooklyn. What was the name of that hollering Dodger fan?"

"Hilda Chester ... back in the thirties and forties."

The boy looked at Jon. "Have you ever heard of her?"

"Sure have. After the Dodgers moved west, Hilda said she wouldn't be caught dead going to see them on the road in Philadelphia ... even though it was only a hundred miles away." He chuckled. "Ask your dad to tell you about the Sym-Phony Band someday."

"Okay. Goodbye, sir."

"Best of luck with your high school team."

"Thanks. We'll need it."

Father and son walked away, probably discussing baseball or that peculiar man who knew so much about a defunct club's equally defunct leather-lunged rooter.

In short order, Jon grew tired of the MLB telecast, so he abandoned the comfy sofa in favor of sauntering through the hotel's dining area, curious to know where breakfast would be served. En route, he remembered his promise to Nikki—to text her as often as he could—so he found a quiet corner to accomplish that task. Factoring in the two-hour time difference, she would be receiving the message at around 11:30 PM.

Texting was the extent of his technological prowess, and it was not something that came naturally to him. He relied upon his right index finger to tap the characters, whereas texters from the millennial generation were skillful at using alternating thumbs to compose their messages. Some of them were as fast as touch typists, but Jon's paragraph took him several minutes to write, thanks to his primitive, hunt-and-peck system.

> Hi, Nix.
> Have gotten registered. Just killing time tonight before going up to bed. Hotel is booked to capacity, but thus far I have only met 3 fellow Mustangs from Darnell High. Lots of DHS events on the schedule for tomorrow. No idea if they'll be worthwhile or boring because I don't know what to expect from such OLD people. ;-)
> The activities start at 10 a.m., so I'll have to eat an early breakfast. Love you, and nighty-night!
> J

He waited for a reply, but the *ding* did not sound until he was already lying in bed.

> Hi, J.
> Appears that you're having a wild and crazy time. Please keep things under control, won't you? :-) Lauren's current boyfriend, Jason II, is letting his hair grow. Looks like a mad scientist in some horror movie. Really don't know what L sees in him, but then I'm not a 16-year-old either. Text me again whenever you can, and I'll

do the same. Couldn't respond earlier because I was watching "Somewhere in Time" on TV and didn't want to leave Christopher Reeve all by himself. (Oh, wait. He does have Jane Seymour, doesn't he?) 'Bye for now, but we'll talk tomorrow. Lotsa love, sweetie.
N

Sleeping conditions on the eighth floor were ideal that night, and Jon dozed off mere moments after reading the text message from Nikki. But around 2:30 AM, he was startled awake by the sound of shouting and laughter beyond his door. Apparently, some unruly revelers had returned to the hotel following their bar-hopping exploits. Worse yet, instead of simply passing by on the way to their own rooms, they resumed their party right there in the hallway.

After trying in vain to muffle this commotion with a pillow over each ear, Jon considered calling down to the front desk. But then, while reaching for the telephone, he heard a familiar chant fill the air. It was rather subdued at first, but then each repeat became louder and louder until bursting forth in a deafening crescendo:

> Mustangs fight for Darnell High;
> V–I–C–T–O–R–Y.
> Blue and orange, be our guide;
> Hoist the colors up with pride.
> Fleet of foot and strong of heart;
> From Darnell High, we'll never part.
> Go, 'Stangs!

He was shocked. So these were his own kind—school chums and acquaintances, voices from the past. Moreover, they sounded very drunk and not at all like the innocent pals he remembered. Is this what he had to look forward to in the two days to come?

Even after silence was restored, Jon Swenson lay in bed for another hour before finally drifting off to a fitful sleep.

•   •   •

Standing in the bathroom of room 819 on Saturday morning, Jon Swenson stared at the reflection in front of him, and the corners of his mouth curved upward. Although no one was likely to mistake him for a lad of twenty-something, he could honestly contend that his appearance was holding up rather well, given the passage of years. Jon wondered how many of those in his graduating class could say as much about themselves. Whimsically, he hoped that the men had experienced a normal aging process, while the women had retained all of their youthful bloom.

Jon picked up his cellphone and began typing.

> G'morning, Nix.
> It's 7:30 and time for breakfast, which is included in the price of my room. I'll just eat a few bites because the meet-and-greet brunch is at 10. That will be our first big chance to renew friendships with old classmates. Last night, we were issued our nametags and photo badges, and those should help us to identify each other. I'm not wearing mine yet but will have them on by 10.
> Love, J

One problem with staying on the eighth floor was that the elevators usually made several stops on the way down to street level. Sure enough, when the doors slid open at the seventh floor, on stepped two couples. They were nicely attired and presumably in their middle to late forties.

The woman closer to Jon spoke in a hushed voice, as if this unfamiliar man might be planning to testify against her in court.

"Did you see what Kayla Jakes wore to the shindig last night?" she asked. "I never thought she was the type."

The other woman glared. "She certainly wasn't like that in high school ... not at all." Upon glancing at Jon, she stopped talking. Did she recognize him? Jon looked up at the lighted numbers, which he hoped would move to the left a little faster. His gaze only hindered the elevator's descent.

On the fourth floor, a family of five climbed aboard. They were casually dressed, perhaps on their way to one of the local amusement parks. Then, at floor number three, these ten occupants were joined by five additional guests of the hotel—two couples and their friend. That amounted to twelve adults and three children—plus four rolling pieces of luggage—all squeezed into a surface area of less than fifty square feet. "Don't anybody inhale," someone joked. Jon was pressed against the rear panel of the elevator, so he allowed the others to exit before doing so himself.

As he walked toward the restaurant, the lobby was brimming with customers. Overhead television screens carried ESPN, so Jon paused for a couple of minutes to watch "SportsCenter." His cellphone emitted its pleasant *ding*, signifying that a text message had arrived.

> Hi, J
> Have fun at today's brunch. Do you think most of the people will have spouses with them? Now that I think about it, maybe I should have come with you to California. Turns out that I'll be alone for most of the day because Rachel's parents have taken Lauren, Rachel, and Monica to the water park. They'll be back by 7 tonight, but that's not exactly the mother/daughter bonding I had in mind. Keep me posted about your reunion bash. Long-distance kisses to ya.
> N

After surrendering his breakfast pass at the restaurant's entrance, Jon proceeded along the serving line. It seemed a shame to consume such a paltry quantity of food at an all-you-can-eat buffet, but he did not wish to spoil his appetite for the mid-morning brunch. Scrambled eggs, bacon, a miniscule scoop of fried potatoes, and orange juice would suffice.

About thirty feet away, seated around an oval table, were eight couples who may well have been from Darnell High School. Something in the way the people acted caused Jon to suspect that half of them were old mutual friends who had not seen each other in decades. They appeared to be engaged in lively chatter, while their spouses just sat back and tried to look as amiable as the situation allowed.

One of the women facing his direction seemed vaguely familiar. Did she occasionally peer at him, or was that just his imagination at work? The longer he stared, the more certain he became of it. Further evidence emerged when this lady addressed the person across from her as "Abby."

Jon ate hastily, laid down an appropriate gratuity for the waitress, and departed from the restaurant. He wondered why he felt so nervous, so reluctant to encounter scarcely recalled contemporaries from his past. Perhaps it was the novelty of it all— leaping headlong into the unknown. Having never been to a class reunion before, he had no idea what to expect.

Back in his hotel room, it occurred to him that he needed a wardrobe modification. He sensed that the dark suit he had worn to breakfast might appear too funereal for such an upbeat occasion as the DHS brunch. All of those men around the oval table had been dressed in stylish, country-club apparel that shunned neckties and favored polo shirts with open collars. With that in mind, Jon went to the clothes rack and pawed through the few changes of attire that he had brought west with him. He draped two sport coats onto the bed and was comparing them, side by side, when the telephone rang.

"Hello?" he said.

"Hi, Jon," came a female voice. "This is Abigail Harker."

"Who?"

"Abby Pierce Harker. Do you remember me from high school?"

Jon swallowed hard. "Of course I do. Hello ... Abby."

"How would you like to escort me to the brunch this morning? My husband has to attend a business meeting across town, and Rhonda Burke said you were sitting all by yourself at breakfast ... looking very miserable and lonesome. How about it?"

"Umm, I'm not sure whether—"

"Come on. It'll be fun," Abby said. "You don't want to go stag, do you?"

"No, but—"

"Then drop by my room ... number 624 ... at about ten till, and we can go down together. Please say you will. I don't enjoy being a solo act."

"Won't your husband mind?"

Abby giggled. "Not if he doesn't know about it. Besides, our little rendezvous will be very innocent. After all, we can't get too outrageous at ten in the morning, with hundreds of people around."

Jon felt himself weakening. What harm could come from mingling in a crowd with an early-middle-aged classmate from high school, someone whom he had never even dated? "Okay, then. I guess I can be your escort," he said.

"My goodness! You don't need to sound so enthusiastic about it."

"I'm sorry. That didn't come out right, but you know what I meant."

"I'll accept that as a humble admission of guilt. See you in an hour or so."

"'Bye." She was really quite witty, this Abby, and much more outspoken than he would have thought. To calm his anxiety about the imminent face-to-face meeting, he resorted to a mental trick that is common among males of the species. He pictured the present-day Abby Pierce as wrinkled, morbidly overweight, and generally undesirable.

How wrong he was. The lady who answered the door to room 624 was every bit as pretty as when she triumphed as homecoming queen of Darnell High School a quarter-century ago. Abby's dark hair was piled high atop her head, her complexion was smooth and creamy, and her figure was shapely enough for a college coed to envy. Very few women in their lower forties would chance wearing such a short skirt, but she met the challenge with effortless aplomb.

Jon blushed at the delectable creature who stood before him. Never in his fondest dreams did he expect her to look like this. "Ready?" he asked. Trying not to act too tongue-tied, Jon invoked a broad smile to mask his jittery nerves.

But Abby could tell, and it seemed to amuse her. "Want to come in for a few minutes?" Clearly, she would not make this awkward moment any easier for him.

"Maybe we should go right down," Jon said. "Everyone will be waiting for us."

She grinned. "No, they won't. They don't even know that we'll be coming together. Anyway, these things never get started on time."

He shrugged his shoulders and, fearing the worst, followed her inside.

"Sorry I can't offer you a drink," she said. "All that I seem to find in here are six bottles of filtered water. Four dollars apiece, according to the tag."

Jon walked over to the window. "You have a good view on this side of the building."

"Except it's two floors lower than your room."

"How do you know that?" He fought back a smile.

"Same number as your telephone, silly. The front desk gave it to me."

"So much for security."

"Let me look at your photo badge," Abby said. She leaned closer to scrutinize it. "Same as in the *Corral*. I wonder why we never saw more of each other during our Darnell days."

"It's a mystery to me. Just flaky teenagers, I suppose."

All of a sudden, Abby darted across the room, scooping up some panties and a bra that were lying on the bed. "Oops! I wasn't expecting company, and my husband is used to seeing how untidy I am." She tossed the underwear into a drawer.

Abby's face had reddened, and—whether genuine or contrived—that bashful grin of hers was very becoming. She picked up a necklace. "Brent forgot to fasten this around me before he went. Would you do the honors?" She turned her back to him and waited.

Jon's fingers became the size of bratwurst, and he fumbled ineptly for several seconds. "I'm not too good at this sort of thing."

"Don't you practice on your wife?"

"Not very often."

"What's her name?" Abby asked.

"Nikki. We've been married for eighteen years ... almost nineteen."

"Kids?"

"Just one, a daughter." Finally, after a formidable struggle of eye-hand coordination, Jon was able to secure the tiny clasp. "There. I think that's got it." He gave a sigh of relief.

"And much appreciated too," Abby said. "I can never manage those by myself, so it's always nice to have a man around to help." She turned toward him. "How does it look?"

Jon gazed at the lovely pendant, an emerald gemstone surrounded by diamonds. Thanks to his assistance with the clasp, it now lay nestled in the cleavage of her low-cut blouse. He raised his eyebrows in tacit approval, and she smiled.

As they were leaving the room, Abby stopped to tell him something. "I wonder if anyone will think we're an item." She giggled, but Jon heard no humor. To him, those provocative words sounded very much like a tease.

•   •   •

Members of the decoration committee had done their utmost to make Banquet Hall C an inviting site for the brunch. Of highest priority to them was the color scheme of blue and orange, emblematic of Darnell High School's Fighting Mustangs. According to the publicity pamphlet, "This venue provides ample accommodations for 680, including our graduates, their spouses/partners, and other friends and guests."

Committee chair Barbara Essegian and her deputy, Michelle Lockerie, monitored the front door, certifying that everyone who entered was entitled to wear a DHS nametag and photo badge. In addition to serving as virtual tickets for admittance to the brunch, these accessories would help attendees to identify fellow classmates throughout the ensuing two days.

Some natural curiosity greeted the arrival of Jon and his pretty companion, the former Abby Pierce. Many in the crowd had seen her dutifully sitting next to hubby Brent Harker at breakfast only a couple of hours earlier, so her surprising choice of an escort caused more than a few heads to turn. In response to this rubbernecking, Jon tried to look straight ahead as he guided Abby toward a pair of vacant spots at the table.

"Welcome, one and all, to Darnell High School's brunch for the Silver Jubilee Reunion," former class president Deborah (Laine) Saunders said over the loudspeakers. "Each of you was presented with a door-prize voucher as you entered the hall, so please be sure to keep this handy for the giveaway that will conclude our proceedings, shortly before noon. There will also be door prizes at the dinner tonight."

The late-morning brunch offered something for everyone, including such delicacies as hash brown casserole, lemon poppy seed pancakes, fruit pastries, spinach puffs, blueberry scones, baked bacon-and-cheese rollups, cinnamon French toast bites, ham-and-cheese sliders, strawberry yogurt parfaits, Monte Cristo sandwiches, maple candied bacon, sweet potato hash, sausage gravy and biscuits, and broccoli cheese quiche.

During the meal, Jon recalled that Abby had been quite friendly, perhaps even frisky, in the hotel room. Now he was seeing another side of her. Once in public, she became sullen and aloof, hardly speaking to him unless it was to answer a direct question. While Jon's self-esteem may have suffered a blow, instinct assured him that it was all for the better. This might be a perfect time to end the mystifying charade before it spun out of control. And then he could enjoy the rest of the weekend in peace, no longer taunted by beguiling images from his late teens.

By precisely just such a margin did he underestimate the allure of Abby Pierce Harker's lovely face and figure. As they were exiting the brunch, she cornered Jon like an agile sheepdog. "I want to apologize for the way I acted in there," she said. "With all eyes on us, I couldn't risk showing too much familiarity. Some of those people are business associates of Brent, and his career depends on them. I hope you understand."

"Don't worry about it. I'm just glad neither of us had to go to the party alone," Jon said. "We'll probably bump into each other again before the reunion is over. Anyway, it's been great seeing you after all these years." If nothing else, this diplomatic stance would give her an easy option to dismiss him from her sight, should that be what she wished.

But Abby had different ideas. "Can't we stay together a little longer before we call it quits?" Grasping his forearm, she flashed a charming smile. "Brent will be in and out for most of the weekend, and I hereby volunteer to monopolize all of your time."

Jon was at a loss for words, so flattered that he could feel his face turning warm. He decided to come clean. "Listen, Abby, you're married, and I feel like some gigolo in a second-rate movie. Believe me, that's not who I am." He gave a shallow laugh. "Want to know how dull and predictable the actual Jonathan Swenson is? After I go upstairs to my room, I'll call Nikki on the telephone. We'll talk about our daughter and probably run out of interesting things to say well before we hang up. That's the *CliffsNotes* version of my humdrum existence."

For a wistful moment, she stared at him in silence.

"Even so," Jon said, "I'm pretty satisfied with my life, for the most part. I really shouldn't complain."

Abby's response, when it finally came, took him by surprise. "That sounds wonderful to me. I wish everybody could be that happy." She looked away. "I should be happy too. I have every reason to be happy, but I'm not. I'm pretty miserable, if you want to know the truth. And I think I'm making Brent miserable, too ... driving him away from me. Or maybe it's the other way around."

She seemed so sad, Jon thought, nothing like he would have expected. In high school, Abby Pierce had everything going for her: looks, intelligence, athleticism, personality. She was voted "Most Congenial" by her peers, and for very good reason. What was it that caused her to stumble so badly during the intervening years? Certainly, it was not a matter of appearance, for Abby remained as beautiful as ever.

They parted company without making any definite plans to meet again. Jon toyed with the idea of competing in the DHS bowling tournament, which was scheduled to begin at two o'clock. To do so, he would need to hitch a ride with someone else because he had not hired a rental car for the weekend. Other than the crosstown bowling alley, all reunion events were to take place right there in the hotel.

He viewed his cellphone while ascending on the elevator and noticed that Nikki had sent him an additional text—undetected before now because the phone was on SILENT. She had some startling news to convey.

Need to let you know that your father is in the hospital. No cause for alarm, though, because it doesn't seem to be anything serious. Your mother called to say that he had nausea and shortness of breath but never lost consciousness. Although the doctor did not diagnose a heart attack, your dad will stay overnight for observation -- just as a precaution, I suppose. Did you enjoy the brunch?

I ate some Chinese take-out, so don't feel too sorry for me. Lauren texted me to say that she is having a fun day with Rachel and Monica. She won't be home from the water park until 7, so it's lonesome and quiet around here.

X's and O's, N

Back inside his hotel room, Jon seated himself at the desk and laboriously tapped out a response to Nikki's text message.

Hi, Nix.

Please let Dad know that I'm praying for him. Since the doctor says it is not serious, I don't think there is an urgent need for me to leave the reunion early and rent a car to drive up the coast. Let me know if his condition worsens. Have you noticed that Mom can never remember my cellphone number and ALWAYS calls our land line? ;-) Here at the reunion, some sort of bowling tournament is up next, followed tonight by (ugh!) the Silver Jubilee Dance. Wish you could be here for that because you're already used to me stomping all over your delicate footsies on the dance floor. Felicitations from out west.

Love, J

Jon walked across the room and opened his laptop. Queued at the beginning of its inbox was an email message from Jeremy Kinnick, who was one of his best pals in high school. Jeremy was a multiple divorcé, having never found a compatible match in four attempts. He wondered whether Jon, a transplanted out-of-stater with no local wheels, might want to ride with him and his girlfriend to the bowling alley. Jon replied in the affirmative, despite his unremarkable average of 135 and not having bowled for almost a dozen years.

At 1:30, Jon climbed into Jeremy's late-model Lexus and sat in the back seat with Barbara Essegian and her husband, Harold.

"Nice to see you again, Jonathan," Barbara said. She had read it directly off his nametag. "Sorry to cheat, but I can't remember everyone by heart."

"That's understandable. I'll bet you'll be glad when all of this chaos is in your rear-view mirror."

She grinned. "Is it that obvious?"

"Not at all. You're running the gauntlet very well."

Her husband laughed. "It's totally crazy. She's been organizing this particular weekend for more than two years."

Harold Essegian turned out to be the best bowler among the thirty-two Darnell High School students and spouses who participated in the tournament. Eight of the lanes were reserved for DHS, and scores ranged from a high game of 281 by Harold, all the way down to a 12 by novice Brianna Hayes. She slowly rolled the ball from between her feet with the use of both hands.

In the mixed-doubles contest, Jon was teamed with unmarried Shannon Finney, who was an experienced bowler and bettered him by more than seventy pins. She was an attractive woman in both face and stature but decidedly masculine in bearing. Jeremy Kinnick assessed her in uncharitable terms. As Shannon was awaiting the ball return, Jeremy leaned toward Jon and whispered, "Your partner is making us look bad. I think she has more testosterone than we do."

Jeremy's girlfriend, Liza Janssen, was the polar opposite of Shannon—so emaciated that she had difficulty hoisting her ten-pound ball and, more often than not, delivered it straight to the gutter. She spent half of her time outside the bowling alley, surrendering, without much of a fight, to a compelling urge to smoke cigarettes.

•   •   •

"You don't actually need to dance at a dance." That is what Nikki Swenson told her husband on the telephone. "Big Brother won't be watching you from a wall screen."

"I don't mind dancing in the old-fashioned way," Jon said, "but I'm hopeless when it comes to these modern gyrations."

"Oh, please! You make it sound like you're already over the hill."

"Sometimes I think I am ... in terms of attitude. Who else would rather watch 'Upstairs, Downstairs' than 'Game of Thrones'?"

"Well, I still love you, even if you are a Neanderthal."

"Maybe I'll just hang around the punchbowl, drowning my sorrows."

"Will this be an alcoholic affair?" Nikki asked.

"Not the punch, I'm sure, but there will be a full-service wet bar. Most of my class probably indulges in adult beverages. I'm the odd exception to that rule." He feigned a gasp. "I think some of them even smoke."

"Nothing more radical than tobacco, I trust."

"Who can say? Like it or not, this is the twenty-first century." Jon thought he could hear muffled voices in the background. "Is that Lauren?"

"Yes, she just got home from the water park. Rachel is here, too, and both of them are as red as boiled lobsters."

Nikki greeted the girls, and they responded with some words that were unintelligible to Jon.

"Sounds like I need to let you go," he said. "Tell Lauren hello for me."

"Okay, Sweetie. Have fun at your degenerate party. All I ask is that you don't go necking in the back seat of someone's 1972 Chevy Vega ... you know, for old time's sake."

"I don't see that happening. It's too cramped in a Vega."

Nikki giggled. "Incidentally, what time will you get here tomorrow?"

"I have a three-thirty flight, and, with the two-hour difference, I think we'll land around nine. So I should be home by ten."

"Goodbye for now, Honey. I love you."

"See you soon. I love you too."

Jon laid down his cellphone and began dressing for the Silver Jubilee Reunion Dance. This was the single event that he dreaded above all others on the weekend's agenda. It was not so much the hobnobbing with utter strangers that bothered him. It was the prospect of being a dullard on the dance floor. His movements, as he perceived them, were strictly from the 1940s, and there would be no swing tunes or foxtrots at the DHS gala. Tonight would be the very farthest thing from a romantic *film noir*. Alan Ladd and Veronica Lake would be stopped at the door.

Before he left the hotel room, Jon gazed again at the image standing before him in the bathroom mirror. His aquamarine turtleneck looked nice beneath the stylish, azure-blue sport coat. His hair was still mostly dark and showed no signs of early receding. And when smiling, as he was now, he appeared to be a good ten years younger than his actual age. Is that how others saw him too? Hopefully so, but such conjecture was pointless, nothing but out-and-out vanity. He was a happily married man and no longer in the hunt. Jon reminded himself that it should be of little concern what the Darnell High School women might think of him. But he was only human.

He heard a knock at his door. When he opened it, there stood Abby Harker. "Ready to take me to the dance?" she asked. Her sparkly, royal blue gown was flattering to the figure—alluring, but within the bounds of good taste.

Jon gave her a playful smirk. "Sorry, but I didn't know that was my assignment."

"Of course it is. Don't you remember when I volunteered to monopolize all of your time?"

"Yes, but I don't recall granting my approval."

Abby could tell he was only joking. "Then again, if you'd rather not, that's fine with me." She turned away but paused after a single step. "I thought you were all by yourself and might appreciate a fellow Mustang to dance with and talk to. Some big-shot producer gave Brent a box seat to the Dodgers' game, so I'm on my own again. That happens quite a lot lately." She squinted at Jon, and the corners of her mouth crept upward. "Oh, I get it. You have another date, right?"

He laughed. "Actually, I've only met a few people so far, and none of them have expressed any interest in being my dancing partner."

"Well, I certainly won't impose, if you'd rather go stag."

"It's not that," he said. "I just don't want people to get the wrong idea ... especially your husband."

"Or your wife, if word ever got back to her about what a blast we had together."

Abby beamed at him, and the sight of it melted Jon's heart. She had haunted his memory for decades, and now that same idealized image was here in person, less than an arm's length away.

"Come on," Abby said. "It'll be more fun this way ... for both of us." She winked. "Besides that, I might get a chance to make a few old flames jealous."

Jon gazed at her for several seconds. "You never give up, do you? You're still fighting your old high school battles."

"Not really, but I do like a good challenge."

"Is that what I represent to you?" he asked.

"Maybe. I never got to know you when we were younger, so this might be an amusing way to spend our time at the reunion. You're here by yourself, and ... as it turns out ... so am I."

Abby had applied make-up very sparingly, but it brought out the loveliness of her eyes, a blue so deep that it caused Jon to inquire whether she wore contact lenses.

"What sort of question is that?" she said. "Absolutely not. My eyes are still twenty-twenty ... like they were in high school when I used to watch you from four rows back in English class."

"You did?"

"Couldn't you feel my stare burning through your letterman's jacket?"

"I didn't know you had designs on me."

"Nothing of the sort, so don't get conceited about it. I liked all the boys ... and played fast and loose with most of them." She lowered her voice. "It might surprise you to know that girls were more promiscuous than guys during our DHS years."

"That's not the way I saw it."

"But you weren't a part of our wild crowd, as I recall."

"No." He could think of nothing to add, so he just gave her a sheepish smile.

Abby eyed her wristwatch. "Come on, or we're going to be late. Can't keep our audience waiting."

Jon joined her in the hallway and shut the door behind him. "Wait a sec. I need to send a quick text." He pulled out his cellphone and typed a few words.

> On my way to the dance. Please keep me posted about Dad.

Abby waited patiently for him to finish, amused by his one-finger typing style. "I have an idea. Let's play like we're on a date," she said. "That's what reunions are for, isn't it?"

"Couldn't prove it by me. I've never been to one before."

She grinned. "So I've noticed."

A moment later, just as Abby took his arm, Jon's cellphone *dinged.* He read its message while they walked to the elevator.

> Feeling lonesome here, but I hope you're having a good time! Let me know how it went.
> Luv u

"What's your wife's name?" Abby asked.

"How'd you know it was my wife?"

"By how embarrassed you were when you saw it."

"Oh."

"What's her name?"

"Nikki. I told you that."

"Is it short for 'Nicole'?"

"Nope. 'Nikki' is right there on her birth certificate, so she tells me."

The elevator arrived, and Abby seemed to be acquainted with four of the people on it. She nodded to them and squeezed the arm of her "date." They stared back with interest but did not say anything to her. None of them wore nametags or photo badges, so perhaps they were unknowns and Abby was only trying to be friendly. In any case, it was a long ride down, with the elevator picking up two or three people at every floor.

Finding the Silver Jubilee Reunion Dance's venue proved to be quite easy. Jon and Abby simply followed their ears toward where the noise was leading them. She was in the highest of spirits, pivoting her head back and forth to see whether anyone recognizable was lingering in the vicinity. He, however, wanted nothing more than obscurity. If only this were a costume party, and he could hide behind a mask. No such luck.

Still, while the whole evening went against Jon's better judgment, there was also a positive side to the equation. Being with the prettiest girl from his graduating class certainly did beat standing in the stag line with old maids and confirmed bachelors. Besides, the first pitch at Dodger Stadium was 6:10, so husband Brent could not possibly make an appearance at the dance before ten o'clock. More likely, he would be out until well past midnight, bending his elbow with the Hollywood crowd at some trendy nightclub.

•   •   •

The Showcase Ballroom was a mass of humanity, pulsating with the ebb and flow of exuberant chatter. Folks who had not seen each other for a decade or two were determined to make up for lost time. Those for whom such reunions were a periodic habit exchanged cordial nods and smiles with their fellow regulars. The dining tables were circular, seating a dozen attendees at each, but that still left plenty of open space for the dance floor and a DJ's audio console.

Although Mr. Swenson and Mrs. Harker were a mismatched couple—each married to someone else—that did not stop Abby from fawning all over her escort. "Oh, yes, we've been great friends ever since high school," she told several observers. "More so now than ever before." No one in the reunion class was bold enough to inquire about the whereabouts of Brent—partly because he was a shadowy figure to most of them, and partly because it would call into question Abby's character.

Being the polite sort, Jon pulled the chair out for her when they sat at the table. "Is that something you do for Nikki too?" Abby asked. Her eyes twinkled with mischief.

"Never," he said. "I don't know any married people who go to that extreme. Do you?"

"Sure … plenty of them. Women like to be treated like royalty every once in a while."

"Does Brent treat you like a queen?"

She laughed. "Used to. Now it's more like a maid, to be honest with you."

He passed her the balsamic vinaigrette, and they began eating their salads.

"How long have you two been married?" Jon asked.

"To Brent? Twelve years. He grabbed me on the rebound." Abby stirred some sugar into her iced tea. "My first husband was an alcoholic, but he never would admit it. He's dead now. Lushed himself to death."

"Any kids?"

"A daughter with Rickie. None with Brent," Abby said. "Brent thinks more about his work than anything else. That's all he ever thinks about. Right at this very minute, I guarantee you that he's more focused on his current movie project than he is on the Dodger game."

"Brent's in the film industry?"

"Yep. That's how I met him. He was dating one of my friends, who at the time was trying to become an actress. Miserable failure."

"What does Brent do?"

"In Hollywood?"

"Yes."

"He used to be a frustrated writer of screenplays, but now he's gone into the editing side of things. That's his true calling, and he loves it. Always working because Hollywood grinds out scripts like sausages."

Jon was impressed. "Has he edited any movies that I would know?"

"Frankly, I don't have a clue. He doesn't let me into that part of his life."

By now, servers were circulating about, bringing plates of food to the reunion guests. There was sliced beef in gravy, stir-fried green beans, twice-baked potatoes with cheese, and hot yeast rolls. Dessert was already on the table—a generous slice of chocolate meringue pie.

To Abby's right sat a handsome man with a neatly trimmed beard. As people customarily do at stilted affairs in public, he started talking with her to open the conversation. "Hello. I'm Colby Reed."

The name struck a chord. "Colby?" She reached out and turned his photo badge toward her. "Colby! Don't you recognize me? I'm Abby Pierce. We dated twice ... until you started going steady with Rebecca Shaw."

"Sure ... of course! How are you, Abby?"

"Not too bad. You?"

"Great!"

"Did you ever get serious with Rebecca?" she asked.

Colby grinned. "Not legally, if that's what you mean. No, she moved to Europe somewhere ... Spain, I think, or maybe it was Portugal. Married a big international businessman and roams the world with him. Last I heard, anyway."

"Are you here alone?"

He blushed. "Pardon me. This is my wife, Talia." Colby motioned to his right, where a black-haired beauty sat with an icy expression on her face. She nodded in Abby's general direction but had nothing to say. Instead, she resumed a discussion with the woman to her right.

Abby ignored the affront. "Colby, do you remember Jon Swenson?"

"Can't say that I do, but nice to meet you." Colby reached across Abby's plate to shake hands. "Sorry. Not very good table manners, I guess."

From that moment on, Jon possessed a good deal less than half of his date's attention. While Colby Reed never seemed to talk with his own wife, he re-established a warm liaison with high school charmer Abby Pierce. "I'm Harker now," she told him, "but what's in a name?"

"Nothing to me. I still think of you as 'Pierce'."

She patted his hand. "Remember that lazy afternoon at Fremont's Arcade?"

"Shhhh!" Colby peered at his oblivious wife. "Some things are better left unsaid."

· · ·

Following dinner, the evening's disc jockey launched into a set of recorded tracks from the early '80s through the late '90s. Colby leaned toward the subject of his renewed friendship. "Care to dance?" he whispered. To Abby's credit, she gave her escort the courtesy of a quick glimpse before accepting the offer. This did not disappoint Jon because the dance tunes were far beyond his skill level. He even considered slipping away from the whole ordeal for good.

It was Barbara Essegian who brought an end to that ill-conceived plan of action. "Mind if I sit here?" she asked.

"No. Not if Abby doesn't. It's her chair."

But Barbara did not sit. "On second thought, let's get some punch."

"Okay. Sounds fine." Jon chuckled. "Is it spiked?"

"Not by me, certainly. I'm not a drinker."

"Nor am I. What a couple of deadbeats we are."

Barbara motioned with her eyes. "On the other hand, there's quite a crowd over at the wet bar. Much more popular than our miserable punch bowl."

They poured the fruity beverage into two cups and, in silence, scanned the scene before them. After Jon took a sip, he posed a mundane question. "How's it going so far, Madame Secretary ... a success?"

"I would say so. No major disasters to report."

"Is Mr. Essegian here?"

Barbara sighed. "My husband is upstairs, in our room. Unless I'm mistaken, he's probably crunching numbers on his laptop. He's a C.P.A., and very good at what he does."

"He's also a great bowler. What's his name again?"

"Harold." It sounded bland, coming from her. "He figured he'd feel out of place in this environment, and he might be right. The bowling alley is a different story."

"Then I take it, he's not a Darnell High Mustang."

"Oh, no. Harold is from all over the country. His father served in the United States Air Force, and the family was constantly moving ... never in one place for more than two years."

"So, how did your paths ever cross?"

Her face turned red. "You'll only laugh."

"No, I won't. I promise."

"Harold rubbed meat tenderizer onto my jellyfish sting."

"He was a lifeguard?"

"Part-time, at Seal Beach. He was studying accountancy in college." Barbara took a sip of punch.

"Do you have any children?" Jon asked.

"Three ... two boys and a girl. Our daughter is a freshman at San Diego State, and our sons are still in high school."

"Not at Darnell, though."

"No, not Darnell. We live thirty miles away, up in Santa Clarita."

A bespectacled man with thinning hair poured himself some punch. He eyed Jon's nametag. "Jon Swenson, I see."

Jon smiled. "That's right. And you're ..."

"Riley Forbish." They shook hands. "We were on the basketball team together ... but you got a lot more minutes than I did."

"Riley, sure! Pretty decent rebounder, as I recall."

"That's all I could do. Too many turnovers to get much playing time." He nodded and began walking away. "Good to see you again."

"You too."

Jon noticed that a song had ended, and some of the dancers were returning to their tables. "Maybe I should get back over there," he said to Barbara.

"How come?"

"I brought a 'date' ... sort of ... and she might be wondering whatever happened to me."

"Abby? I wouldn't worry too much about her. She always lands on her feet."

Such a catty remark—especially when coming from someone as meek as Barbara Essegian—had razor-sharp teeth. Jon's eyes widened, and he could not resist pursuing the matter. "How much do you know about Abby Pierce?"

"Just whatever I've learned over the past quarter-century or so."

That took Jon by surprise. "You two stay in touch?"

"Hardly! In addition to being the Reunion Committee Chair, I'm also President of our DHS Alumni Association. I receive lots of correspondence ... some of it not meant for public scrutiny, so to speak."

"Spicy gossip?"

"Deeper than that," Barbara said. "Quite a bit is fully substantiated and from reputable sources. I can't go into any detail, but suffice it to say that Abby Pierce ... excuse me, Mrs. Harker ... won't be wondering about your whereabouts for very long. Believe me, she's not the lonely sort."

Jon finished drinking his punch, and he laid the empty cup on a collection tray nearby. "Still, I feel some sense of obligation to Abby, having escorted her to this event."

Barbara rolled her eyes. "You're both staying in the very same hotel, for goodness sakes. Basically, all you did was share an elevator ride with her, nothing more ... and Abby probably pushed the 'down' button."

Jon laughed. "She did, as a matter of fact. What does that have to do with anything?"

"Not much. Just a character trait, her Type-A personality on display." Barbara reached toward him, and they shook hands. "Very nice talking with you, Jonathan. Glad you could come, after all these years of sending your regrets."

"Well, L. A. is a long way from my home now."

"Your wife didn't care if you made this trip without her?"

"Didn't seem to. In fact, she's always encouraging me to come." He smiled. "I don't think she senses any great danger. I'm not the wandering type."

"It's not you I'd be worried about."

●   ●   ●

By the time Jon went back to the table and sat down, all remnants of the meal had been cleared away by the efficient dinner staff. Two chairs on either side of him were unoccupied, which meant that the closest person to his right was Talia Reed, who possessed an exotic beauty that suggested a half-Asian lineage. Comeliness aside, she was a dour presence, aloof to the point of impudence. Jon caught her eye, nodded hello, and was promptly rebuffed with a haughty sneer. That was the last overture she would get from him.

Abby was nowhere to be seen, although the sheer bottleneck of dancers made it difficult to determine whether she was among them. Strobe lights and an overhead bank of atmospheric dimmers compounded the problem. Within twenty minutes, Colby Reed returned to the table, alone, and bravely endured what he knew was sure to come, a glowering reception from his aggrieved wife. Better to suffer it in public than behind closed doors.

Jon bided his time by being force-fed a steady diet of dance tunes. To an oldies radio announcer, each track sounded interchangeable with the others, products of manipulative promotion. But his sonic melancholy changed when the loudspeakers eventually carried a song that was familiar to him— "Head Over Heels" by the Swedish group ABBA—and Agnetha Fältskog's soaring vocal embraced him like a long-lost friend. How strange that no one beyond the dance floor even seemed to hear it. Jon felt like an anachronism, woefully out of touch with modern times.

Colby leaned toward him, as if he were about to confide some classified information. "Abby wanted me to tell you that she'll be back as soon as she satisfies her conga line of dance partners." He raised his eyebrows, the visual equivalent of a wolf whistle. "I think Abby Pierce is the only girl in our class who hasn't aged."

"Healthy genes, I guess."

"Not just that. She works hard at staying fit. Spends lots of time in the gym, so she says, and I can believe it." Colby made sure that Talia was not listening. "In case you haven't noticed, Abby's muscle tone is as firm as a twenty-year-old."

"Brent's a lucky guy," Jon said.

"Who's Brent?"

"Her husband. I thought you knew him."

"Nope. I didn't even know she was married." Colby eyed him more closely. "Then why'd she come here with you?"

"Brent's at Dodger Stadium."

"So, how did you get chosen?"

"I happened to be handy at the right time, and she didn't want to attend this soirée by herself. Besides, I get the impression that Abby enjoys playing the field, which she couldn't do with a husband nosing around."

Colby grinned. "Reunions are a good excuse to act like you're still single. Some of those guys are trying to get Abby plastered."

"No kidding?"

"Can't you see her over there?" He pointed toward a rowdy cluster near the DJ console.

"Yeah."

Colby shook his head, more awestruck than disgusted. "She's got a drink in one hand and hasn't missed a beat."

What he alleged did prove to be accurate. Abby was quite wobbly when she finally returned to her chair. "Jon-Boy, you're missing all the fun," she said. "Hurry over there before time runs out."

"Sorry, but that music's too fast for me."

"So's the company, I'd wager." She giggled at him.

"No doubt," Jon said. Nervous and humiliated, he cleared his throat. "Listen, I think I'll be calling it a night, if that's okay with you."

"Aw, please stay! Don't be a party-pooping spoilsport." Abby's slurred speech made that sound extremely funny to herself. She bent over laughing, which caused the top button of her dress to come unfastened.

"Seriously, I'm about ready to leave," Jon said. "Can you find your way back to room 624 all right?"

"No!" Abby shouted. "No, I can't!" Heads turned toward her. "I'll be needing some assistance from you, or I'll get lost for sure." She giggled again, the liquor exerting its hold.

Noticing this, Jon gave an apologetic look to those around him.

That was when Abby stood up and gently tapped her tea glass with a spoon. "Ladies and gentlemen, Jon Swenson and I are going up to my bedroom right now, and no one can stop us. Not even my husband, who is at some stupid baseball game instead of at this dance with me."

Colby jumped to his feet too. "Take her hand, and I'll grab the other one," he said to Jon. "We need to get her out of here ... fast!"

Jon did as he was instructed, very nearly cutting his finger on the prongs of Abby's opulent wedding ring.

"Come on, Ab," Colby said in a baby voice. "You'll be fine in the morning." He smiled to the crowd as Jon helped him usher their unruly classmate from the ballroom.

"Where are you taking me?" Abby asked. Her mind was addled, as if awakening from a surrealistic dream. "We haven't even had the door prizes yet."

"You'll be fine in the morning," Colby said again.

• • •

Abby was surprisingly docile until they exited from the elevator onto the sixth floor. Then she broke into song, chanting the weekend's most ubiquitous refrain at the top of her lungs:

> Mustangs fight for Darnell High;
> V–I–C–T–O–R–Y.
> Blue and orange, be our guide;
> Hoist the colors up with pride.
> Fleet of foot and strong of heart;
> From Darnell High, we'll never part.
> Go, 'Stangs!

She sang it over and over again, never imagining that this quatrain was anything but well received by those already in their rooms for the night.

At the door numbered 624, Colby interrupted Abby's unmelodious crooning with a simple question. "Do you have your room key?"

She pointed to Jon. "I gave it to that gentleman there. He was going to use it later tonight."

"No, you didn't," Jon said. "It must be in your purse."

Abby knelt down and turned her purse bottom-side-up, scattering its contents onto the carpet.

Colby spotted the plastic card and swiped it through the room's scanner. Then he propped the door open with one foot while Jon used the side of his hand to slide Abby's toiletry articles back into her purse.

"What now?" Jon asked.

"I don't know. Let her sleep it off, I guess." Colby began dragging the girl by her shoulders, and Jon joined in the effort.

Abby was, by now, digging in her heels, fighting their every move. "I don't want to go to sleep. I haven't won any of my door prizes yet."

"Hush, girl. You can win them later," Colby said. With some struggle, they managed to place her onto the bed.

"I don't want to wrinkle this expensive dress, Jon-Boy. Hand me my nightgown."

Jon shook his head. "Don't worry, Abby. It won't hurt the dress for a few hours ... until Brent comes back."

Abby began pouting. She sat up in bed and reached behind for the tiny metallic slider to unzip her full-length party gown. "Will somebody please help me?"

Colby looked at Jon and laughed. "Here is the moment of decision for us."

"Wait a second," Jon said. He searched his cellphone for ESPN. "Looks like the Dodger game is a final."

"Uh-oh." Colby turned to the woman. "Pay close attention, Ab. There's no time to lose. If you roll onto your stomach, we'll pull your zipper down and then leave the room. And you can take it from there. Got it?"

"Got it!" She consented a little too willingly, Jon thought, and his instincts were well founded.

Not only did Abby fail to roll onto her stomach, but she started wiggling out of her stunning gown from the bottom hem upward. This worked well until she reached her bosom, and the bunching material caused a snag.

Jon got the merest glimpse. "Are you not wearing a ... ?"

"Why should I? This gown is self-supportive."

"Uh-oh," Colby said again.

Abby gazed at the men. "We're all adults here. There's nothing to be bashful about."

Colby shifted into high gear. "Listen, Jon. This is definitely a compromising situation. Go to the elevator and intercept her husband, if he happens to show up."

"Why should I go? Abby's my date, not yours."

"But I don't know what her husband looks like."

"Neither do I."

"Then there's no choice. We both have to leave ... and I mean now!"

Abby panicked. "You can't leave me here all alone. I'll strangle myself in this straightjacket."

"Shhhh! Do you have a picture of your husband?" Jon asked her.

"In my billfold."

Colby tossed the purse to her, and she knew right where to find the photo. "This is Brent." Both men studied it.

For the first time, they could sense that Abby was enjoying this little escapade. "Okay, who gets to stay?" she asked. "He'll be the winner, I promise."

Colby held a quarter in front of Jon's eyes. "Flip?"

"I always guess wrong."

"Good! Call it." The coin spun into the air.

Jon vacillated between his choices. "Tails."

George Washington's likeness lay face-up on the bedspread, mocking him.

"Or we can count on the Los Angeles traffic to save our bacon," Jon said. "Besides, Brent might have gone to some bar."

"Too risky. You lost, fair and square. Now, go."

Outside the room Jon went, trudging all the way back to the elevator. No one came into view for ten minutes, and that first person was Colby Reed. He was smiling but mute.

"Well?" Jon asked him.

"Mmmmm."

"What happened?"

"Like I said, our lovely Abby Pierce has some very nice muscle tone."

That was too much for Jon to take. "Now it's your turn to watch the elevator while I go back inside."

"That wasn't the agreement, pal. Anyhow, it's too late."

"Why?"

"She's sound asleep ... under the covers."

"How much ..." Jon struggled for breath. "How much did you see?"

"More than I expected."

"Tell me."

Colby grinned. "Sorry, but I'm not allowed to betray the confidence of a woman in distress."

"Distress! She was loving every minute of it."

"By the way, she wondered where you were. 'Nothing wrong with a *ménage à trois*,' is what she said." Colby chuckled. "I didn't know our Abby spoke such beautiful French."

Jon frowned. "And I was down the hall on look-out duty."

"Believe you me, I'll pay in spades for this innocent fling," Colby said. "Now I have to face Talia, and she'll try to drag it out of me. She's very good at that ... tenacious."

"You'll tell her everything?"

"No. I'll stop well short of that. Discretion is the better part of valor."

"How so?"

"I'll paint us as tonight's heroes, taking Abby away before she totally ruined her reputation, such as it is. I'll leave out the raciness, for my own survival as a married man."

Jon gave a loud sigh. "You know, when all is said and done, I think Abby came out on top. She probably had the most fun of anyone at this reunion ... teasing the Darnell High boys, just like old times."

"You may be right about that," Colby said. "She's a firecracker with a short fuse. I wouldn't have missed this for the world."

"Easy for you to say, having won the coin toss."

Back to the Showcase Ballroom they went, and several people inquired about Abby Harker's health. "She'll be fine," was their standard reply, "after a few hours of sleep and the inevitable hangover."

The men went their separate ways, Colby reclaiming his chair at the table and Jon meandering over to the refreshment spread.

"Abby won a door prize," Barbara Essegian said to Jon, "but she forfeited it by not being here in person."

"Do you remember what it was?" he asked.

"An iPad tablet."

"Uh-oh! That'll disappoint her."

"Serves her right."

Jon gave that some thought. "There's really no reason to mention the iPad to her, so I hope you won't."

"Why not?" Barbara asked. "How can you be so considerate to her after the way she treated you?"

"Oh, she's all right."

"No, she's not. From what I can tell, she's just a glorified hooker."

Those words came as a shock. "I don't think you should call her that," Jon said. "There's a lot more to Abby than you could possibly know. Deep down, she's a very unhappy person." He fought back a wave of emotion. "For my sake, try to give her the benefit of the doubt."

"If you say so, Jonathan, but my heart's not in it."

"Thanks. I kind of feel sorry for that girl. Her life hasn't turned out the way she had hoped."

Barbara's face darkened. "I guess we could say that about most of us."

●   ●   ●

Both Nikki and Lauren were awake and waiting for Jon when he parked his Ford F-150 in the garage at 10:20 on

Sunday night. After greeting them with hugs and kisses, he heard his wife say, "You look fine, Honey, so I'm assuming that everything went well."

"Can't complain ... except for the dancing, of course."

"But you didn't ..."

"No. I sat out every one of them, from start to finish."

Lauren sighed. "Oh, that's a silly thing to do. You'd probably be a great dancer, if only you'd give it a try."

"I don't plan to make a fool of myself in public, thank you." He smiled at his daughter. "It sounds like you had a busy time, too ... the concert and water park."

"Caliper Squid was awesome, but my ears are still trying to recover."

"And you have quite a sunburn there."

"Really?" She looked at her arms. "I thought it had disappeared by now."

"Almost," Jon said. "It's not very noticeable at all." He knew how self-conscious teenagers were about appearance.

"That's a relief." The girl sought further assurance from her mother and received it with a nod. "Well, I'm going to bed. We're glad you're home, Daddy." Lauren waved to her father and ran up the stairs.

Wearily, Jon rubbed his face with open palms. "I'm pretty sleepy too. Jet lag, I guess."

"Please stay up with me for a while," Nikki said. "I want to hear all about it."

He took a deep breath. "All right, but not for very long. I'm beat."

They went to the living room and sat closely together on the sofa, her right leg crossing over his left.

"I missed you," she said.

"Same here."

"Did you renew some old acquaintances?"

"A few. Only three or four."

"How come? A Silver Jubilee Reunion should have been a big draw."

"I don't know," he said. "Maybe I didn't have as many friends in high school as I thought I did."

"What about the girls? Did any of your former flames show up?"

"None that I dated."

Nikki picked up on that distinction. "How about girls that you admired from afar?"

"Abby Pierce was there. She was every guy's goddess during my junior and senior years."

"How'd she look?"

Jon cautioned himself to be careful. "She looked pretty good."

"Just pretty good?"

"Okay, pretty darned good." He blushed at his own response.

Nikki giggled. "You know, this Abby of yours could not be all that old, so give her some credit."

"Hey, she's not 'mine,' by any stretch of the imagination. Her husband works as a film editor in Hollywood, so they live in a different world from ours."

Suddenly, Nikki seemed to be playing with him. "Does Abby have a nice figure ... ancient though she is?"

"For her terribly advanced age ... yes, her figure is fine."

"Just fine?"

"Okay, darned fine. Is that what you want me to say?"

Nikki gave him a playful grin. "This old girlfriend seems to be a sensitive topic, so I thought you might want to talk her over with me while she's fresh on your mind."

"Sounds to me like you're jealous," Jon said, "and you don't even know the girl."

"That's ridiculous. I was only teasing you, and somehow I stumbled upon a hot button."

Such marital conversations can fester, no matter how lighthearted, so Jon figured that now was the time to set the record straight. "Listen, Nix, let me spill the beans about this mysterious Abby Pierce or we won't be able to get any sleep tonight. And I have to go back to work in the morning."

"If that's what you want, I'm all ears. Please proceed, counselor." At least she still retained a sense of humor. That was a good sign.

"First, may I have some coffee?" he asked.

"Don't stall. You know the caffeine would keep you awake."

"Then pour me some Sierra Mist, will you? And the reward for your prompt service will be the complete, unadulterated saga of Abigail Harker, née Pierce."

"Ooh, sounds steamy! I'm glad Lauren is already in bed."

Jon's request for a soft drink gave him a few minutes to consider how to convey his story—and how much to leave out of the telling.

Nikki hurried back to the living room, tall glass of lemon-lime beverage in hand. "Here you are, kind sir. The floor is yours."

Her husband took a refreshing swallow, cleared his throat, and began. "If you think this is going to be a confession of sins, you'll be disappointed."

"Okay by me."

"I'll start by admitting, right up front, that Abby Pierce is a knockout. Even at middle age ... if that is what forty-two is ... she remains in her prime, at the top of her game. Someone told me that Abby is an exercise junkie, and she has the muscle tone to prove it."

"How interesting. Is she married?"

"Yes, but her husband was at the Dodger game last night, so she was unattached."

Nikki frowned. "Care to rephrase that?"

"All right then, she was ... unaccompanied."

"That's better."

"Anyhow, I didn't ask Abby for a date. It just happened."

"You had a date with her?" Nikki was no longer amused. "Your charming tale is getting a little too serious."

"Relax! It wasn't a real date. Basically, all I did was escort her to the Silver Jubilee Reunion Dance."

"Was she staying in your hotel?"

"Yes."

"On the same floor?"

"Two floors below me."

"How do you know that?" Nikki asked.

"I had to pick her up yesterday morning for the brunch."

"So, you actually had two dates with her."

"No, I wouldn't say that."

"Did you ever go to her hotel room?"

"Yes."

"Inside?"

"Only for a few minutes," he said, "but I didn't see anything that I shouldn't have."

"And what exactly was the content of your so-called date?"

"Last night?"

"Yes, the dance."

"Going down together on the hotel elevator and then walking her to the ballroom. That was the extent of it, pretty much."

"No dinner?"

"Sure, we had dinner. It was a dinner-dance." He took another sip of the drink.

"Did you sit together at the dinner?"

"Yes, I believe we did, as a matter of fact. She sat between me and a high school friend of hers. I never actually knew Abby at Darnell High. I knew who she was ..."

"Every guy's goddess."

"... but I never even talked to her."

"Did she know who you were?" Nikki asked.

"I think so. She was in my English class, four rows behind. Anyway, to make a long story short—"

"Did she come on to you while you were there at the table?"

"Ah! That's where I'm in the clear. She spent almost the whole dinner talking to Colby Reed."

"Is he a married man?"

Jon laughed. "His wife was sitting next to him on the right, and he paid no attention to her at all. She was pretty steamed ... especially after Colby and Abby went over to the dance floor."

"I don't blame her," Nikki said. "Did his wife ask you to dance? That's what I would have done."

"No. She was a cold fish. Never smiled or had a friendly word for anyone."

"So, Abby danced the night away?"

"Not the whole night. Eventually she staggered back to the table ... drunk as a skunk."

That raised Nikki's eyebrows. "They had alcohol at the dance?"

"A full-service wet bar. Didn't I tell you that on the phone?"

"I guess maybe you did."

"Drinks were free ... or built into the registration fee ... and obviously Abby made good use of them. She got loudmouthed and out of control. It was kind of embarrassing."

"What happened to her?"

"Colby and I had to drag her out of the Showcase Ballroom ... or we don't know what she might have done. Her vocabulary was getting crude."

Nikki's eyes widened. "What did she say?"

"Suggestive stuff. For one thing, that she and I would be going up to her bedroom, and nobody could stop us."

"She mentioned you by name?"

"I'm afraid so ... right in front of everyone."

"Oh, terrific! But you got her out of the ballroom all right?"

"We finally did. Abby fought us part of the way, but mostly she was just dead on her feet, totally out of it. Colby and I laid her on the bed and left her there to sleep it off."

"Do you think she stayed in her room?"

"Probably. A hand grenade couldn't have woken her up," Jon said. "I know for a fact that she never did go back down to the Showcase Ballroom. She missed out on her door prize."

"I'll bet she had the mother of all hangovers this morning."

"No doubt."

"Were you able to see her before you left?" Nikki asked.

"Never did. I guess her husband, Brent, must have taken her home."

"Were you hoping to say goodbye to her?"

"Sure. Why not? I might never see her again, and everything we did was perfectly harmless."

Nikki pondered that for a moment. "You're right about one thing, Honey. I think I am a little jealous of your weekend with a sexy girlfriend."

"Oh, please! Abby is still quite a looker ... I can't deny that ... but she is also one mixed-up individual, very insecure and unhappy in her life. She'll never think of me again and probably can't even remember my name. As she told me before we went to the dance, all she really wanted to do was tease the boys of Darnell High School, like old times. And she's a master at it ... like an artist or a surgeon, twisting them around her pinky finger."

"You should know," Nikki said.

He looked down and nodded. "I was had, just like the rest of them."

"Glad you went?"

"I'm not sure, but I suppose so. I made some new memories and clarified some of the old. One in particular."

"Your dream girl."

"Oh, please! That was a long time ago. I was very immature."

"Not like now, huh?"

Jon's eyes darted toward his wife, and he was met with a blank stare of sarcasm. "This weekend could have been much worse," he said. "I think you would have been extremely proud of me ... at least for the most part."

Nikki shook her head and laughed. "Grown men are such little boys."

Jon laughed, too, because he had to agree. "I'm only glad that the next big milestone for Darnell High won't be for another twenty-five years."

"Good," Nikki said. "Maybe everyone's libidos will have calmed down by then."

"That's possible, I guess."

She smiled at him. "But let's hope ours are still going strong for a while yet ... at least until the Golden Reunion."

"I'm with you on that."

• • •

L iterally overnight, Jon Swenson's existence settled back into a sedate normality. He slept well, awakened to his alarm at 4:30 AM, went to work on Monday morning, and assumed his regular drive-time board shift. Life could not get much more routine than that.

The radio station's ratings had remained static for over a year, firmly ensconced at the second lowest ranking in the market. Station management had no realistic hopes of upward mobility, so their only viable objective was to forestall a descent to the very bottom. Their plan—if indeed they could be accused of having one—was to stubbornly adhere to the status quo. In keeping with that policy, Jon continued to perform just as before, with reasonably steady numbers to show for it. He even had a substantial fan base, listeners who embraced him as a surrogate friend as they drove to work or got the kids ready for school.

When not on the employment clock, Jon used every spare moment to craft his current movie script. The previous effort, *Kiss Me Where It Hurts*, had been stonewalled by apathetic agents and studio functionaries. That did not faze him. For his own sanity, if nothing else, he leapt right into the teeth of another project. This latest screenplay was tentatively called *A Ring and a Prayer*, a play on words that alluded to a chart-topper from 1943 by the Song Spinners. But that working title was almost certain to change. Few people today had any grasp of, or interest in, wartime pop culture. Jon was an ardent exception—and he had the recordings of Al Bowlly, Vera Lynn, Glenn Miller, and The Andrews Sisters to prove it.

Each day, after arriving home, Jon made it a practice to check the mail straight off, usually within a minute or two of greeting his wife. On one particular Tuesday afternoon, Nikki seemed distant, possibly even resentful. A mysterious letter had arrived.

"Who's it from?" she asked. Her gaze was locked on a light-blue envelope that released a floral scent into the air.

Jon glanced at its return address and began to slice open the top end. "We'll soon find out."

"The city was Westwood," Nikki said. "That's near Los Angeles, isn't it?" She studied his face.

"Right. The UCLA campus is there." He unfolded the paper inside and suddenly froze.

"Anybody we know?" she asked.

"Just an old school friend ... someone I saw at the reunion." Jon refolded the letter. "I'll read it later."

"Nice part of town?"

"Westwood? Yes, very much so."

"He must have quite a bit of money."

"Who?"

"The person who wrote to you."

"Oh, sure. I guess so." Jon looked at the stovetop. "What's for dinner? Is that pulled pork I smell?"

Nikki continued to stare at him. "Uh-huh. Please let Lauren know that we'll be eating in about fifteen minutes."

Jon went up the stairs, envelope still in hand, and saw that his daughter's bedroom door was closed. "Hi, Sweetie," he called. "Dinner will be ready in fifteen minutes."

"All right, Daddy," Lauren shouted. She opened the door and pirouetted around like a fashion model. "Thanks for the wonderful gift." She was wearing a new backpack, which was blue in color with the stylized words THE BEATLES stitched in white, horizontally, between a Union Jack and a broad yellow stripe.

"Like it?" Jon asked.

"Sure. They're one of my favorite groups. From pre-historic times, I mean."

He grinned. "Don't worry. I knew what you meant."

"I'll start using it whenever my Spider-Man one wears out."

"Fair enough."

Lauren ran forward and kissed him on the cheek. "Really. It's very nice, Daddy, and I appreciate it very much."

After changing into more comfortable clothes, Jon re-opened the incriminating envelope from California, wondering how he was to explain the letter. But the more he thought about it, the bolder he became. Why should he feel guilty? He had done nothing wrong at the reunion, and any *rapprochement* that occurred with Abby Pierce Harker was unilateral. He allowed his eyes to absorb the handwritten, feminine script.

Hello, Jon, from "Contrite Land." ☺

I feel terrible about the way I acted at the dance, and I want to personally apologize to you. There was no excuse for my conduct—and in public to boot. Something just hits me whenever I get a few drinks too many, and (despite what you may think) that is really not very often. I was bummed by depression at the time, with Brent ignoring me for his job and Colby showing up with a beautiful wife in tow. Honestly, this behavior will never repeat itself, if and when we meet again somewhere down the line.

I hope all is going well for you and that you have not given up on your screenplay aspirations. You know, my husband Brent might be able to help you sell a script or two. He's on speaking terms with most everyone in the production end of Hollywood and could pitch your stories to the decision makers. He couldn't actually go to bat for you, but he might toss your manuscript "over the transom," as it were. From what I have heard, that is half the battle—getting someone to take a look at written words on the page. Tell me if you are interested in pursuing this idea, and I'll bounce it off Brent. Can't promise anything, but it might be worth a try.

Other than the ill-fated (for me) Silver Jubilee Dance, I think our DHS reunion was a hoot. Did you have fun as well? It was interesting to see the old gang—and I use that adjective advisedly. Everyone but you and I aged sooooooooo much! You were not a part of our wild crowd during high school, but I had my eye on you just the same.

Sorry we did not meet until 25 years later, but I think that made the occasion even more special.

Drop me a note sometime and let me know how life is treating you these days. If you want me to ask Brent for assistance on your behalf, all you need to do is say the word.

Warm wishes,

Abby

arph-arph@yahoo.com

That night's dinner was tense. Although Nikki tried to hide her annoyance, Jon could sense that jealousy was churning right beneath the surface. Just to be safe, he would wait until the two of them were alone before showing her the correspondence from Abby Harker. There was no reason to subject Lauren to the potential ugliness of such a divisive issue. Another decision that he made during the mealtime's prolonged silences was to stick up for himself and present no inkling of shame or remorse. It was Abby who wrote to him, not the other way around. Despite how the letter might appear to Nikki, he was innocent of wrongdoing, merely the recipient of an unsolicited note from a high school classmate.

Lauren, perhaps sensing some friction in the air, ate more quickly than usual and turned to her mother. "Need for me to dry the dishes?"

"No, Honey. You run along upstairs."

So, the stage was set for Jon to bring up the knotty matter of today's mail, and naturally he tried to put a positive spin on it. "By the way, that letter was from someone in California who might be able to help me sell a screenplay."

Nikki feigned disinterest. "Oh?"

"I would think you'd be happy for me."

"What's his name?"

Jon took a deep breath. "Don't get the wrong idea, but the person who sent the letter is a *she*. Her name's Abby."

"The same Abby that you mentioned before?"

"That's right ... Abby Harker."

"How can she help?"

"She can't, but maybe her husband can. He's a film editor who used to write movie scripts." Jon waited for a reaction but got none. "Anyhow, I don't see what harm it would do to shop my manuscript around."

"Which one?"

"*Kiss Me Where It Hurts*, I guess. None of my others are anywhere near ready."

"Is that your favorite?"

"It's hard to say. They're like my children, so I can't pick one. I do think it has the most commercial appeal."

To his shock and immense relief, Nikki's iciness thawed into a smile. "This is kind of exciting. My husband ... the writer of a Hollywood movie!"

"Now, don't go jumping so far ahead. I haven't even given the manuscript to Brent yet, much less sold it to a producer."

"Is that the man's name ... Brent?"

"Brent Harker," Jon said.

"Did he go to your high school too?"

"No, just his wife."

"Abby Harker."

Jon nodded his head. "Her name was Abby Pierce back then."

"Did you two ever date?"

"Nope. We never even spoke to each other. Abby and I ran in different crowds."

"In other words, she was fast."

Jon laughed. "Are you implying that I was a dork?"

"Not exactly, but more introverted than this Abby seems to be."

"Why do you say that?"

"She's certainly not a shrinking violet, dropping you a note from clear on the other side of the country." Nikki paused for a moment before continuing. "Incidentally, why did she send a letter instead of emailing you?"

"The reunion program only listed postal addresses," Jon said. That was certifiably true, so he suffered no remorse at contriving a fib.

"What does this Abby person look like? Do you have her picture?"

Suddenly, Jon could feel the conversation taking a wrong turn, but he was unable to steer it back on course. He answered with a question of his own, much too defensively. "Does it matter?"

This had precisely the opposite effect from what he intended. "No, not really," Nikki said. But now, of course, she was locked onto one thing alone—the physical attributes of Abby Pierce Harker.

Jon tried to play down the whole matter. "All I have is the reunion program."

"And your high school yearbook."

"Sure ... that too. But it's a quarter-century old."

"May I see them?"

"Why?"

"I'm just curious."

Refusing to comply would only raise suspicions, so he had no choice but to cooperate. "Let me go find them," he said.

Soon Nikki was staring at one of the cutest eighteen-year-olds she had ever seen. And the more recent image did not help whatsoever—an even prettier woman in her lower forties. "Was that PhotoShopped, or is that how she really looks in person?"

Jon played it safe. "It's a very flattering picture of her. Good photographer."

"But she's a beautiful girl?"

He sighed. "Listen. All I'm going to do ... maybe ... is send one of my scripts to her husband. What difference does it make how beautiful Abby is? I'll probably never see her again."

"And you say Abby's husband ..."

"Brent."

"... is in the film industry. Was Abby ever involved in showbiz?"

"I don't think so."

"I mean, is that how they met?" Nikki asked.

"I'm not sure. The topic never came up. Someone told me that Abby is in real estate."

"Do they get along ... Abby and Brent?"

"Not noticeably well. They go their own separate ways, for the most part." He studied her face. "Why the interrogation?"

"That's not what this is. I just don't want to see you get taken for a ride."

"How so?"

"You don't know anything about these people. Do you really trust them to act in your best interest?"

"It's not much of a gamble. My pitiful attempts haven't gotten me anywhere, as you know." Jon looked down at the carpet. "I can't even find an agent on my own, so maybe I'll try going through an insider."

•   •   •

Ten days elapsed before Jon finally decided to accept Abby's suggestion, and he sent her an email to that effect.

> Hello, Abby.
> I enjoyed reading your letter. Glad you had a good time at the reunion. I did, too, for the most part. Mingling in crowds was never among my favorite things to do! Many thanks for offering to give Brent my screenplay for possible submission to a film producer. Feel free to read it yourself beforehand. Then, if you think it has merit, pass it along to Brent. How do you prefer to receive it -- as a printed manuscript or an electronic attachment (.docx or .pdf)? Just let me know, and I'll get it to you ASAP.

All my best,
Jon
(What's with that comical email address? You
must have some dogs.)

Abby's reply arrived within one minute.

Hi, Jon.
Yep, two dogs, but I had the email address long
before I had either of them. My middle name
is Renée, so the initials naturally come out as
ARPH, and "arph-arph" just seemed like the
clever thing to do! Please send me your movie
script as a PDF attachment. Brent can always
print it off, if that's what works best for him.
Abby

And Jon emailed her back.

Actually, let me give the screenplay a quick
once-over before I send it to you. I haven't laid
eyes upon it for several weeks, and I might need
to tweak it here and there. Stay tuned!

Jon surprised himself by how many textual changes were
necessary. This was not a good sign, of course, but then no
self-respecting writer is ever satisfied that a document is truly
finished. Two days later, he proceeded to store his revised
screenplay in a computer folder called "Kiss Me."

Nikki was watching "House Hunters International" on
television when he joined her in the living room. Although
their viewing tastes seldom converged, this was one program
that they could enjoy together. Nikki liked the show's personal
relationships, whereas Jon liked the travelogue aspect.

He sat next to her on the sofa and eyed the screen. "So,
where are we?"

"Nassau, in the Bahamas. This is the third house. The first two were high-rise condos."

"I'll take either one of them ... sight-unseen," he said.

"With price tags of 1.9 million and 2.3 million, respectively."

"On second thought ..."

A commercial break interrupted the program. "Is your manuscript ready to send?" Nikki asked.

"It's ready, but I wonder if I am."

"What do you mean?"

"Reading it over again, I'm not so sure that it's any good."

"You should have more confidence in your writing," she said. "I think it's a terrific script ... better written than any movie we've seen all year."

"But we're talking Hollywood bigwigs here, ruthless guys who play hardball. And they don't care whose guts they splatter in the process."

"That's okay. You're pretty thick-skinned by now ... much more than you used to be."

"Chronic rejection will do that to you."

"When do you plan to send the screenplay?" Nikki asked.

"Tomorrow, I guess."

"Is he expecting it?"

"Brent?"

"Uh-huh."

"I told him ... well, actually I told his wife ... that it would be coming a couple days ago."

"What's her name again?"

"Abby Harker."

"Oh, yeah ... the pretty one."

Jon shrugged his shoulders. "She's just my conduit for submitting the film script."

"Do you write back and forth to her?"

"Just about business. She and her husband are my only hope for getting a foot in the door. I'm tired of writing stuff that nobody reads."

"Will Abby read *Kiss Me Where It Hurts?*"

"I've asked her to read it," Jon said, "but who knows if she actually will? People can promise to do anything and then not follow through."

"Do you think she'll like it ... hypothetically?"

"I can't speak from a woman's perspective. It's not a chick-flick, by any means." He touched Nikki on the nose. "You liked it, didn't you?"

"You know I did. I'm your biggest fan."

"But you're not exactly an objective witness either. This Brent guy may hate it ... or he might never read it at all."

Shortly after 9:30 that night, Jon typed out an email for Abby. He read it over, time and time again, to make sure that its tone was right.

> Abby,
>
> Sorry this is a few days late. My screenplay for "Kiss Me Where It Hurts" is attached. Read it over, whenever you have some spare time, and let me know what you think about its potential. Then -- unless your personal review is strongly negative -- please give it to Brent for his thoughts. If Brent likes it, I hope he can forward the file to some filmmaker(s) who might bring it closer to production. Many thanks for your help!
> Best,
> Jon

He attached the PDF file, mouthed a silent prayer, and clicked the SEND button. Now, all he could do was wait, and nagging doubts were sure to cloud his thoughts. Was the screenplay worthy of consideration? Would Abby dislike it and refuse to give the file to her husband? Would Brent laugh it out of contention?

Abby must have been one of those people who live with their cellphones, day and night. She responded to his email almost at once.

Hello, Jon.
Thanks for the screenplay, which I'll be sure
to read during the next week or so. My review
will not count for much, I'm afraid, as I have
no personal connection to the film industry. It
goes without saying that Brent will be the key,
and I'll try to forward the PDF to him pretty
soon. Hopefully, we'll have his verdict within
four weeks. That is about his average speed for
turning one of these spec scripts around.
Warmest wishes for your success,
Abby

And Jon responded, with more frivolity than he actually felt.

Hi, arph-arph.
A million thanks for serving as a messenger
girl for this budding playwright. My fingers
are crossed that you'll enjoy the story that I've
written. (It's very hard to type that way!) Please
give me your honest thoughts. With any luck,
you might recognize a few of the characters as
being rather true-to-life.
Cheers,
Jon

• • •

About one week later, Jon Swenson sat at his cubicle desk
while making a cold call on the telephone. When it became
clear that Miranda Soto had no intention of advertising her
hair salon on the radio, Jon thanked the woman politely and
hung up. No reason to waste any more of her time with useless
salesmanship. This was the part of Jon's job that he disliked

the most, pushing himself upon unreceptive businesspeople who only wanted to be left alone. He certainly did not envy the full-time sales staff, those colleagues whose entire livelihood depended upon convincing clients to invest hard-earned money in thirty-second sound clips to promote their products.

The intercom *beeped.* "Jon! Who's the lead singer of Herman's Hermits? 'No Milk Today' is ending, and I need to back-announce." The voice sounded frantic.

"How much is it worth to you?" Jon asked.

"Chocolate shake."

"Peter Noone."

"Got it!"

Jon knew that he would never receive that shake, but he enjoyed making the "rookie" squirm. It was a station tradition, and he himself endured it almost two decades earlier. The ten-to-two man was twenty-five-year-old Ronnie Delaney, whose mellifluous voice was the envy of every male counterpart on the announcing staff. Whenever an authoritative tone was needed for a commercial spot, account reps requested him more than anyone else.

Ronnie Delaney had little in common with Jon Swenson—only their mutual fondness for Sweden's top musical export, ABBA. Both announcers possessed all of ABBA's songs in their CD collections (including those from the miraculously recent *Voyage*), not to mention well-worn copies of Carl Magnus Palm's authoritative book, *ABBA: The Complete Recording Sessions.* Each day, the men quite often chatted about this 1970s supergroup during the off-mike time that their shifts overlapped.

Strong friendship or not, the pair's temperaments could hardly have been more dissimilar. While Jon might best be described as straitlaced, Ronnie was very much of a swinger. In the course of his leisure hours, Ronnie could usually be spotted at one or more of the local bars. Despite his tender years, he was already a heavy drinker and liked to chase the skirts. Whenever he was scheduled to perform air work on weekends—Saturday one week, Sunday the next—he was likely to bring his current female conquest, whoever that might be, right into the broadcast studio. She would sit alongside him, silently adoring his every movement and syllable. Station management were rarely around during his weekend stints, so nothing was ever done to curtail this mockery of professional conduct. He probably could have talked his way out of it anyway. That was Ronnie Delaney in a nutshell.

At the other end of the personality scale, Jon Swenson would never have countenanced such willful behavior in the workplace. That said, even Jon had to admire the younger man's gumption, his freedom to grab life by the throat on a grand scale. Being married had something to do with it, of course, for that brought a sense of responsibility and perhaps a certain austerity of expression—particularly when it came to interacting with the opposite sex. That is what now made Jon's present situation so confusing for him.

Late one Tuesday afternoon, as he was about ready to leave for home, an email notification appeared on his computer at the radio station. He opened Outlook to see a newly arrived item topping his inbox. Entitled simply "Yay," it was from Abby Harker.

> Hello, Jon.
> I think your screenplay is FABULOUS!!! I started reading it three days ago, off and on, and finished this morning. It was funny, intriguing, suspenseful, and bittersweet all at once. I guess my favorite characters would have to be Jason (the would-be hit man) and Alfonso (the goofy hamburger flipper), but Monica (the cop's love interest) was right up there, too, as were Norris (mister goody two-shoes) and Sheila (who can't speak the truth to save her life). The story feels quite cinematic to me, but of course I'm strictly an amateur, on the outside looking in. I'll forward the file to my husband right away but

can't promise to hear back from him anytime soon. That's just the nature of his business, I'm sorry to say. Oh well, at least "Kiss Me Where It Hurts" has cleared its first significant hurdle -- me! ☺ I hope Brent will be as pleased with it as I am.

Warmest wishes from La-La Land,
Abby

It was all Jon could do to refrain from whooping out loud, something everyone at the station would have heard through the paper-thin cubicle walls. He read the email again, savoring Abby's positive review while reminding himself that even the kindest words meant little unless they were translated into an actual production contract. That eventuality was so far down the line that it seemed inconceivable. For the time being, this virtual "high five" from a well-positioned friend was fulfillment enough.

As typically happens in cases of high anticipation, no response came from Los Angeles for three weeks. But then Jon wrote an email to Abby and heard back almost immediately.

Hi, Jon.
Sorry this matter has taken so long to be resolved, but Brent has been awfully busy with two simultaneous productions and could not break loose from them to give your spec script adequate attention. He started it once but became sidetracked through no fault of his own. Initial comments were favorable -- I can tell you that much -- but such a lot of time has passed that I'm afraid he will have to begin again from square one. Be assured that "Kiss Me Where It Hurts" has not been scrapped from consideration. That is a promising indicator!

All my best wishes,
Abby

Jon let his wife read the message, but Nikki saw little in it to bring much optimism. "This seems like a smokescreen," she said, "to keep you wondering what her husband might say ... somewhere in the distant future, if ever."

"Could be, but it won't do any harm to wait. I'm sure a film editor is very busy, and you can't expect Brent to drop his studio projects for an amateur's feeler. Besides, Abby says he started reading my script and had to set it aside. He had good intentions."

"Maybe so, but don't be too gullible. Just because this girl in California gives you some fanciful story doesn't necessarily mean there's an ounce of truth in it." Nikki began walking away but then stopped. "To be honest with you, I'd be surprised if her hotshot husband even bothers to read your screenplay, much less recommend it to a studio."

The slightest smile crept across Jon's face. "Don't be so sure about that. Abby can be mighty persuasive."

"Oh?" Nikki's eyes widened. "In what way, exactly?"

"*Pfff!* You don't have to worry about me. This is strictly a business deal."

"How well do you really know this Abby person?"

"Not very well at all ... I admit that," Jon said, "but I still believe she'll come through. It might take a while, but she won't let her husband forget about my script."

"And why exactly is that? What stake does she have in this? None at all."

"Abby loved *Kiss Me Where It Hurts*. You saw what she wrote, describing it as 'fabulous' in all caps. That counts for something."

Nikki giggled at him. "Oh, please! Next, you'll be spouting the Darnell High School fight song."

"Listen, Nix ... being a former classmate of hers can't hurt. Who knows? Going to that reunion might bring dividends. Maybe it was meant to be. I sure wasn't having any luck shopping my scripts around without an insider to help."

This little talk with his wife, openly discussing Abby and Brent, had a positive effect on Jon. He was now willing to admit to himself that further advancement of the screenplay was beyond his control. At least for the present, he would try his best to dismiss the entire exasperating matter from active deliberation, more than pleased to finally allow his psyche to relax. It proved to be a subtle change—and one of short duration.

The following Saturday night was daughter Lauren's orchestra concert at the high school auditorium. She was section leader in the second violins, a position of considerable responsibility among the strings, subordinate only to the concertmaster. Exactly where Lauren had gotten her musical ability was a mystery to both Jon and Nikki. Neither of them played an instrument or possessed a particularly fine singing voice.

They traced their daughter's talent to an early piano instructor, whose younger sister taught violin and viola *gratis*— purely for the love of serious music. Lauren soon gravitated away from the piano and toward the violin. A natural string player, she made remarkable progress in the relatively short span of six years, already mastering some of the treacherous solo pieces of Bach and Paganini.

The concert's program was challenging for a high school ensemble, and the second violins were positioned front and center. Lauren and her section were called upon to collaborate in Britten's "Sentimental Sarabande" from *Simple Symphony*, Schubert's *Ave Maria*, the middle movement from Mozart's Piano Concerto No. 12, Copland's "Corral Nocturne" from *Rodeo*, the second movement from Bizet's Symphony in C, and Holst's "Jupiter" from *The Planets*. Lauren's good friend, sophomore Devon Forbes, would perform as soloist in the Mozart concerto.

Prior to his first downbeat, the orchestra's youngish conductor, only eight years removed from high school himself, advised the audience to make certain that their cellphones were either off or in SILENT mode. Jon, for one, was grateful to hear this announcement. He had forgotten to silence his phone, and it would have issued an intrusive *ding*—for a text notice—during a particularly quiet passage of the Bizet. Although muted, the phone nonetheless displayed a message from Abby Harker on its illuminated screen. Even the dimmest light will catch one's eye in a darkened auditorium, so Nikki turned toward her husband. He shrugged it off, and she gave this mundane incident no further regard.

Not until the brief intermission—while Nikki was chatting with the mother of one of Lauren's fellow string players, a cellist named Philip Hedge—did Jon finally read the waiting message. It was indeed from Abby in California.

> Hi, Jon.
> No late word on your screenplay, I'm afraid. Brent is on location in Montana, so he will not be able to devote any attention to unsolicited projects. Honestly, his cavalier attitude about such tangential matters is becoming a big pain in the ... ankle. He certainly seems able to find ample time for his "social" affairs, but more on that later. I'll try to keep you posted about the script.
> Best,
> Abby

Instantly, Jon was again preoccupied by musings upon *Kiss Me Where It Hurts*, despite his best efforts to let the chips fall where they may. He also found himself ruminating over the enigmatic disposition of Mrs. Abby Pierce Harker. Although there were times when Jon wished that he had never even met Abby, he was also keenly aware that his only realistic chance to land a movie deal ran directly through her to husband Brent. Mindful of playing with fire, how much was he willing to gamble for this fleeting opportunity? Clouding Jon's thought process even further was the vexing truth—if only he would admit it to himself—that he considered Abby to be quite irresistible.

•   •   •

As every morning drive-time announcer can attest, sleep is a precious gift that cannot be taken for granted. With his daily alarm set for 4:30 AM, Jon Swenson had learned, through harsh experience, that retiring for the night after 9:30 often proved to be problematic for him. His mind did not function well amidst a sleep deficit, no matter how minimal, and his microphone performance suffered accordingly.

One Thursday morning, after staying up much too late to watch *The Red Shoes* (1948) on Turner Classic Movies, Jon relied upon cup after cup of strong coffee to tackle his six-to-ten shift. He was the only person at the radio station for the first two of those hours, so it was his unwritten prerogative to stoke the caffeine content in his own favor. But then, as if fulfilling Newton's Third Law of Motion, this prodigious intake of liquid brought forth an equal and opposite reaction: multiple trips to the urinal.

When he returned to the control room at 7:40 AM, there was a recorded message for him on the station's antiquated landline voicemail system. "Hi, Jon. This is Abby Harker," it began. "I'm in town and would like to join you for lunch, if that might be possible. You have my number, so please give me a call at your earliest convenience."

Jon could hardly believe his ears—and not in a positive sense. Nothing good could come of this, except of course for the sale of his movie script, and it was much too soon for that to be even a remote possibility. Still, he had no choice but to call her back. Alleging that the message was never received would only delay the inevitable. Abby could easily track him down, perhaps in a most inopportune setting. Besides, she had traveled fourteen hundred miles to see him, and for him to lie low after such a formidable effort on her part was an unthinkable snub.

His hands were tied until off the air, which meant that ten o'clock was the earliest that he could call Abby back. But what would he say to her? The voicemail message provided no details, so he could only speculate. Did she have further information about his screenplay? Was she in some sort of trouble and in need of his help? Or was her presence in town what might be charitably termed a social visit? He spent the next two and a half hours deciding how he would respond to whatever it was that Abby had in mind.

When his on-air duties concluded, Jon seated himself at the desk in his cubicle. Here was where he made daily sales calls anyway, so no one would think it unusual for him to be on the phone. He also knew that the adjacent cubicle was vacant because Ronnie Delaney was now at the microphone in the control room. With those two factors smoothing the way, this telephone call figured to be about as private as it ever could be during business hours at a radio station.

Holding his breath, Jon dialed the number.

"Hello?" It was Abby's voice all right, but she sounded to be in a very public place. Children could be heard playing in an outdoor setting.

"Hi, Abby. I got your message ... obviously."

She giggled. "Why do you say that? You could have called me for no apparent reason, couldn't you?"

"Not likely. Remember, I'm a married man." Jon hoped some humor might lighten the tone. "By the way, where are you calling from? It sounds like a school playground."

"I'm lounging around the hotel's swimming pool ... filling in my bikini tan line, you know."

Jon tried, unsuccessfully, to ignore such a picture. "Is that what you Californians do to occupy your free time?"

"Pretty much. Say, do you have any lunch plans for today?"

He knew it was useless to conjure up an excuse. "Not really. Only my brown bag."

"Care to entertain a voluptuous guest instead?" Abby, too, was opting for a lighter touch, and Jon was glad to hear it.

"Sure ... fine. Shall I meet you somewhere?"

"Just give me the location," she said. "I've got a GPS, and I know how to use it."

"Some fast-food joint, I guess. I only have an hour." He thought for a moment. "What about In-N-Out Burger? You have those in SoCal, don't you?"

"That's where it all started. I've been to the original one in Baldwin Park. They even have a museum."

Jon told her the local street address, and their meeting was set for 12:30.

The next couple of hours dragged on, filled by a few inconsequential sales calls, and Jon's nerves wound more tightly with each passing minute. What would Abby look like? What was her intent? Most troubling of all, would anyone he knew see them together at the restaurant?

He arrived in the crowded parking lot right on time but had no idea whether Abby was already inside, waiting for him. When he opened the eatery's glass door, he allowed his eyes to scan over the customers in search of a familiar face. Maybe she was caught in traffic or unable to find an available space to park. But then someone tapped his shoulder from behind, and he heard Abby's voice: "That's what I like about this place ... the simple menu."

Jon laughed. "And the moderate prices."

"Yes, that too."

She flashed him a lovely smile, and his knees felt weak. "It's great to see you again," Jon said. Abby was as stunning as ever, and he hoped that his red-faced grin was not giving her the wrong signals. "Shall we?" He motioned toward the lengthy queue.

"We'll go Dutch," she said.

"Think again. You came halfway across the country."

Their lunch together went well—that is, after they finally acquired an open table. They sat across from each other, enjoying identical meals of a hamburger and French fries.

Jon opened the conversation with, "I hope you didn't drive all this way," and she answered with, "Nope. Airplane and rental car. That's my Honda over there ... the metallic blue one."

She pointed toward a sporty Acura TLX that could be seen through the window, and Jon nodded his approval. "My goodness. You must have paid extra for that."

"A little bit. It goes on my husband's expense account anyway, so nobody really cares ... least of all me."

Jon was unsure whether to laugh or frown at her sassy comment, so he did neither. "Let me get us some ketchup."

He walked over to the counter and began filling two thimble-sized containers with the red condiment. This gave him a couple of minutes to assess his situation from afar. There sat Abby, chewing a bite of her hamburger while looking at a cellphone. Above her tight-fitting blue jeans was a curvaceous gray top that brandished the MGM logo, complete with a growling lion. Nice choice, Jon thought. Nothing bespoke the Golden Age of Hollywood quite like that.

"You're probably wondering why I'm here," she said. He had just returned to the table and was sitting down again.

"That did cross my mind."

Abby dipped a French fry into the ketchup. "To be honest with you, I'm not quite sure myself. One of two main things, probably."

What an odd thing to say. This beautiful woman had traveled fourteen hundred miles for some reason, and now she could not even verbalize why. Jon tried to put her at ease, something he certainly did not expect to do. Their respective situations had been flipped, and now it was Abby who appeared to be flustered.

"Does it have anything to do with my screenplay?" he asked.

"Not directly, although you might say it's involved."

Jon hesitated before probing further. "But you're not here just to see me, are you?"

Abby fought back a smile. "Don't worry. My intentions are entirely proper, I can assure you."

That came as both a disappointment and relief. Any normal, forty-something male would be flattered to have his high school heartthrob track him down so many years later. And yet, the wife of that same man might not find such a renewed acquaintance to be charming or even acceptable.

"So, why are you here?" Jon asked again. "Not that I'm complaining."

Abby pursed her lips. "You're going to think I'm making this up. It's all so crazy."

"No, I won't. I promise."

"Well, my husband ... I don't think you ever met Brent at the reunion ..."

"He was at a Dodger game."

"Anyway, he's on location for a movie shoot in Montana, and I have the run of our house for at least three weeks." She leaned closer to Jon. "I'm pretty sure that Brent is getting some on the side, so to speak, and I even know who it is. One of the continuity girls has the hots for him." Abby's cellphone emitted a *ding*, but she ignored it. "I thought this might be a perfect time to show him that I can play that game too."

"To make him jealous of you?"

"Yep."

"And I'm the pawn?"

She reached out and patted his hand. "No, absolutely not. I just want Brent to realize that I don't plan to be a trusting housewife while he's lounging around a mountain retreat, shacking up with some sweet young thing."

"So, you packed your suitcase and left?"

"Only for four days. Our neighbor is feeding the dogs."

"Where are you staying?"

"At the Homewood Suites ... very nice and paid for."

"Brent's expense account."

She grinned. "Right."

Jon had nearly finished his hamburger when he bolstered his courage enough to tell Abby about a nagging concern. "I can't be in on this. I mean, if my wife ever found out that you were in town ..."

"She won't."

"How can you be so sure?" He looked around the restaurant. "There could be somebody in here right now who might tell her, 'I saw Jon with the prettiest woman on Thursday. They were eating lunch together.' Nikki would never understand or forgive me."

"Don't worry. I could explain it all to her."

"No!" Jon said, much too loudly. A few customers turned toward him, so he lowered his voice. "I need to keep you two apart, at all costs." A touch of anger had crept into his eyes. "Listen, Abby, my marriage is too important to me."

"Aw, that's a shame ... I mean keeping us separated from each other." She bit off half of a French fry. "I was hoping to meet Nikki someday."

"Sorry, but that won't be possible." He glared at her, but she brushed it aside, and their mealtime discussion ended on reasonably good terms. It was nearing 1:30, time for Jon to make his way back to work.

"When are you on the air?" Abby asked.

"Weekday mornings, from six to ten."

"What station? I'd like to hear you."

"94.5 FM. It's oldies pop, though, so you probably won't much care for the music."

"Don't be too sure. As you know, I come from the very same generation as you." Abby gave him a cute smile, her eyes a shimmering topaz blue.

The remainder of Jon's afternoon was rather uneventful. He settled back into the normal workday routine and envisioned that his winsome visitor was probably basking alongside the hotel's swimming pool. To hear Abby tell it, being AWOL from California for a few days should teach Brent a stern lesson in obeying their sacred marital vows. And filling in her bikini tan line would be more productive than sight-seeing around town.

All too soon, however, Jon was regretting his complacency. Nikki confronted him the very moment he parked their truck in the garage and came inside. According to her account, somebody had left a mysterious package on the front porch before ringing the doorbell and then speeding away in a fancy sports car. What little she could say for certain was that this unseen person was not from USPS, FedEx, or UPS.

Instinctively, Jon thought it best to make light of the entire incident. "Maybe it was a postal contractor," he said, "someone who makes special deliveries for one of those companies. Sometimes these part-timers use their own vehicles."

"But everything seemed so secretive," Nikki said, "the way that car zoomed away from our house ... almost like James Bond was driving."

Jon picked up the rectangular parcel, which was neatly wrapped in brown paper but showed no return address. He could feel his resentment rising, perturbed at Abby Harker for being so careless—seemingly unworried about the damage that one false move might bring to the Swenson marriage.

"What do you think it is?" Nikki asked.

"Probably one of my manuscripts. I've gotten so many rejections lately that I can't keep track of them all." He laid the package back down.

By now, Nikki's curiosity was bursting. "Aren't you even going to open it? I'm dying to know what's inside."

"Okay, but I promise you it's no huge mystery. Hand me the scissors." He cut his way through the paper and slid out a stack of letter-sized papers, all printed on just one side. "Yep, just as I figured."

Nikki cocked her head to see the title page. "Which screenplay is it?"

"*Kiss Me Where It Hurts.*"

"What does that little note say?"

Jon turned a yellow slip right-side up and read aloud its handwritten message: "I thought you might want to have this extra hardcopy for your files. Brent printed out two sets."

"Who's Brent?" Nikki asked. She contrived a look of innocence.

"Brent Harker, I'm sure. I told you about that film editor from Hollywood. I met his wife at the reunion but never did see him." Jon laid the slip down. "At least he still has a copy of my script. That's a good omen."

Nikki looked him squarely in the eye. "But who put this on our front porch? Does Brent Harker know somebody here in town?"

"Like I say, maybe he hired a delivery service, and some contractor handled it."

"Do contractors drive around in shiny blue sports cars?"

"Could be."

Jon carried the papers into his study and placed them atop some other returned manuscripts. A sense of relief overcame him, like a bullet had narrowly missed striking a vital organ. Even so, tomorrow he planned to read Abby the riot act—unless, of course, there were extenuating circumstances that had caused her to perform with such reckless abandon.

• • •

The following morning, a Friday, Jon's announcing was no better than a novice broadcaster, so self-conscious that he flubbed some innocuous words in an early news brief and then stuttered audibly during current conditions of the 7:00 weather forecast. His only hope was that Abby Harker was not listening at the time, either because she was still asleep or had forgotten to jot down his radio station's frequency. Experience will tell, however, and Jon's performance at the microphone steadily improved to the point that he was soon his old self again.

"'Hey, Mr. Tambourine Man,' from The Byrds in the summer of 1965," Jon told his audience, "with that distinctive twelve-string Rickenbacker of Jim McGuinn ... later to be known as Roger McGuinn. Before that, we heard a nice cover version by Judy Collins of The Beatles' 'In My Life.' And I'll wager that John Lennon and Paul McCartney would have approved."

All through the 8:00 hour, familiar faces paraded by the control room's sound-proof glass, as station employees arrived for their duties, heartened by the thought of TGIF and the impending weekend. One of the on-air talent was announcer Ronnie Delaney, who caught Jon's eye and made a circular OK sign with his thumb and index finger. There was no time to ponder what this odd pantomime might signify, for a pair of live commercials were waiting to be read.

A bit later, Jon had just finished announcing his next triple-play set—"You Were on My Mind" by We Five, "Without You" by Harry Nilsson, and "Woman Helping Man" by The Vogues—when the control room's hotline rang. This happened with great regularity, of course, because its primary purpose was to allow listeners to make song requests and dedications. But when Jon eyed the caller ID, its vaguely familiar cellphone number made him swallow hard.

"Hi, 'Request Line'," Abby said. "Can you meet me for lunch again? Otherwise, I don't know when I can give you my news. It's very important."

"That's fine because I need to tell you something important too. Try to be at the downtown Applebee's around twelve thirty. Will that work?"

"Sounds good. I'll look up the address because I know you're on the air." She paused for a couple of seconds. "Did you get the package I left?"

"That's one thing I want to discuss with you," Jon said. His attitude was decidedly icy, but it was difficult to tell whether she even noticed.

"Okay, I'll be there." Abby's voice remained quite cheerful. "You're great on the air, by the way."

Jon could not help but soften. "Gee, thanks for that 'impartial' review. What time did you tune in?"

"About a quarter to eight, I guess. Why?"

"Nothing ... just wondering when my audience doubled to two."

She laughed. "Don't talk like that. I'll bet your ratings are pretty strong. Dinosaur that I am, I like the music quite a lot."

Sometimes Jon found himself forgetting that Abby Harker was nearly his own age—in fact, less than two months short of it. She appeared to be in her lower thirties, if that, and he supposed it was those regular work-outs at the gym that kept her so trim.

Both of them selected the same food item off the restaurant's menu: oriental chicken salad, prefaced by a shared appetizer of boneless wings with honey barbecue sauce. Orders in hand, the waiter left their booth but quickly returned. "I forgot to ask if you wanted fried chicken or grilled." He was looking at Abby at the time, so she answered him, "Grilled, please."

"And your husband?" He turned to Jon.

"Fried, please ... but we're not married." It was anybody's guess who turned redder in the face, the waiter or Jon, but Abby took scant notice of the mistaken identity.

Small talk between the pair ensued, each sensing that the gist of their encounter could wait until after the entrées were served. Meanwhile, Jon stole a few peeks at his pretty guest. Abby's generously contoured blue top matched the color of her eyes, and that was probably not by sheer accident.

With their oriental salads now sitting before them, Jon figured that this was the perfect chance to shift gears. "I want you to know that my wife saw you deliver the manuscript yesterday." He took a sip of sweet tea while awaiting her reaction.

"Oops. I tried to make it a quick drop." That was all Abby said.

"Actually, she didn't see who you were, but that sports car is hard to overlook."

Abby beamed. "I love that Acura. Brent has one, too, only in a bright red. Good thing I can drive his standard transmission."

This girl was missing the whole point, Jon realized, so he tried to steer her back on course. "I should probably tell you that Nikki gave me the third degree over what you did."

"Is that your wife's name?"

"Nikki ... yes. I told you that."

"Is it short for something else?"

"Nope, just plain Nikki."

"Just plain Nikki, huh?" Abby grinned at him. "I won't tell her you put it that way."

Jon's patience was wearing thin. "Look, I don't think you're being very serious about this. Why in the world did you bring the manuscript to my house ... in person ... when you could have just given it to me yesterday at lunch?"

"I forgot that I had that extra copy with me until this morning," she said. "I needed a few gallons of gas anyway, and your house was less than three blocks from the Shell station."

"If you ask me, that was a pretty stupid thing to do."

Abby was visibly hurt by the accusation. "Well, excuse me for disrupting your life. I was only trying to help." She began staring at a tennis tournament on one of the television screens.

"No, I didn't mean it like that. It's just that my wife ..."

"Nikki."

"That's right ... Nikki. She can get sort of jealous at times ... like any woman ... and seeing you on our front porch would have been big trouble. You're a very attractive girl."

Those seemed to be the exact words that were needed, for Abby snapped out of her doldrums at once and eyed Jon's salad. "Do you mind if I try the fried version?"

Jon slid his bowl toward her, and she speared a tiny piece of chicken. "Mmm, that's good, too, but I think I prefer the grilled."

And so, the advantage was lost. Jon gazed at Abby's mesmerizing face and found it impossible to fight back a smile.

"Anyway, no harm," she said. "Nikki would never dream that I came all this way to deliver a screenplay."

Jon conceded that point. "I did finally manage to ease her suspicions, but it was an uncomfortable chat, to say the least."

Abby nodded her head. "Good for you. She should know, after all these years, that you're not the philandering type of husband. Too bad I can't trust Brent around other women. I guess that's one of the hazards of showbiz."

A single stalk of celery remained on the appetizer plate, and when Abby leaned forward to claim it, her shirt's neckline drifted open a bit. Jon's eyes locked in, naturally, but Abby was considerate enough to shrug the incident away. She crunched down on the celery.

"What's that news you wanted to tell me?" Jon asked. "You said it was very important."

"It is ... believe you me!"

The waiter chose that very moment to drop by their booth and offer them refills of iced tea. Jon waived him off, but Abby accepted. She opened an extra packet of real sugar to stir into her already-sweetened beverage.

Jon glanced at his wristwatch. The lunch hour was nearly at an end, so he gave his guest an interrogative prompt. "Well?"

"Well ..." Abby paused to heighten the suspense. "I have decided to move away from California if things don't work out between Brent and me. The state's gone crazy anyhow, so it'll be easy to leave. No regrets."

Jon's jaw dropped. "You seem pretty casual about this. Would you get a divorce?"

"Easiest thing in the world."

"How would you earn a living?"

"Alimony, of course, which is called 'spousal support' in California. I won't spill any tears over it. Brent brings in a hefty income, so he can afford to help me. He probably spends a tidy bundle on his recreational flings." Abby popped the final inch of celery into her mouth and continued talking while she chewed. "I also have my real estate license, so I can always fall back on that, if times get really tough."

"So ... what happens next?" Jon asked.

"The tennis ball is in Brent's court. I'm fed up with his sneaking around with the bimbos. As a general rule, most film editors stay pretty close to the studio, but not Brent Harker. Oh, no, he wants to be on site for every shoot because he says it gives him a better feel for the project. And he's a palsy-walsy drinking buddy with all the producers and directors, so they have no problem with having him around."

Jon was not sure how far—or loudly—to pursue this line of discussion. It was, after all, quite personal and not for public consumption. He ventured forth anyway, but now hardly above a whisper. "What makes you suspect that your husband is sleeping around? Is there any proof?"

"No lipstick on the collar, if that's what you mean. No strands of blonde hair on his sport coat. Brent is too careful for that."

Abby continued to speak at full volume. "Actually, I have some unofficial spies in the business who keep me posted."

A slight chill swept over Jon. Here he sat, eating a clandestine meal with this beautiful woman without his wife's knowledge. He glanced around the dining area and bar. What if some gossipy acquaintance happened to spot him and Abby together, and word somehow got back to Nikki? Perfectly irreproachable this lunch may be, but would his wife see it that way?

Abby noticed his unease, so she, too, lowered her voice several decibels. "I'm telling you all of this because I don't have anyone else to confide in. Most of my friends are also close to Brent, and they would probably stick up for him. The Hollywood crowd takes its wedding oaths very lightly. Closet romances are just part of the game."

"Has Brent always been like this?"

"Unfaithful, you mean?"

"Yes."

"That's hard to say. He's probably taking more chances than he used to do ... still cautious, but not quite so meticulous in his planning."

Jon let that simmer for a moment. "And you think your disappearance from the scene ... dropping off the face of the planet for a while ... will make him think twice about taking you for granted?"

"Maybe so. It certainly can't hurt."

Her idea seemed like shaky reasoning to Jon. "How will he even know you're gone?"

"Oh, he keeps close tabs on me, with trivial five-minute calls every couple of nights. And I think a few of my friends report back to him ... sort of an amateur spy network. I'm pretty sure Brent will know when I'm away from home, and he'll get plenty worried."

Jon took this as a constructive sign. "At least that shows he still has some strong feelings for you."

"Not for me. Brent only wants to be sure that somebody is there to feed the dogs."

• • •

When Ronnie Delaney's Friday board shift came to an end at 2:00 PM, he immediately joined Jon Swenson for a cup of coffee in the staff break room. Creatures of habit, this was part of their daily routine.

They had been there for about ten minutes when, for some reason, Jon remembered a trifling incident from several hours earlier in the day. "You never did explain why you gave me that OK sign this morning."

"That what?"

Jon curled his index finger and thumb together in circular fashion.

"When was this?" Ronnie asked.

"About eight fifteen ... when you were just getting to work."

Ronnie's face broke into a wide smile. "Oh, yeah! How could I ever forget her?"

"What do you mean, 'her'?"

"That gorgeous gal who was in the lobby. She told me she was here to see you."

Every now and again, listeners did drop by the station—to say hello to their favorite announcers or get autographs—but that was not the case today. "Nobody came in to see me," Jon said. "She mentioned me by name?"

"'Jonathan Swenson' was how she put it. I told her to phone the hotline, and you would be the one who'd answer."

Now it was beginning to make sense. "Was she wearing a blue blouse, about the same color as her eyes?"

"I didn't notice its color ... only the shape."

Jon smirked. "That sounds like something you'd do."

"Who was she, a fan?" Ronnie asked.

"Not really. I went to high school with her, about a quarter-century ago."

Ronnie nearly choked on his coffee. "The girl I saw this morning has been out of high school for twenty-five years?"

"Yep, Abby Pierce was her name back then. I ate lunch with her today."

"Well, she certainly takes great care of herself, from top to bottom," Ronnie said. "And I don't think she was wearing a bra."

"You've got a wild imagination."

"Maybe so, pal, but I didn't imagine that ring on her left hand."

Jon conceded the point. "Guilty as charged. I did indeed go to lunch with a married lady."

"Does Nikki know about this liaison of yours?"

"I hope not, for the sake of our household tranquility. All I did was eat a salad with one of my old classmates."

Ronnie snickered like a man on the street viewing saucy French postcards. "An 'old classmate,' huh? Well, she sure didn't look old to me ... and I don't think Nikki would think so either."

"You got that right. She's seen a recent picture of Abby, taken at the reunion."

"What did she think of it?"

"She was impressed, like anyone would be. But it didn't seem to make her jealous."

"Don't be so sure about that," Ronnie said. He was taking his final sip of coffee when a sudden thought struck him. "How long will this 'old classmate' of yours be in town?"

"Two more days."

"Keep me in mind if you need anyone to entertain her. I'm always willing and able to help you squirm out of a ticklish situation."

Jon rolled his eyes at him. "You, my friend, are all heart."

The captivating Abby Pierce Harker made herself scarce for the rest of that afternoon, and it crossed Jon's mind that she might be planning to drop in on him at a most unfortunate moment and place. She really had nothing to lose, he figured. The mere fact that she was away from her California home was accomplishing what she had set out to do. What difference would it make to her how much residual damage she caused in the process of salvaging her own marriage?

And yet, surely Jon was assigning more ill intent to Abby than was her due. Deep down, beneath the cheerful façade and Hollywood trappings, she was a rather unhappy person who had not led a storybook life. That much became clear at the Silver Jubilee Reunion Dance when she flirted with everyone in pants before tying herself to the wet bar. But Jon knew there was one thing that Abby was not. Beyond all reasonable doubt, she was not vindictive. She would never deliberately ruin someone else's successful marriage out of her own spite or envy. Jon was almost sure of it.

• • •

Ronald Blinn Delaney, the radio station's youngest full-time announcer, was an impressively fast worker when it came to the ladies. What made Ronnie so special in this respect was that he always secured his prey by such honest means, attracting to his side virtually any member of the opposite gender who captured his fancy—regardless of marital status. He did so with tenderness and sophistication, never stooping to an approach that was the slightest bit crass or suggestive. Matinée-idol handsome and sounding for all the world like Orson Welles, this twenty-five-year-old possessed what might be termed a magnetic personality, and he had learned to brandish it to his best advantage.

With rare exceptions, Ronnie was scheduled to tackle a six-hour board shift on alternate Saturdays, from 6:00 AM to noon. This was his favorite time slot because all of the business offices were empty, and seldom did management nose around on weekends. Ronnie considered this biweekly stint to be his very own personal playground. More often than not, he would invite a female acquaintance to join him in the control room on such euphoric days. So professional was he in mastering this high-wire act that, for the most part, his risky indulgence went undetected by the audience. Ronnie looked forward to these recurring delights with even more eagerness than his alternate Saturdays off.

In sharp contrast to this youthful newcomer to the airwaves, veteran Jon Swenson had amassed seventeen years of broadcasting experience, ample seniority at the station to excuse him from ever working on Saturdays and Sundays. Jon's monthly timecard was doggedly repetitious—Monday through Friday from six to ten; ditto; ditto; ditto—and that was how he liked it to be. Weather permitting, he used his Saturday mornings for catching up on neglected yardwork, of which there was typically plenty to occupy two or three hours. He liked to roll up his sleeves and get to it, even if the tedious outdoor chores only amounted to battling a flock of relentless weeds.

The fly in the ointment was Jon's cellphone, which was no respecter of weekend privilege. His fingers were deep in soil when he heard that maddening device's ringtone jump to life—the sound of John Barry's "Wednesday's Child" from *The Quiller Memorandum*. Quickly, he tossed down his trowel, withdrew a glove, and fumbled for the phone's home button. The ID showed that somebody from the radio station was trying to reach him.

Jon answered the call with a pettish grunt. "Yes?"

"Jon-Boy! Ronnie here."

"What's up? Something wrong?"

"No. As a matter of fact, everything's great. Can you drop by the station for a few minutes? There's something I need to give to you, and now is the only day."

Jon gave a long pause. "Can't I just pick it up on Monday? We'll both be there anyway."

"No. It needs to be this morning, and you'll see why when you get here."

"But I'm in my smelly work clothes."

"How soon can you make yourself presentable?"

"Maybe an hour."

"That'll work."

"This better be good, R. D.," Jon said. "I'll wring your neck if it's some sort of elaborate prank."

"You won't be sorry you came."

"Do I need to bring anything?"

"Just your smiling, cheerful self."

"This better be good," Jon repeated. Grumbling, he removed the other glove, gathered his tools, and went inside.

Nikki was in the kitchen, stirring some spaghetti sauce, which gently bubbled on the stovetop. "Finished so soon?"

"Ronnie called from work and wants me to come to the station for something."

A whiff of his sweaty shirt made her wince. "Are you going like that?"

"I'll take a quick shower and change clothes." He spied the spaghetti sauce. "Yum! Is that for dinner?"

Nikki nodded her head. "Lauren's having a sleepover tonight ... with three other girls ... so I'm cooking enough to feed all six of us."

Jon grimaced at the thought. "Why didn't you warn me? I could have flown off to Alaska or somewhere."

"It won't be that bad, Honey. Lauren promises to keep them all upstairs, and we'll never even know they're around."

"Isn't she a little old for a sleepover?"

"I think it's really more of a glorified gossip session, if you want the truth. That's what we always did as sixteen-year-olds ... and we were very good at it too."

It was 10:30 when Jon finally arrived at the radio station's parking lot. He drove around to the rear of the building, near the authorized-card entrance for weekend access. Just as he pulled into an available space and turned off the engine, a gleaming image to the right caught his eye. Positioned two spots away from his truck was a metallic blue Acura TLX. This was not necessarily Abby's rental vehicle, of course, but the timing made him wonder whether its proximity to the station was something more than a coincidence. As he went into the building and then walked down the long corridor that led to Studio A, Jon's feelings were unclear, even to himself. By now, it was self-delusional to claim that Abby was not a delight to his eyes, but how much longer could he risk meeting with her in secret until the luck ran out?

"Studio A" was a classy name for what amounted to nothing more than the rado station's single, solitary control room. Jon's home away from home, it lay behind a heavy wooden door that was reputed to be soundproof—that is, unless someone was laughing loudly in the hallway. Jon stopped at the door and waited for the ON AIR light to go dark. But several seconds passed with the sign still illuminated, so he assumed that Randy must be reading the weather forecast or a sixty-second commercial spot. Finally, it was permissible to enter.

The first face that Jon encountered was that of Abby Pierce Harker, who sat, with her legs crossed, on a plastic, straight-back chair. Abby smiled at him for a moment but did not rise. That left it for Jon to approach her instead, which he was perfectly willing to do. But when he leaned down to say a word of greeting, Abby stunned him with a kiss on the cheek.

"Hello, Jon. I'll bet you didn't expect to find me here." She looked lovely and demure.

Jon was dumbstruck, so he turned to his fellow announcer for an explanation.

Ronnie patted him on the shoulder. "I figured Abby was probably lonely, being so far from home ... all by herself and with no one to comfort her but you, an old married man."

Jon grinned sheepishly, looking from one to the other. "But how did you get ahold of her?" he asked Ronnie. "I never gave you her cell number."

"The station's telephone log. I just scrolled down through the incoming calls from yesterday morning. After a few wrong numbers ... bingo! ... I finally hit paydirt."

A 1967 recording of Al Martino's "Spanish Eyes" was coming to an end, so Jon wondered aloud if his colleague needed to back-announce.

"Nope. It's a double play," Ronnie said. Sure enough, The Lovin' Spoonfuls' "Do You Believe in Magic?" began airing after a two-second pause.

Jon thought back to the old days, before automation, when the disc jockey had to manually cue up each record. But that seemed eons ago. "So, what have you two been doing in here?" he asked. Neither of them answered for an uncomfortable moment.

"Oh, Ronnie has just been terrific!" Abby finally said. "He rolled out the red carpet for me, bringing coffee and doughnuts. It's been great fun to watch him run the program, and I'm proud of myself for never making him flub ... not once ... during any of his announcements."

"Even when I let her sit on my lap," Ronnie added. He winked at Abby, who giggled quietly to herself.

For some unaccountable reason, that last comment really got under Jon's skin, although he managed not to let it show. Without expression, he took a step forward. "What do you have for me?"

Ronnie seemed confused. "I don't get it."

"You told me on the phone that you wanted to give me something," Jon said. "That's why I came all the way over here on my day off."

Ronnie gave a shallow chuckle but could see that his friend was in no mood for jokes. "Sorry, pal, but that was just an excuse to get you over here ... a clever ruse, you might call it." He gazed at the girl. "Abby told me she wanted to see you again, and she can't very well swing by your house. She doesn't think Nikki would appreciate that."

Jon felt another pang of affection for his high school classmate. She looked so sweet and bashful sitting there in the control room, reveling in the presence of two professional broadcasters, both of whom happened to be male. Privately, he would have enjoyed nothing more than to slip away with Abby for a quiet afternoon together, safe in the knowledge that she would soon be leaving for the West Coast. But he also knew this particular reverie was out of the question.

"Hey, why don't we hit a lively spot that I know about?" Ronnie asked. His eyes were full of excitement, as if the thought had struck him from out of nowhere.

Jon frowned. "A bar?"

"Not really. More like a small café that serves drinks on the side."

Jon turned toward Abby. "Personally, I don't think that's such a smart idea. What about you?"

"Absolutely! Sounds like fun," she said.

Ronnie raised an index finger, signaling for both visitors in the control room to silence themselves. Then he back-announced the past two songs, voiced a live thirty-second spot, played a recorded commercial, gave the current time and temperature, and introduced a triple-play set of vintage renditions from the war years by Duke Ellington, Jo Stafford, and Harry James.

Ronnie closed the mike and, without missing a beat, revealed his plan. "Okay, gang, listen up. I get off at noon, and Sheila Sims will be coming in for her shift. I'll take everybody in my car, if that's all right, because I'm the only one who knows where we're headed."

"Nope. I'm going to bow out," Jon said. "My daughter is hosting a sleepover tonight, and I'll need to help."

Abby stood up, taking hold of Jon's arm. "Aw, don't be such a spoil sport. I'll only be in town for one more day, and ... who knows? ... you may never see me again. Please come. It'll be fun."

"Come on, Jon-Boy," Ronnie said. "You can just drink a Coke, if that's what bothers you about my little escapade."

Jon could feel his face turning red. "It's not that so much." He looked directly at Abby. "I'm afraid that other people ... not to mention names ... might not know when to quit. Remember what happened in L. A.?"

Now it was Abby's turn to be embarrassed. She glanced at Ronnie but then stared down at the floor in silence.

"We're all adults here," Ronnie said, "and we can handle our liquor." Suddenly, his patter resembled a Knute Rockne pep talk. "I'll be driving, and I definitely take that very seriously.

Believe me, I know when to say 'when.' I'll be the good cop, so to speak, making sure no one steps over the line of sobriety." He clapped his hands and gave two thumbs up. "So, what do you say, boys and girls? I want to make this afternoon something memorable."

Abby waited for a response from Jon, but he simply shook his head.

"Please come with us. It'll be fun!" she told him.

That remark took him by surprise. "In other words, you'll be going with Ronnie no matter what ... even if I'm not there?"

"Sure. Why not? This is my last whole day in town, and I would hate to waste it by sitting around the hotel room. I'm already depressed enough by what's happening at home."

"I'll tell you what," Ronnie said. "Let me call a friend of mine to join us there. Her name's ShaunaKaye Gibbs, and she's always ready to party ... especially if I'm paying her tab. Great looking too!"

Abby squeezed Jon's arm again, harder than before. "Please come with us. It'll be a double date with none of the pressure. We all know you're a thoroughly married man."

But there was plenty of pressure right now—peer pressure— and Jon began to weaken in the choke hold of this tag-team assault. Finally, he agreed to go, but only if he could call home first. Otherwise, Nikki might be worried sick about him. It was so unlike Jon to do anything without her.

•   •   •

The place was called Vinnie's Wursthaus, and its neon logo featured a dancing sausage in German *Lederhosen*. While few observers would probably denigrate the dining area as a "dive"—having squeezed past its most recent health inspection— the dimly lit bar that stretched the length of its distant wall attracted a loathsome clientele that was likely to keep any decent person away. Its *faux Schwarzwald* décor was populated by three Oktoberfest beer maids in low-cut blouses.

"Don't let that rowdy bunch back there sway you about my secret watering hole," Ronnie Delaney told his three guests. "The food here is actually pretty good ... and look at the size of those *Bierkrüge*." Most of the high-top tables around them supported enormous German mugs, with pitchers of beer standing at the ready.

Jon Swenson recoiled from the sight. Not only was he a non-drinker, but he could imagine many better ways to spend his Saturday afternoon than having to fight his way out of this dismal joint. And yet, a quick glance at Abby Harker and ShaunaKaye Gibbs told him that these two saw nothing wrong with their new environment, no doubt a hard-earned product of social conditioning.

ShaunaKaye could not have been older than twenty, so it would be interesting to see whether the staff at Vinnie's would demand proper identification before serving her any alcohol. Ronnie was spot-on about her looks. She was a living doll, very slim with short, black hair that crested in bangs over the eyebrows and swept forward on each side. Her breathtaking appearance reminded Jon—though certainly no one else at the table—of former screen star Louise Brooks, whose brief career in silent films burned so brightly but then faded almost overnight.

The dining room's wait staff were more modestly attired than the bar maids, and they did not make such a show of leaning over the table to deliver their goods. All four customers in Ronnie Delaney's party ordered sandwiches of various descriptions, and the food was really quite tasty. Everyone but Jon requested steins of beer, and ShaunaKaye was indeed carded for age. At the risk of being branded a momma's boy—or something worse—Jon contented himself with a tall glass of Dr Pepper.

Predictably, Ronnie sneered at Jon for his abstinence, but at least he made his jab sound good-natured. "Thanks for taking one for the team, Jon-Boy. This means you can drive us all back to the station in my car, and I don't have to be worried about it."

He hugged the reserve pitcher of beer in a loving embrace, and the others, including Jon, laughed at his antics.

In terms of quaffing down the Pilsner, Jon noticed that Abby was keeping pace with the others, and it was not an agreeable sight. To his way of thinking, a woman drinking beer was offensive to the eye—the very antithesis of femininity—and this afternoon's meal would be difficult to wipe clean from his memory. Still, he made a genuine effort to cut his three companions some slack, realizing that he was a member of the headstrong minority.

Stein after stein of German brew was brought to the table, with Ronnie assigning each purchase to his credit card. Time and again, the host and "his girls" (as he put it) traipsed off to the restrooms in quest of relief. Although Ronnie's own enunciation continued to sound perfectly sober, the two women drifted into a befuddled haze of slurred diction that would have been adorable if it were not so sad. And, needless to say, the ladies themselves found it to be uproariously funny. They became the chummiest of ephemeral pals.

"How long have you known Ronnie?" Abby asked her new best friend.

ShaunaKaye consulted her Fitbit and giggled. "Let's see. About a week," she said, "give or take a week or two. What about you an' Jonsy-boy?"

Abby tried to organize her thoughts before speaking. "We two of us went to the same high school, you might say ... but you couldn't actually say 'together,' though, because we steered clear of each other, almost always. I thought he was a cute hunk, obviously, but kind of square, too ... know what I mean? ... not wild enough to keep up with my boozy crowd, that's for sure."

Jon squirmed on his perch atop the high stool but countered with nothing in his own defense—mostly because everything Abby described did boil down to the truth. It was Ronnie who softened the blow. "Don't be so hard on him," he told the others. "Even way back then, if you can believe this amazing fact, Jon-Boy here predicted to the world that he'd probably be needed someday as our designated driver."

"Good thing this ain't real spirits," ShaunaKaye said, "or I'd be asleep with my head on the table."

Abby grinned at her. "Or drownding in your beer mug. Ronnie'd have to preform mouth-to-mouse restitution on you." She shook her head at the nonsensical wording but was unable to do any better.

"Wouldn't mind a bit ... not a bit," Ronnie said. He smiled at ShaunaKaye and pursed his lips into a kiss.

The girl popped him a cartoon kiss in response. "And I'd be a good patient ... promise!"

Ronnie stood up and motioned for the Teutonic waitress. Then he polled the table. "Shall we do it once again, gang?"

The two girls nodded their consent, but all four eyelids were drooping. Abby managed to say, "Sure! Why not?" Jon wanted to glare at her but was outnumbered.

Even after this final "one for the road," Ronnie pronounced himself fully competent to chauffeur his happy band back to the radio station. Jon concurred with his friend's self-appraisal, so he seated himself in the front passenger seat, with Abby and ShaunaKaye bringing up the rear. The return trip, much to everyone's good fortune, necessitated no top-speed interstate highways to navigate, and Ronnie appeared to have little trouble staying within his lanes. Clearly, he had plenty of past experience to draw upon, a questionable résumé item that may have provided a modicum of protection from harm.

After expressing goodbyes in the radio station's parking lot, the foursome went their separate ways. That is to say, Ronnie Delaney and ShaunaKaye Gibbs departed in the announcer's Chevy Malibu—to points unknown—while the other two were left behind, standing equidistant between their respective vehicles.

"I guess this is it, then," Abby said to Jon. "My plane leaves at eleven ten in the morning." She gazed not directly at him but just off to one side.

It pleased Jon to hear that every last remnant of Abby's beer-drenched slurring had vanished, and he noticed that tears were welling up in her lovely blue eyes. "I've enjoyed seeing you again," he said.

Abby smiled at him. "Thanks for tolerating me these past few days. I put you in some tricky situations, making you tell your wife a whole slew of white lies." She struggled to find the right words. "Your friendship is valued more than I could ever say."

"Would it be possible to see you another time before you go?" he asked.

"Not unless you wave *bon voyage* from the tarmac."

Jon shrugged off her flippant remark. "Maybe I could slip out for a while this evening ... to give you a proper farewell. I can use my daughter's sleepover as a good excuse for grabbing an hour or so for you." Instantly, he regretted the rash suggestion, which would commit him to more than he was really prepared to offer.

"No. I'm tired of playing hide-and-seek with Nikki," Abby said. "We're not doing anything immoral, so why should we feel guilty about seeing each other?"

That rebuff, gentle though it was, took Jon by surprise. Abby was indeed refusing to meet with him again that night, and his ego was shaken more than he cared to admit. To ease the sting, he resorted to a nimble change of subject. "Have you heard anything from Brent?" he asked. "Taunting him was your whole purpose for this trip."

"Nope, nothing. But of course I blocked his calls, so he couldn't reach me, even if he tried."

"Do you think he knows you've been away from home?"

"Oh, he knows, he knows. Brent's spies ... mutual friends of ours ... keep me under close surveillance, I'm sure."

"Maybe he came home to search for you."

"Good. I hope he did ... all the way from Montana. That would serve him right ... and separate him from that slutty continuity girl for a while."

Abby stared at Jon for the briefest of moments. Then she stepped forward and, rising to her tiptoes, kissed him softly on the lips.

Jon felt himself blush. "Goodbye, Miss Abby Pierce," he said. "I'm glad we both went to that reunion."

"Same here, Mister Jonathan Swenson. Go, Mustangs!"

"Go, Mustangs!"

Abby continued to smile up at him. "I'll never forget what you've done for me, and I hope this won't be the last time we'll be together."

•   •   •

Although Abby Harker was still very much in the picture, only two miles away, nothing remained for her to do but turn in the rental car and catch her scheduled flight to southern California. That being the case, Jon hoped that he was finally in the clear and entitled to breathe a well-deserved sigh of relief. He even went so far as to presume that his life with Nikki might return to normal this very evening, when daughter Lauren would be hosting three other teenagers at a sleepover party.

But a quick resolution was not meant to be. When Jon playfully approached his wife to "report for duty," she saw no humor in his military oath or salute. As a matter of fact, Nikki acted downright chilly toward him, possibly even suspicious of his motives. Jon thought back, wondering why she was suddenly so aloof, and then it struck him. His one careless blunder had been taking so long at the radio station after assuring her that Ronnie just wanted to give him something. Jon had telephoned home, like any dutiful husband would do, but his flimsy tale of needing to help synch the database's music files did not ring true.

Trapped in his own deceit, Jon realized that becoming overly quiet now would only serve to confirm his presumed guilt. Instead, he pushed straight ahead. "Want me to pick up a batch of those breadsticks we like?"

"No, thanks," Nikki said. She did not bother to turn toward him. "Rachel can't stomach butter, so we'll need to use an ordinary loaf of French bread, and I'll put garlic powder on the slices." She flashed him a quick look. "If you're really willing to help, you can chop an onion for the salad." Then she began fiddling with some forks in the silverware drawer.

Jon's strategy, from here on out, was to offer his assistance and yet not seem unduly accommodating. Otherwise, Nikki might suspect that he was trying to cover a multitude of sins. Husbands and wives were forever playing psychological chess with each other, regardless of how long they had been married, and he and Nikki were certainly no exception to the rule. Sometimes it actually seemed that couples who tried to walk the straight and narrow resorted to such trickery even more than those who spent their time sidestepping the lethal venom of an adulterous affair.

The sleepover was soon taking shape better than Lauren had expected. Demonstrating admirable punctuality for a group of teenagers, Rachel Hearne, Monica Burgess, and Valery Lippmann all arrived within a brief twenty-minute span, between 5:35 and 5:55. They came one at a time, each with a parent dropping her off. Valery already had her driver's license, but the other two (as well as Lauren herself) only had their learner's permits. Just as Lauren had promised her mother, all three visitors went straight upstairs at once. The four girls had attained that independent age when adults were considered to be largely superfluous—except of course at mealtimes, which on this occasion was scheduled for 6:30.

Homemade spaghetti was the featured attraction, and everyone seated at the dining room table raved about Nikki Swenson's made-from-scratch meat sauce. Also served another specialty of hers, green beans with sauteed onions and tiny bits of real bacon, along with a garden salad beneath her very own concoction of Italian dressing.

Small talk was at a premium because all three guests were bashful, reluctant to engage their elders in conversation. At one point, the silence became awkward, and that compelled daughter Lauren to lead the way.

"I'm thinking about buying a new bow," she said to Valery. "Mr. Brigham tells me that a better bow can make a big difference in how the upper register projects."

Valery was a violist who studied with the same teacher as Lauren. "I've heard that, too, but they're pretty expensive."

"Not anywhere near as expensive as a new instrument."

Nikki turned to Rachel. "Is the garlic bread okay, dear? Your mother told me that you don't like butter."

Rachel made a face. "I can't stand it! For some reason, I've always hated the taste of butter. But I love garlic, so this is great."

Now that Lauren, Valery, and Rachel were joining in the table talk, Monica was emboldened to inquire about something that she had noticed an hour earlier. "Did you get a new car, Mr. Swenson?" She had taken a bite of garlic bread and spoke with her mouth full.

"No. What makes you say that?"

Monica swallowed and reached for her iced tea. "There was this awesome car parked in your driveway when my father brought me over here."

"At our house?" Jon asked. Puzzled, he stood up and walked toward the front window. "There's no car in the driveway. What did it look like?"

"A super-sleek sports car of some kind. I thought it might be yours."

Jon grinned. "Sorry, but no such luck."

Nikki asked the girl, "What color was it?"

"Blue ... sort of shiny."

Nothing further was spoken about the unidentified car, mostly because Jon saw fit to change the subject—and none too smoothly either. This bumbling evasion aroused Nikki's curiosity, and she gazed intently at him for what seemed to be forever. When she finally relaxed her silent wrath, Jon was overcome with remorse about the deceit he had invoked to evade the truth. After all, Nikki was the only innocent party involved in this complicated mess.

Once the four young people finished their meals, topped off nicely by an ice cream drumstick apiece, they went upstairs to Lauren's bedroom and the adjacent sleeping quarters for guests. Within mere minutes, the discordant sounds of video games, pop music, and boisterous laughter could be heard down in the kitchen. The sleepover party was in full swing.

Jon was determined to adhere to his strategy. That entailed assisting with the dinner dishes and counter wiping, while stopping short of going overboard to the point of becoming too obvious. Besides, he needed to sequester himself well out of earshot range—and Nikki had excellent hearing, particularly when enhanced by the super-power of spousal suspicion.

Finally, shortly past eight, conditions grew favorable for him to slip away for a few minutes. Into his study he went, closing the door behind him and staring at the numeric pad of his cellphone. This promised to be a more labyrinthine issue than simple texting could resolve, so he punched in the appropriate digits and waited for a live person to answer.

"Hi, Jon," Abby said. "Want me to come over?"

"Don't be so cute. I'm about to get my head chopped off."

"I dropped by your house earlier, but some teenaged kids kept showing up, so I figured a party was brewing."

"I told you about the sleepover, and you know it." Jon's voice pulsed with anger, but Abby sounded oblivious.

"Want to meet me somewhere for a drink?" she asked. "Oh, sorry. I forgot you don't do such awful things."

"Look, Abby. I'm married, and my daughter is hosting a party tonight."

"That would make me want to get out."

"Well, that's where you and I are different," he said. "I have a sense of responsibility."

"Are you accusing me of being selfish?"

"I never said that."

"But that's what you implied."

Jon could not think of how to respond without sounding cruel.

"It's just that I'm lonesome," Abby said. "I have a whole night ahead of me, with nothing to do and no one to do it with."

"That's a crying shame, but I can't afford to leave the house. Nikki is already watching me like a hawk."

"Okay then, let's just gab on the phone. That's the next best thing to being there. My plane has a late-morning take-off, so I really don't need to hit the sack until around midnight."

Jon snubbed the bait. "Nope. Like I said, our daughter is having a party, and I should be downstairs to help her, however I can." This time he described Lauren as *our* daughter instead of *my* daughter, a minor tweak to remind Abby that she was not conversing with a bachelor in search of some wild nightlife.

"Okay, okay," she said, "I can take a subtle hint. You don't want to be disturbed."

"Sorry, but that's about the size of it."

"I just need some male companionship tonight ... before flying back to my empty house ... and I seem to be striking out with you."

"Sorry."

"Oh, well, I can always hang around the hotel lobby and see who turns up."

"Don't do anything stupid," Jon said. "There could be some maniac out there, just looking for trouble." He thought for a moment. "Abby, you're too attractive to be chasing after whoever happens to show up on your doorstep ... beautiful enough to be in the movies."

As usual, that shameless flattery seemed to fulfill Abby's craving for adulation, at least for now. Maybe it would hold her until she was in the air. Jon felt like a heel for toying with her emotions, but he had his own life to lead. And he had his wife and daughter to think of too.

• • •

In less than a week, Nikki's concern about the blue sports car had all but vanished. Or maybe that was just how Jon chose to view it. He never did know for certain whether she made any connection between the two sightings—Thursday's delivery of his manuscript and Saturday's sleepover. As time would tell, he should have given his wife more credit than that. It was better to fear the worst than to become complacent and careless.

Jon fully expected to receive word from Abby almost immediately upon her return to southern California, but there was nothing forthcoming but an eerie silence. As the days went by, this became frustrating for him because lots of questions were left unanswered. For instance, had her ninety-six-hour sojourn caused Brent to rush home on a frantic search? Had this taught Brent a harsh lesson, to put blinders over his promiscuous eyes? And had Brent resolved to stay closer to the studio instead of exposing himself to the temptations of location filming? On a more personal—that is to say, egocentric—level for Jon, had the Harkers' troubled marriage doomed any prospects for *Kiss Me Where It Hurts?* He decided to give Abby a little bit more time to contact him before taking the initiative himself. It was just like her to make him squirm.

Beyond his recent, face-to-face interactions with Abby Harker, there was no further fallout from the Darnell High School Silver Jubilee Reunion until a link containing over three hundred images of the occasion circulated online. Jon appeared in many of the photos, alongside scores of other DHS Mustangs, but what really caught his attention was the fact that Abby's likeness was nowhere to be seen.

What were the odds that any one person, out of sheer happenstance, could be so completely blackballed from visibility? It was as if "Miss Pierce" had not even attended the event at all. Abby was certainly not camera shy—quite the opposite—so there was only one credible explanation: the custodian of these pictures was Barbara Essegian, Reunion

Committee Chair. Barbara had something in for Abby, even finding a perverse delight in wanting to notify her that she had forfeited her door prize of a new iPad. How sad it was that petty jealousies could smolder for so many years. Such was the pain of half-forgotten slights from a quarter-century ago.

For three relatively tranquil weeks, any thoughts of Abby receded to something akin to "out of sight, out of mind." But this came to a sudden halt. Over coffee one afternoon, announcer Ronnie Delaney astounded Jon when he divulged, in the course of an otherwise prosaic conversation, that he was maintaining a fairly regular correspondence with "that cute friend of yours from California."

Jon's eyes widened. "Abby Harker?" He laid down his cup so fast that some steaming liquid sloshed over the rim.

"That's the one ... Abby."

"Texting or email?"

"Yes."

"Which?"

"Both."

Jon had no legitimate reason to be angry about this development, but angry he most certainly was. "Why are you chasing after Abby? She's nearly old enough to be your mother."

"Not really. Much older sister maybe."

"Even so, Abby is no cougar ... at least that I'm aware of."

Ronnie's grin was accompanied by a sly wink. "What can I say, pal? I'm just spellbinding, that's all."

"Did she say anything about her homelife ... about her husband?"

"Nope. She never even mentioned Brent."

That, too, took Jon by surprise. "How do you know her husband's name?"

"You must have told me."

"I don't think so. There would have been no reason for me to tell you about Brent."

"Then maybe Abby typed his name," Ronnie said. "How should I know?"

Jon could feel his ire rising. "You two are getting pretty chummy, aren't you?"

Ronnie grinned again. "Can you blame me? Abby is a first-class hottie."

That was a valid argument, Jon conceded, and he decided to let the matter rest. What right did he have to feel so possessive about Abby Harker anyway? In terms of her extracurricular activities, she enjoyed a "free agent" standing. If anything, Ronnie Delaney had more of a claim on Abby than Jon himself did, for Ronnie was a bachelor while Jon was a married man.

The radio station was now in the midst of an autumn ratings period, and all that an "oldies" provider could offer for enticement was a poll that might hold the audience's interest long enough to register in the numbers game. This was the seventh consecutive year for "The Top 100 Songs of the Golden Era." For two months now, listeners had been submitting their favorite songs to the station's website, and these titles were compiled, on a weighted basis, into a computerized listing that represented how today's public felt about the hits of yesteryear. Only one submission of fifty songs per listener was permitted.

The countdown's parameters stretched from the middle 1950s through the late 1970s—or, roughly, from Elvis Presley through ABBA. Quite often, of course, many of the same titles appeared regularly in the poll, year in and year out, but it was curious to note that the very elite vote getters (the annual Top Ten) generally swapped places more than might be expected. And never yet had the same song won First Place a second time.

The on-air countdown was scheduled to begin at 8:05 AM on Monday, with Jon Swenson announcing number 100 in the poll. Then, for ten consecutive hours each workday, until 5:05 PM at the end of the second week, a new title would be revealed. This meant that Jon would disclose two titles daily, Ronnie four titles, and Sunny Shade (pseudonym of MacKenzie

Bastrop) the next four in sequence. Presumably, the suspense would be riveting—or so station management hoped—and the one listener whose submission most closely agreed with the final rankings would win a $5,000 prize. Inasmuch as no one in the audience was likely hear every announcement live, a running list of titles was posted online for easy access.

Jon had already been working for two hours on Monday when it came time for him to start the process rolling. After reading five minutes of news and weather at the top of the hour, he aired a catchy jingle for "The Top 100 Songs of the Golden Era." Then he voiced the appropriate intro: "And now ... as voted by you, our listeners ... here is hit number 100 on this year's survey." That is when the 1964 song, "She's Not There" by The Zombies, began playing, and Jon could sit back and enjoy this familiar tune for a brief 2'21"of his drive-time shift. An hour later, he introduced number 99, all 4'28"of the 1971 song "Me and Bobby McGee" by Janis Joplin.

There was no accurate way to determine what effect this referendum might have on the local ratings, but the early feedback was promising. During the first week of balloting alone, more than thirteen hundred posts jammed the website's pages of comments. The only negative remarks were those occasional complaints about the 1950s or 1970s being under-represented in the polls. To virtually no one's surprise, songs from the innovative 1960s had an effortless knack of taking care of themselves.

When all was said and done, a dazzling list of "The Top 100 Songs of the Golden Era" had ratcheted up enthusiasm from the oldies crowd to what was, for them, a fever pitch. As clear evidence of that, the final PDF compilation was downloaded by over seventeen thousand people in the station's listening area, a transmission signal that extended to a radius of just under forty-five miles. The ultimate winners, the coveted Top Ten, were revealed during the survey's concluding Friday, and they included the following titles:

10. "Peggy Sue" - Buddy Holly
9. "House of the Rising Sun" - The Animals
8. "You Can't Hurry Love" - The Supremes
7. "You Were on My Mind" - We Five
6. "Happy Together" - The Turtles
5. "A Day in the Life" - The Beatles
4. "Good Vibrations" - The Beach Boys
3. "Dancing Queen" - ABBA
2. "The Sounds of Silence" - Simon and Garfunkel
1. "California Dreamin'" - The Mamas and The Papas

And so, the streak still maintained its viability: no song had occupied the number-one position twice in the seven years of polling. Last year's winner, "Dancing Queen," tallied a respectable third place this time around. But most impressive of all, "The Sounds of Silence" maintained its active record of finishing within the top four slots every single year of the survey's existence.

•   •   •

No sooner had Sunny Shade declared "California Dreamin'" to be the latest champion—followed by an airing of the winning song itself—than Ronnie Delaney barged into the control room, dispensing streams of silly string from a can in each hand while humming into a vibrating kazoo. Sunny's microphone was still open, so this improvised celebration went out over the air and brought convulsive laughter from Madame Disc Jockey. Only the most attentive listeners could identify Ronnie's off-key rendition as anything sung by The Mamas & The Papas, but the winning tune was indeed receiving an encore performance.

"Thank you so much for that glorious exhibition of unbridled spirit, Mr. Ronnie Delaney," Sunny told the listeners. "This being radio, I'm sure no one in the audience could guess who had burst upon the airwaves at such a dignified moment. I can assure you that it was our midday announcer, though he might wish to remain anonymous after such a humiliating display of tone-deaf musicality."

Sunny Shade had a droll sense of humor, a quick wit, and a phenomenal command of the English language. But when removed from her announcer's chair, thirty-year-old MacKenzie Bastrop was quite the opposite of her broadcasting alter ego. Poor MacKenzie possessed hardly any discernible personality whatsoever. For four hours each weekday, from 2:00 to 6:00, she could entertain with the best of them, but displace her from where she felt at home—safely behind the microphone—and instantly she turned into a bowl of quivering gelatin. Wildly popular on the air, with the station's highest-rated time slot, she was woefully unable to win any friends once she left the control room and allowed its heavy door to swing shut behind her.

To Ronnie Delaney's credit, he tried repeatedly to earn MacKenzie's camaraderie in the staff lounge, but before long he realized that this was a losing battle. Now he simply sat at a separate table, killing time by staring at his cellphone. MacKenzie was a loner, always by herself, always reading from the classics, never viewing a handheld electronic device. She would reply if someone spoke to her, but the words came grudgingly. Her face was plain, her figure spindly, and her spectacles scarcely thinner than the glass bottoms of soda bottles. But she had redeeming features, too, including long, feminine fingers, gorgeous straight brown hair that reached to below her rump, and perfect teeth that were white enough for a television commercial.

Jon Swenson had comparatively few dealings with MacKenzie Bastrop, not so much because he was intent on avoiding her as because their work schedules diverged to both extremes of the day. He was the morning drive-time guy, and she was the afternoon drive-time gal, each with a rush-hour audience to charm or inform through the travails of dense traffic. One Thursday at 1:30, following his lunch hour, he made it a point to go into the staff lounge when he knew that MacKenzie was sure to be there, eating a Spam sandwich, unsalted potato chips, and a green apple while reading her Austen, Brontë, or Melville.

"May I sit across from you, Ms. Bastrop?" Jon asked. He pulled out a chair.

"Do I have any choice?" She acknowledged the intruder with the briefest of glances but then looked back down at her book.

"Sorry for the imposition, but I think our station's DJs should get to know each other a little better. You're sort of a mystery woman around here."

"Am I?" MacKenzie attempted to resume her reading, even going so far as to place her finger atop the operative paragraph.

Still, Jon was adamant to break through her invisible barrier of isolation. "What's the book?" he asked.

"I'm trying to read Edith Wharton's *The Age of Innocence*, but it takes some concentration to keep all the characters straight."

"I saw the movie ... from the early nineties, with Daniel Day-Lewis and Wynona Ryder ... and it was very good."

"I'll take your word for it," MacKenzie said. "Personally, I'm a voracious reader and don't have time to waste on films."

"If you don't mind my saying so, that's kind of an elitist attitude."

"Oh?" MacKenzie finally looked up again, but her expression remained dour.

Jon grinned. "Do you mean to say that you've never seen *Citizen Kane* ... *Casablanca* ... *The Best Years of Our Lives* ... or *The Godfather*? I can't imagine my life without them."

"More power to you. I certainly don't have any objection to your seeing those movies, so why do you want to foist them onto me? That seems to be very self-absorbed." She returned to her reading, and Jon decided to change his approach.

"What did you think of this year's poll?"

Sighing, MacKenzie inserted a bookmark and admitted to enjoying mid-twentieth-century pop music quite a lot. But she appended a disclaimer. "I would have chosen 'Monday, Monday' instead of 'California Dreamin'."

"For the top spot?"

"I didn't say that. I just meant for a contender from John, Denny, Michelle, and Cass." She had a serious look on her face. "My number-one pick would always be 'Pretty Ballerina' by The Left Banke ... or maybe 'MacArthur Park' by Richard Harris. But I'm being rather eccentric there."

"Nothing wrong with that. I like people who think for themselves instead of just swallowing what the promoters are pushing. Today's music is rubbish ... nothing but some recording studio's synthesized assembly line." Jon awaited her reaction and thought he could detect the merest hint of a smile. Yes, he was sure that the corners of MacKenzie's mouth were trending upward ever so slightly.

"It's been nice chatting with you," she said, "but I really need to get back to my Wharton."

"I understand." Jon slid his chair away from the table and rose to his feet. "Maybe we can continue our discussion one of these days, Ms. Bastrop. You seem to be a very contemplative person."

"Should I take that as a compliment?"

"Please do. You seem to be interested in the same things that are important to me."

"Only not the movies."

He grinned. "No, not the movies. Listen, someday I'd like to get your list of recommended books ... just for personal enrichment, you might say. I'm a sucker for period novels, for instance, but don't know where to turn."

"You came to the right person," MacKenzie said. She did so in a benevolent way, not at all boastful.

As he left the staff lounge, Jon concluded that he liked this MacKenzie Bastrop very much, even if she was still carrying some unjust burdens from years ago, which announcer Sunny Shade was able to set aside for four hours of each day.

• • •

"They're back together again," Ronnie said. To issue this statement, he had strolled around the corner and peeked into the office cubicle that stood next to his own.

Jon squinted back at his friend. "Who are, the fighting Harkers?"

"None other. Abby sent me a text this morning, and she mentioned Brent by name, instead of how she normally refers to him ... 'you know who.' That seemed significant to me, so I thought you should know."

"Maybe ... but what makes you think they're living together? Just because she says 'Brent' doesn't mean they're sleeping under the same roof."

"Or in the same bed."

"Right."

Ronnie picked up his cellphone and showed the screen to Jon. "See this picture? Abby just sent it to me, so I assume it's fairly recent." It was a photo of two people, standing in front of what appeared to be the grandiloquent entrance to a motion picture studio. Abby was on the right, looking as beautiful as ever, and a handsome, actorish man stood beside her, their arms interlocking. This man was a head taller than Abby, and he sported a rakish, two-day growth of beard. "Is that Brent?" Ronnie asked.

"I'm not sure," Jon said. "All I've ever seen of Brent is a mugshot that Abby carried in her billfold."

"I thought you met him at the reunion."

"Nope. He was at a baseball game the night of the dance, so Abby was on her own ... running free ... and she took full advantage of it, believe me."

Ronnie frowned. "So I guess this doesn't prove anything then. That guy could be some boyfriend of hers."

"Could be. She probably has dozens of them."

"And here I thought this might be an earthshaking piece of information for you."

Jon shrugged his shoulders. "Why would anything Abby and Brent do as a couple be earthshaking for me?"

"Because if they're together again, maybe there's still some hope for that movie script of yours."

"Okay, I see your point," Jon said. "And so, presuming that the man in the picture is really her husband ... and presuming that Abby and Brent are really reconciled ... and presuming that he ever actually reads my screenplay ... and presuming that Brent really has any pull in Hollywood ... then I'm on the fast-track to fame and fortune."

"Precisely. My clever sleuthing might spell the crucial difference for you ... between wining and dining the world's biggest movie moguls, and hawking arthritic pop tunes at an oldies radio station."

Jon laughed so hard that his eyes began watering. "That's a very funny way of putting it. Well played!"

And Ronnie agreed. "That was rather good, wasn't it?"

The upshot of this little exchange was that Jon made his fellow announcer promise to notify him whenever something new arrived from Abby Harker. This was a task that Ronnie happily consented to do, for it gave him the satisfaction of posing as a pseudo gumshoe while, at the same time, keeping active his provocative correspondence with the pretty Californian.

"But why doesn't she just write directly to you?" Ronnie asked.

"I really don't know. I must've said something wrong to her when she was here in person. Or maybe she's afraid Nikki will get jealous if she finds out that I have a 'pen pal' on the side ... especially one who's as great looking as she is."

"Makes sense."

Owing to an odd coincidence, within a week of Ronnie's pledge to share his Abby-related texts and emails, this propitious source of information dried up entirely.

"She's stopped writing, Jon-Boy. I haven't heard from Abby in quite a while," Ronnie said, "not since last Friday, to be exact."

"Have you written to her? I hope she's all right."

That drew a tiny smile from Ronnie. "One of the last times I wrote to her, I attached a photo of myself ... nothing risqué, but I was in my Speedo ... standing next to my apartment's pool with Gretel."

"A girlfriend?"

"My Labrador retriever. The problem is Gretel loves the water, and my landlord gets furious whenever I let her swim with me ... all that canine hair collecting in the filter. But I know which car is Raghav's, so I can pick and choose when to let Gretel dog-paddle."

"Who took the picture?" Jon asked. "Was your arm long enough for a selfie of yourself and the dog?"

"Missy Lynch and I were having a pool party. Do you know her? She's been here at the station once or twice."

"Only on weekends, I suppose."

"Uh-huh ... so you've probably never met her." Ronnie pursed his lips and stared at the wall, as if recalling a pleasant memory. "Missy is a sweet kid, a sports and phys-ed major at college ... and she looks terrific in a bikini."

Jon smirked. "Maybe you can teach Gretel how to take pictures of you two."

"I've got plenty of those already."

"No doubt."

Unlike Ronnie's apartment, the Swenson household had no swimming pool, though Nikki often suggested that they build one in their backyard. Two trees would have to be removed, but they were sickly and difficult to maintain anyway, especially when local rainfall totals dipped to a marginal level.

Nikki's go-to argument in favor of the pool idea was that Lauren might become even more popular among her peers than she already was. "Not that I'm overly ambitious for her ... a soccer mom ... but she could host parties that would create enough fun-filled memories to last a lifetime."

Jon was not buying it. "I don't mind high school girls hanging around the pool with Lauren, but when the boys start doing that, it becomes an entirely different matter. Girls, water, and boys do not mix very well. It's a volatile combination."

"Nonsense. You should trust your daughter more than that."

"It's not Lauren that I don't trust. It's the boys. I was one of them myself, once upon a time, and I remember how it was."

Nikki grinned. "How, exactly, was it? Did you participate in some wild pool parties back in your day?"

"I wouldn't call them wild, but I could see how things might spin out of control without much warning."

"Were you easily spun?"

"Not me, but one of my best friends was necking with a girl on the shallow-end steps."

"How far did it go?" Nikki asked.

"Shelly Mason's mother came out and put a stop to it, or who knows what might have happened?" Jon said. "My friend was mortified at the time, of course, but then he went around bragging about it at school on Monday morning."

"Well, we can't keep Lauren locked in her room until graduation. She has a level head on her shoulders, and so do most of her girlfriends. In my experience, that's the more important side of the equation. Boys don't have as much self-control."

Jon nodded his head. "You're probably right about that, I must admit."

"Maybe we could install the swimming pool and restrict the under-twenty crowd to females only."

"What about ancient folks like us?"

Nikki touched her husband on the tip of his nose. "No problem there. Most of us have long since forgotten how to make out."

•   •   •

Two days after Jon established a semblance of friendship with MacKenzie Bastrop in the staff lounge, he happened upon her again at the very same table. As always, she was sitting alone, with her eyes focused upon the text in a massive tome. She had finished reading Edith Wharton's *The Age of Innocence* and was now a quarter of the way through her next literary challenge.

Jon stood by the chair that was opposite hers and waited in vain for MacKenzie to become aware of his presence. Finally, he proceeded to utter one word: "Gum?" He tossed a stick of Wrigley's Juicy Fruit onto the tabletop with a disruptive plop.

Instantly, she snapped out of her author-induced trance and looked up at the visitor. "No, thanks," she said. "I don't chew gum."

"Just tobacco, huh?"

MacKenzie hinted at a smile. "Hardly." She picked up the stick of gum and handed it back to him. "Thanks just the same."

Jon unwrapped the gum and placed it into his own mouth. "What are you reading today? I see that *The Age of Innocence* is no longer in the batter's box."

"*Tess of the D'Urbervilles* by Thomas Hardy."

"I saw the movie," Jon said.

"So I might have guessed."

"It was actually a three-part television miniseries from the late nineties, starring Justine Waddell. And very good too."

"I'm glad you enjoyed it, but I prefer to be immersed in the author's original concept, with no film director interpreting it for me."

"I don't see why you can't do both. Read the book, then see the movie ... in that order."

MacKenzie disagreed. "Doing both is unrealistic in the busy lives we all lead."

"How come?"

"I'm sure you've heard the maxim, 'So many books; so little time.' I subscribe wholeheartedly to that doctrine." MacKenzie swept a loving hand across the Hardy classic. "I would rather read one great book than watch twenty great movies. Otherwise, I'd be shortchanging myself."

Jon mulled that over and nodded his acceptance. "Have you had a chance to come up with a list of recommended titles for me yet?"

MacKenzie retrieved from her purse a quarter-folded sheet of paper, which she laid flat to spread on the table. "I hope this will suffice. It's single-spaced on both sides ... a hundred novels and their authors."

Jon stared in awe. "This is super. I'll start reading one of them by the weekend. Care to give me a top choice?"

"You can't go wrong with any of them. Just close your eyes and pick."

"Okay, will do. Many thanks, Ms. Bastrop."

"Call me Mack, if you don't mind."

"Not Sunny?"

"Only if you're in the control room. That's where Clark Kent becomes Superman."

"Great Caesar's ghost!" Jon said. MacKenzie did not appear to understand his esoteric comment, so he told her about Perry White, the *Daily Planet*'s editor-in-chief. "See? I'm stronger in at least one area of fine literature than you are ... namely, author Jerry Siegel of DC Comics."

"Ouch! I probably had that coming to me."

Jon seldom listened to Sunny Shade's two-to-six program. The first half of it normally found him either catching up on sales calls in his cubicle or chatting with Ronnie Delaney in the staff lounge. Then, as a general rule, he walked out to the parking lot for his drive home. Even in the truck, he did not tune to his own station but rather to some political pundits on talk radio. No doubt Jon was somewhat jaded after seventeen years of spinning records and speaking into a microphone. The very last thing he wanted to hear in his leisure time was another disc jockey at work.

Everyone told him that he was missing something special, for this Sunny Shade persona (with her oxymoronic name) was reputed to be head and shoulders above the station's other on-air talent. Just for once, Jon made it a point to break routine and listen to his own station on the way home. Sunny had two strikes against her, for Jon was cynical enough to suspect that she was vastly overrated. Still, he tried to remain as objective as possible.

"That was an oldies double play," Sunny told the audience, "as fluid and graceful as Fox to Aparicio to Kluszewski. With brothers Phil and Don Everly vocalizing ... and no less than Chet Atkins on guitar ... we time-traveled back to 1958 for 'All I Have to Do Is Dream.' Another blockbuster ... nearly as big as the Everly Brothers' chart topper ... was '96 Tears' by Question Mark and the Mysterians. In 1966, the question on everybody's lips was 'Who is this pop star called Question Mark?' and the answer was the pride of Saginaw, Michigan, Rudy Martínez. Far from one-hit-wonders, Rudy and his group ... featuring Frank Rodríguez on a lively Vox Continental organ ... actually scaled the singles charts with five separate hits."

It was almost a foregone conclusion that the station's top disc jockey would not remain employed locally much longer before moving on to a larger market. Ironically, the only thing offsetting Sunny Shade's undeniable gift of gab was MacKenzie Bastrop's sullen personality. Sunny's audition tapes would earn rave reviews, but how would MacKenzie present herself to a prospective boss in the stressful setting of a job interview? On second thought, maybe she already had reached the pinnacle of her career ... and what was wrong with that? MacKenzie could enunciate to her heart's content while on the air and then retreat to a make-believe existence, created in novel form by one of the world's great literary masters. She had the best of both worlds.

• • •

Ronnie Delaney was in the staff lounge, savoring a caffeine-rich can of Mountain Dew. "Hey, Jon-Boy," he said, "remember last week, when I told you that I sent Abby a picture of myself and my dog?"

Jon nodded. "Standing by the swimming pool."

"Today I received one from her."

"A picture?"

"Yep, from none other than our mutual friend, Abby Harker ... and, brace yourself ... she's wearing a swimsuit."

That captured Jon's attention as few statements possibly could. He thought for a moment, holding back a smile, and ventured a follow-up question. "A one-piece?"

"Two."

The answer stirred Jon's imagination to boiling, but he also heard it with a tinge of disappointment. He desperately wanted Ronnie to tell him that it was a one-piece suit—very modest and conservative—and yet now an opposite vision was thrust upon him. In order to maintain his rational mind, Jon always endeavored, with variable success, to minimize the pin-up girl aspect of his DHS classmate.

"I probably shouldn't see that picture," he said. "It can't do me any good."

Ronnie could not believe his ears. "Are you crazy? You'll always be wondering."

"Abby didn't send it to me, so maybe she doesn't want me to see her like that."

"Like what?"

"In a ... compromising pose ... one that might spoil our relationship."

Ronnie laughed aloud. "Oh, right! And if you don't look at this photo, you'll still see Abby as the innocent sweetheart next door, trying to decide whether to join a convent. Believe me, she has other things on her mind than selling Girl Scout cookies."

"Okay. I really shouldn't, but go ahead ..."

The photo was taken at a southern California beach. Abby was standing between two dogs, with a medium-sized wave cresting far behind them. Her swimsuit was not an "Itsy Bitsy Teeny Weenie Yellow Polka Dot Bikini," as Brian Hyland's song immortalized in 1960, but it was revealing enough to accentuate the curves of Abby's tan figure, with particular emphasis on her youthful muscle tone.

"See? There's nothing X-rated about it," Ronnie said. "That shot wouldn't survive the first cut of a girlie mag. It does show that every inch of her is one gorgeous female, though."

Jon had to agree. "Abby is photogenic ... no question about it."

"That's an understatement. I'm surprised to hear she's never been an actress ... or at least a world-renowned model. And she's even better looking in person."

"Can't argue with that," Jon said. "Why did she send you the photo anyway?"

"She didn't give a reason, but I guess it was because I sent her one of my own."

Jon motioned toward Ronnie's cellphone. "Did she include any text to go along with it?"

Ronnie pressed the home button and scrolled down the screen. Reading again what Abby had written made him chuckle. "Listen to this, Jon-Boy: 'Here's a pic of my dogs at the seashore.' As if all I really cared about were those mutts of hers." He studied Jon's face. "Want me to forward the picture to you? It just takes a couple of clicks."

"Better not. I'd have a tough time convincing Nikki that I wanted to see Abby Harker's dogs."

Nevertheless, Jon did take Abby's photo home with him—in his mind—and there it would reside for the foreseeable future. Even if his memory offered the command of UNSEE, there was no chance that he would ever opt to use it.

Quite soon, Jon would have the opportunity to speak with his heartthrob once again. Early on the ensuing Saturday morning—at a time that equated to 5:55 AM PDT—Jon was outside, trimming two overgrown bushes, when the ringtone of his cellphone alerted him to an incoming call from HARKER, BRENT. It was shortly before 8:00, local time, so wife Nikki and daughter Lauren were probably still upstairs, asleep—a weekend luxury for them both.

Jon walked around to a rear corner of the house, opposite the two bedrooms, before answering. "Hello?" He spoke at full volume, for there was no need to keep his voice down back here.

"Hi, Jon. Sorry to rouse you from a sound sleep."

"No, I've been awake for nearly an hour. Lucky me, I'm now outside, trimming hedges."

"As you might have guessed, this is Abby Harker."

"So I noticed on the caller ID."

"It said ABBY?"

"Actually it showed HARKER, BRENT, but I figured it was you."

"Smart boy." There was an awkward silence.

"What's up?" Jon finally asked her.

"Sorry it's been so long since you've heard from me. I have a distinct feeling that your wife does not appreciate my existence on this earth."

"You know how women are. As I recall, you're not amused by your husband's perceived girlfriends either."

"But there's something physical between them, whereas you and I haven't done much more than talk."

Jon did not respond, sensing that it was inadvisable to pursue such a dangerous line of discussion. "How did you know this would be a good time to call me?"

"I just guessed that you'd have your phone on SILENT overnight, and later on you'd see the MISSED CALL notice. Has Ronnie Delaney told you that he and I have become texting BFFs?"

"He didn't put it exactly that way, but I gather that you two are pretty close in terms of sharing gossipy news." Jon thought before continuing. "Ronnie showed me a photo of your dogs."

Abby chuckled. "Did you enjoy seeing them?"

Jon could not resist. "That depends on what you mean by 'them'."

"The dogs, of course."

"Oh, sure, they were very eye-catching, both of them."

Abby laughed aloud, and it seemed clear that she adored every second of Jon's flattery. "Maybe you're wondering why I called today," she said, "after such a long lull from my end."

"It did take me by surprise."

"I want to bring you up to date on my life, in case you're interested. I don't know how much Ronnie told you."

"Not much."

"To begin with, my husband is back in town ... but it did not result from my excursion to see you."

"So, it was a wasted trip?"

"Oh, no ... I wouldn't say that." Her answer sounded almost like purring, and Jon took it as a compliment. "Brent never even knew I was gone, as it turned out."

"Then what made him come back? Worried about the dogs?"

Abby's voice connoted a smile. "Please give me more credit than that. I actually think Brent missed me."

"He's crazy if he didn't." Too late, Jon cautioned himself to tone it down a bit.

"Why, thank you." Abby still seemed to be soaking up the unsolicited praise like a sponge. "Then again, it could be that I'm reading too much into Brent's motives. Maybe that hot-to-trot continuity girl decided to throw him overboard, and I'm catching my own husband on the rebound."

"I doubt it. I mean about the 'rebound' part," Jon said. "Brent probably missed you, and now he's home to stay."

"I sure do hope so. It's been like a second honeymoon around here."

"That's great to hear. Keep up the good work."

"Oh, it's not work ... believe me!" She punctuated her remark with a playful laugh.

Jon wanted to come up with something clever, but instead he just swallowed his words. A naughty rejoinder here, of all places, might send the wrong signal.

Abby waited graciously but heard nothing from Jon. "Brent is going to start reading *Kiss Me Where It Hurts* again," she said. "That's the real reason I called because I thought you'd like to know. He's got the ear of two people at the studio, a man and a woman. I don't know what he calls them ... producers maybe ... but anyway they're big-wigs who assign future projects."

"That's terrific! Thanks a million for reminding Brent about my story. I know he's plenty busy editing that Montana film, so I appreciate anything he can do to advance my chances of being considered."

"Don't grant Brent too much weight in the decision-making process, though," Abby said. "Like I've mentioned before, about all he can do is toss a new product 'over the transom,' as they say in the biz. What happens after that depends on the quality of the manuscript itself ... not to mention an unbelievable streak of good luck. It's really amazing that any movies ever get made."

"I'm thankful for whatever you and Brent can do in my behalf. Otherwise, *Kiss Me Where It Hurts* is dead in the water."

"I'll keep you apprised of any developments. Brent has promised to read your manuscript within the next couple of weeks ... and I'm going to hold him to that." She giggled. "I have a very strong way of pressing the issue."

"By the way, whenever you want to contact me in the future, it's probably best to go through Ronnie Delaney. Just let him know that you're trying to reach me, and I'll give you a call or text. I get the impression that Ronnie is more than happy to be your go-between."

"He's a nice boy ... a little young for me, but very nice," Abby said.

"Don't sell Ronnie short. I think he'd like a poster of you to hang on his bedroom wall."

• • •

Sixteen-year-old friends Lauren and Valery wanted to perform special music at an area church, but there was a serious snag that prevented this from happening. Music ministers at the city's five competing megachurches had little interest in orchestral instruments. Their concept of Christian music sounded very much like rock concerts to the uninitiated public—with guitars, drum sets, synthesizers, and a half-dozen overmodulated vocalists. Pulsating amps and flashing strobes magnified the on-stage charisma. Perhaps it was providential that the lyrics appeared on overhead monitors, or no one in the congregations would have guessed what was being sung.

On a more positive note, the local high school had a regionally acclaimed music program that—in addition to the requisite marching band for football halftimes—featured an orchestra with a full compliment of strings. There was also an offshoot string quartet, embodied by Lauren Swenson (first violin), Olivia González (second violin), Valery Lippmann (viola), and Philip Hedge (cello). In all honesty, they were not yet proficient enough to "play for pay," but these amateur musicians desired to honor God in a traditional setting that paid homage to the old hymns.

As they embarked upon this mission, Philip reported back to the others that locating suitable repertoire would not be a major obstacle. According to him, many public domain (i.e., free of charge) quartet reductions existed that would suffice very nicely. In view of this pleasant surprise, the main concern would be to identify an outlying church that might welcome such an old-fashioned ensemble into its sanctuary. The group decided to adopt a democratic approach—very common in chamber music circles—with each member placing two telephone calls.

It was Olivia who stumbled upon the most promising venue, a country church that was located just two miles outside the city limits. Best of all, its pastor gave his enthusiastic approval. "We're a very small church ... but slowly growing," he told her. "Our typical Sunday morning has about fifty people in attendance. Would you need a piano?"

"No, sir, just four music stands."

"We begin at ten thirty, so if you could get here no later than ten o'clock, that would be great."

"Do we see the minister of music?" Olivia asked.

"Actually, we're in between music ministers right now."

Olivia paused for a moment, wondering how to phrase her next question. "Do you want us to send you an audition tape?"

"No, I trust you. We'll let you play three pieces, scattered throughout the service. One will be the offertory."

"Thank you very much, sir," Olivia said. "Sorry, but what is your name again?"

"Baker Turpin."

"Doctor?"

He laughed. "No, I'm afraid not. I did go to seminary, but I stopped with my master's degree."

It turned out that Baker Turpin's tiny church was having difficulty retaining a minister of music because of a dire lack of funds. Even the most inexperienced college graduate expects to be paid for time devoted to preparing a choir, organ, piano, and handbells—and understandably so. But any salary, no matter how infinitesimal, makes a big impact on a small church's budget. And now, along comes a high school quartet that is willing to perform for free. How could Pastor Turpin possibly turn them down? He saw it as an answer to prayer.

So did the quartet, and they downloaded their music parts— "Be Thou My Vision," "Come Thou Fount of Every Blessing," and "Amazing Grace"—that same night, which was a Sunday. They practiced separately at first, but by Tuesday evening at Valery's house, they felt ready to take a stab at full rehearsals as a foursome. It did not go well. Rhythms were off, intonations were off, and more squeaks inhabited the occasional rests than were passable for anyone but floundering sixth-grade beginners.

Lauren called a halt to the unproductive session and proposed a contingency idea that would postpone the quartet's performances for a seven-day cushion. That seemed a reasonable Plan B, but Olivia told her how much she would hate to break the bad news to Pastor Turpin.

"Maybe a miracle will happen," Lauren said, "and we'll sound like the Borodin Quartet by Sunday." No one so much as tittered, for the path ahead was fraught with musical hurdles.

"If worse comes to worst, we can always trim our participation down to two pieces," Philip said.

"What would go?" Valery asked.

"My vote would be for 'Be Thou My Vision,'" Olivia said, "but 'Come Thou Fount' is not very secure either. Maybe we bit off more than we can chew."

Philip glanced around at the other three. "Shall we meet again on Thursday?"

"Only for a couple of hours," Lauren said. "We all have homework."

"Can we use your house this time?" Valery asked her.

"I'm not sure. I'll check with my mother and let everybody know."

Valery nodded her head. "Do you have music stands?"

"Just mine."

"Everybody bring your own," Philip said, "but we'll use the church's on Sunday. It's the least they can do for a bunch of struggling ... and unpaid ... musicians."

Individual progress was made in the intervening forty-six hours, such that confidence was restored when the foursome met again as a group on Thursday evening. After a quick run-through of "Be Thou My Vision," Valery whooped her endorsement. "Hey, gang, that wasn't half-bad," she said. They were upstairs, practicing in the guest room because no other space at the Swensons' home lent itself as well for a rehearsal of four people. A string quartet, being totally acoustic, had no need for electronic pickups, microphones, or amplifiers, so the physical needs were minimal—just four chairs, four music stands, and the sheet music.

The final rehearsal was on Saturday afternoon, and it too went well. Some measures sounded better than others, of course, but overall there were no glaring weaknesses. The four musicians agreed that all three pieces would be played for the morning service. Now they could relax a little, get a good night's sleep, and awake refreshed and ready to perform.

Except that living through an actual event is often not as straightforward as our anticipation of it has prepared us to confront. Lauren's cellphone alerted her to an incoming call at 9:00 AM. She rushed over from the breakfast table and noted the chilling ID that was displayed: HEDGE, PHILIP.

"Uh-oh," she answered.

"Yep, we have a major problem," Philip said. "My dad's van won't start ... dead battery ... so someone else is going to have to take us."

"Valery has her license."

"I already called her, and she doesn't feel very self-assured about driving us to the church. Besides, her little car won't hold four people and their instruments ... especially my cello. Can your father or mother drive us there?"

"I don't know ... maybe. They're planning to go anyway ... to hear us play ... but it'll be awfully crowded with six people and the instruments."

"What kind of car do they have?"

"A Toyota Highlander," Lauren said. "It can hold enough people ... no problem ... but I'm not sure about carrying the instruments too. Our Ford F-150 is out of the picture because I'd hate to just throw the four instruments into its flatbed."

"So, we don't have much choice. I can straddle my cello if I have to. I've done it many times before by moving the rear seat as far back as it'll go."

Lauren could not believe her ears. "In its hard-shell case?"

"I didn't say I was comfortable. I could hardly walk when I got out."

"All right. I guess we can make the Highlander work. Like you say, no other choice."

"And," Philip said, "you three pansies can balance those wimpy little Strads on your laps."

Somehow, like a proverbial clown car, they all managed to squeeze themselves inside, with Philip's cello lying lengthwise atop the legs of both him and Olivia. Jon stopped his SUV near the church's entrance, allowing the four musicians to extricate themselves and their music cases from the vehicle. Then he drove himself and Nikki around to the gravel parking lot, where they waited for other churchgoers to show up for the 10:30 service. Neither of them wanted to be among the first to arrive, for they were acquainted with no one in the congregation and felt awkward about conversing with complete strangers.

It so happened, however, that the church's members made their ill-at-ease visitors feel welcome and very much at home. Oddly, every person in the sanctuary—bar none—was wearing a suit or a dress instead of what the Swensons were accustomed to seeing in their own church: t-shirts, baseball caps, and flip-flops for the men and pullover tops with pulverized blue jeans for the women. Even the pastor, Baker Turpin, wore a tasteful suit and tie rather than athletic sweats beneath an NFL sweatshirt.

Without any introduction, the string quartet seated themselves in folding chairs up front and opened the service with "Be Thou My Vision," receiving a warm ovation for their efforts. Counting heads, Jon tallied that forty-seven people were in attendance, excluding the pastor and musicians. Ten minutes or so later, the quartet came forward to their chairs again and played "Come Thou Fount of Every Blessing" for the offertory music. Following Pastor Turpin's sermon, a message on "How to Share Jesus Christ with Your Immediate World," the string quartet performed "Amazing Grace" as the invitation.

Baker Turpin was about to conclude the morning service when a sudden thought came to him. He invited the quartet to stand and receive yet another round of applause. No one was more surprised than Lauren, Valery, Olivia, and Philip when the pastor asked his ushers to pass the plates for an impromptu love offering.

All told, the musicians' voluntary appearance brought them a tidy $62 apiece. Philip looked at his musical colleagues and expressed aloud the idea that each of them was thinking: "Thank you so much for this generous gift, Pastor Turpin, but we would be honored for you to add the money to your general fund. It was our pleasure to bring you these instrumental hymns, and we hope they added some beauty to the preaching of God's word."

•   •   •

Nowadays, whenever Jon thought of Ronnie Delaney's dealings with Abby Harker, his mind automatically drifted to the title of a 1971 movie with Julie Christie and Alan Bates.

Real life, thankfully, was much less incriminating than *The Go-Between*, which was based on a novel from 1953 by English author Leslie Poles Hartley. For instance, no illicit love affair had actually occurred, and there was no clashing of the social classes. Indeed, apart from the title, about the only things this film and reality had in common were that, in each case, the leading lady was very beautiful and had more than her fair share of faults.

Two days after Jon's daughter performed at church with her string quartet, Ronnie pulled his fellow DJ aside in the staff lounge to tell him that Abby had sent him a text. "I can't show you all of it, but I'll read the part that is not steamy ... in other words, the part that pertains to you."

"Gee, thanks a lot."

Ronnie located the lengthy text from Abby and, within it, scrolled down to the one paragraph that he judged to be tame enough for Jon's tender ears to bear. Despite eight or nine other people sitting in close proximity, Ronnie did not bother to lower his voice.

> Please tell my DHS pal that Brent has finished reading the screenplay for "Kiss Me Where It Hurts." He likes it pretty well but has a few suggestions that might make it even more salable. Would Jon be able to fly here in the next couple of weeks and hammer out these problems with Brent and two script doctors? They insist on meeting face-to-face rather than remotely. Please say yes. Otherwise, Brent is afraid that he would have to pass.

Jon looked around the room, hoping that nobody overheard this thoughtless recitation, which was intended for him alone. "Does she want me to reply directly to her or use our infamous go-between?"

Ronnie grinned at him. "What am I here for, pal? Always willing to assist a damsel in distress."

"Don't tell Abby anything yet," Jon said. "I can't just promise to go hopping on a plane without any preparation. I would need to check with Nikki first ... not to mention arranging to be away from work for a long weekend, without pay. All of my vacation days are gone."

"I can put Abby off for a while," Ronnie said, "but sooner or later she's going to pressure me to get an answer from you. Who knows how long Brent will be at home and on speaking terms with his wife? If you want my unbiased opinion, I don't think their marriage was built on very solid ground."

From that point on, a second West Coast excursion threatened to monopolize every waking hour of Jon Swenson's existence, and his mind was in turmoil about how he should present the idea to Nikki. A mature approach would be to tell her the absolute truth—or as close to it as realistically possible. He could explain to her that movie editor Brent Harker wished to meet with him and two so-called "script doctors" to fine-tune the screenplay before submitting it to the studio's decision makers. Abby Pierce Harker's name need not even enter the conversation.

Three days went by, during which Jon procrastinated and drank way too much coffee, in the mistaken belief that this might steady his nerves. The caffeine binge turned out to be counterproductive—an empty psychological crutch—creating nothing beyond an elevated case of the jitters and an urge for more frequent visits to the lavatory. As he returned to the control room from his third such trip since 6:00 AM, Ronnie Delaney trapped him in the hallway for a quick confab.

"Abby wants to know why you're not responding to her request to talk with Brent," Ronnie said. "She knows that I showed you her text message."

"I just haven't found the right time to inform Nikki, that's all," Jon said. He tried to break free. "My music's ending."

Ronnie blocked his way by playfully outstretching his arms. "No, it isn't. That's only the beginning of 'Sunshine Superman' by Donovan, and it's four and a half minutes long."

"Okay, here's the unadulterated truth. I'm a colossal coward when it comes to telling my wife that I consider some other girls, besides her, to be attractive. Abby Harker, it goes without saying, is one of them. Wouldn't you be the same way, if you were a happily married man?"

"But this is a business deal. Nikki will understand."

Jon laughed aloud. "That's where you're wrong, pal. Nothing ... nothing ... outflanks the bounds of matrimony. And that's probably a healthy thing, now that I think about it."

Ronnie could only shrug his shoulders. "Meet me in the lounge at two. I've got something else to tell you."

"About Abby?"

"You'll find out later. See you at two."

Jon went to the staff lounge a half-hour before that because he wanted to visit with his bookish friend, MacKenzie Bastrop. This was Friday, and he had not seen her in several days.

"How's *Bleak House* coming?" Those were the first words out of MacKenzie's mouth, with no preliminary small talk. She was very serious about the world of literature.

"Fine," Jon said. "Dickens really had a way with characters, didn't he?"

"Absolutely. What page are you on?"

"About two hundred, I think."

"You need to pick up your speed. Even the best novels, when neglected for too long, grow chilly and distant."

"I'm trying, but there's a wife and daughter to consider. All I can do is shove good ol' 'Charlie D' into the mix on a fairly regular basis." Jon hoped that injecting a tad of humor might lighten the topic somewhat—and it worked.

"That's very true, and I commend you for the laudable effort." MacKenzie's eyes were dancing with high spirits, something he had never seen from her before. It struck Jon that she now saw him as a literary disciple, and he did not want to let her down.

"I'll give it my best, MacKenzie. You have my promise."

"Feel free to call me 'Mack,' if you prefer," she said.

"Sorry ... Mack. You've told me that before, but I forgot."

"Don't worry about it. Either Mack or MacKenzie is fine, but please don't call me Sunny Shade off the air. Sunny is someone for the audience to have as a friend ... but she and I are two entirely different people."

MacKenzie departed from the staff lounge at a quarter to two, and Ronnie Delaney arrived there at a quarter past two. Exactly in between—at 2:00 straight up—came the changing of the guard in the control room. That was when Sunny Shade presented five minutes of news and weather to open the fresh hour, which kicked off musically with Andy Kim's "Baby, I Love You" from 1969.

Jon was still sitting at the same table, nursing yet another cup of coffee, when Ronnie pulled up a chair and sat down. "Abby Harker wants to know what's up ... why you haven't replied to Brent's invitation for tweaking your screenplay."

"Like I told you this morning, I haven't bounced the idea off Nikki yet. Getting her on board is not as simple as you'd think, and there's a good chance she might assume that I have a hidden agenda."

"An agenda named Abby."

Jon nodded at the rhetorical comment. "I've made quite a mess of things, and I probably give the appearance of being guilty of something. But a lot of the problem was Abby's own fault. She's the one who sent a perfumed letter from Westwood to my home address. And she's the one who parked a flashy car in front of my house ... not once but twice."

Ronnie interrupted. "But her biggest fault, as we both know, is just being so awesomely beautiful. Any wife in her right mind would try to keep her man away from a girl who looks like that."

"So, you can see my predicament."

"What of it? That doesn't change anything. When are you going to 'man up' and take your medicine?"

"Soon. I've been waiting to catch Nikki in a perky mood, but that doesn't seem to be happening anymore."

"Ever since when?"

"About the time of Lauren's sleepover ... if I had to pinpoint a time."

"Any connection?"

"That bright-blue sports car ... first at our curb and later in our driveway," Jon said. "It's almost like Abby was deliberately trying to force a wedge between Nikki and me."

Ronnie flashed his friend a knowing glance. "Perish the thought."

"What's that supposed to mean?"

"I mean, who can really say what feminine wiles are going through Abby's head? She's been having marital problems of her own, so maybe she wants to share the pain with an old classmate."

Jon inhaled deeply and sighed. "Sometimes I wish I'd never even gone to that blasted reunion."

"No, you don't. I know you better than that." Ronnie walked over to buy a can of Mountain Dew from the vending machine. He opened its pop-top and sat back down. "Don't kid yourself, Jon-Boy. You would've always wondered about your school heartthrob."

"It sure would've made my life a lot simpler, though."

Ronnie sipped his soda and swallowed. "Granted ... but *Kiss Me Where It Hurts* would just be a doorstop instead of a viable script."

Jon's coffee was only lukewarm by now, so he downed the final mouthful. "What was the 'something else' that you needed to tell me?"

"It's sheer bribery on my part," Ronnie said, "but for your own good."

"Well?"

"If you break the news to Nikki tonight ... that you have a chance to visit with studio producers, or whatever they are ... I'll let you gaze upon the other five photos that Abby sent to me."

Jon turned red and laughed. "Who do you think I am, a junior high kid with smutty magazines under his bed? Give me more credit than that."

Ronnie grinned at him and held out his hands, palms up. "It's up to you. Otherwise, you'll never see them."

"Are they 'adult' pictures?" Jon asked. "Why else would you be dangling them in front of me like my whole world depended upon seeing them?"

"Down, boy! Abby and I are not good enough friends for her to send me that kind of images ... not by a long shot. But I can tell you that they are gorgeous pictures of her, in that same bikini, taken by a professional photographer at the beach. Maybe she plans to use them as audition photos for modeling gigs."

"I'll give you this much," Jon said. "You do have my curiosity."

"Okay, then, it's up to you. Either you tell Nikki tonight, or these beautiful photos are sealed forever."

Jon sneered at that. "No way are you going to erase any pictures of Abby Harker from your phone."

"That's very true, my friend. No, I'm saying that these additional shots will be sealed from your view ... and only yours. Tell Nikki about California tonight, and you can salivate over Abby's pictures tomorrow. You won't regret it. She looks super in them, believe me."

Jon squirmed in his seat. "Don't get me wrong. I was planning to tell Nikki about Brent's offer when I get home tonight. I really was. So, these photos have nothing to do with the timing."

"That's fine ... no questions asked. But it won't do you any good to lie about telling her. Once you see the pictures, I'll text Abby that you're going to follow through on this, and Brent will be organizing the meeting. Then it'll be too late for you to back out."

"You drive a hard bargain."

"Somebody has to get you moving on this right away. Abby says Brent is not patient about film projects, and he won't wait much longer."

"Just remember this," Jon said. "I'm not considering the trip to L. A. because of a handful of photos. They're nothing but icing on the cake. I was going to talk with Nikki tonight anyway."

Ronnie smiled. "Whatever you say."

• • •

Jon felt like a death-row inmate trudging to the gallows. He could see Nikki in the living room, watching "America Says" on Game Show Network, so he circled around behind the sofa for the right moment to interrupt. A minute later, GSN went to a commercial break, so there would be no better time.

"I heard back from that film editor in Los Angeles," Jon said. "He likes my screenplay 'pretty well.' Those were his own words."

"That doesn't sound very encouraging."

"No, but he says a good script consultant or two might be able to make *Kiss Me Where It Hurts* more appealing to potential buyers."

"Is he going to show it to them?"

"Not without me being there in the room too."

Nikki had a surprised look. "In California?"

"That's where all of this would be done ... and no video conferencing allowed. They won't even consider putting more work into this property unless I'm there, in person, to advise and consent."

"Are they going to pick up the tab for your plane fare?"

"Not a chance. I'll be the one begging, with hat in hand. They know who's in the position of power, and it sure isn't me."

Nikki muted the television remote. "Are you seriously planning to take this step? Do you really think it's worth it?"

"Don't you? Unless I can get it sold, my screenplay is just a hundred pages of Courier typeface that nobody will ever see. And what a waste that would be."

"But a trip to California might be an even bigger waste ... of time and money."

"Could be, but I feel like I need to take this chance. Otherwise, I'm condemning *Kiss Me Where It Hurts* to the trash heap without a fair hearing."

"Is this the guy who's married to your high school sweetheart?" Nikki asked. Her eyes narrowed.

Jon's laugh sounded shallow and defensive. "Abby Harker is hardly my old sweetheart. She's just a girl who used to go to Darnell High School with me. We never even spoke a word to each other during those four years."

"But you hit it off rather well at the school reunion, didn't you?"

"Her husband, Brent, was at a baseball game, and Abby needed an escort. I just happened to be a handy classmate for her to drag into service."

"Is that really how you felt about it ... indentured servitude?" Nikki had caught her husband in a fib, and she knew it. "You seemed pretty fond of her when you first told me about the dance."

"I've had more time to think about it by now. Looking back, I'm sure that she used me for her own amusement ... to tease the other boys, just like she used to do to them in high school."

"But she didn't tease you?"

"Maybe a little, like I told you at the time. I didn't fall for it, though."

A look of hurt crossed Nikki's face. "You do what you want. I won't stop you. But your trip to Hollywood had better be for business purposes only ... with no playing around, if you catch my drift."

"You should know me better than that, after all these years. You act like you don't trust me."

"I don't know what to think anymore."

That sounded ominous. "I don't get it," Jon said. "What's changed between us?"

"Maybe nothing at all ... just some circumstantial evidence."

He swallowed hard but tried to mask it. "What kind of evidence?"

"Mindy Oates ... my friend from church ... thought she saw you at In-N-Out Burger. You were eating with a very pretty young woman."

"Occasionally I take a client out for a quick lunch. That must have been one of those times."

"A client?"

"Someone who is considering the purchase of commercial air time."

"Is that who this was?"

"I guess." Jon felt terrible, lying to his wife like this, but he was boxed into a corner and could see no other way out. Besides, if he stretched the truth far enough, Abby was technically a client of sorts. She was married to a potential business associate, should *Kiss Me Where It Hurts* sell to the studio where Brent Harker was employed.

"And then there's the matter of a blue sports car that showed up twice at our house," Nikki said. "What do you know about that?"

"You mentioned a blue sports car to me, but I never saw one at our house. You told me it was a delivery guy."

"I thought so the first time, but then it showed up again."

"Same car?" Jon asked.

"I can't say for sure. Only Monica Burgess saw it the second time ... when she got here for the sleepover."

Jon shrugged his shoulders. The evidence—such as it was—made a rather feeble case, and even Nikki could probably sense how unconvincing it all sounded. Nonetheless, her suspicions remained firmly in place.

She pressed the remote's MUTE button again, and the television audio returned. John Michael Higgins resumed the emceeing of his game show, and the Swensons' West Coast controversy stalled to an inconclusive halt. Jon sat alongside his wife for a few minutes, neither of them paying much attention to the program.

It was Nikki who finally broke the silence. "Go ahead and fly out there, if you think it's for the best."

"I don't have much confidence in this trip," Jon said, "but there's no other way to reach the studios. Brent Harker is my only contact."

There was a strained pause of perhaps fifteen seconds before Nikki finally turned to respond. "What if I went with you? Would that be another option?"

This jarring suggestion had never crossed Jon's mind as a real possibility, and his reply sounded indecisive. "Fine with me," he said, "but can you get off work?"

"Could be. I have some personal days coming to me."

The more Jon thought about it, the better this seemed to him: a perfect solution, the ideal way to mix business with pleasure. If nothing else, such an arrangement would quell any amorous temptations that might arise—or at least hold them to a minimum.

Within twenty-four hours, everything was set for both of them to travel west, pending any last-minute change of plans. Jon was pretty certain that he was doing the right thing, and Nikki knew for a fact that she would be more at ease accompanying her husband than leaving him on his own in some beauty queen's crosshairs. Briefly put, she trusted her husband to behave properly much more than she trusted this film editor's wife.

There was no time to lose, so Jon telephoned Ronnie Delaney's cellphone on Sunday afternoon. Not until the fourth try did Ronnie finally answer.

"Hi, Jon," he said.

"Go ahead and tell Abby that I'll be able to meet with Brent on Friday."

"So, you finally got permission from the missus, huh?"

Jon ignored the sneer in Ronnie's voice. "Didn't have to. It may interest you to know that Nikki is very supportive of my writing ambitions. In fact, lots of times it's Nikki who pushes me along when I'm ready to give up."

"Have you informed the front office?"

"Not yet, but it should be a slam dunk," Jon said. "Irving Koslov has sat in for me a couple of times in the past with no ill effects. He's young but ready for prime time."

"I'm not so sure about that. The only shift he's ever filled on a regular basis is Saturday and Sunday afternoons ... and I've heard some complaints from the girls in radio copy."

"Like what?"

"That he flubbed the pronunciations of two of our sponsors, for example."

"Did anyone bother to correct him?"

"On 'Heidenheimer Jewelers,' yes ... but then he pronounced 'La Taquería del Sur,' the Mexican restaurant, as 'lah tah-QWER-ee-uh del sewer.'"

"Okay, so he never took Spanish in high school. You can't hold that against him."

"Irv's not very bright, that's all," Ronnie said. "He should be professional enough to check his pronunciations before opening the mike. Sponsors don't enjoy hearing their company names butchered over the air ... not when they're paying exorbitant money to advertise. I sure wouldn't want to eat at a place that's connected to the sewer."

"Good point. Anyhow, I'll ask Pridgen for some time off when I finish my shift tomorrow. And meanwhile, you can shoot Abby a text, stating that I'll be there next Friday through Monday. That way, her husband can organize a face-to-face with those two consultants.'"

"What do they call them again?"

That embarrassed Jon, but he spat out an answer. "Script doctors."

"They must really think your screenplay is sick," Ronnie said.

"Oh, well. At least they didn't refer it to the ICU."

• • •

And so, the die had been cast. The Swensons would be flying to LAX for a four-day weekend on the outer fringes of the film industry. Jon had never met Brent Harker before, so that was a source of considerable trepidation. Just how does an outsider speak to an established figure in Hollywood? He imagined what he might say to Brent and what degree of familiarity he should adopt in doing so. Too bold would seem like arrogance, and too reserved would denote a lack of confidence. At the script meeting, would the four men be seated around an intimidating circular table, or would it take place in Brent's editing suite at the studio? Either way, Jon was sure to hear nothing but negativity from the consultants, for that was the essence of their job.

While Lauren's parents were away, this would be the first time for her to be truly alone for such an extended period of time. She had slept at various friends' homes for occasional evenings, but never had she been on her own for almost four days straight. To soften the blow somewhat, over-protective Nikki arranged for her daughter to eat dinner with the families of schoolmates on both Friday and Sunday nights. She also instructed Lauren not to accept a date for Saturday night. As always, any child of Jon and Nikki would be expected to attend church services on both Sunday morning and Sunday night. She could ride there with Tammy Neil, who was a senior at the high school. Mother and daughter agreed on one thing—that this long weekend might be a valuable experience for a sixteen-year-old.

On Monday morning, when Jon watched Ronnie walk by the control room window, he tried to get his attention but failed. Twice during the next two hours, he peeked into the staff lounge, but Ronnie was nowhere to be found. Not until 9:58 AM, news copy in hand, did Ronnie finally speak to the morning drive-time announcer. The Dave Clark Five's biggest hit from late 1965, "Over and Over," was bringing the hour to a close.

"Hey, Jon-Boy," Ronnie said. "Is everything still looking good for your trip to see Abby?"

"I'm not going there to see Abby. I might not even bump into her the whole time I'm in California."

Ronnie grinned. "We both know that's not true. I'm sure you'll manage to squeeze in some 'Abby time' while you're there. I certainly would."

"I have no doubt about that, but of course you're a bachelor on the prowl ... in sharp contrast to my more stable situation."

"Oh, really? You'll be a married man who's more than half a continent away from the prying eyes of his wife. No ball and chain reaches all the way from here to the West Coast."

This would not be a good time to divulge that Nikki was planning to tag along with him, so Jon simply dismissed Ronnie's statement with a shake of the head. Then he played the hourly station ID, followed by the news intro's dramatic jingle. Straight up 10:00 was the time, and Ronnie Delaney was on the air.

The week leading up to her West Coast trip proved to be a busy one for Nikki Swenson. She shopped for some summerish clothes, including a swimsuit, and purchased a mid-size piece of rolling luggage. By Monday afternoon, all of her envious colleagues at work knew about the upcoming adventure. Far from being a marital obligation, she viewed the sojourn as an opportunity to take in the sights of fabled La-La Land, while leaving her banking worries fourteen hundred miles behind.

On Wednesday morning, Ronnie told Jon that another text message had arrived from Abby. "It's mostly private ... for me only ... but here's the part that deals with you." By careful scrolling, he permitted Jon to read a short excerpt.

> Tell Jon I'm thrilled that he's coming to SoCal to talk with Brent. Calling in the expertise of script doctors is probably a favorable indication that "Kiss Me Where It Hurts" has some worthy qualities going for it. While he's here, I hope the visit will not be all work and no play. I plan to show him around the L. A. area because a lot has changed since that sad day when he left to go away to college.

Jon tried to look pleased with what Abby wrote, but he dreaded the prospect of spending four days immersed in what amounted to a double life, desperately keeping two women separated from one another while maintaining a carefree bearing that ensured that both remained blissfully unaware.

The only way out of this dilemma was to tell Abby, right up front, that Nikki Swenson would be accompanying her husband on his West Coast trip. Jon had enough trouble fending one woman off the other while Abby was secretly here in town, but the L. A. situation would be even more volatile, for there Abby would be calling the shots on her home turf.

When he informed his announcing pal of these plans, Ronnie was flabbergasted. Why would Jon, being of reasonably sound mind, wish to take his wife along with him to Fantasyland—especially when the gorgeous Abby Harker would be there to greet him with open arms? It made no sense to the playboy bachelor. "Okay, I'll let Abby know tonight," Ronnie said, "but my heart's not in it. You could have had four days of ecstasy in paradise. Lots of men would dream about a perfect set-up like this, but you're throwing it all away."

Jon stood his ground. "You keep forgetting one thing. I'm not going to California to see Abby. I'm going there to see her husband, Brent."

"Oh, yeah, and those script doctors. Personally, I think you need to see another kind of doctor ... a psychiatrist ... but that's just my opinion."

This remark struck Jon as very funny, and he slapped Ronnie on the back. "Maybe so, my friend, maybe so. I guess my hormones no longer run as rampant as yours do. One of these days, you'll find the right woman, and you'll settle down too."

"I hope I never get that old."

Thursday was the day before Jon and Nikki were to leave on their flight to Los Angeles International Airport, but Ronnie was not forthcoming with any news from the West Coast. Again and again, he told Jon the same refrain: "Nope, nothing yet." Clearly, Abby was not in a texting mood. Just after 2:00, Jon begged Ronnie to write to her one last time that day, impressing upon her the importance of knowing whether she had gotten word of the revised arrangement that included Nikki. But Abby Harker was too clever to make this any easier on her DHS classmate. From her end, there was nothing but a spiteful silence.

Not until 9:30 that night did Jon finally receive the long-awaited call—from Ronnie's cellphone to the Swensons' landline—and Jon answered it in his study with the door closed.

"Abby got the message," Ronnie said.

"Any response from her?"

"Nothing but a polite acknowledgment. That's all it amounted to."

"Do you mind reading it to me?" Jon asked. "I should know where I stand before Abby and I meet face-to-face again."

"Okay, here's what she said ... word for word. 'This comes as quite a surprise. I figured that Jon would be traveling by himself on such a business trip. Hopefully, Nikki understands that she is not invited to attend the filmscript meeting. Maybe she is just accompanying Jon for a short vacation, and of course that is perfectly fine.' Do you want me to text her back with anything?"

"No, don't bother. I have all the details that I need to locate Brent at his studio, and he'll take me to the script consultants."

"Will you rent a car while you're there?"

"For all four days. We got a special deal that gives us one extra day, free of charge."

"Can't beat that. Are you and Nikki already packed?"

"Yep, ready to go when our five o'clock alarm wakes us up."

Ronnie grimaced at the thought. "Five o'clock! I couldn't do that, no matter what time my flight left."

"That's sleeping-in for me," Jon said. "I usually get up at four thirty."

"You're a better man than I am, Gunga Din." This was the only line Ronnie knew from Kipling, but it applied well here.

Jon thought of one other thing. "Before I forget, please tell Mack that I'll be walking up the entire length of the 'Music Box' steps while I'm out there. She wanted me to see them."

"Who's 'Mack'?"

"MacKenzie Bastrop, the two-to-six girl ... you know, Sunny Shade."

Ronnie made a scoffing noise. "I call her 'Old Stone Face.'"

"Oh, she's all right, once you get to know her better."

"What are these famous steps?"

"The outdoor staircase that Hal Roach used for his Laurel and Hardy film called *The Music Box*."

"I won't remember all that," Ronnie said, "so I'll just tell her you plan to see 'the steps.'"

"That's fine. Mack doesn't care for movies, but she is a Laurel and Hardy fan. She'll know what you mean."

"Well, best of luck, pal ... with your screenplay and with Abby Harker."

"Thanks, but what does Abby have to do with it?" Jon asked.

"I think you know what I mean."

•   •   •

The flight to LAX was scheduled to take just over three hours. Then the Swensons would need to secure a rental car and drive to their hotel. For his own sake, Jon thought it best not to stay at the same facility that Darnell High School had used for its Silver Jubilee Reunion. There would be too many memories for him to suppress in his own mind, too many incidents that he would need to soft-pedal for Nikki. Instead, he selected a conveniently located lodging that was really quite nice for the medium asking price of $210 per night. He and Nikki both agreed that this was not an outrageous rate for the inflated vicinity of downtown Los Angeles.

After the couple registered at their hotel, the very first thing that Nikki did was telephone Lauren to ask how her Friday went. This call was made easier by the two-hour difference between Pacific and Central Time Zones, for Lauren had already arrived home from school and had been driven over to the Fischmann household for dinner.

As teenagers are wont to do, Lauren acted a little peeved that her mother was checking up on her—and right in front of the host family. "I'm fine ... school was fine ... and Karlie and

I are having fun playing a new video game she just got for her birthday." That was the essence of their conversation, although Nikki did manage to fit in a quick "We love you, Baby. Please be careful. I'll call you once a day to make sure everything is okay."

That evening, Jon and Nikki enjoyed a seafood dinner at the nearby Red Lobster restaurant, during which Jon's cellphone silently vibrated in his pocket three times. Fortunately, the Swensons were sitting across from each other in a booth, which enabled Jon, at the first opportunity, to lay his phone on the bench seat in order to view the screen. All three calls were from HARKER, BRENT. He stifled a sarcastic smile. So this was how the weekend was to be.

Jon could only guess whether these calls were from Brent Harker himself or from Abby. He no longer had the luxury of filtering his communications through go-between Ronnie Delaney, which meant that any random moment held the potential to bring disaster upon him. Gradually, he became more and more convinced that it was Abby who had placed the calls. Were Brent trying to reach him, perhaps to reschedule their conference, he could have resorted to either texting or email. The caller must have been Abby. And so, one whole day earlier than Jon had hoped, his double life had already begun in earnest.

The meeting with Brent and two script consultants—Jon refused to accept the term "doctor"—was set for 10:00 on Saturday morning at Conference Room #4 of Arr-Tee Studios. This twelve-year-old production company was named for its founder and titular president, Reinhardt Georg Tetsch, who rarely made a physical appearance on the four-acre grounds. But R. T.'s spirit breathed down the neck of every employee on his payroll, and Brent Harker had the battle scars to prove it.

Jon Swenson, being an outsider, was totally unaware of this, so he held no preconceived notions of what to expect. All he possessed were his manuscript, called *Kiss Me Where It Hurts*, and a GPS that would guide him to the film studio. In truth, he also had a stomach full of butterflies, which was only natural for someone so oblivious to the inner workings of hardball movie-making. He decided to adopt a positive attitude, seeing these consultants more as collaborators than as confrontational adversaries. Wearing a thick skin would be a definite plus.

Nikki was anxious to see the sights of Hollywood, but the onset of nightfall made this a difficult time for travel-weary, out-of-town visitors to attempt much exploring. She and Jon would spend their first night in Los Angeles almost like they were still back home, watching either Game Show Network or Turner Classic Movies on television. This hotel offered an upper tier of channel selections, which made the room charge all the more reasonable. Dreading his morning meeting, Jon went to bed at 10:00 PM, and Nikki followed a half-hour later. She fell asleep quickly and soundly, but he tossed and turned for three hours before finally drifting into an intermittent slumber that lasted until around 5:30 AM. It was a good thing that theirs was a king-sized bed, or Nikki would have awakened as unrefreshed as her husband.

Both parents used Nikki's cellphone to chat with their daughter before going downstairs to breakfast. Lauren had slept, on a comfortable camping cot, at the house of sophomore Karlie Fischmann, whose mother then drove her back home after a family meal at IHOP the next morning. Lauren would be able to sleep in her own bed on Saturday before joining a high school girls' night at the home of Sonya Toliver immediately following the Sunday evening church service. Senior Tammy Neil would drive her there.

Jon was something of a wreck on Saturday morning, following his restless sleep the night before. He tried not to worry about his appearance, for he was not being asked to perform in front of a movie camera. His presumptive career would take place behind the camera, if he was permitted on the set at all. Screenwriters were considered to be distinctly inferior lifeforms when it came to a movie crew's hierarchy. Why that should be was a long-standing mystery in cinematic lore. After all, the film would not even exist were it not for the person who created its story out of whole cloth. But once a screenplay was sold, it was out of the hands of its writer forever, and studio hirelings were free to alter the plot however they wished. Oftentimes, as many as a half-dozen writers would be involved in transmogrifying the original screenplay into an unrecognizable feature that accorded to their own peculiar visions and whims.

Breakfast was included in the price of the Swensons' room, something they had come to regard as a prerequisite when making hotel selections. Jon ate some eggs and sausage, fried potatoes with onions, a small bowl of oatmeal, and a blueberry muffin. He now felt more invigorated than he would have thought possible just a half-hour earlier. Upstairs he went with Nikki, trying to assure himself that all would be well. After adding a necktie and suitcoat to his business attire, he glanced at the full-length mirror and pronounced himself to be as presentable as he ever could be. There was no time for procrastination here. He had to leave right away for what might prove to be the most momentous appointment of his life.

In their rental car, Jon drove himself and Nikki to the Arr-Tee Studios, which did not look anything like what he had envisioned. There was no pretentious archway above the entrance, nor was a grizzled guard named "Pops" stationed there to wave the celebrities past. Instead, a nondescript driveway led to a *cul-de-sac* that dead-ended in nothing grander than a semi-circle of six squatty huts. Happily, this underwhelming presentation gave Jon a marginal boost of confidence. The only thing even remotely intimidating about the site was its theatrical artwork. The Arr-Tee Studios logo dominated the rooftops of all six single-story structures, and full-color scenes from past productions adorned their front surfaces.

When Jon halted their rental car on the *cul-de-sac*, he climbed out with a leather valise under his arm. Inside the valise was a copy of *Kiss Me Where It Hurts*, which he feared would be torn to shreds—figuratively—by the three people whose purpose it was to whip the manuscript into shape. He stood for a moment, as grim and lifeless as a statue, while Nikki walked around to the driver's side to wish him good luck. "Don't worry about those script doctors, Honey. Whatever damage they inflict on your screenplay, you'll always have your own version of it on your computer. I'm with you all the way."

"What'll you do while I'm being kicked in the teeth?" he asked.

"I'm going to Rodeo Drive in Beverly Hills ... to see how the other half lives."

"Don't spend all of our savings. You know, Lauren might want to attend college some day."

"What time should I pick you up?"

Jon grinned. "You mean off the mat?"

"Let me put it this way," Nikki said. "When will you be ready to be accompanied back to the hotel by your stunningly beautiful chauffeur?"

"In that case, let's go right now."

Nikki rolled her eyes. "Really, though ... how long do you expect this meeting to take? Do you think they'll treat you to lunch in their commissary afterwards?"

"I don't even know if they have one."

Again he stared at the buildings, only now they had become much more imposing than his first glance had made them appear. For starters, these structures extended back at least two hundred feet from the asphalt roadway. Likewise, each supported a small but artistic sign, high above, that identified the nature of its interior components: Studio A, Studio B, Studio C, Properties, Conference Rooms, Administrative Offices. Jon would report to the fifth building from the left.

"I'll give you a call when the bloodbath is over," he said. "Park in any of these spots out front."

She nodded her head. "Is this when I'm supposed to say 'Break a leg'?"

"Nope. That's just for people in showbiz ... and I'm a long way from there, as I'll soon find out in no uncertain terms."

"Be positive, Honey. They wouldn't even be here if your screenplay didn't have some merit. Give them the benefit of the doubt."

Still, a nagging suspicion would not go away. It told him that Brent Harker was only performing this charade to satisfy the persuasive demands of his resplendent wife. Poor Jon was nothing but a naïve pawn, falling for every single move in Abby's egocentric game of manipulation.

•   •   •

Entering the building marked "Conference Rooms" was more difficult than Jon expected. The door was locked, and no one came to the front when he knocked. He considered walking around to the side, in order to peek in a window to wave for assistance, but windows were not to be found. Seeing no other choice, Jon resigned himself to trying the structure to his right instead, the one identified as "Administrative Offices." Its entrance door opened freely, so he went inside and approached the front desk. There sat a beautiful young woman, age twenty-five perhaps, who greeted him with a friendly smile.

"Yes, sir. How may I help you today?" she asked. A can of Diet Coke stood near her, and she had been flipping through an *American Cinematographer* magazine.

"I have a ten o'clock appointment to see Brent Harker," Jon said. A digital clock on the wall read 9:58 AM.

"I'm sorry, but Mr. Harker is not here yet. He called to say that he would be about twenty minutes late. Mr. Friedenburg and Ms. Wallick are already next door, in Conference Room #4, though, if you would like to go meet them before your meeting. I can unlatch the exterior door remotely from here." She picked up an electronic remote, resembling one that might open a locked vehicle.

"No, thanks. I should probably wait for Mr. Harker to arrive. He can introduce me to the others."

"That's fine, sir ... totally up to you." She pointed toward some vending machines behind her. "Would you like a can of soda or a candy bar while you wait? Whatever you want is on the house."

"Oh, no, but thanks just the same." He smiled at the young lady, whose name plate on the desk read "Ms. Levoir," and she was quick to smile back. Arr-Tee Studios certainly was an accommodating company, Jon noticed, but he was careful not to let his guard down from all the cushy treatment. This might very well be the oral surgeon's anesthetic before extraction.

Not long thereafter, a rather tall man with closely-cropped beard entered the front door and nodded at the receptionist. "Hi, Mandy. Will you let Randall and Trisha know that I'm here? We'll be over there in about five minutes."

"Right away, sir."

The man turned toward Jon, who was the only other person in the room, and extended his hand in greeting. "I'm Brent Harker, and you must be Jonathan Swenson, the playwright of *Kiss Me Where It Hurts*."

"Yes, sir." Jon stood up, and they shook hands.

"Please call me Brent. We're very informal around here, as a general rule." He took a step back from the guest. "As my wife probably told you, I was pretty impressed by your screenplay, but I think it could stand a few bits of refinement here and there."

"Thank you, sir."

That brought a grin. "Brent."

"Sorry ... Brent."

"I've asked a couple of our script supervisors to join us for this little meeting of ours. Randall Friedenburg and Trisha Wallick both know what they're doing ... and, more to the point, they are well aware of what it takes to turn a very good script into a dynamite one that will earn a profit on our investment." He chuckled. "That's the only reason we exist ... to make money. That may sound crass to you, but it's the unvarnished truth."

"I understand."

"With that in mind, Jonathan ..."

"Jon is fine."

"Okay ... Jon." Brent's smile darkened just a bit. "Are you willing to accept some changes that might be bounced off you? Most will be minor, I'm sure, but there could be one or two more substantial ones."

"All I can say is that I promise to remain open-minded. I guess that's what any writer will tell you."

Brent nodded his head in agreement. "Yes, absolutely. After all the work you put into your product, it will always be a rude awakening to learn that this beautiful offspring of yours is imperfect. And I should know, having written a half-dozen masterpieces of my own that were not successful."

Jon acknowledged the statement but did not think it appropriate to respond.

Brent motioned toward the door with his right hand. "Shall we proceed to the electric chair?"

"All right. At the very worst, I hope to come out of this alive."

"Most everyone does," Brent said. He turned to the receptionist. "Will you unlatch it for us, Mandy? I left my clicker at home."

"Of course, sir." Mandy pointed the remote to her right, toward the building next door, and pressed a button. "All right, sir, it's open."

The spacious parking lot out front, stretching along the cul-de-sac, was mostly empty, but Jon figured that was pretty normal on a Saturday. The only vehicles there were a bright-red Acura TLX, which Jon knew must belong to Brent Harker, and a Chevrolet Tahoe and Jeep Wrangler, which must have brought the two consultants. "After you," Brent said. He swung the front door open for Jon to enter.

From that point on, the film editor became an entirely different person. Now he was all business and no congeniality. He bypassed Jon in the hallway and walked straight ahead at full speed, expecting his invitee to follow behind as best he could. Brent turned sharply to his left and went inside a room marked "Conference 4." Its wooden door was connected to an overhead closer that slammed shut less than a second after Jon safely entered.

The man and woman who were already waiting there had been munching from snack-packs of Cheez-It and Chex Mix, respectively, while drinking from cans of Pepsi, all acquired from vending machines that stood at the back of the room. The pair did not trouble themselves to rise when Brent made his appearance, so Jon assumed that the editor held no executive power over them.

"Sorry to be so untidy, Brent, but Mandy promised us that Mr. Tetsch would pay for anything we wanted," the woman said.

"And we took her up on that," the man added.

"So I see," Brent told them. "Well, it won't break R. T. to fork over some of his loot while he's still around."

All three of the film people gave knowing grins. While doing so, the woman straightened up her area somewhat, and the man, too, pushed his litter to one side.

Then Brent spoke again. "I apologize for being a little late, but I was stuck in traffic. It's times like these when I really miss Montana."

"You're preaching to the choir," the man said.

Brent turned toward Jon. "Folks, this is Jonathan Swenson, the author of *Kiss Me Where It Hurts*, which I presume you've both read by now." They nodded their heads.

"And Jon ... that's what we'll call him from now on, just Jon ... these are Trisha Wallick and Randall Friedenburg, two of our very best script doctors."

That terminology rankled Jon, but he was in no position to lodge a complaint.

"It's up to us, as a group," Brent said, "to put some polish on this rough draft of Jon's and, if possible, make it more acceptable to the boys with deep pockets."

Now Jon was beginning to seethe, but he did so stealthily and without a sound. The nerve of these supernumeraries—all three of them probably failed scriptwriters—to label his heartfelt labor of love as a "rough draft" made his blood boil.

"Who wants to get the ball rolling?" Brent asked.

"I'll start," the woman said. "Jon, why do you have your protagonist be a former NFL cheerleader? Aren't you painting yourself into a corner by limiting her intelligence like that?"

Brent turned to the author of *Kiss Me Where It Hurts*. "What say you?"

Jon cleared his throat. "For one thing, why do you assume that a cheerleader has to be dimwitted? As a woman yourself, you should know better than that."

The room temperature dropped ten degrees.

"That's not the point," Trisha Wallick said. "It's what the filmgoer thinks that is important. Most of the public would not expect someone from that background to be a Rhodes Scholar."

"Maybe not, but Genevieve has lots of redeeming qualities that set her above other people with better educations. She's street-smart, for instance, and not gullible enough to fall for the party line."

Randall Friedenburg raised a finger. "On that same point, Jon, does an NFL cheerleader really make enough money to be self-sufficient? Wouldn't Genevieve also need a full-time position to make ends meet?"

"Certainly," Jon said. "As you'll recall, having carefully read the screenplay ..." The temperature dropped another ten degrees. "... she worked as the corrupt district attorney's administrative assistant until she was laid off, as a result of knowing so many inside secrets."

Brent jumped in at this point, choosing to guide the discussion elsewhere. "Let's restrict ourselves to the structure of *Kiss Me Where It Hurts*. Is there any problem with the sequencing of its three acts?"

"Frankly," Randall said, "I don't detect any division between the three acts ... or that there are three acts at all."

Brent prompted the defendant. "Jon?"

"To be honest with you, I did not create *Kiss Me Where It Hurts* as a three-act play. This is not the legitimate theater that we're talking about. There are no curtains to interrupt the flow."

Randall glanced at Trisha, who shrugged her shoulders.

"We should still construct our screenplay within a master plan of three acts," Brent said, "even though the divisions between them may not ... indeed, should not ... be as apparent as curtains in a theater."

Jon knew this three-act philosophy to be true, judging from the screenwriting manuals he had consulted over the years, but it still made little sense to him.

Trisha stabbed the tip of an index finger onto her copy of the manuscript. "Our recommendation ... and I think I speak for all of us ... would be to reconstitute this screenplay in a framework of three acts, preferably by basing it on a fully developed outline as your roadmap. You can't go far wrong with that."

Brent looked from one consultant to the other. "Any other glaring weaknesses that need to be addressed? I'm sure Jon here will be receptive."

Randall put on some reading glasses and flipped to an interior page of his copy. "Yes ... here on seventy-nine, near the bottom, I don't buy the way Kendrick speaks to that priest. It's just not realistic. No son of a dockworker would pop off like that ... not in mid-twentieth-century Baltimore."

Trisha nodded her head with great conviction. "And, while we're at it, I would point out that Kendrick is much too easily swayed by those PTA women who visit Bobby's fourth-grade classroom. No self-respecting man in 1947 would take that kind of verbal abuse from a woman. Today, perhaps yes ... but not in the immediate post-war years. He was an Army captain and no doubt used to ordering men around."

And so it went for two and a half hours, with sitting-duck Jonathan Swenson fielding potshots from three critics who seemed to find nothing whatsoever that might be construed as positive in *Kiss Me Where It Hurts*. On sheet after sheet of a legal-sized yellow pad, Jon dutifully wrote down all of these suggestions, as if they were the inerrant words of holy scripture.

When the brutal session was over, Jon could not resist firing a barb at the others for a change. "Can any one of you point to something that you actually liked about *Kiss Me Where It Hurts?* I don't mean that in an impertinent way, but I would sincerely appreciate anything at all as a cornerstone, upon which to erect a new story over these ruins."

After a short pause, Trisha volunteered a favorable comment. "I'll be happy to admit that the title is not too awfully bad."

But even this, a rather left-handed compliment, was quickly countermanded by Randall. "I don't like that title very much at all, to tell you the truth. Too clever by half, in my opinion."

"I'm afraid I must agree," Brent said. His smile was kindly rather than spiteful, so perhaps this was yet another scrap of constructive criticism. "Titles are nothing but hooks ... and surely our marketing division can dream up a replacement moniker for your property."

But was it really his property at all? Here before Jon was a coming attraction of how hardball movie-making would be played, and he wondered what techniques might be used to grow a thicker skin.

•   •   •

Once Randall Friedenburg and Trisha Wallick had driven their vehicles away from Arr-Tee Studios, Brent Harker and Jon Swenson returned on foot to the building marked "Administrative Offices." And Brent returned to his earlier persona—quite friendly and approachable. He led Jon to a rear room in the editing suite, where his office lay, and preliminary plans were arranged for the pair to meet at least one more time while the would-be screenwriter was still in California.

"I don't want you to feel like you were sucker-punched next door," Brent said. "Script doctors know exactly what they're looking for in a property, and they don't mind being blunt to the point of rudeness. It must have seemed like an ambush to you."

Jon remained a bit dazed by the experience, but he did manage to respond. "Yeah, I was prepared for the worst ... and this didn't even live up to my lowest expectations. If you want to know the truth, right now I'm tempted to throw *Kiss Me Where It Hurts* into the nearest dumpster fire."

Brent grinned. "Don't do that. There's hope for it yet." He poured a cup of coffee for each of them. "Cream? Sugar?"

"No, thanks ... just black."

"Some of your comments, in defense of the script, made a good deal of sense to me," Brent said, "but of course Randall and Trisha would never be honest enough to see it your way. They both know their stuff but are sort of hidebound when it comes to innovative story lines. Take about one quarter of their recommendations to heart, and discard the rest. Sometimes I think they're just trying to show everyone how brilliant they are."

Into the room came the pretty front-desk girl—whose full name, time would tell, was Amanda Levoir—and she laid a stack of manuscripts atop the bookshelves.

Brent looked her up and down. "Hi, Mandy. More spec scripts?"

"Yes, sir, I'm afraid so. Nothing very interesting, though, according to Mr. Dykes."

"Everyone is a playwright!" Brent said. Then, recalling who was seated beside him at the work table, he softened his cynicism. "Sorry for that, Jon. I think your property has some true promise." He grabbed the girl by her arm as she was leaving. "Say, Mandy, schedule a dinner spot for me and Abby tonight at seven, will you? Mr. Swenson has traveled halfway across the country to be manhandled by a couple of experts ... so I think I owe him that much at the very least."

Mandy laughed aloud. "Yes, sir. Will Mr. Friedenburg and Ms. Wallick be joining you?"

"No, please. I don't think that would be wise. Just Mr. Swenson, thanks."

"Yes, sir." Mandy exited the room with both men hypnotized by her swaying hips.

"She's a doll," Jon said.

Brent smacked his lips. "You noticed, huh?" He stared at the closed door. "I think it's important for a film studio to have attractive employees, so the 'beautiful people' will feel right at home. It's just a matter of image, really ... making a good first impression."

Jon was vacillating between whether to tell Brent that there would be four for dinner, not three, or to inform Nikki that an impromptu business dinner with Brent Harker had been scheduled but did not include her. He knew which choice would be the more honorable, of course, but was he socially adept enough to entertain both women at the same table? His better self told him that it was about time to stand up to the ghost of his past—no matter how beautiful and intriguing Abby might be. For now, though, he would take the easy way out and simply procrastinate. With any luck, something might happen during the next five hours that would render his decision moot. Maybe a meteorite would crush him into microscopic particles.

Jon chimed Nikki's cellphone with a new message, texting that she could drop by Arr-Tee Studios to pick him up at any time, now that the script meeting had concluded. Meanwhile, Brent Harker had plenty of other jobs to tackle in his office, so he excused Jon to return up front until his ride arrived.

"You probably won't mind seeing Mandy again," Brent said.

Jon grinned. "No ... not at all."

"You've arranged for someone to pick you up, right? Otherwise, I can have a staff member take you to your hotel or wherever else you need to go."

"No, don't bother with that. There's somebody on the way right now."

"I'll text you in a couple of hours, to let you know where we can meet for dinner," Brent said. "Nothing fancy ... probably just a chain restaurant of some sort."

"Sounds fine. That's where we like to eat anyhow."

That caught Brent's ear. "We?"

"My wife and I."

"Is she here in town?"

Jon feigned a look of surprise. "Yes. I thought you knew that."

"No. I presumed that you were on your own. By all means, invite her to come along tonight."

"Okay, but she's probably made other plans. Nikki has never been to L. A. before, so she's trying to hit the hot spots ... which to her means shopping."

"Is that your wife's name?"

"Yes ... Nikki."

"N-I-C-K-Y?"

"No, she spells it N-I-K-K-I."

Brent scribbled that, in pencil, onto the cover of *Kiss Me Where It Hurts*. "Is that short for anything ... like Nicole or Nicolette?"

"No, it's just Nikki."

"Well, I hope she can come. I'd like to meet her ... and I'm sure Abby would too."

Jon nodded his head, teeth firmly gritted. Then, feeling that a reply was needed, he supplied one that was noncommittal. "Same here, Brent. I'll be sure to let her know."

Up front in the entry room, occasionally answering the studio's landline telephone, Mandy Levoir sat very primly with her legs crossed. Beside her left elbow lay an *American Cinematographer* magazine, the same issue that she was reading that morning. Jon noticed this when he came forward from the editing suite.

"Hello again, Mr. Swenson," the girl said. "Have you had a nice day?"

Jon gave a weary sigh. "Not very. I've had better."

"Oh!" She appeared to be genuinely concerned. "What went wrong? I hope it was nothing that we said or did." She smiled, and the whole room brightened.

"No, no ... certainly not."

"That's good to know ... and quite a relief too. We pride ourselves on treating our clients with the utmost respect."

"Then I guess that doesn't include your script doctors."

Mandy squinched her pretty eyes. "Our what?"

Jon gave her the proper term. "Your script consultants."

"Oh, yes ... them. They're not big favorites around here, especially among the writers."

"Does your offer still hold ... about the snacks and drinks?"

"Yes, absolutely. Please help yourself ... no charge ... and show me what you got, so I can subtract it from the inventory."

Jon walked behind her to the vending machines and came back with a Pringles Snack Stack cylinder, a PayDay bar, and a can of Coca-Cola. Mandy jotted down those three items for later, when she would have a spare moment to deduct them from the computer stats. Jon took a couple of minutes to idly stand by the front desk, appreciating how beautiful this receptionist was. Her complexion and teeth were as flawless as any model's—and without the benefit of PhotoShop. Her green eyes sparkled with a happy spirit, and her straight brown hair was so long that it nearly reached to the seat of her chair. Mandy seemed to enjoy being looked at, and no wonder.

"You're a very pretty girl," Jon said.

"Thank you, sir." Her smile widened.

"Are you studying to be an actress?"

She giggled. "No, sir. I don't have any talent along those lines."

"You sure do have the looks to swing it."

"Thank you."

"I hope you don't mind my saying so. It's just that you're in the film production business, so I guessed you might be trying to work your way up through the ranks."

"No offense taken, sir. In fact, I'm flattered that you even considered the possibility."

Jon glanced down at the girl's left hand, which displayed an engagement ring and wedding band. "How long have you been married?"

"It'll be two years in August. We tied the knot right after I got out of summer school at college, one week before graduation."

"Where did you get your degree?"

"San Diego State ... but I'm actually from Arcadia."

"What does your husband do?"

"He's a police detective."

"L. A. P. D.?"

"Yes, sir."

Jon bounced that around in his mind. "Do you worry about him a lot?"

"Every minute."

"I wish law enforcement would get better support ... from the public and the state government."

"Same here."

"Pardon me for saying this, but California has a terrible reputation in that respect,"

"And well deserved too," Mandy said. She lowered her voice to a confidential level. "I can't express my true feelings around here very often. As you may know, the movie industry is extremely far to the left."

Jon winked at her. "I understand. Hang in there."

Mandy smiled up at him, and he walked back to his chair, where he opened the beverage's pop-top and began munching on the snacks. Not long thereafter, Jon's cellphone *dinged* a text signal, and the message read:

> Hi, J.
> On my way, so please be waiting outside around 1:30 or 1:45, depending upon this delightful traffic.
> Love, N

Jon flipped randomly through some pages of the yellow pad, refreshing his memory about the innumerable shortcomings that *Kiss Me Where It Hurts* was reputed to have. He bolstered his spirits by recalling what Brent had told him about disregarding three quarters of the suggestions. Still, even the remaining quarter was quite a lot of revision to consider. Much of what the consultants had recommended was utter nonsense, in Jon's objective opinion, but a handful of their proposals were valid and could be added to the plus column. In any case, suggestions were not decrees. Despite what Trisha and Randall might believe, Jon Swenson was still the writer.

• • •

When Nikki turned the rental car to the left, from a busy boulevard onto the property of Arr-Tee Studios, she noticed that her husband was already waiting for her outside. He stood, unsmiling and carrying a leather valise in his right hand. She came to a halt and rolled down the driver's window. "I don't see any broken bones or a bloody nose," she shouted over the road noise.

Jon climbed into the passenger seat and slammed its door. "Nothing as conspicuous as that ... but there are plenty of internal bruises."

"Uh-oh, sorry to hear that." She began to drive the car. "Hungry?"

"Starving! All I've eaten since breakfast are some potato chips and a candy bar."

"That beats me. I haven't had anything."

Los Angeles traffic was horrendous, as usual, but Nikki was able to position their car in the right lane, hoping to find a good place to stop for their midday meal. Countless blocks went by—largely occupied by dust-covered industrial firms—until they happened upon a metallic diner that resembled an abandoned railroad car. "How about this?" Nikki asked.

"Suits me."

The restaurant was crowded with blue-collar workers, apparently on their lunch hours, so the Swensons had to wait at the front for an available booth. When one came open, they were ushered to it by a skinny blonde with tattoos over every square inch of her visible skin—except for the face, which instead featured multiple piercings through each eyelid, a painful-looking bolt through her tongue, and a golden, horseshoe-shaped nose ring. "Your therver will be with you thoon," she lisped.

Greasy, old-fashioned double hamburgers and French fries were the order of the day in this place, and that was fine with both Nikki and Jon, who sat across from each other. They agreed that these 1960s-style delicacies were some of the best burgers and fries they had ever tasted. In a throw-back gesture to romance, the couple decided to share a tall chocolate milk shake. Although delicious, it proved to be far too thick for their straws to function properly, so they resorted to the use of two long-handled spoons.

"Did you learn anything productive at your meeting?" Nikki asked.

"Not much. As Brent told me later, sometimes his so-called 'script doctors' are kind of egotistical ... mostly interested in showing everyone how brilliant they are." He stirred the milk shake. "A couple of the pointers might help, I guess, but if I accepted every one of their recommendations, the credits for *Kiss Me Where It Hurts* should probably read WRITTEN BY RANDALL FRIEDENBURG AND TRISHA WALLICK. The whole confab was pretty humiliating for me, in addition to being a big waste of time."

"And money," Nikki said.

"That, too, obviously ... coming all the way to the West Coast."

"At least you know where you stand now."

"Do I?" Jon's question summed up the meeting in two words and sent his morale reeling. "Let's just drop it. Nothing can be done now to turn things around."

"Has Brent Harker given up on you?"

"No, I don't think so. In fact, he's invited both of us to dinner tonight."

Nikki smiled. "Really? That's a good sign for sure."

"Oh, don't get too excited, Nix. I'm afraid this dinner with Brent is more of a consolation prize than a firm offer."

"Will he be coming alone? Or is his wife planning to be there too?"

That seemed like a snippy way of putting it, so Jon responded in kind. "Yes, I'm pretty sure Abby will be planning to join us."

Although Jon had blurted out the invitation with little regard for its complications, he was instantly satisfied with himself for including Nikki in the occasion. Without question, she would always deserve top billing in his life. But what hazards might accrue in positioning her and Abby at the same dinner table? Jon shuddered to think about the near future and how carefully he would need to tread. And yet, staging a face-to-face encounter between the two was bound to happen sooner or later, and putting it off would only make matters worse. Besides, surely Brent Harker—who had never even met Nikki—would serve as a neutral buffer between them.

A text from Brent came to Jon's cellphone at 5:35 PM.

> Hello, Jon.
> I had no idea where you might like to eat tonight, so I asked Abby for ideas. She recommended Applebee's and Olive Garden. Do either of those sound good to you and Nikki? Let me know which you prefer (or another one entirely), and I'll give you the street address for the nearest location.
> Cheers, Brent

Mention of Applebee's brought back pleasant memories that Jon had no burning desire to repeat in the company of his own wife and Abby's own husband. The best he could hope for was to make it through the dinner unscathed. Inciting a lovers' quarrel in front of Brent would be the death knell for his screenplay—and perhaps his marriage as well.

Nikki and Jon mulled over the dinner suggestions and settled upon Olive Garden, whose Tuscan ambiance would be fully in keeping with her dressy outfit—not to mention,

Jon privately mused, Abby's apparel as well. Both women would feel comfortable in those surroundings, as would their proud escorts. Jon texted his dining choice to Brent, who replied immediately with the GPS address.

Rarely, if ever, had Jon Swenson been more neurotic than when readying himself for that night's dinner with the Harkers. Even his afternoon meeting with the script consultants was a cakewalk compared to this incendiary event. He wanted Nikki to look her absolute best—like the evening gown competition in a beauty pageant—so he insisted that she wear the sparkly, low-cut, Kelly green formal gown that she had brought along for whatever special occasion might present itself while they were in and around Hollywood. Furthermore, he knew Abby well enough to feel quite certain that she would be in full feather for this golden opportunity to strut her stuff.

In contrast, men were such pampered creatures. All they had to do was throw on a suit and tie and be done with it.

• • •

All this time, while Jon Swenson was out west in search of his screenwriting dreams, two major developments at the oldies radio station were anything but routine. For one thing, Ronnie Delaney had fractured his right leg in a motorcycle accident. Luckily for the station, this mishap occurred on a Sunday afternoon, and Ronnie was professional enough to report for duty, wearing a fourteen-inch-long cast, the very next morning.

Actually, "mishap" is probably the wrong term to use. More accurate would be "madness for speed." It seems that Ronnie was pushing his Yamaha YZF-R3 to its very limits—or at least to the rider's limits—on a closed track with hairpin turns and concussive moguls. His bike landed on top of him with the unforgiving force of gravity, although thankfully distributing most of its 375 pounds elsewhere in the dirt. This was not Ronnie's first broken bone, nor undoubtedly would it be his last.

The most sympathetic co-worker came as a total surprise to him. The person who succeeded Ronnie daily at 2:00 was known to the public as Sunny Shade, and her on-air personality was that of a chatty gadabout who was welcomed to radios all over town. Away from the microphone, however, MacKenzie Bastrop crawled into her shell and became a poster girl for unsociable conduct. That all changed when she spotted Ronnie in his plaster-of-paris prison, precariously balancing one buttock atop a chair in the staff lounge.

"Ooh, my poor dear!" this unfamiliar Ms. Bastrop shouted at him. She charged forward and clasped Ronnie's right hand between both of her own. "What did you do to yourself?"

"Oh, it's nothing, really ... ''Tis a flesh wound,' as the Black Knight said in *Holy Grail*." Ronnie laughed at his own joke, but MacKenzie did not appear to comprehend what was, to her, an arcane reference. He brooded for just a moment, shaking his head with sadness. "Not a Monty Python fan, I see."

"Hardly," MacKenzie said. "My taste in British humor lies on a loftier plain than that troupe."

Ronnie drew back in mock astonishment. "I ask you, what could be loftier than Monty Python's Flying Circus?" Then he held up a hand. "Wait! Don't answer that ... or I'll only demonstrate my vast ignorance."

She actually flashed a smile, something he had never witnessed from her before. MacKenzie was not pretty, as conventional perception might rate her. She was quite tall—nearly six foot, Ronnie estimated—and her frame was a bit too thin for aesthetic gratification. She wore tiny glasses that were distinctly unbecoming, causing her eyes to appear beady and even reptilian to the casual observer. But there was an aura of self-satisfaction about her that commanded attention. MacKenzie was comfortable in her own skin, and she cared not a whit how anyone else might view her physical attributes or accept her literary predilections. Against every fiber of his masculinity, Ronnie Delaney was warming up to this androgynous outcast. In her own unique way, he conceded, MacKenzie Bastrop was not too terribly unsightly.

Only a few minutes went by before MacKenzie was treating Ronnie as if she were his private duty nurse and he were her sole patient. And, to no one's surprise, not very many days went by until she began introducing him to the niceties of classic fiction. At this point, Ronnie dug in his heels. The essence of his reading material extended no further than various Dashiell Hammett yarns, *The Complete Calvin and Hobbes*, and transcriptions of Rod Serling's "The Twilight Zone." He also possessed a peculiar fetish for committing to memory the dialogue from all twelve scripts of "Fawlty Towers."

One might assume that Ronnie quickly fled from his governess's overzealous attention, but one would be wrong. He found it to be quite refreshing after a long day's announcing, sort of like sinking into a warm bubble bath on a rainy Sunday afternoon. Ronnie felt like crown royalty when in MacKenzie's presence, and he did nothing to dissuade her from serving as compassionate mother for the next six weeks of rehabilitation. At their appointed time together in the staff lounge—9:00 to 10:00 AM—she habitually fêted him with plastic-wrapped cinnamon rolls and steaming cups of coffee. Never did she accept any recompense for her expenditures, even when Ronnie insisted. Why should he object to this generosity if it made her so very happy?

"How's the leg?" she would never fail to ask him.

"Better," he would tell her.

Among the many autographs that his cast acquired over the ensuing weeks were well over a dozen names with feminine, stylized flourishes in their penmanship. Men signed their names too, of course, but Ronnie seemed to have reserved the cast's front side for the female acquaintances in his orbit. He instructed these chosen girls to stand between his legs when adding their names. That way, their signatures would be readable from his own vantage point, with a self-absorbed disregard for any other onlooker in the world who might wish to view his assembled "cast" of characters right-side up.

The very first signatory was MacKenzie Bastrop. She signed in the normal fashion, kneeling in front of him with pen in hand, but she inserted a tiny heart above the "i" in her given name. As any of her timeslips would promptly reveal, this was not her usual way to write in cursive. Before long, others on the staff began to question what relationship might exist between MacKenzie and Ronnie, who had become inseparable during their daily hour together.

The finest detective in that respect was weekend announcer Irving Koslov, who was substituting for Jon Swenson on Friday and Monday. Irving passed the figurative baton to Ronnie on each of those two days, and he made it a point on Friday to ask whether MacKenzie was "hotter" than she looked. He said it with a grin, as men would do, granting Ronnie the privilege of tossing the matter aside just as playfully, if so inclined.

Ronnie was so inclined. "How should I know?" he said. "We're just pals. I never even see Mack except for that one hour before I go on the air."

"So, you two are not dating?"

Ronnie was indignant. "Me and MacKenzie Bastrop? Give me a break!"

But he remained friendly with MacKenzie and did not allow the tawdry suspicions of fellow employees to cloud his strong attraction to her. He even began reading a book that she recommended very highly for a novice classicist, particularly one who revered the imaginative stories of Rod Serling. Penned as far back as 1818, this was *Frankenstein; or, The Modern Prometheus* by Mary Shelley, wife of the short-lived British poet Percy Bysshe Shelley.

Besides Ronnie's motorcycle crash, a second major development at the radio station—one that could impact everyone on the payroll—was its proposed change of format, from DJ-hosted oldies to automated pop hits. Understandably, owner Myron Kapp and his wife, Cecilia Borden Kapp, were never satisfied with their station's anemic ratings numbers, and they had long considered the tempting notion of trimming the budget by ridding it of so many full-time salaries. According to the internal accountants, this could be implemented within ten days or so, and the budget would adjust to become less than sixty-eight percent of its former self.

But could Myron and Cecilia pull the rug out from under their loyal workers after twenty-two years? They knew most of them and their families personally—even going to church on Sundays with some and socializing in the evenings with others—and they would need to give the majority of them pink slips at the end of this pay period. Mr. and Mrs. Kapp were seventy-nine and seventy-six years old, respectively, and it would be very distasteful to devastate the lives of so many people who looked to them for their sustenance.

The final decision would be made sometime during the week and then revealed early on Friday. Irving Koslov, pinch-hitting for Jon Swenson as the morning drive-time announcer, received the official, telephoned proclamation from the lips of Myron Kapp himself.

"Are you sitting down, my boy?" he asked.

"Yes, sir ... in between songs."

"I hate to be the bearer of bad news ..."

"Uh-oh."

" ... so I've decided to give you some good news instead."

"Oh?"

"We are to be, for the foreseeable future, an oldies music station. I want you to pass the word along to your colleagues, as best you can. You'll have all of today for doing that."

"Yes, sir, will do. That is good to hear!"

"But not over the air, please. This is an in-house matter, and we don't want our audience to become too skittish about the years ahead."

"Yes, sir. Thank you, sir," Irving said. "I'll let everybody at the station know. My mouth can be pretty big when I've got some breaking headlines to spread."

• • •

There was a thirty-to-forty-minute wait for a table at Olive Garden on this busy Saturday night, so the Swensons sat on one of the half-dozen twelve-foot-long cushioned benches near the greeters' stand. Nikki cradled in her hands an electronic notifier, which would vibrate and illuminate to signal that it was their turn to be taken to the dining area.

The only snag was that Brent and Abby had not yet made an appearance. Although the restaurant's waiting area was teeming with people, both seated and milling about, so far Jon had detected no sign of them. "I'll keep my eyes peeled," he said. "We probably can't go to our table until they get here."

Nikki would be no help in spotting them because she had never met either of the Harkers. Thirty-five minutes into the wait, she registered her annoyance. "I would have thought they'd be here before us," she whispered. "They're familiar with this area and the traffic patterns." She sighed, quite loudly. "Maybe they're just the sort who like to arrive fashionably late. Some insecure people get a cheap thrill out of that masquerade."

Jon did not wish to dignify Nikki's derisive comment by responding to it, so he turned his head away from her and toward the front door. Why were women like that anyway? Who could really say what caused the Harkers to be late? It was very nice of Brent to invite him and Nikki to dinner, something he certainly did not have to do. And yet, here was Nikki, grumbling about some petty error in timing that would soon be forgotten. Again, he scanned faces in the crowd.

And there she was! Jon's heart raced when he spotted Abby from afar. She looked glorious in an elegant, blue, corded lace gown. It was full-length and sleeveless, with an alluring V-neck. Alongside her, Brent was tastefully attired in a complementary blue suit that was accented by ultra-thin black pinstripes. No seating space was left on any bench, so the Harkers remained standing across the congested room. Abby did not appear to see Jon, but Brent acknowledged him with a quick nod.

A couple minutes later, the hand-held device alerted Nikki that their time had come, so she showed it to her husband and stood up. Jon also rose, while motioning toward Brent to follow them behind the hostess. "There they are," Jon said. He pointed in the general direction, but naturally she had no idea which man and woman were the Harkers.

Their booth for the evening was situated at the extreme rear of the dining area, a considerable distance away, and this gave the two women a brief opportunity to size each other up as they walked. When the hostess stopped at their table, the couples began to seat themselves in a chivalrous sequence—that is, women first. However, Abby induced her husband to slide across the seat prior to her, so it happened that Brent was facing Nikki, and Abby was facing Jon. The scene was set for a very pleasant meal, assuming that the looming personality clashes were kept in check.

"Did you have any luck with your shopping?" Brent asked Nikki. He did not really care, but at least this would open the lines of communication.

"Too much luck," she said. "I'm afraid my luggage will be breaking the weight barrier, à la Chuck Yeager."

Brent seemed confused, so Nikki elaborated. "It's similar to the sound barrier ... only not as loud."

He gave her a charitable grin. "Don't feel too bad about that. I almost never beat the fifty-pound limit anymore ... and I do a lot of flying."

Abby turned to Nikki. "I wish you could have come to your husband's class reunion. He was the life of the party."

Jon cringed at the thought. "That's so untrue it's funny. I felt like a fish out of water ... flopping around on some wharf."

Abby gazed at him with dreamy eyes. "But you were kind enough to be my escort to the dance, and I'll never forget that."

"Some escort! I never even danced ... with you or anyone else."

Nikki looked straight ahead, at Brent. "Jon said you were at Dodger Stadium that night … and couldn't attend the dance." She wanted to keep up her end of the conversation.

"Yep, that's where I was all right … four rows behind home plate. No contest where I'd rather be … at some high school reunion or a Dodger game." He gave his wife a blank stare. "Oh, well, Abby probably had more fun that way, didn't you, Babe? You know, without me hanging around, clipping your wings."

Abby considered for a moment before answering his loaded question. "I'll never tell. Frankly, I don't recall much about that night, except how nice Jon was to me."

"And Colby Reed," Jon said.

"Oh, yes … Colby. I think we dated a couple of times during our senior year."

The Swensons exchanged glances with each other. Both knew of Abby's weakness for adult beverages and how she brought embarrassment upon everyone in the Silver Jubilee Reunion class. From all indications, Abby now retained only the sketchiest memory of Colby's assistance in dragging her away from even further disgrace.

A waitress arrived at their booth, mumbled a three-syllable name that no one caught, and requested the drink preferences.

"Just water for us," Jon said. He indicated the Swenson side of the table.

"A *pinot noir* for me, please," Brent said, "and a sweet *sauvignon blanc* for my wife."

Abby smiled at the waitress. "And we'll let you know when we need refills."

Jon and Nikki did not have particularly broad palates, so each of them ordered basic meals for themselves—spaghetti with meat sauce, prefaced by the *pasta e fagioli* soup. Brent and Abby, however, began with an appetizer of shrimp *scampi fritta*, followed by the *capellini di mare* and seafood *brodetto*, respectively. The names of these Italian dishes rolled off their tongues like natives of the Mediterranean. Any impartial bystander would have been impressed by such poised *savoir-faire*, and that included the unschooled couple seated across from them.

Before long, the dinner talk became centered upon that afternoon's meeting with the consultants, whom Brent continued to call "script doctors." Oddly enough, it was Abby who introduced this topic to the table, but she did so in a very smooth, unobtrusive manner that bespoke no ulterior motive beyond the desire for casual chatter.

"How did you like the studio?" she asked Jon.

"Oh, fine. Arr-Tee is much larger than it appears from the street."

"And isn't that Mandy Levoir a beautiful girl?"

In answering, Jon was careful not to make eye contact with his wife. "You bet she is ... prettier than most movie stars."

Brent intruded with a more substantial theme. "I think we managed to come up with one or two useful suggestions, didn't we, Jon?"

"I guess so, but that's awfully hard to say at this point ... until I bake them into the mix and see how it tastes."

"Please give that three-act structure a shot ... even if it seems like a foreign concept to you. And it wouldn't hurt to have a printed outline ready before our discussions go any deeper. The big boys will want to see it, sooner or later, so you might as well have one handy."

"Who are these 'big boys'?" Nikki asked. She did so in all honesty, for it seemed like a logical question to her. Instantly, though, she regretted trespassing on the film editor's private territory.

Brent looked askance at her—as if she were a pesky toddler—and replied in the most elementary terms that he could muster. "I was talking about our ATS producers, the higher-ups who get to choose which stories you'll be watching at the local movie theaters." With that, he dismissed Nikki and turned to Jon. "Any idea when you might be able to develop a revision for them? No huge hurry, but I'd like to know what your general timeframe is."

"I'll dive into that right after I get back home."

"How much trouble will it be to make these revisions?" Abby asked.

When Jon looked at her, he could not help but smiling, and quite broadly, too—so broadly, in fact, that he hoped Nikki did not take notice. Abby Pierce Harker was every bit as beautiful as he remembered her when she opened the door to room 624 of the Los Angeles hotel. Like before, her dark hair was piled high atop her head, and her unblemished complexion was lovely and smooth. The corners of her mouth curled up ever so slightly, as if she were bemused at those around her—an affectation that reminded him of Vivien Leigh in her role of Scarlett O'Hara.

He snapped out of it. "I'm sorry, Abby. What did you ask?"

"I was wondering how much trouble it'll be to make the revisions to your screenplay."

"Not much, I don't think ... compared to all the time it took to come up with my first draft and the next few versions."

"Why do you need three acts?" she asked.

Brent glared at her, no less fiercely than if Abby had poured her entire glass of wine onto his seafood. "Because that's what will hold the entire story together," he said. "It gives the screenplay a backbone, so it won't be as amorphous as a jellyfish. Please don't muddle the issue, Honey. Filmmaking is not in your wheelhouse, despite what your husband might do for a living."

To Jon's great surprise—and no little disappointment—Abby accepted the criticism with a calm resolve. She simply laid down her fork and took a sip of the *sauvignon*. Above the rim of her long-stemmed wine glass, Abby's deep blue eyes, now shifting to Jon instead of her husband, remained perfectly dry and clear.

Brent swallowed another bite of the *capellini*, after savoring it to the utmost, and unconsciously stroked his well-manicured beard with the left hand. "Tell me this, Jon. If I were to switch the genders of your two protagonists ... Genevieve and Damon ... would *Kiss Me Where It Hurts* still be a viable story? This is a time-honored writer's trick that can sometimes expose narrative defects before they become fully ingrained and beyond repair."

"That might be interesting to try, but I think my characters' genders are already fully ingrained. For instance, I can't imagine portraying Damon as a former NFL cheerleader."

"Not if he has much hair on his chest," Brent said. He laughed good-naturedly at his own joke. "And I do see your point there. That would create an entirely unwanted angle for your story." Both of the women giggled, too—a cheery departure from what had gone before—and this lightened the whole tone of the meal, at least for the time being.

But that was enough levity for Brent. "Actually, though, I'm talking in just the most general terms ... switching genders as if viewing *Kiss Me Where It Hurts* from an altitude of thirty thousand feet. Sometimes this clever technique can provide the writer with a fresh perspective on his creation, whereas he may have been too close to the project until then."

"Or *her* creation," Abby said.

Brent was visibly annoyed. "Excuse me, Dear?"

"You said *his* creation, when really it could just as likely be *hers*."

"Fair enough. I just thought that would be understood. In this particular case, it would be *his*."

Abby did not give in. "Unless the genders were switched."

Brent sighed at his wife, but then he could no longer fight back a smile. "Point well taken, my love. Sometimes I'm just a chauvinistic brute."

With the exception of two or three mildly tense moments between the Harkers, the rest of this evening meal was an amiable experience for everybody at the table. As they were unwrapping and relishing the complimentary after-dinner mints, Brent expressed his delight in meeting Nikki Swenson. This was a host's automatic remark that conveyed little conviction. More sincere was his encouragement for Jon Swenson to stay in touch. "Let me know when you have a revision ready for the studio brass to evaluate."

"You mean the 'big boys,' don't you?" Nikki asked. She did so with a perfectly straight face.

Brent blushed at her sarcasm. "*Touché!* I probably deserved that," he said. "Sorry I was such a wise guy earlier, but I tend to get way too serious whenever a discussion concerns the studio's bottom line." He nodded sideways, toward his wife. "If this production company goes under, then so do we."

A few minutes later, as they were saying goodbye in the parking lot, Brent shook Jon's hand and gave him a colorful Arr-Tee Studios business card. It was three dimensional, embossed with his personal email address and direct cell number. "Keep this in your wallet. Maybe you and I can do business some day."

"I hope so. Thanks for the great dinner."

"Yes, thank you very much," Nikki said. Brent smiled at her, and they shook hands.

During that brief second, Abby slipped Jon a folded scrap of paper. He read it, in private, a half-hour later at the hotel, while Nikki was brushing her teeth in the bathroom. The message, written in an attractive, feminine penmanship, said, "Meet me tomorrow at AMMP about 11. I'm telling you this now so you can make plans." At first glimpse, Jon wondered what the acronym AMMP could possibly stand for, but then he recalled something Brent had talked about over dinner.

· · ·

Teenager Lauren Swenson had never spent an entire night alone before, so this Saturday would be a milestone on her road to maturity. Breakfast at a local IHOP restaurant began the day, a treat provided by the parents of schoolmate Karlie Fischmann. Lauren had slept on a cot in Karlie's bedroom overnight, and, predictably, the girls did not fall asleep until after 2:00 in the morning.

Ten-year-old Caleb Fischmann was partially responsible for the girls' lack of pillow time, for he engaged in a series of childish pranks that were designed to spook his older sister and her friend—and did so rather effectively. Towheaded Caleb was proud to claim responsibility for why Karlie and "that Swenson girl" were so drowsy over breakfast. Karlie's parents, David and Jillian, suspected as much and manifested their displeasure by curtailing his weekend access to all video game controllers. Caleb, of course, was able to evade their punishment by simply gaming on his cellphone instead.

It was nearly 11:00 AM when her host family brought Lauren back home. By that time of the morning, severe weather was brewing, just off to the west of town, and David Fischmann was worried about the girl's safety. "Will you be all right on your own?" he asked. "You're welcome to stay with us until the bad weather blows through."

"Oh, I'll be fine," Lauren said. She exhibited an outward air of confidence, but her reply was little more than bluster. Deep within, she was quite fearful of the approaching thunderstorm—especially after the Fischmanns departed, and she was truly alone. What caused her nerves to be on edge was how dark the house had become in daylight, and at such an unnatural hour. Hail was now rattling against the windows. The wind was flexing its muscles, too, gusting up to forty miles per hour. A tree limb began striking the roofline, gently at first but then swelling to the deafening barrage of a sledgehammer.

Over the years, Lauren had heard on television weathercasts that the safest place in a house during tornado watches was an interior space away from any windows. For that reason, she went inside a closet beneath the staircase, bringing with her a flashlight and battery-powered radio. Soon thereafter, in the wake of a blinding flare of lightning and its resounding boom, the house's electricity ceased to function. The closet's interior, even with the door wide open, was now as black as midnight.

And then there came a loud pounding of another sort. Someone was knocking frantically on the front door, yearning to be rescued from the onslaught of this deluge. Lauren peered at the security camera's monitor to see who it was. Positive identity was hard to determine because the person, evidently a young man of medium build, was facing to one side while trying to keep the horizontal rain from blowing into his eyes. Finally, the boy noticed an overhead surveillance camera and waved his hands toward it in the fervent hope that he would be recognized.

The camera's high-quality lens showed Lauren that this "stranger" was Bradley Tallin, a fellow high school student in the junior class. He appeared to be drenched by the unremitting downpour and desperate to be let into the dry house. Quickly, Lauren retracted the deadbolt and allowed Bradley to step inside. Although dripping onto the hardwood floor, the important thing was that he was away from the rain, hail, and lightning.

"You must be crazy, Brad!" Lauren said. "What are you doing outside in weather like this?"

"My truck got stuck in a ditch, and I was stranded."

"Where is it?"

"Just a couple of blocks over ... but that's a long way in this kind of weather. A ton of rain came down in the past five minutes." With both hands, Bradley wiped water from his forehead.

"You're right about that. Why'd you come here?"

"I remembered where you live, and I just took a chance that you'd be home. Otherwise, I'd probably look like a drowned rat by now."

"Wait here. Don't muddy up the carpet." Lauren ran to the laundry room and returned with two bath towels, which she tossed to Bradley. "Take off your shoes and socks."

After wiping his face and arms, he sat down on the wooden floor and did as she requested.

"I can't ask you to stay because my parents aren't here," Lauren said.

"But I sure can't go outside with all this happening." He motioned toward the front door.

"No, of course not. I just meant that you'll need to leave whenever the storm lets up."

"Roger that."

Another flash lit up the room, followed almost immediately by a deafening crack of thunder. The wind continued to grow in intensity, and the civil defense sirens were beginning to wail.

"There's trouble on the way," Lauren said. "Follow me."

"Roger that."

She ran toward the closet again, with Bradley close behind.

"Shine that flashlight toward me," she told him. Lauren turned on the radio, hoping to get a weather update. She heard mostly static until finally acquiring a strong signal. "I think that's my daddy's station."

The oldies radio station was carrying a recorded message from the National Weather Service. "A tornado has been sighted or indicated by weather radar," the robotic voice said. "There is imminent danger to life and property. Move to an interior room on the lowest floor of a sturdy building. Avoid windows, and protect yourself from flying debris."

Lauren shut the closet door, and the tiny room was plunged into total darkness. Bradley giggled. "Point the flashlight at my mouth, and you can see my teeth chattering."

"Hey, you're shivering. Are you really that cold?"

"I'm not just pretending." His voice wavered as he spoke.

"We sure don't want you to come down with pneumonia."

"No, I doubt that, but I feel like I fell into a cold lake."

"Let me grab some dry clothes for you." Flashlight in hand, Lauren left the closet and ran upstairs to her parents' bedroom. Once there, she snatched a few mismatched articles of her father's clothing—shirt, pants, underwear, socks—and ran back downstairs. "Here. Change into these."

"Do you think I should?"

"Just do it ... and hurry. No one's going to see." She laughed at him. "If you're worried about me sneaking a peek, you can keep the flashlight over there by you." Again she closed the closet door, and the room went pitch dark.

Lauren could hear Bradley as he changed into her father's clothes. "Okay, I'm done," he said. "I don't think they fit very well."

"No problem."

The wind was howling, almost triple figures in velocity, and Lauren prayed silently for their health and safety. Something struck the kitchen window like a thrown rock, and there came the sound of shattering glass. Lauren opened the closet door just long enough to assess the damage. Sure enough, the flashlight showed that one of the window panes was demolished from top to bottom. A foot-long piece of tree limb lay beneath it, and rain was streaming freely inside. Nothing could be done about that now. At least the floor was vinyl and would not suffer any water damage.

Into the closet Lauren returned, shutting the door behind her. "Did something get smashed?" Bradley asked.

"Yep. A piece of flying wood hit one of the windows ... probably broke off from a tree."

Thirty more minutes passed, and the storm audibly lessened in ferocity. Lauren opened the closet door and ventured into the kitchen. About half of its floor was covered in an inch of water. Bradley came out, too, wearing an oversized flannel shirt, khaki jeans, and woolen socks.

"Don't walk through the water," Lauren said, "or you really will catch pneumonia."

"Roger that." This was one of Bradley's favorite expressions—coming not from the military or police in his case, but from its common usage in dramatic television shows. He thought the phrase had an official and authoritative ring to it. Also, of course, he presumed that it might impress someone of the opposite sex.

As suddenly as the severe storm arrived, it departed just as quickly. "Do you think your truck will be all right?" Lauren asked.

"Hopefully so. The hail might have caused some small dents, but at least there were no trees or buildings near where the truck was stuck. Pulling its tires out of the mud will probably be the toughest part." Bradley pondered for a few seconds. "I'm sure my dad can bring his four-wheel-drive Silverado and a strong rope. That should do the trick."

For now, he and Lauren collected the shards of glass and mopped up the kitchen floor. Then they turned their attention to the open window, affixing lengthy strips of shipping tape to fasten two layers of cardboard over the gaping hole. While this was not an ideal, waterproof solution to the problem, at least it would keep flying insects from coming inside until something more permanent could be done. That would need to wait until Lauren's parents returned home from the West Coast.

•   •   •

With few exceptions, Jon and Nikki Swenson's normal practice at home on Sunday mornings was to attend their local church, where they had been members for the past fifteen years. But when traveling, particularly to a great cosmopolitan center like Los Angeles, that praiseworthy routine sometimes was not feasible to maintain. Instead, they considered it permissible to sleep late, enjoy the hotel's free breakfast, and then spend the rest of the day behaving like common tourists.

One thing was for certain. However they chose to occupy their time, there would be no escaping the southern California traffic, which was dreadful even on a Sunday. The stated goal for Nikki was to finish her previous day's shopping spree, an excursion that was cut short when Jon needed to be picked up after his meeting with Brent Harker and the script consultants. So intent was Nikki to resume her bargain hunting that she even wrote down some of the more likely street addresses for eventual use by their GPS.

But spending a whole day in department stores and dress shops held no interest for Jon, and he explained to her that he preferred to forge his own trail. Being a fair-minded wife, she fully understood and, if the truth be known, preferred a solo jaunt anyway.

"There's an obvious problem," Nikki said. "How can we go two different directions with only one rental car between us?"

"Bus, train, or taxi for me ... maybe all of the above. Don't worry, though. I'll figure it out, somehow." Another practical matter had to be considered, too, and it made Jon smile at his wife. "Remember that anything you buy today will have to be taken back with us on the plane ... and we don't have an unlimited amount of space and weight."

Nikki nodded her head, as if to acknowledge that she was aware of this issue. "I'm sure that anything we can't take with us can be shipped."

"For a stiff price."

"But it'll be worth it because lots of fashions are one-of-a-kind and not available online." She glanced again at her GPS addresses. "By the way, what are you thinking about seeing?"

Jon seemed hesitant to say. "Brent mentioned a place that kind of intrigues me. It's called the Academy Museum of Motion Pictures."

Nikki chuckled. "That does sound like something Brent Harker would recommend."

"I know, but it could be a good idea for a one-day visit."

And so, the day's itinerary was set. Nikki would go her way and Jon his, with plans for them to meet back at their hotel around 5:00 PM.

Despite the comfortable, king-sized bed, Jon had trouble sleeping that night. For almost two hours, he could hear people noisily walking back and forth in the room directly above theirs, and it made him envision what they must be doing. Were they working off a heavy meal, breaking in some new shoes, or boosting their pedometer score? In any case, it was very inconsiderate.

As for Nikki, she outwitted the problem by the simple expedient of inserting a pair of earplugs. "Sorry, Dear," she said, "but they're all I brought along, and we can't very well share them." Her cellphone's alarm was set for 8:15 AM, thus guaranteeing that she would have most of Sunday to pursue her accumulation of, as she saw them, priceless artifacts.

Due to Jon's abbreviated sleep, he was startled to hear his wife's alarm notification—entitled "Emergency Alien Fast Alert"—

at such a blaring volume. Worse yet, her phone was sitting atop the end table on his side of the bed, and he did not know how to squelch the pandemonium. With his heart still pounding from the shock, he tossed the phone to her, and she silenced it by gently touching the screen. Only then did she finally remove her earplugs—while chuckling at Jon in spite of herself.

Nikki's plans for the day were clear. "I'll try to leave by ten," she told him, "and that'll give me almost seven hours to have fun."

"Is that what shopping is for you ... fun?"

"Certainly!"

Jon shook his head in disbelief. "Men and women are from different planets. Going shopping all day would be a form of slow torture for us."

"The only thing that bothers me are those uppity females from the Westside neighborhoods ... like Brentwood and Bel Air. They think salespeople are their personal servants, just there to make them feel important."

After breakfast, Nikki kissed her husband goodbye around 10:15 and then left to locate their car in the parking garage. Meanwhile, Jon took a minute to re-read the handwritten instructions that Abby Harker had slipped to him the night before: "Meet me tomorrow at AMMP about 11." Obviously, that would be impossible because of his lack of transportation, so Jon sent her a text message to say that he was stranded at the hotel.

Abby responded with a text of her own.

I'll swing by for you at 10:45. Be waiting at the entrance, and look for a dark blue Subaru.

She drove up right on time—in fact, about four minutes early. Her car was easy to spot, a stylish Subaru BRZ that was cobalt blue in color.

"Nice car," Jon said.

"Thanks. Brent bought it for me last month as a birthday gift." She raced the engine with pride and grinned at her passenger. "Care to take the wheel?"

Jon's face turned a bit red when he declined the invitation. "Better not. It's hardly even off the showroom floor."

As expected, Abby was a fast driver who weaved in and out of traffic, never signaling her next move. But she was also alert to everything around her and had a quick reaction time that steered clear of any precarious situations.

"How long do I have you?" she asked.

To Jon, that sounded like an odd way to phrase her question. "What do you mean?"

"When will Nikki expect you back at the hotel?"

"We agreed to meet there at five o'clock."

Abby nodded her head. "About six hours." Her voice was so quiet that Jon could hardly hear it.

The Subaru sped around a corner and into a public parking lot. Abby flashed a card at the unmanned toll booth, and immediately its boom barrier went up for admittance. "We have an annual pass," she said.

The Academy Museum of Motion Pictures was located next to the Los Angeles County Museum of Art in the Miracle Mile's Saban Building on Wilshire Boulevard. Offering four floors of gallery space, two theaters, a restaurant, and a gift shop, the AMMP was designed by Italian architect Renzo Piano, winner of the 1998 Pulitzer Prize.

Among the cinematic treasures in the museum's collection were the "Rosebud" sled from *Citizen Kane*, Dorothy's ruby slippers from *The Wizard of Oz*, both R2-D2 and C-3PO from *Star Wars*, the Dude's robe from *The Big Lebowski*, a full-body animatronic of E. T. from the film of that name, the Mount Rushmore backdrop from *North by Northwest*, some animated pencil drawings from *Bambi*, and "Bruce," the sole surviving shark from *Jaws*.

At one point in their visit, Jon confided something that he felt needed to be said. "Don't take this wrong, Abby, but I feel bad about coming here with you. I told Nikki that I was coming to the Academy Museum, but I let her believe that I'd be here by myself."

Abby gave him a mischievous smile. "Then we're all even. I never told Brent that I'd be here with you."

"Would he mind?"

"Not at all. We have a very open marriage ... maybe too open, as it turns out." She reversed the viewpoint. "Would Nikki mind?"

Jon could not even bear to imagine that scenario. "I think she'd explode like Vesuvius. She'd probably never trust me again."

"Let's just make sure she never finds out," Abby said. Again, she had that playful look. "Sometimes it's kind of fun to sneak around on your mate. It can be very thrilling ... the suspense that any minute you could get caught."

"Have you ever gotten caught?"

"Lots of times ... especially if I've been drinking, and my guard is down." She curled her lips in thought. "Of course, I have an advantage over you because I know for a fact that Brent is doing the same thing behind my back ... and I can always use that for extortion."

Suddenly, Jon felt very vulgar about what he was doing on the sly. He was really not like this, and he knew it without a doubt. If only Abby Pierce Harker were not so beautiful and exhilarating. Her melodic voice was like music to the ear, and her smile would brighten the gloomiest room. He was addicted to her, even though he realized that this was only a childish crush, a teenage infatuation that was left over from high school.

Jon and Abby ate grilled chicken sandwiches with potato salad at the museum's restaurant and then completed their traversal of the various exhibits. They stopped just inside the exit doors for a talk.

"You still have three hours of freedom," Abby said. "Would you rather visit LACMA next door or come home with me for a while?"

Jon stalled for time. "What is LACMA?"

"That's the Los Angeles County Museum of Art. It's quite an impressive venue, if you go in for that sort of thing." Her eyes lit up when she smiled at him. "But I'd really like to show you my DVD collection ... and, of course, our two dogs always love to have company."

"What are their names?" Jon continued to tread water in the deep end.

"D. W. and C. B. They're named after two famous movie directors, Griffith and DeMille. We usually call them 'Dee' and 'Cee' for short."

"Is Brent at home?" Jon braced for Abby's reply, hoping against his every fleshly desire that she would say yes.

"No. He's at SoFi Stadium for the Rams game. Brent has season tickets for them and the Chargers, so almost all of his Sundays are taken by football from August to December."

"Do you ever go with him?"

"Not very often. Usually he takes a business associate along." Abby thought of something fundamental to add. "You should know that these two seats at SoFi actually belong to Arr-Tee Studios, not to Brent and me. We could never afford them, but the company can. Fortunately, Reinhardt Georg Tetsch couldn't care less about sports of any kind ... except soccer ... so Brent came out smelling like a rose."

"What time does the game start?"

"Kickoff is at one twenty-five, so that gives us all afternoon."

Hearing this, Jon felt very uncomfortable, and it must have shown.

"I mean all afternoon to look at my DVDs and CDs," Abby said. "I also have some Darnell High memorabilia to show you." She stared at him for a moment, but he seemed indecisive. "Unless, of course, you'd prefer going to LACMA. Our passes are good for that too."

"Which do you want to do?" Jon asked. He knew what her answer would be, but at least it was not his choice. Maybe that qualified him for a widow's mite of credit from his conscience.

"I'm dying to show you some things," Abby said. "Come on. Let's go."

• • •

"D. W. and C. B. came from the same litter of nine. They're more mongrel than pedigree, but we wouldn't have it any other way." Abby was scooting them away from the open door with her foot. Initially, the two miniature schnauzers barked at Jon, but when Abby commanded them to quiet down, they did as they were told and began treating the visitor as just another member of the household.

"Here. Throw this tennis ball," Abby said. "Cee and Dee love to chase after it, fight over it, and then bring it back to the person who threw it ... even if he happens to be a stranger, like you. They'll do it for as long as you're willing."

Jon sat down on a padded arm of the sofa and tossed a tennis ball across the living room floor. The two dogs scampered after it, sliding on their sides to capture the ball in their mouths. Sometimes the victor would be C. B., and sometimes it would be D. W.—according to Abby's spotting skills—but Jon was not sure which identical dog belonged to which name.

Ten minutes into the canine game, Abby made an announcement that stirred Jon's imagination. "I'm going to change into some shorts. You don't mind, do you?"

Jon stammered for a second, but then replied. "Of course not. Go ahead." He picked up the tennis ball. "The dogs will keep me entertained."

Abby returned to the living room in a fashionable outfit of shorts and halter top, in place of the summery blouse and blue jeans that she was wearing earlier. "If this makes you feel overdressed now, I can loan you a pair of Brent's athletic gear. He's big on tennis and racquetball."

"No, thanks. I'm fine."

She reached over and patted him on the leg. "I must admit that we both look pretty good for forty-year-olds, don't we?"

Jon's only response was a grin. He was not so sure about his own appearance, but Abby Harker looked stunning. He could envision her posing for a magazine ad, playing volleyball in the sand on a Caribbean beachfront.

With Abby leading the way, they went into Brent's study. That is where she and her husband each had their own DVD shelves of favorite movies. Inevitably, there was some overlapping of titles, but for the most part their collections represented two very distinct, idiosyncratic tastes.

"We both like discs instead of streaming," Abby said. "There's something nice about having the physical boxes standing there." She looked up at Jon. "What's your favorite movie of all time?"

The question was point-blank, so his eyes widened. "That's almost impossible to say. I probably couldn't narrow it down to less than a dozen."

"But that's not the question." Her face had an impish expression that made Jon smile. "You must play by the rules, Mr. Swenson." She reached over and took his hand. "Well? Tell me."

Although flustered, Jon did manage to mumble a sensible title in reply. "Okay. Then how about *Paper Moon*? That's a film by Peter Bogdanovich, with Ryan O'Neal and his daughter, Tatum. It's from the early seventies." He waited for Abby's response but got next to nothing from her.

"I haven't seen it," she finally said. "I've watched that director's *The Last Picture Show* ... which was terrific, of course ... and also his *What's Up, Doc?*, but never *Paper Moon*."

Jon felt that a further explanation was in order. "I'm not declaring *Paper Moon* to be the greatest film ever produced, but I would say that it is currently my favorite movie."

"I understand. That was my question, after all, so I'm obliged to accept the answer. Who am I to say that it is not your favorite?" Abby's face was just a couple of inches from his own, and he could smell the enticing fragrance of her perfume. He recognized the silver necklace around her neck. It supported the same lovely pendant that he had admired during the class reunion—an emerald gemstone surrounded by diamonds.

"And what's *your* favorite movie?" Jon asked. "It's only fair." He drew away from her as smoothly and imperceptibly as he could.

"I'd have to say *Somewhere in Time*, I guess, but that changes all the time and never stays the same for very long. Again, this would be my personal favorite film at the moment, which is a lot different from calling it the greatest movie ever made."

"That's one of my wife's favorites too," Jon said.

His remark had no appreciable effect on Abby, who brushed past it as if she could not be bothered. "I'm very fickle about selecting a favorite movie. The title of choice just depends on what my present mood happens to be. For instance, I must be feeling very romantic right now to pick a movie like *Somewhere in Time*."

Jon swallowed hard and tried to swing the topic elsewhere. "Too bad about Christopher Reeve's accident. It was at an equestrian competition in Virginia. I read that if he had fallen one centimeter farther to the right, he wouldn't even have been seriously injured. But if he had fallen one centimeter farther to the left, he would have been killed."

"Tragic," Abby said. "He was a talented actor ... and, in my book, the very definition of handsome."

Jon frowned at her. "More importantly, Christopher Reeve's foundation helped to improve the quality of life for thousands of people dealing with paralysis."

"You sound like a public service announcement."

"Well, it's true, and I give him a lot of credit for that ... for not just giving up on life."

Far from being profoundly moved, Abby began staring into the distance, as if in a daydream. "He and Jane Seymour made a beautiful couple, don't you think?"

"Sure. I can't deny that."

"Just imagine the offspring they would have produced. It boggles the mind."

Jon was at a loss for words, and his esteem for Abby, high school heartthrob or not, was dialed back a notch or two in that single instant. And yet, her undeniable charm continued to carry the day.

The next hour was an engaging journey through cinematic history. Feeling very much in her element at center stage, Abby proceeded to call attention to many of her DVD titles by taking their boxes off the shelves and laying them, spines up, in a majestic gallery of honor. Many were consensus greats, such as *Gone With the Wind*, *Citizen Kane*, *Casablanca*, *The Best Years of Our Lives*, and *Chariots of Fire*. Others were not so widely known and universally celebrated, such as *Brief Encounter*, *It's a Wonderful Life*, *Whistle Down the Wind*, *The Trip to Bountiful*, and *A Summer Story*.

"Were you a movie buff even before you met Brent?" Jon asked.

"Oh, yes, definitely. In fact, that's how we were first introduced. Brent was studying writing and editing in the Film Department at UCLA, and I was studying acting and design in the Drama Department. Both disciplines are part of the UCLA School of Theater, Film, and Television. It's nationally distinguished as one of the top programs around."

"You wanted to become an actress?"

Abby laughed. "Originally, yes, but I quickly learned that I was not enough of a ham to make the grade. The really good students love to be in the footlights and don't fear the auditioning process. Just the thought of that petrified me, so my interest had shifted more to stage design by the time I graduated."

"And Brent?"

"He started out as a budding screenwriter but soon became disenchanted with the futility of it all and switched over to the editing side of the business." She grinned at Jon. "Sorry to paint such a bleak picture of what's in store for you."

"That's fine. I could already see the handwriting on the wall ... to borrow a quote from the Book of Daniel."

That took Abby by surprise. "Are you a student of the Bible?"

"I try."

"There was a time when I decided to read through the entire Old and New Testaments in one year," she said, "but I only got as far as Leviticus. That did me in."

"Do you and Brent go to a church?"

"Not very often, I'm afraid. We're lucky to make it there three times a year." She giggled. "I guess you could say we're not very committed to saving our souls. We should be, but we're just not."

"That's no laughing matter." Jon seemed gravely ernest, and Abby's first instinct was to resent his self-righteous attitude.

"Let's drop it," she said. "What's that old maxim? 'Never talk politics and religion.' No one should meddle into someone else's spiritual well-being."

Although Jon knew that not to be true, he yielded to her shortsighted concept of eternity.

"Let me show you something I'm quite proud of," Abby said. She leaned forward, so far in fact that a good portion of her breasts came into view beneath the halter top. Realizing what had happened, she became amused at Jon's reaction. "No, not these," she said with a wink. She adjusted upward the polyester/spandex material. "I'm referring to my CD collection." Again she leaned forward to open her cabinet of music discs.

To Jon's great surprise and delight, her taste in popular music appeared to parallel his own quite closely. A hefty percentage of her CDs contained songs from the late 1950s through about 1980. Heavy on "greatest hits" compilations, the artists ranged, in terms of chronology, all the way from Bill Haley and His Comets to ABBA. Among a couple hundred others, there were anthologies by The Association, The Beach Boys, The Beatles, The Bee Gees, The Byrds, The Cowsills, Creedence Clearwater Revival, The Dave Clark Five, Elton John, The Everly Brothers, Herman's Hermits, The Hollies, The Left Banke, The Lovin' Spoonful, The Mamas and The Papas, The Monkees, The Seekers, Simon and Garfunkel, The Turtles, and We Five.

"What's your favorite group of all?" Jon asked.

"John, Paul, George, and Ringo, of course."

"I can't argue with that."

"And in the case of The Beatles, not only are they my favorites, but I would also consider them to be the greatest, most influential group ever."

"Same here. Not even close."

They spent almost two hours listening to tracks by these groups, supplemented by a good number of solo male and female vocals, of whom John Denver and Petula Clark were Abby's particular favorites. If she had any further schemes up her sleeve for testing Jon's immunity to seduction, she did not reveal them during this lazy afternoon with no one else around. And what setting could have been more conducive to giving it a whirl? Jon appreciated Abby's change of heart in what could very well have been a compromising situation. Or was she simply stymied by his antediluvian embrace of principled behavior in mixed company?

As the clock neared 4:30, they tuned a radio to 710 AM, which was the Rams' flagship station, KSPN. The game had almost reached its two-minute warning, so Abby prepared to take Jon back to his hotel. Hopefully, his wife would not already be there waiting for him to arrive. That was unlikely, though, because shopping, as Nikki saw it, was one pastime that was not constrained by a game clock.

•   •   •

College student Irving Koslov was fitting in quite nicely as a substitute weekday announcer—working for Jon Swenson on Friday and Monday while Jon was away in California—but Irving could ill afford to miss any more of his undergraduate classes. He was a junior history major, with emphasis in the modern American era. He prided himself on being able to recite the first and last names of every President of the United States, in order, within a span of forty-five seconds, a parlor trick that earned him five dollars from anyone skeptical enough to doubt that he was able to accomplish the feat. He could also list their years in office, but that was a more leisurely stunt, which was neither timed nor rewarded.

It was Irving who first received the glad tidings from owner Myron Kapp that the radio station would retain its current format as a broadcaster of oldies music. And he did a commendable job of spreading the word among other employees. What he did not do very well at all was rehearse the pronunciations of sponsor products. He had occasionally made such careless flubs during his regular weekend shifts, and now he did it again at a peak period of listenership. When he encouraged listeners to purchase their children's clothing from Beauchalet Department Store, located at Kirkland and Belknap, he mistakenly said "byoo-CHAY-let" and "BELK-nap." This infuriated the franchisee, who threatened to withdraw all advertising from the station. Sales rep Candace Thatcher, who had landed the Beauchalet account just two months ago, completely sympathized with her client and demanded that station manager Rudy Flynn remove "this irresponsible kid" from the air at once.

Rudy tried to defuse her anger. "I'm sorry to hear that, Candy, but the problem will take care of itself. Young Mr. Koslov will be back to weekend duty after ten o'clock this morning. He's a college student, just trying to earn some extra spending money."

"That boy is doing more harm than good for us ... even if it is just the weekends." Candace's voice crackled with irritation.

"This will be corrected soon, I promise you. From now on, we'll make Irving pronounce all sponsors' names for us before he does his Saturday and Sunday shows. If he doesn't pass muster, he won't be allowed on the air."

When Ronnie Delaney entered the control room for his 10:00 AM newscast, Irving would hardly speak to him. "What's up, Irv?" Ronnie asked. "Something wrong?"

Irving was so angry he could not sit still. "Oh, nothing against you. One of our salespeople reamed me out on the phone."

"How come?"

"Apparently, I didn't say the sponsor's name right, and she went ballistic."

"Candy Thatcher?"

Irving looked startled. "How'd you know?"

"She's famous for doing that. I've had a couple of run-ins with Candy myself. I think her most recent divorce ... of three ... has pushed her over the cliff." Ronnie tapped his news sheets into an orderly stack. "Who was the sponsor?"

"Uh ... something called byoo-CHAY-let Department Store."

Ronnie grinned at him. "Better try that one again."

"She told me it's French, but how was I supposed to know that?"

The 10:00 to 2:00 air shift had a new feature, beginning on this Monday. It was a five-minute nostalgia package called "Behind the Hits," a daily exploration of how the most famous oldies songs came into being. Ronnie himself put these concise narratives together, using various internet resources, and each segment would precede the actual playing of its song. BTH was a 50/50 sponsor package, with Ronnie—wearing his salesman hat—earning a robust half of the advertising fee. He was industrious that way, and his powerful announcing voice assured that this would be a superior, professional-sounding product.

The first installment of "Behind the Hits" aired at 11:15 and told about the painfully brief existence of an American rock group known as The Mamas and The Papas. It then segued into the story behind their 1967 hit "Twelve Thirty," subtitled "Young Girls Are Coming to the Canyon." Written by John Phillips two years earlier, the song's title made reference to a broken steeple clock in "dark and dirty New York City," while its subtitle evoked the Los Angeles neighborhood of Laurel Canyon. By the time "Twelve Thirty" was released by Dunhill Records, The Mamas and The Papas had all but self-destructed, victims of marital infidelity by group members John Phillips and his wife, Michelle Phillips. This eventually morphed into a love quadrangle that dragged the other members, Cass Elliott and Denny Doherty, down with them.

On the same Monday afternoon, staff announcer MacKenzie Bastrop made it a point to arrive in the control room well before her 2:00 shift would begin. She wanted some time for expressing to Ronnie Delaney how much she enjoyed hearing his initial episode of "Behind the Hits." MacKenzie waited for a triple play to commence, and then she went inside and pointed an index finger at Ronnie. He was sitting in front of the microphone, with his right leg, bound in its cast, elevated across the seat of an armless chair.

"Good show!" she said.

Two and a half hours had passed since BTH aired, so Ronnie was unsure what MacKenzie meant. "How so?"

"I think your new feature will be a big success, if 'Twelve Thirty' is any indication of the typical quality. In fact, I wouldn't be surprised to hear 'Behind the Hits' being picked up by other stations as well ... and in other markets, too, maybe even nationally."

Ronnie laughed out loud. "It's a little too early to be dreaming about that. I just hope to make a few extra bucks right here."

"Really. I think 'Behind the Hits' has coast-to-coast potential if every one of the shows is as good as this one."

"That remains to be seen. Who knows how far it can go before I start running out of interesting material?"

MacKenzie laid her news copy on the desk. "I'd think there are plenty of stories for five or more years ... easy."

"I hope you're right."

She glanced at the digital wall clock. "Could you use a partner ... to help do the research and put the shows together?" she asked. "I'd be willing to pitch in, for a small share of the profit."

Here was a new MacKenzie Bastrop to Ronnie, more aggressive and sure of herself—in short, more like her alter ego of Sunny Shade. This girl seemed able to toggle her personality back and forth like a light switch.

"Right now, I think 'Behind the Hits' is a one-man show," Ronnie said, "but I'll let you know if I run into any trouble keeping up ... and that could happen. Thanks for the offer."

He closed out his shift and started the news intro's dramatic jingle. That provided adequate time for "Nurse Bastrop" to gently guide Ronnie's leg off the chair, so he could hobble to one side and allow her to sit at the microphone near the news copy. With tearful eyes, she watched him ambulate out the control room door.

And then, after five minutes of news, a commercial, and the weather outlook, Sunny Shade's four-hour program of golden oldies was on the air. She was back in character, energetic once again, and eager to please an audience that idolized her every nuance.

•   •   •

With the exception of a single pair of casual shoes—a bargain at $79.99—Nikki had restricted her shopping to four very small items of negligible weight. Her checked-through piece of luggage amounted to just forty-eight pounds, inspiring her to tease Jon that she was tempted to go back to the stores for thirty-two ounces of stockings and make-up.

"How about two pounds of peanut brittle to share with your loving husband?" he asked.

Nikki crinkled her nose at him. "We should be worried about our own weight, too, you know."

The Swensons had a 10:10 plane booked for their three-hour flight back home, so they set an alarm for 6:30 AM. After the free hotel breakfast, they hitched a ride on the airport shuttle and arrived at LAX in plenty of time to negotiate through the TSA screening. As always, Jon sat next to the window, which was fine with his wife. Viewing the world from an altitude above Mount Everest made Nikki uneasy, so she was content with occupying the middle seat. A sixty-something lady took the aisle position, and this woman spent the entire flight reading two romance novels, the kind with steamy cover illustrations that showed fetching heroines tearing off the shirts of their brawny lovers. By all indications, she was not offended by these graphically articulated tales.

Jon and Nikki were home by 3:00, and the first thing they noticed was the missing window pane, which was covered over by a makeshift square of cardboard and clear tape. Then they saw a handwritten note lying on the kitchen counter. "We had a bad storm on Saturday night, almost a tornado," Lauren wrote. "A heavy piece of wood flew through the glass, but I patched up the hole as well as I could." She was careful to leave out any mention of Bradley Tallin, as that might give the wrong impression of how she spent her time "alone." Her parents were unlikely to believe an implausible story about Bradley's truck being stuck in the mud.

When Lauren came into the house after school, she began to say how sorry she was for the messy kitchen—that is, until her father held up a hand to stop her. "Don't apologize. Listen, Sweetie, we appreciate the damage control. That was very ... adult ... of you, and it makes us much more confident that we can leave you here by yourself whenever we need to be away." His commendation made Lauren feel a bit deceitful, but revealing the truth would not have been taken the right way either. "We'll get somebody over here this week to install new glass," Jon said. "I think Abel Sosa and his brother do that kind of work."

After the whirlwind trip to Los Angeles—and the humbling script criticism—Jon felt somewhat relieved to return to his morning drive-time shift on Tuesday. He was also rather curious to know whether young Irving Koslov had encountered any serious problems while substituting for him. He did not have to wait long for an answer because Ronnie Delaney wobbled into the control room less than thirty seconds after Jon completed his 8:00 news and weather block.

"What happened to you?" Jon asked. He was stunned to see his friend reduced to walking on crutches.

"Motorcycle mishap. I was only going about fifty, but the terrain was not exactly level. Anyway, that's my excuse."

"Broken leg?"

"In two places ... but it could have been a lot worse if the bike had landed on my head." Ronnie pointed down to his cast. "Want to sign it?"

Jon knelt down to do so. "How long will you be carrying that thing around with you?"

"At least six weeks ... best-case scenario."

It was time for Jon to back-announce the preceding two songs, so he held up an index finger to silence Ronnie. "From the tumultuous year of 1968, that was 'Son of a Preacher Man' by Dusty Springfield, her very last top-thirty solo hit. Before that you heard The Vogues, a popular American quartet from the Pittsburgh area, with their 1969 remake of 'Earth Angel,' which was originally a 1954 release by the L. A. doo-wop group, The Penguins."

Inasmuch as the play list was already established in the computer, there was no need to search for what songs to transmit next. After two minutes of commercials, the oldies music resumed with a triple-play set of 'New World in the Morning' by Roger Whittaker, 'Lodi' by Creedence Clearwater Revival, and 'You Light Up My Life' by Debby Boone. In the meantime, it was back to chatting for Jon Swenson and Ronnie Delaney.

"How did Irv handle my slot?" Jon asked. "No major disasters, I trust."

"The bad news is that he made two announcing flubs. The good news is that only one sponsor was involved."

Jon grinned. "How did he manage to do that?"

"He mispronounced Beauchalet as 'byoo-CHAY-let' and also the store's street, Belknap, as 'BELK-nap.' Candy Thatcher blew a gasket, as you might expect, and now Rudy plans to put Irv on a sort of probation ... making him pronounce all sponsor names before his weekend shifts."

"Poor guy. Irv means well. It's just that he gets a little lackadaisical." Jon's face brightened. "Have you ever heard Irv recite every American President's first and last name in forty-five seconds flat? It's pretty amazing, so I'm sure he has a good head on his shoulders. I hope Rudy gives him a second chance."

"He will. Candy was just venting upon the nearest target, and Irv happened to be in her line of fire." Ronnie pivoted on his good leg to walk away on the crutches.

"You're getting pretty agile on those stilts," Jon said.

"Not too bad, but I've had a couple days of practice." Ronnie thought of something he wanted to say. "Hey, be sure to drop by the lounge after I get off the air. There are two important things I want to ask you about."

Jon arrived in the staff lounge three minutes before Ronnie. This arrangement was ideal because both knew that MacKenzie Bastrop would be in the radio station's control room, and Ronnie wanted to clear up some confusion about who this peculiar woman was and why she was so determined to act as a maidservant for him during his struggle with the physical ailment.

"You know, MacKenzie has changed quite a lot," Ronnie said. "She didn't use to give me the time of day, but now she won't leave me alone ... ever since taking pity on me after the motorcycle wreck. She even wants me to start calling her Mack. Do you think I should?"

"It's up to you," Jon said. "Has she become chummy with the other employees, too, or just with you? As I recall, she wouldn't speak to anyone at all when she was off the air."

"That's why this whole thing seems so bizarre. She's just as standoffish with other people as before ... a recluse who wouldn't throw a life preserver to a drowning man. What's that kind of person called?"

"Misanthrope?"

"That's it. She's a misanthrope." Ronnie motioned his head toward the overhead speaker, from which the voice of Sunny Shade could be heard. "But now, all of a sudden, this girl has adopted me as her little brother and won't give me a minute's peace when I'm at work. I appreciate her concern for me, but it's kind of annoying too."

Jon squinted at his friend. "Do you have any warm feelings for her?"

"MacKenzie Bastrop? You've got to be kidding! She's definitely not my type, and I don't know where she got the idea that I'm interested in her ... if that's what she thinks. I just want to unload her, but I don't know how to do that politely. She's even forced me to start reading *Frankenstein*."

"Oh, yeah? How far along are you?"

"Just about fifty pages. That's really not my cup of tea, but it would hurt her feelings for me to tell her so."

Jon nodded agreement. "I'm nearly finished with *Bleak House* by Dickens ... but the difference is I'm actually enjoying it."

"So, what should I do about her? I'm getting desperate."

"How much longer for your cast?" Jon asked.

"I already told you ... six weeks at least, and there could be another couple of weeks after that."

"In that case, my friend, I'd say MacKenzie Bastrop is all yours for another two months of mothering, so get used to it."

"Nope. I'll just need to get downright rude, I guess. No wallflower like MacKenzie is going to cramp my style." Ronnie raised his head high and grinned. "After all, Jon-Boy, I've got something of a reputation to uphold among the young ladies. It just doesn't look good to be shackled by an albatross."

"Try to let her down gradually, and maybe she'll get the message."

"Hmm, maybe so."

"What else did you want to ask me about? You said there were two things."

Ronnie's grin became wider. "How did it go with Abby out west? Is she eating out of your hand yet?"

"That was not my goal," Jon said. "I went out there ... along with Nikki, by the way ... to gather some recommendations for my screenplay."

But Ronnie had scant interest in that part of the trip. His eyes gleamed with anticipation elsewhere. "Were you ever alone with Miss Abby?"

"Thank you very much for asking about my screenplay, good buddy. I appreciate your distress over my writing career. And yes, since you are so deeply concerned, the script consultants did offer some recommendations for me. Not only that, but the husband of Mrs. Abby Harker added a few of his own."

Undeterred by cynicism, Ronnie plowed ahead. "Did you find a quiet corner, just for you and Abby to commune with nature?"

"Sometimes you have a one-track mind, don't you?"

"Just whenever beautiful girls are involved," Ronnie said. "How did Abby look? Was she as gorgeous as when she went to that German restaurant with us?"

"Sure, I'd say so ... absolutely." Jon thought back. "Who was that girl you brought there?"

"To Vinnie's? Her name is ShaunaKaye Gibbs, but I don't think I'll be seeing much of her again ... at least for another six or eight weeks, if you know what I mean."

Jon knew exactly what he meant. "Getting back to Abby, though, she's really not as wild as you might fantasize. We spent an entire afternoon together at her house, just by ourselves, while her husband was watching the Rams game at SoFi Stadium."

By now, Ronnie was nearly hyperventilating. "Let me get this straight. You had Abby all for yourself for several hours?"

"Yep."

"In a house with a wet bar ... and a bed?"

"Several beds. And a swimming pool, a film room, and two dogs. What about it?"

"And nothing happened between you?"

"Sure, it did. We looked through both of Abby's disc collections ... DVDs and CDs. You would have been impressed by them."

"I don't understand you," Ronnie said. "Sometimes I wonder if you're a living and breathing human being. That Abby Harker ticks all the boxes for me."

Jon shrugged his shoulders. "I just happen to have a smidgen of self-control to draw upon."

"When it comes to Abby, all of my self-control goes out the window."

"What if you were married, like me? Would that make a difference?"

Ronnie's eyebrows raised. "That's hard for me to say. Maybe if I was sober and could think straight."

"So, you admit that boozing it up impairs your ability to make wise decisions," Jon said. "That tells me what your biggest challenge might be in the next few years. I think you have a potential drinking problem."

"So what? We're talking about Abby Harker here, not me."

"And Abby has the same problem."

Ronnie beamed a broad smile. "That's just one more thing that Abby and I have in common. Don't even ask me what I would have done while Brent was at the football game."

"I can imagine."

•   •   •

Nikki Swenson had achieved enough seniority at GoldSpire Bank to earn her own workspace, complete with an executive desk, a private entrance door, a dedicated extension of the company's outdated landline, and a wide-screen monitor for instructional videos. She and the other loan officers occupied the entire span of the main lobby, directly facing the wall-to-wall tellers' counter. Employees who served in lesser positions were consigned to interchangeable cubicles at the rear.

Nikki's work neighbor—and nominal boss—pursued his duties in the office adjacent to hers on the east. Tony Zeigen had been on the payroll of GoldSpire for three years longer than Nikki—that is, since day one of the bank's existence, though it had a different name back then. He was rather tall, at six-foot-three, and his wiry build concealed a surprising muscularity. Tony's facial features were quite handsome, with prominent cheekbones, arresting eyes, and a black mustache that complemented the other characteristics perfectly.

To Nikki's eyes, Tony Zeigen looked very much like British actor Simon Williams, who played the role of James Bellamy in the early 1970s television program "Upstairs, Downstairs." Jon was of the same opinion—and he should know, being a loyal fan and DVD owner of that classic series. He had met Tony many years ago and subsequently rubbed elbows with him at various parties and social functions in connection with the GoldSpire properties. The Swensons had been guests of Tony Zeigen and his wife, Allison, on two separate occasions. One was Tony's recent "Big 5-0" birthday bash, which drew a crowd of almost a hundred, and the other was a wedding reception for the Zeigens' daughter, Belinda.

"Hang around for a while after work on Thursday," Tony told Nikki. "It won't take very long ... just a half-hour or so." He was leaning against her open door, about a dozen feet away. "You and I need to figure out how to expedite the loan process for low-risk applicants. All things equal, they should sail through without any unnecessary speed bumps ... and that's just not happening as we now stand."

"Okay. Where should I go?"

"My office, I guess. Eileen Fortunato has a couple of recommendations, but I don't know whether they'll speed things up. They may have just the opposite effect."

Nikki thought nothing more about this meeting until Thursday morning, when she noticed it on her electronic calendar. And then, with all of her loan accounts needing attention throughout the day, it slipped her mind again at quitting time. Tony Zeigen poked his head inside her office to remind her.

"Are you coming?" he asked.

"Oh, I'm so sorry. Yes, I'll be there in a couple of minutes."

Tony was waiting for her with special treats for them both, a chocolate-filled doughnut and a cup of black coffee. "These are your favorites, as I recall."

"My goodness! How did you know?"

"Just a lucky guess." He shuffled some papers on his desk.

"Really?"

"No. They're my favorites, too, and I noticed our similar tastes." His smile was kindly, nothing deeper than that. There was a second chair placed next to his on the same side of the desk. "Have a seat, and we'll get started."

Nikki did as he requested but took the liberty of sliding her chair away from his by a couple of inches.

"Have you had time to look over Eileen's recommendations?" Tony asked. He shuffled the papers again.

Nikki had a blank look. "You never gave those to me."

"Yes, I did. I laid two sheets, stapled, on the corner of your desk."

"Sorry, but I never saw them. Are you sure?"

Tony sighed. "Never mind. We can go over them now." He picked up two sheets, stapled, and began reading out loud. Nikki did her best to follow along, but the convoluted steps made little practical sense to her. "These look pretty good on paper," Tony said, "but I'm not confident that they'll fly in the real world."

Nikki concurred. "We certainly can't access the applicant's financial history at the drop of a hat. Eileen makes it sound so simple."

Tony took a bite of his doughnut. Then, after pondering the issue further, while chewing and swallowing, he gazed directly into Nikki's eyes. "Which is why I value your opinions so highly. Some of our 'yes' people don't voice their true thoughts ... and they wouldn't do so, even if their lives depended upon it." He slid his left hand onto her right hand. "But you're different, and I appreciate it."

Nikki was shocked but tried not to show it too dramatically. She could not move her hand without causing a scene, so she did the next best thing. She frowned at him and made a request. "Would you please pass me my coffee? I drink right-handed."

Tony looked embarrassed, but there was no way to reverse what had already happened between them. All he could do was proceed with the meeting as if his horse was back in the starting gate. Maybe Nikki would presume that their touching hands had no significance whatsoever—simply a chance encounter on this random desktop. The more natural and unruffled Tony behaved from that moment on, the more Nikki began to suspect that she was overreacting to his silly gaffe.

As it turned out, their proposed half-hour meeting lasted only twenty minutes, hardly long enough for each of them to eat a doughnut and drink a cup of coffee. Nothing of substance was settled, except that Eileen Fortunato's suggestions would be tabled for later consideration.

Nikki did some soul-searching as a result of her *tête-à-tête* with Tony Zeigen. While this may have been an exploratory session for him, it was a cautionary one for her. From now on, she would be sensitized to even the tiniest signs of affection from his direction, and he would have to be on his best behavior. Incidental contact might be forgiven on a basketball court but not in a place of business.

The problem was, Nikki knew that Tony was an authentic gentleman through and through—and a very good-looking gentleman at that. If only she were honest enough to admit it, she was flattered that he would show some tenderness toward her. They were workmates on one level, but caring friends on another. Maybe she should not be so unapproachable. After all, she felt pretty certain that her own husband had a harmless infatuation on the side—that pretty wife of his film studio contact—so why shouldn't she, too, have some innocent fun?

Just over a week elapsed before Tony Zeigen made another effort to see where he stood with Nikki Swenson. As he was walking past her ceiling-to-floor window, suddenly he slammed on his brakes and performed a spit-and-polish right turn, finishing with a broad grin that made Nikki smile. And that was all. He resumed walking and, from that day forward, never mentioned the episode to her.

But now Tony knew, beyond question, that Nikki had a soft spot for him—no matter how deeply buried—and someday conditions would be right to exploit it. Meanwhile, he could begin laying the groundwork, subtly at first but then with more and more focus on the prize.

"You got a letter from Tony," Jon told his wife. This was about a week later, and he was standing in the kitchen, thumbing through the day's mail.

Nikki gave him a casual glance. "Tony Zeigen?"

"It would seem so." The return address was plain for anyone to see.

"It must be an invitation of some sort. You know the Zeigens ... social climbers." But she went too far when the envelope continued to lie there unopened.

Jon decided to press the issue. "So, you think it's an invitation, huh?"

"I'm sure that's what it is, but I'll open it just to make sure." She had no other choice, now that a federal case had been created. Were Jon scientifically measuring her hand movements, he would have calibrated that the fingers of both of them were trembling ever so slightly. Nikki sliced open the envelope's sealed edge and withdrew the contents. Pretending to read, she summarized the message in the very broadest of terms. "Oh, that's nice of them. They've invited us to come to their son's graduation from Purdue."

"That's in Indiana," Jon said.

"Right. But still, I think it's very nice of them to ask us to attend."

"What's their son's name again?"

Nikki felt sheer panic shoot through her like an electric shock. Her duplicity was sure to be exposed. And yet, against all odds, her memory cells came through when she needed them most. "Jeremy, I think."

He laughed. "Well, what name does it say?"

She looked at Tony's letter again. "Yes, it's Jeremy all right." The boy's actual name was Jerome, but it would have to be Jeremy for now, and Jon fell for the pseudonym.

Later that night, in the privacy of the master bedroom—while Jon was downstairs watching *The Shootist* on Turner Classic Movies—Nikki reopened the letter and read it for the first time. She envisioned the debonaire Simon Williams speaking directly to her, perhaps with a cigarette holder in one hand and a gin and tonic in the other. But the actual words fell sadly short of that imagery.

Just a quick note to let you know how much I have appreciated working alongside you for these past twelve-plus years. Often we neglect to tell our colleagues such things until they transfer somewhere else or even retire. It is much better to do so while both are still pulling the same tug-of-war rope together, in tandem. Thanks for everything.

With warmest regards,
Tony

Nikki did not know quite what to make of this strange piece of mail—whether to take it at face value as a business communiqué or to treat it more guardedly, as an enshrouded declaration of love from a secret admirer. Whichever she chose to do, it was a foregone conclusion that Jon would never lay eyes upon the letter. He was apt to read into it more than was actually there. Worse yet, he might grasp the reality that lay beneath its counterfeit surface.

It remained to be seen how Tony would comport himself from here on out, now that he had expressed, with suspicious timing, his sincere appreciation to Nikki for her fine work ethic and team spirit. The more she thought about it, the more certain she became that this unprompted letter was nothing but an effort to becloud any residual memories of the touching-hands incident. And it might have worked, too, were it not for the fact that Nikki was already attuned to some marital questions of her own.

·   ·   ·

E ver since Jon's trip to Los Angeles, the occasional texts and emails from Abby Harker—whether direct or through Ronnie Delaney as go-between—had dwindled to nothing, and her silence distressed Jon so much that he began to reproach himself for causing a breach of friendship. Over and over in his mind, he replayed every moment to determine what went awry while he was alone with Abby in California. Had he said something wrong to her? Did she resent that he spurned her advances? Did she finally conclude that he was still too tame for her, just as he had been in high school? Although Abby was no longer running with a fast crowd, surely that is where her true tendencies lay.

After much soul searching, Jon resolved to back off from his shaky relationship with her, even as a conduit for his writing ambitions. *Kiss Me Where It Hurts* seemed fully developed as it now stood and would accommodate none of the major changes that Brent and the script consultants proposed. If Abby was interested in sustaining her long-distance liaison with Jon, she was entitled to do so, but it would be her choice and not his.

Ronnie Delaney was much more proactive in that respect. All along, he had maintained the lines of communication with Abby, describing his motorcycle crash to her in great detail—perhaps embellishing it a bit to paint himself as second only to his legendary hero, Evel Knievel, whose name Abby was barely old enough to recognize. At one point, their correspondence threatened to get entirely out of hand. That was when Abby's photographs of herself had become more and more racy. Being a self-described "tease," she loved few things in life better than to tantalize her cadre of young men. But she also knew exactly when to quit, leaving them pining for more.

As had become their usual routine on weekdays, Jon and Ronnie met for a round of small talk in the staff lounge on Wednesday between 2:00 and 3:00. But on this particular occasion, instead of ABBA, "Seinfeld," or classic movies—their most often discussed topics—the day's chat went directly to Ronnie's favorite subject of all: Abby Pierce Harker. Jon grabbed a cup of coffee and a cinnamon-apple pastry for each of them, due to the twenty-five-year-old announcer's temporary incapacitation.

"I can't show you the pictures that Abby sent to me yesterday," Ronnie said. "She made me promise to keep them under wraps."

Jon tried to appear disinterested. "Then why are you telling me about them?"

Ronnie did not answer. "They're really something," he said. "Even her husband hasn't seen them, so she says."

"I'm not surprised. Why would Brent need to see pictures of his own wife?"

Again, Ronnie ignored the rhetorical question. "Abby must have hired a professional photographer because these are super quality. Of course, the subject matter is what really brings them to life."

"Yep, I know what you mean. There was a silent-screen actress named Clara Bow, who had 'it.' In fact, that was the title of her most famous movie ... *It* ... just that single word."

Ronnie's curiosity was piqued. "Was she good looking?"

Jon smiled. "In my opinion, Clara Bow and Louise Brooks ... both from the silent era ... are two of the most gorgeous actresses ever. You can't take your eyes off either of them when they're on screen. Their beauty was timeless."

"Then, I'd have to say Abby also has 'it,'" Ronnie said.

Jon nodded his head. "I've always thought so, even though I lost track of her for a quarter-century after high school."

Ronnie took a bite of his pastry and spoke while chewing. "Do you think I'm too young for her?"

Jon chuckled. "Who can really say? We're talking about Abby Harker here, and she doesn't play by the rules."

"I don't know what power she has over me," Ronnie said, "but I can't seem to get very interested in girls my own age anymore."

"She can do that to you. Some women just have that special magic."

Ronnie stared down at his leg cast. "I'd give all of these other signatures for just one from Abby ... maybe in bright purple ink." He sighed. "It's probably those hot photos that have me caught in her web. Sometimes, she's all I can think about."

"Does Abby ever talk about me in her messages to you?" Jon asked. "I haven't heard from her since I was out there in L. A."

Ronnie grinned at him. "Sorry, but nothing for you. Maybe she prefers younger men ... yours truly, for instance. The next time you and Nikki fly to southern California, please take me along in your suitcase. Brent wouldn't have a chance against me."

Mention of Brent Harker caused Jon's face to darken. "I'm pretty sure I'll never get another face-to-face meeting with him. Strictly off the record, my gut feeling is that Brent has decided that *Kiss Me Where It Hurts* is not salvageable after all, so any future contact with me would be pointless."

"What does Nikki think about your screenplay?"

"She's more optimistic about it than I am."

"Want me to put a bug in Abby's ear?" Ronnie asked. "I sure don't mind. Any excuse to write to her is all right with me."

"Be my guest. I have half a mind to text her myself. I think I may have insulted her on that Sunday afternoon."

"When Brent was at the Rams game?"

"Yes. Abby was playing rather loose with me, but I wouldn't take the bait."

Ronnie leaned toward his friend. "Are you sorry you didn't follow through on your baser instincts?"

"No. I'm proud of myself for keeping her at arm's length. It wasn't easy."

"You didn't even kiss her?"

"Not in California," Jon said.

"You've never kissed Abby?"

"Just once, as I recall ... when she left here to go back home."

Ronnie squinted with doubt. "Come on! You don't know for sure?"

Jon shook his head. "She may have kissed me when she was drunk at the reunion dance ... but I'm not totally sure about that."

"I wish I could be as nonchalant about her as you are. Her kiss lit me up like a Roman candle."

Jon was stupefied. "Wait a second! You and Abby actually kissed when she was here?"

"Yeah. What about it?"

"In town for those three or four days?"

"Right. We kissed two times, to be more precise."

"Two times!" Jon's smile was filled with wonder. "Sir Ronald Blinn Delaney, I tip my hat. You really are a fast worker."

"She was worth it."

"Had you two been drinking?" Jon asked. "I can't imagine Abby kissing you when sober."

Both of them laughed, so loudly in fact that everyone in the staff lounge looked their way.

"You'd be surprised what Abby is willing to do," Ronnie said, "even when she hasn't had a drop."

Jon waited for more, but the younger announcer gave him nothing but a prideful grin.

"Incidentally," Jon finally said, "I'm thinking about cutting off all contact with her. She hasn't bothered to write in a long time, and keeping in touch with Brent seems like a dead end."

Ronnie had a doubtful look. "Oh, sure. That's easy to say right now, but you haven't seen her photos yet." He took another bite of the pastry, washed down by a sip of coffee.

"What do you mean, 'yet'?" Jon asked. "I thought you promised Abby that you wouldn't share the pictures with anyone. Even her own husband hasn't seen them."

"I'm keeping the latest batch on hold ... for extortion purposes, you might say. I'll release them whenever I need for you to do me a big favor, but not until then."

"How big of a favor?"

"Huge!" Again, Ronnie laughed aloud.

"They must really be something," Jon said.

"They are, my friend ... they really are." Ronnie smiled while waving his cellphone in front of Jon's eyes. "I'm surprised my phone isn't hidden behind a cloud of smoke."

• • •

Another week passed without a single text or email from Abby to Jon. Ronnie, on the other hand, was still receiving his usual spate of messages from her, sometimes as frequently as twice a day. Jon was now firmly convinced that Abby was ignoring him, and there was no use telling himself that her detachment was of little concern. He missed their playful banter and wondered whether a quick word to her might reopen the channels of communication.

Jon continued to see nothing improper about maintaining a friendship with this fellow DHS alum. Everything between them was completely innocent and G-rated, and he had proven beyond any doubt that even the most inviting of circumstances did not lead to conduct he would later regret. Jon's resistance to temptation when he was alone with Abby in her home had given him a well-deserved feeling of pride. Conversely, it may also have led to Abby's inclination to cast him aside as a likely partner in passion, if indeed that is what she was seeking.

Even Jon's own wife might have accepted his dalliance with a high school classmate, were it not for one incontestable fact: Abby Pierce Harker was so exceedingly pretty. Due to Abby's regimented exercise routine, sensible diet, and advantageous chromosomes, she was able to sustain the vibrant beauty that had given her a leg up on popularity all of her life. Like most girls who are blessed with uncommon good looks, Abby was spoiled. She sailed through her various stages of physical development with a "Get Out of Jail Free" card in her pocket, and she played it quite lavishly, too, whenever difficult situations arose. If Nikki Swenson did not view Abby as a serious rival for Jon's attention, that was probably only because of the miles that separated them.

Besides, Nikki was confronted with comparable problems much closer to home. While Jon was forever understating his interest in and involvement with Abby Harker halfway across the country, Nikki was having to do the same for someone who practically worked shoulder-to-shoulder with her. Senior Loan Officer Tony Zeigen was finding all manner of opportunities to chat with his attractive colleague, whose office existed beyond the thinnest of walls.

To Tony's credit, he knew exactly when to apply the brakes. He was far too clever to be accused of workplace harassment or any such infringement of Nikki's rights. Only on the rarest of occasions did he so much as brush against her, those times when physical contact seemed trifling and unavoidable. He was "Tony" to her, and she was "Nikki" to him, but there was nothing intimate about it. Almost all employees on the bank's staff were on a first-name basis with each other, and no one thought anything of it.

"Would you please sign something for me, Tony?" she asked. This was the first piece of business on Monday morning, so her short-distance phone call had caught him before more pressing issues would take precedence.

"Okay, Nikki, I'll be right there." Tony breezed around the corner, from his door to hers, in a matter of seconds. "Fast enough for you?" he joked. When he leaned forward to sign the customer's waiver sheet, he stood less than one inch from Nikki. The unblemished skin of his face carried with it a pleasant fragrance that delighted her sense of smell.

"What is that you're wearing?" Nikki asked. "I think Jon might like to have some for himself."

"I'm not sure ... some cologne that Allison gave me for Christmas." He stood straight up and smiled. "I was going to ask you the same thing about your perfume."

Nikki's eyes danced for joy. "It's called 'Soleil Brûlant' by Tom Ford, and I love it. Jon wouldn't have a clue what to buy me in the *eau de parfum* area, so I picked it out for myself."

"Wise choice. I wouldn't have a clue either, but I'll keep this in mind for Allison. She'll be shocked by my good taste in perfumes. What's the name again?"

"'Soleil Brûlant.' Here, I'll write it down for you."

"Thanks. That's not easy to remember." Tony ran an index finger across each half of his thin mustache. He probably did so unconsciously, but it produced a rakish impression nonetheless.

Nikki took note while handing him the perfume's name. "You don't have any more of those chocolate-filled doughnuts, do you? I got away from home without a bite of breakfast."

"No. They were just a one-time surprise for our meeting." Tony looked worried. "You didn't eat anything?"

"Nope. Just a quick cup of coffee. Our daughter had orchestra practice at seven thirty, and I needed to drop her off at school. By the time I got back home, I had to turn right around and leave for here. Jon goes to the radio station at about five thirty, you know, so he was no help."

"I'll tell you what. Let me shoot over to Taco Bell and get you a couple of breakfast burritos. I'll buy one for myself, too, just to show you how greedy I really am." His smile was contagious. "Please. I won't take no for an answer. We could lose business because of your growling stomach."

Nikki's face became red. "I'm sorry. Did you really hear it?"

"No, but that's what mine does when I don't eat a proper meal before work." He hurried to her open door. "Don't go anywhere. I'll be right back with the goodies."

The ensuing week brought countless other acts of kindness from Nikki Swenson's neighboring loan officer. Each may have been trivial on its own, but when added together, they amounted to a meaningful sum of the parts. Nikki did not know how to reciprocate, if that is what was demanded of her in such a sticky situation. She wanted to appear appreciative to Tony—who was, after all, her ranking superior—but she was unwilling to sacrifice her independence as a free agent in the labor force. To make matters worse, Tony Zeigen was handsome enough to "tickle her fancy," as an earlier generation might have put it. She was charmed by his attentive nature, an honorable quality that she had never noticed in him before.

By the time Friday arrived, Nikki had come up with a new game plan for curbing Tony's freedom to roam unimpeded in her personal territory. To a greater extent than ever before, she would bring both of their families into the picture. Maybe that would shift the focal point away from any thoughts of an office romance.

"How is Jerome doing these days?" she asked. "Is he still at Purdue?"

"Oh, no. Jerry graduated two years ago. He's the manager of a truck rental place on the outskirts of Fort Wayne, Indiana."

"Is he married?"

"No, but it looks like he's well on the way to becoming engaged. He's been dating the same girl, exclusively, for over a year. She's a dental hygienist."

"Jon and I dated, off and on, for nearly three years. How about you and Allison?"

This line of questioning appeared to disagree with Tony's intentions at the moment. "I don't know ... about six months, as I recall. She graduated a semester behind me."

"Did you go to the same high school?"

"No. We're from different parts of the country ... Kansas and New Jersey. We met at college." Tony glanced at Nikki's wall clock and made for the door. "Do you have any plans for lunch?" He asked this very blandly, almost as if it were an afterthought.

"Madison, Kassondra, and I are meeting at Panera Bread. Care to join us?"

"No, thanks. That sounds like a hen party to me." He grinned at Nikki, who simply nodded her head without a word.

As he walked away, she felt bad about derailing his lunch idea—especially after the many thoughtful things he had done for her all week long—but neither could she allow him to continue imagining that she was receptive to his warmhearted overtures. Toying with her affections must come to an end at once, she decided, and clearly it was not going to be Tony Zeigen's doing.

The first three days of the next work week were commonplace. In fact, Tony and Nikki hardly saw each other, except from a distance or among several other people. On Thursday morning, however, when the lobby was crowded with customers queuing in the teller lines, their eyes did meet. Tony was striding from the copier room to his workspace, but he thought of something and stopped. Just then, as Nikki walked out her door and into the lobby, her reading glasses fell to the carpeted floor. She bent her knees to retrieve them and straightened up again.

And there stood Tony, about thirty feet away. He was a head taller than anyone else in the lobby, and his handsome face drew Nikki's attention. She smiled at him, and he gave her a raffish wink. Instantly, something in her heart mellowed, and she began to think that responding to his ungainly moves might be rather a lark. After all, she told herself, an office flirtation was almost always in good, clean fun—and especially so when both of the principal subjects were happily married. Yes, she would do it, but at the same time never forgetting how hazardous a game she was playing. And, of course, that is what would make the adventure so exciting.

The next time they talked, Nikki had great difficulty subduing her beaming smile. She felt strangely elated, but also quite silly—like a bashful teenager who was tongue-tied in the presence of the high school quarterback. Everything Tony said caused her to giggle with delight. He was really quite something, this Tony Zeigen, a witty raconteur who brought sunshine to her otherwise drab workaday treadmill. Suddenly, Nikki felt like she was being courted all over again, a thrilling sensation that she had not experienced in many years. Being with Jon did not make her heart race like this anymore.

Perhaps it was inevitable that the pair would join hands over lunch someday. This likelihood finally became a reality at 11:30 on a chilly Tuesday morning when Tony suggested that he take her for a quick bite before they were due to attend an executive meeting across town. "My treat," he said, "and I'll drive."

"Do you think that's wise?" The moment Nikki said it, the image of Jon's face came to mind. Her remark had sounded just like Sergeant Wilson speaking to Captain Mainwaring on the television series "Dad's Army," and Jon surely would have imitated the voice of John Le Mesurier.

"Why not?" Tony said. "We can just treat it like a pre-business lunch. Even if someone sees us together, we'll have an ideal pretext."

This was taking matters a step further than what had gone before, and it could prove to be a very risky gamble. Nikki remembered when a friend told her that Jon was spotted eating with "a very pretty young woman" at In-N-Out Burger. Something in Jon's instinctive response—insisting that this woman was only a client—seemed much too defensive. Nikki was well aware that the same thing could happen to her.

Tony drove her to a small café just outside the city limits. This unpretentious sandwich shop had garnered rave reviews in the Sunday newspaper column on area restaurants. Unfortunately, the weekend's five-star ratings also encouraged a mass of hungry diners to give the place a try. Tony and Nikki were among them, and suddenly choosing such a remote location did not seem like a very good idea. This lunchtime drive required much more effort than simply breezing over to a fast-food joint on the corner. Too late now.

They remained near the entrance door for almost thirty minutes, waiting for a table or booth to become available. Tony did not appear to be particularly edgy, but Nikki's eyes darted back and forth, dreading that a familiar face might come into view. With each newly arriving customer, Nikki died a slow death, but thankfully this café must have been a bit too far out of town to draw anyone from her own circle of friends. Their lunch hour was nearly over when the duo were finally seated—at right angles to each other at a table for four.

"What time is it getting to be?" Nikki asked. She was worried because their meeting was scheduled for 1:30.

Tony glanced at his phone. "Just twelve twenty-five, so we should be fine. Everyone at the bank knows we're headed to Polk City after lunch."

"But not that we're going there together."

"There's no law against it. We'll be saving on gasoline consumption ... helping to rescue the planet from going extinct."

Nikki frowned. "I hope you're not one of those."

"I was kidding." Tony reached over and touched her gently on the nose. "Listen, Nikki, you need to lighten up. Eating with me is not a criminal offense. You're not going to death row."

Nikki lowered her voice so far that Tony could barely hear her. "This just makes me very nervous. Playing cat-and-mouse behind my husband's back is not something I'm very experienced at doing."

"Implying that I am?"

"I didn't say that."

Almost two whole minutes of strained silence passed between them. Nikki and Tony were sitting quite near each other, but they stared straight ahead, eating their sandwiches and sipping their tall glasses of sweet tea.

It was Tony who broke the impasse. "Do you know what one week from today is?"

"I'm not sure. Am I forgetting something important?"

"I would say so, yes."

"Something to do with GoldSpire Bank?" Nikki asked.

"GoldSpire and its subsidiaries."

She crinkled her nose at him. "Okay, I give up. Tell me."

"The Southern Regional Banking Conference."

"I thought that was next month."

"Nope ... seven days from now," Tony said.

"How long will you be gone?"

"Four days ... and then the weekend, of course, if I choose to spend it there in Atlanta."

Nikki wondered whether she should become too personal. "That'll make our bank a pretty dull place ... not having you around."

He smiled. "Thanks. I would feel the same way about you."

Once again, silence descended upon their table.

"Can you get away for most of next week?" Tony asked. "It would be on GoldSpire's dime."

Nikki remained at a loss for words.

"Strictly business," Tony said. He hoped that would clinch the deal. "We'd be back, bright and early, on the following Monday."

"Gee, I'm not sure. Jon and Lauren will be awfully surprised. Do we need to book our own planes?"

"Don't worry about anything. I'll take care of all the arrangements ... round-trip flights, rental car, hotel rooms."

Nikki was relieved to hear that he used a plural noun when referring to the lodging accommodations. "Does Allison know you'll be going?" she asked.

"Oh, sure, she knows. I attend this meeting every year at about the same time. Don't you even notice when I'm gone?"

Nikki blushed. "Not until lately."

He reached over to lay his hand on hers. This time, she did not pull away.

• • •

On Tuesday afternoon at 1:05, announcers Jon Swenson and MacKenzie Bastrop were sitting across from each other at a table in the radio station's lounge. Jon had finished reading *Bleak House* by Charles Dickens the night before, and he told MacKenzie how much he enjoyed it. He also wondered what classic novel she might suggest for him to read next. This discussion took place during one of the four hours in which their off-the-air time coincided—that is, when Ronnie Delaney was in the control room. Other than Ronnie, Jon was the only employee on the entire staff who took the trouble to speak with MacKenzie on more than a sporadic basis.

"How about something by F. Scott Fitzgerald?" MacKenzie asked. "He was best known for his keen insight into the issues of class and identity during the Jazz Age. He wrote five novels in all, but I would recommend *The Great Gatsby* for starters."

"Sounds good to me, Mack. I've seen a filmed version of it ... from 1974, with Robert Redford in the title role. I thought it was pretty good, so I'll probably like the book too."

"No doubt about it. I'm sure it's much better than the movie." MacKenzie was unlikely to give much, if any, credence to a humble strip of celluloid.

Not to be outdone, Jon contributed a few more good words for the screen version. "Most of the reviews I've read were positive and claimed that this film was very faithful to the novel."

MacKenzie remained unconvinced. "Then why not just read the novel to begin with? There will be a much greater sense of fulfillment when you turn the final page."

"I suppose it's a matter of how much time you need to invest. It might take me a whole week to read *The Great Gatsby*, whereas the movie only lasts a couple of hours."

"But what is missing after the screenwriters and editors get through fooling around with it? Personally, I enjoy going straight to an author's own conception of his or her story ... not how some Hollywood-type thinks the story could have been improved."

"Point well taken," Jon said. There was no reason to argue about it because he knew that MacKenzie was never going to change her opinion about the relative merits of books and their films. Moreover, he realized that she was standing on very firm ground. Few indeed were the movies that constituted improvements over their literary sources.

Jon was about ready to leave the lounge when MacKenzie raised an index finger. "Don't run away," she said. He turned around and, for the first time, viewed MacKenzie as a very lonely person—nowhere near as self-reliant as the false image she had cultivated. "Seeing as how you are receptive to my tastes in the written word, maybe you'd also like to hear what I have to say about 'serious' music."

"You mean the Three B's?"

MacKenzie nodded. "That's right ... Bach, Beethoven, and Brahms. Not to mention a bunch of others."

That subject was of little interest to Jon, but he did not wish to offend a hard-won friend by rejecting her zeal without a fair hearing. Fearing the worst, he sat back down and forced himself to listen to MacKenzie's discourse. After all, how bad could this possibly be? She would be on the air as Sunny Shade within forty minutes, and a portion of that would be required to familiarize herself with a "rip-and-read" newscast for 2:00.

"All I ask is that you listen with an open mind," she said.

Jon shrugged his shoulders, not knowing how else to respond.

"You seem to have some capacity for valuing classical literature, so I feel rather certain that you'll also be sensitive to what the greatest musicians in history have composed ... and I'm not talking about Lennon and McCartney or even Rodgers and Hammerstein, great as they were in their chosen fields of rock and musical theater."

Jon shrugged again. "Okay. Go ahead and hit me." He gritted his teeth in an exaggerated fashion.

MacKenzie laughed at him, just as Jon hoped she would. "I don't blame you a bit," she said. "I was skeptical at first, too ... until I immersed myself in a whole new sound world, allowing the full orchestra to wash over me like an ocean wave. The classical masters were brilliant at their craft, and the music they created for their own time still speaks to us today."

"I've heard some pieces by Beethoven and Mozart," Jon said, "but, to be honest with you, I can't pretend that they meant very much to me."

"Don't tackle the big stuff right off the bat. My advice would be to begin with overtures. They're generally short and to the point. Sample some overtures by those two composers you mentioned ... they each wrote a slew of them ... and also the overtures of Rossini and Suppé. They're all winners, and you can't go wrong with any of them."

Jon frowned with doubt. "I don't have the patience to research these classical composers and their thousands of pieces of music," he said. "Call me lazy, but who are your dozen or so favorites? That would make it a lot more manageable."

MacKenzie rubbed her chin, pondering how to help. Then she opened her valise and tore out a yellow sheet of lined paper. "I'll write them down for you ... and you can pick and choose."

That sounded fine to Jon.

She applied pen to paper, writing a series of numbers down the left side of the sheet. "I'll put a composer's name next to each number, from one to twenty, and then stop when I fill up all the spaces. These are in no particular order ... just how they happened to hit my brain." She began filling in the names of her favorites. "Mozart ... Schubert ... Haydn ... Beethoven ... Bach ... Handel ... Dvořák ... Rimsky-Korsakov ... Rachmaninoff ... Copland ... Brahms ... Schumann ... Tchaikovsky ... Barber ... Saint-Saëns ... Chopin ... Bartók ... Vivaldi ... Wagner ... Prokofiev."

"Pretty impressive!" Jon said. "And that was just off the top of your head?"

MacKenzie grinned with pride. "Yes, but there are plenty more composers that I left out ... Grieg and Albéniz, for example, and Bizet, and Sibelius ... and this doesn't even include the great opera composers, such as Verdi and Puccini."

"I haven't ever listened to much classical music, and it's probably too late to start."

"Why do you say that?" she asked.

"It seems overwhelming ... the sheer size of what's out there to hear."

"I'll let you in on a secret. There's an internet channel that you can listen to anytime, day or night. It's called Radio Swiss Classic, and the selections cover all periods of music. This will expose you to almost the entire repertoire that has been recorded."

"So, it's a painless way to become an expert?"

She laughed. "Not really an expert ... but after a few months of listening, I guarantee that your musical soul will be enriched. Radio Swiss Classic is free of charge, too, and it's there for you 24/7. Just put it on in the background, and you'll be surprise by how much you learn."

"What's the catch?"

"No catch," MacKenzie said. "Well, maybe just one. The announcements are not in English. You'll have to try hearing the composers' names and their compositions in either French, German, or Italian ... your choice. After a little practice, you'll have no problem with that."

Jon looked at the wall clock. "You need to get your news together, don't you?"

MacKenzie closed her valise. "Sorry to always go on and on about famous novels and classical music. I enjoy sharing my enthusiasms with people I like."

"I'm glad to be one of them," Jon said. He accepted her list of favorite composers, folded the sheet into fourths, and tucked it into his shirt pocket for later reference. "Radio Swiss Classic, huh? I'll give it a go ... maybe even tonight."

MacKenzie smiled at him. "You won't like everything you hear ... nobody would ... but there's plenty of great music on that channel, and the leg work has already been done for you."

•   •   •

Again it was airtime for the five-minute package called "Behind the Hits," Ronnie Delaney's daily feature that was becoming so very popular among local listeners. Producing five of these informative programs every week was a challenging routine for Ronnie, for he needed to reserve the radio station's recording studio for two-hour blocks each Sunday afternoon—and that was in addition to the one hour each weekday morning when he would apply the finishing touches. Ronnie was adept at audio engineering, so the sound quality of his program was exemplary. Despite his broken leg, he navigated around the studio with enough agility to showcase his professional skills. This was not so important to him on weekday mornings, but Sunday afternoons were a different matter. On Sundays, Ronnie was never alone in the recording studio. That was his time to strut his stuff for pretty girls, whose ages ranged from his own, twenty-five, down to a certifiable eighteen.

Today's installment of "Behind the Hits" aired right after the 11:39 commercial break and told about "Love Is Blue," one of the biggest instrumental hits in pop-music history. Recorded in France by Le Grand Orchestre de Paul Mauriat in late 1967, "Love Is Blue" reigned at number-one on America's *Billboard* charts for five consecutive weeks—during February and March of 1968—the second longest streak ever for an instrumental, behind only Percy Faith's "Theme from A *Summer Place*" in 1959. "L'amour est bleu" premiered as a French-language vocal, written by André Popp (music) and Pierre Cour (lyrics). As Luxembourg's entry in the Eurovision Song Contest of 1967, it was performed by Greek singer Vicky Leandros and finished in fourth place, behind England's winning entry, "Puppet on a String." French bandleader Paul Mauriat was born in 1925 and died in 2006. His brilliant, harpsichord-inflected arrangement of "Love Is Blue" continues to live on as an instrumental classic.

While this episode of "Behind the Hits" was being broadcast, MacKenzie Bastrop dropped into the control room and had five full minutes to pick Ronnie Delaney's brain about Mary Shelley's *Frankenstein*, the novel that she recommended for him to read. Ronnie professed to have finished it two days earlier, which made MacKenzie smile warmly with satisfaction.

"I'm proud of you," she said.

"No problem. It was pretty good. I've always liked that kind of story. Anything in the sci-fi realm is fine with me."

But the more they discussed *Frankenstein*, the less MacKenzie believed that Ronnie had read very much of this book. For one thing, he recalled Mary Shelley's description of the laboratory slab, on which the monster was "born," whereas the novel actually leaves that scene to the reader's imagination. He also mentioned Dr. Frankenstein's lab assistant, Igor, whereas his name in the novel was Fritz. Worst of all, Ronnie grunted incoherently and walked stiff-legged on his cast, imitating Boris Karloff's staggering gait as the film monster. In the novel, author Mary Shelley penned a humanoid that eventually became articulate and ambulatory.

Evidently, Ronnie Delaney had abandoned his reading assignment and opted instead for the 1931 film adaptation. Although MacKenzie did not let him know that she saw through his crude deception, never again would she invite him into her private world of literary masterpieces. Still, she felt more sorry for Ronnie than she felt betrayed, and his transgression was too mild to disqualify him as a friend. MacKenzie sadly conceded that some people are just not meant for appreciating the finer things in life. Through no fault of their own, they simply set their sights too low.

Truth to tell, Ronnie had more immediate concerns on his mind than Frankenstein's monster from the year 1818. For one thing, he was ratcheting up his correspondence with Abby Harker, and each seemed to thrive on the other's brazen innuendos and double entendres. Most enticing of all was the half-baked idea, floated by both of them at various times, that another personal meeting could take place someday. It seemed far-fetched and unrealistic due to the thousand-and-a-half miles of separation, but each kept the idea alive in their texts and emails.

When Ronnie told Jon Swenson about this outrageous notion of theirs, Jon contrived a feeble laugh. But it was nothing but a defense mechanism, invoked to stave off his anger at how Ronnie was making more inroads with Abby than he himself could ever hope to achieve. Ronnie was a free man, after all, unencumbered by the constraints of wedlock. He was also young and libidinous, two traits that Abby no doubt valued very highly as she advanced into her early forties. All Ronnie saw—or even cared about—was that Abby's beauty was second to none. She caused him to think of nothing else. Abby Harker fulfilled his every desire, and thoughts of meeting her again in the flesh dominated many of his waking hours.

Jon, meanwhile, had reached a point where he could wait no longer to hear from Abby. Ronnie's constant references to the latest batch of suggestive photos—"You've never seen anything like these"—were causing his patience to wear thin. Come what may, Jon decided to drop Abby a note, seeing as how she seemed unwilling to take the initiative herself. He would compose it so as to keep her guessing about his motives for writing. The premise had to be his screenplay, no doubt, because *Kiss Me Where It Hurts* was by now the only tenuous thread that linked them together. The Silver Jubilee Reunion, with those memories of a few common activities that they shared, was receding farther and farther into the past.

Determining what form of communication to use was an easy choice for him to make. He considered texting to be too personal, as compared to emailing, and such intimacy was the very last thing he wished to express. The way Jon envisioned it, texting would cause Abby's cellphone to *ding* with close contact, and she would be aware that he was right there at the other end, counting the seconds before her reply would appear in his hands. Jon had no desire to let Abby feel that she was in charge of the situation—even though she really was—and so, by default, emailing it would be. But what should he say? How should he even begin? Sweat was forming on his palms, as if he were some jittery *Wunderkind*, sitting down at the piano in a sold-out Carnegie Hall.

"Hello, my long-lost friend" might be dispassionate enough to serve as a cheerful opener, so he keyed in those letters. And already Jon could sense that he had settled upon the most efficient platform for this particular mission. Editing passages on a full-sized computer keyboard was so much simpler than on one of those tiny touch screens—especially for a holdover from the twentieth century who never learned how to type with his two thumbs.

> Hello, my long-lost friend!
> I have not heard from you in several weeks (even through Ronnie, our designated go-between), so I thought this might be a good time to re-establish a chat line. I hope you and Brent are doing well in sunny SoCal and that neither one of you has forgotten about me entirely. I have made a few changes to "Kiss Me Where It Hurts" that I'm sure Brent will endorse when he sees them. The "script doctors" were too ruthless for my liking, but they did offer some productive suggestions that I weighed very seriously. If Brent rejects my changes (or the whole screenplay, for

that matter), I would still like to maintain our friendship, which is something I value quite highly. Shoot me an email or text whenever you can. Ronnie has kept me in the loop about your current activities, and he has even allowed me to see a chosen few of the photos you have sent to him. Wow, you should be a professional model!
Please keep in touch,
Jon

After reading over his prospective email several times and making a dozen or more minor adjustments, Jon finally regarded it as worthy to be viewed by his high school heartthrob. It seemed evasive enough to make Abby wonder what his true intentions might be for writing it and yet ingratiating enough to stroke her craving for adulation. For a long while, his cursor hovered over the SEND button, but then he clicked the mouse. Away flashed the message to her computer in California, and now it only remained to be seen what kind of impact Jon's carefully selected words might have, if any, on his cross-country relationship.

Jon checked his inbox with compulsive regularity for the next two days until finally, at his 9:30 bedtime on a Thursday night, he laid eyes upon a reply from the familiar email address of arph-arph@yahoo.com. With scarcely a nanosecond's delay, he opened the message and viewed his first words from Abby Pierce Harker in more than three weeks.

Hello to my favorite screenwriter!
I apologize for being MIA for so long, but there were a couple of reasons that made this necessary. Number one was because you seemed afraid that Nikki might read your emails, whether by mistake or on purpose. Secondly, I hesitated to include anything very private when I channeled my messages to you through our

go-between, Ronnie Delaney. He was very kind to offer his help, but slipping a brief passage or two into what I wrote to him had the effect of diluting what I was writing to you. I probably won't be able to send you anything else for quite some time because we're flying to Honolulu pretty soon and then visiting ALL SEVEN of the major Hawaiian Islands for a travelogue that Brent's company is bankrolling. Arr-Tee Studios will not actually shoot the footage, but it is sponsoring the advertising campaign (a tourist bureau or chamber of commerce sort of thing) and will promote and distribute the finished film. Reinhardt Tetsch himself invited Brent to come along with the production staff, and he also insisted that Brent bring his wife -- probably to keep him out of mischief. ☺ This is mind-blowing for me because I've never been west of Avalon! Glad you enjoyed my photos. If you want to see more, just let me know after I return to the mainland.

Love,
Abby

Having read Abby's email message at such a late hour, Jon had difficulty falling asleep in a timely fashion that night. He hoped that his tossing and turning did not keep Nikki awake for very long because his cellphone's 4:30 AM alarm rarely failed to awaken her as well—at least for a short while—and sometimes she had trouble returning to sleep prior to her own phone's 6:00 AM alarm.

As for Jon, sleep deprivation was sure to make itself felt in his announcing job. It always did. But he accepted this latest round of insomnia with good cheer, for Abby's sweet face danced through his consciousness until he finally drifted into a dreamless slumber.

• • •

Two miniature schnauzers, named D. W. and C. B., barked furiously and came running when a delivery man rang the doorbell. But all the man did was leave a package on the front porch and return to his truck. The dogs calmed down within half a minute, just as if nothing had occurred.

During their barking frenzy, Brent Harker was in the master bedroom with a woman who was not his wife. They were spending a Saturday afternoon together while Abby Harker was across town at a screen test. Although devoid of any professional acting experience, Abby hoped to build a late-blooming career because of two unique qualities that she trusted would set her apart from the others who were auditioning for this role. She was utterly beautiful in whatever pose was asked of her—whether clad in the classiest evening gown or the skimpiest swimsuit—and her husband, Brent, manned one of the most responsible positions with a mid-major independent called Arr-Tee Studios.

Abby waited for her name to be called. She was sitting with six other women, all in their late thirties or early forties. Without exception, each of these hopefuls was undeniably pretty as a film camera would view her, but three—by Abby's unofficial count—had temperaments that would cause every sane producer to remove them from serious consideration. Such swaggering, self-important females would cause dissension on any movie set, despite the fact that none had, to date, ever accomplished anything of note beyond regional commercials or bit parts in television sitcoms.

An excessive amount of time seemed to pass between auditions, and Abby wondered how long each screen test took before the next woman was beckoned to the "cattle call." Was there more going on behind the scenes than she could have imagined? The same, identical lines of dialogue were to be recited by each of the candidates, and no more than ten minutes would have been required for that, even at the slowest conversational pace.

The only contender who bothered to speak with Abby in the green room was a lovely brunette whose foreign-sounding name was called when just two of the others remained.

"Wish me luck," she told Abby. Grimly, with precious little hope in her arsenal, she disappeared through a doorway with script in hand.

Twenty-one minutes later, according to the clock/timer app on Abby's phone, a dumpy woman in her late fifties opened the door again to request the next auditioner. "Abby Harker," she said. "Please bring your script along with you, dear." At least she was polite about it.

Abby followed the lady into a hallway that led to what appeared to be a photo gallery of some sort. Two men and one woman, with notepads in front of them, were seated at a long, folding table that looked like a piece of furniture that had been borrowed from a Little League banquet.

"Please lay your script on that music stand, so you can run over the dialogue again before we begin," one of the men told her. "I'll be reading the lines for Guillaume, and you will be speaking the lines for Marta." The man sounded lethargic, as if he no longer cared what became of this role. He took a deep breath and slowly exhaled. "Any attempt at what we loosely call 'acting' will be greatly appreciated. Your part will be declaimed by heart ... in other words, from memory. You have five minutes to prepare, starting now."

Abby Harker was one of seven competitors for a minor supporting role in a movie called *The Doe-Eyed Country Lass*. This modest part in a low-budget potboiler consisted of just six lines, spoken mostly within a Swiss tavern that would soon thereafter be the setting for a deadly, life-altering fracas. The audition material was not excerpted from the film's existing script, which seemed strange to Abby until the man informed her that "this will tell us everything we need to know about you."

After precisely five minutes, a red recording light came on, and the readings began. Abby, as Marta, interacted reasonably well with the seated Guillaume, and she was pleased to have accomplished her main goal, that of remembering all her lines. The bonus of interjecting some emotion into the duo drama fell rather flat, primarily due to Guillaume's monotone delivery.

"Thank you, Ms. Harker," the seated woman said. "Just for the record, what are your preferred pronouns?"

"I beg your pardon."

"For instance, do you prefer to go by 'she/her'?"

"Obviously. Don't I look female to you?" Abby grinned, but she was the only one of the four who did so. The panel seemed uptight and without humor.

"Thank you, Ms. Harker," the seated woman repeated. She pointed toward a side door and then looked down at her papers.

Three days passed before Abby heard back from the production company of *The Doe-Eyed Country Lass*. A tersely worded form letter informed her that she did not get the role.

> We regret to inform you that the part of **Sondra** in our current production of **The Doe-Eyed Country Lass** went to another candidate. Thank you for auditioning, and best wishes in your future endeavors.

That was perfectly fine with Abby. She did not much care for the people behind it anyway, and she could afford to be more patient than other aspiring actresses. Brent earned a nice enough salary to support both of them rather comfortably. Abby would treat this lost Saturday afternoon as a valuable experience to build her future upon, a preliminary screen-test for better things to come.

However self-serving Brent Harker's motives may have been, he had begun using his moderate degree of clout at Arr-Tee Studios to sign Abby up for a series of further auditions. All of these were for minor roles in tiny-budget properties that, at best, might garner two stars out of ten on the ratings scale. Even so, they would look more noble than they deserved on a growing résumé of film credits.

Abby's next screen test was at an accountancy firm in Orange County, far enough away for Brent to count on six hours of uninterrupted euphoria. He had met a twenty-three-year-old blonde surfer girl whose tanned body sculpted her bikini with all the desirable curves. She was contracted to play the leading role of a tomboyish athlete whose love life thrived near the coastal waters of San Diego's Pacific Beach. The title of this Arr-Tee Studios picture was *Catch Me If You Dare*, and its target audience was the date-night teenager crowd. Truth be told, the script was only one slim step above "Valley girl" mentality. And yet, this was a film that Brent Harker would no doubt enjoy editing very much because of his personal involvement.

Actress and real-life surfboard hugger Tina Coyle was more than a novice in the motion picture industry, for she had appeared in seven national releases in the past three years, in addition to numerous parts in stage dramas and musicals throughout Ventura, Los Angeles, and San Diego Counties. She could sing reasonably well, having taken voice lessons from a private instructor in Oxnard. But her primary talent was decorative, as on-screen eye candy for adolescent-to-thirty-something males who had enough discretionary income (or parental allowance) to splurge on a movie ticket or two for Friday night.

In her private life, Tina had a weakness for dogs of all shapes and sizes. She owned a golden doodle named "Dipsy" but enjoyed the smaller breeds just as much. In fact, her beloved Yorkshire terrier had died just six months earlier at a superannuated sixteen. This was her first visit to Brent Harker's home, where D. W. and C. B. ruled the roost. Tina petted and romped with Dee and Cee for so long that Brent began to wonder whether there would be much time left for anything else. To avoid further stoppage of play, he double-checked to make sure that his cellphone was on SILENT mode. He had wine in the cooler, for that is the way his guest liked it best.

An accountancy office in Orange County was not the most customary place for a video audition to be staged, but this particular role would be in an advertising campaign for Howard Klingmann & Son, Financial Advisors. There were to be six thirty-second commercials in the series, and each would feature the same fictitious character, named Meredith. She would be seen in a half-dozen different photogenic locales, such as Griffith Park and Catalina Island, and her pitch would be how gratifying it was to be debt-free in today's volatile economic climate. This hypothetical Meredith woman was a member of the smart set, patently upper-crust and enjoying life to the fullest because of an absence of monetary worries. Meredith, it need hardly be said, relied upon Howard Klingmann & Son for management of her financial planning and investments.

Did Abby Harker fit the part in terms of appearance? Most assuredly, and that was a critical factor in the selection process. She had to look like a person of Meredith's standing would look and to comport herself in Meredith's poised, self-confident manner without seeming haughty. No husband would ever be portrayed in this advertising campaign, tacitly insinuating that truly independent women of a certain age should turn to Howard Klingmann & Son for advice. Four other attractive women were competing for the recurring part. Two were tall, willowy, and exceedingly beautiful. Two were short, shapely, and exceedingly beautiful.

A tall, willowy woman was called to read first for the ad agency rep, and she was succeeded by a short, shapely woman. Next came Abby. She walked, as had the others, into an austere cellblock, with white walls that impounded nothing but a television camera. Committing her lines to memory was a snap, especially since eleven seconds of each spot were devoted to the canned, unvarying intro and outro. To facilitate their tryouts, the applicants were given elegant props—a stylish handbag, elbow-length white gloves, and a chic hat. Presumably, this made it easier for them to get into character.

"Abby Harker?" This was an echoey male voice from the overhead speaker.

"Yes, sir," Abby said.

"You may begin when the recording light turns red above the camera." The studio became deathly quiet, but only for a fleeting moment. "Stand by. Abby Harker, take one, in five ... four ... three ... two ... one ..." The recording light turned red.

At twenty-one seconds, Abby's first reading was a bit too measured to fit inside the allotted time window. Also, she did not emote quite enough self-confidence. "Not bad, Ms. Harker, but please deliver more pomposity," the voice said. "Picture Meredith as being a high-roller in Vegas. The men pant after her, but she is oblivious to them all. Okay, stand by. Abby Harker, take two, in five ... four ... three ... two ... one ..."

Abby tried it again, while quickening the pace and adding a thick layer of arrogance. "That's better, Ms. Harker, but we still need you to speak down to the audience. They love it and will follow you anywhere. Stand by. Abby Harker, take three, in five ... four ... three ... two ... one ..."

This time, she must have nailed her lines because The Voice was ecstatic. "Perfect, Ms. Harker. You look and sound the role." He paused as Abby laid the props on a table, ready for the fourth applicant to attempt a reading. "We'll be in touch."

Anxious to tell her husband how well the audition had gone, Abby dashed away in her cobalt blue Subaru BRZ, at least ten miles per hour above the posted speed limit. Brent was alone by now, and he expressed to Abby how proud he was of her. He vowed to procure other screen tests, in order to harness the positive momentum. A secondary purpose, left unsaid, was to secure for himself some recreational time with an assortment of young lovelies.

• • •

It was becoming more and more apparent to sixteen-year-old Lauren Swenson that the harmony of her homelife had declined in the past couple of weeks. Her parents were outwardly courteous to one another, but no longer did they tease or laugh as they had always done before, as far back as she could remember. Little did Lauren know that her father was preoccupied with a flirt in California and her mother with a flirt in the very next office.

Two full days had gone by since Nikki's lunchtime chat with Tony Zeigen, and yet she still had not found just the right moment to tell Jon about the upcoming conference in Atlanta. Her time for delaying was over because a few arrangements needed to be made. "Do you have a minute or two for me to give you some news?" she asked.

"Sure. I'm just killing time," Jon said. He was sitting in front of his computer, which displayed a candid photo of James Stewart, Henry Fonda, and Margaret Sullavan.

"I think GoldSpire is sending me to Atlanta next week," Nikki said.

"To Atlanta! How come?"

"The annual SRBC."

"What's that?"

"The Southern Regional Banking Conference. It's an assembly of banking executives that lasts for six days, starting on Tuesday."

Jon tallied those six days in his mind. "A conference that lasts over the weekend? That's kind of strange."

"Well, there are probably just a few sessions on Saturday morning, and then most of the attendees will be expected back at work on the following Monday. Officially, it's probably only five days."

"Would you fly out on Tuesday morning?"

"Yes. I'm sure that first day is mainly for registration ... allowing people to get there from all over the fourteen-state area. It's a pretty big deal."

"How come you've never gone to this conference before?"

"I'm not sure. For some reason, our branch office has never invited me to attend the SRBC until now. Maybe that means I'm moving up in the world."

Jon rubbed his face with both hands, as if waking up from a sleep. "Hmm, I guess this makes me Mister Mom for a while. What'll I fix Lauren and me for dinner all of those nights? I'm not used to being in charge of the kitchen."

"Don't worry. I'll draw up a list of things you can make. But I'll also allow for a couple of outings to restaurants. You won't mind that, I'm sure, and neither will she."

Jon idly scrolled through his Twitter posts, which consisted mostly of baseball history, old-time radio, and vintage movie accounts. "How many of you will be making the trip to Atlanta?"

This was the question that Nikki had dreaded more than any other. "Just the two of us ... Tony Zeigen and I, as far as I know. Tony is the top-ranking loan officer at our branch, and he picked me because I designed the spreadsheet that we all use to track the flow of interest-bearing monies among our constituents."

"Oh?" Jon had no idea what his wife was talking about, but it sounded plausible.

"In fact, that is one of the topics on the docket for Thursday afternoon."

He turned toward her. "Will you be a speaker?"

"Yes. I just saw the agenda online ... and there I am!"

Jon smiled at her. "Let me see it." They departed from Twitter and onto the GoldSpire Bank website. Under Southern Regional Banking Conference, they went to Thursday's schedule and found, at 1:15 PM, the names of two presenters: Sheila Connors Drake and Nikki Hiller Swenson. "They even have your maiden name," Jon said.

"I suppose it looks more masterful that way ... or at least official."

"Is Tony a presenter too?"

"No ... but he was on one of the steering committees that appointed me to session leadership. I owe this SRBC assignment to him."

"Good for Tony." Jon's comment, while supportive on its surface, sounded hollow and not quite totally sincere. In fact, the more Nikki thought about it, his tone of voice definitely leaned toward the cynical. "Will you two be flying to Atlanta together?" Jon asked.

"I believe so. He's handling all of the travel and accommodations."

Jon grinned. "Two hotel rooms, I presume."

Nikki rolled her eyes at him. "Of course two rooms. What a silly notion. I'm not even sure Tony and I will be in the same hotel ... although I would guess so."

"That would make it simpler." Again, Jon's biting irony simmered beneath.

Nikki could sense, and rightly so, that her wisest move now would be to cut their discussion short. All she had set out to do was inform her husband about the impending trip, and that had been accomplished. Exactly where the topic veered out of control, she was not certain, but riding that train of thought was a perilous gamble—even for a couple who had been married for almost nineteen years and presumed that they knew each other so well.

The next morning was a Friday, and Tony Zeigen dropped into Nikki's office to inform her that all arrangements had been made. Their flight would depart at 9:40 AM on Tuesday, and they would be staying at a Holiday Inn Express near the airport. In passing along this information, Tony seemed unusually affectionate, both in word and deed—twice caressing her hand—and Nikki enjoyed every minute of the attention he showed. Had her large window not looked directly into the lobby, they may have taken even more liberties still.

"Can we ride to the airport together on Tuesday?" Nikki asked.

"Of course. I'll pick you up at seven thirty. Will that give us enough time to go through security?"

"Better make it seven. I'd rather have too much time on our hands than too little. The TSA lines can be unpredictable."

Tony frowned. "That'll work fine for me. Allison and I are in separate bedrooms nowadays, so my five o'clock alarm won't bother her at all."

That was more information than Nikki really needed to know, but perhaps it did clarify why Tony's eyes were wandering off the reservation. "Sorry to hear that," she said. "I hope things can be straightened out between you two pretty soon."

"I hope so too. The best I can recall, it was a silly argument that grew into a gargantuan one ... way out of proportion to how it started." Tony gazed at Nikki, as if appealing for sympathy. "To be honest with you, I was mostly to blame, but I'm having a hard time admitting it."

"How come?"

He sighed. "Sometimes Allison is not very forgiving when I apologize. That makes me mad ... and then the whole thing starts all over again."

"How long have you and Allison been married?"

"Twenty-four years. What about you and Jon?"

"Eighteen."

"Allison is my second wife. Did you know that?" Tony flashed her a wry smile. "Yep, I was married for three years to a gal from Memphis whose one goal in life was to be an exotic dancer. She wanted everyone to stare at her figure."

"Whatever happened to her, or did you lose track?"

"She became an exotic dancer. So, I guess her fondest dreams came true."

"Aw, what a sweet ending that is. It almost makes me cry."

Tony recognized sarcasm when he heard it. "Don't waste your tears. She was always into booze and drugs ... even way back when ... so I'd hate to think what she looks like now. She probably operates a bordello on the Mississippi."

"Thus ends the fairy tale," Nikki said. "Good thing you dumped her."

Tony blushed. "Actually, I must confess that she dumped me." He chuckled at himself. "I guess that doesn't say much for my taste in girls back then."

She pretended to punch him in the jaw. "Oh, well, we all need to grow up."

"Some of us are still trying," he said.

In the present circumstances, Nikki did not feel it proper to respond.

•   •   •

B oth Swensons awoke when they heard Jon's cellphone *beep* its alarm at 4:30 on Tuesday morning. This was Jon's normal time to rise for his announcing stint anyway, so it was no major hardship for him to roll out of bed at such an early hour. But Nikki's everyday alarm would not have roused her for another ninety minutes, so she was bleary-eyed and uncommunicative. Their improvised meal—toaster waffles with syrup—was a very quiet affair, for Jon's questions at the table earned him only the most perfunctory of replies. Something was amiss, he thought, because usually his wife was more talkative in the mornings than he was—at least on those rare occasions when they ate breakfast together on a weekday.

Maybe Nikki was nervous about her trip to Atlanta. She had not been sent to an out-of-town meeting for four years, and that winter's three-day seminar only required a journey by car of one hundred miles. Relatively speaking, this year's conference was a complex venture, involving two airline flights and adequate luggage to handle six days of clothing changes. Besides that, Nikki was to be one of the scheduled presenters this time, so there was no room for error in any of her preparations.

On that Tuesday, Jon backed his truck out of the garage at 5:30 AM, as always, and encountered the usual light traffic on the way to work. This was one reason why he preferred the early morning slot to other announcing duties that he had performed at the radio station—and he had done them all at one time or another. Also, of course, he enjoyed being the only person there for the first couple of hours. It gave him a chance to perform his announcing duties in peaceful solitude for half of his shift.

Jon had just completed his second hour of hosting the morning show when, across town, Tony Zeigen rang the Swensons' doorbell. Nikki greeted him with a quick nod and wave, but no show of warmth could be dared on the front porch in this suburban neighborhood. Too many eyes might be watching, and torrid gossip traveled fast, especially if inflated well beyond the truth.

Tony loaded Nikki's heavy luggage into his car trunk as effortlessly as a seasoned longshoreman. With admiration, she watched him hoist her three suitcases into place and then shift them around until there was no wasted space. He was remarkably strong for someone of his height who only weighed 180 pounds. Nikki found herself enjoying the sight of Tony's biceps, as they rippled beneath the short sleeves that he chose to wear on this pleasant morning of seventy-one degrees.

People did not dress up for airplane flights anymore, so Tony felt justified in going casual, and Nikki certainly had no objections to that. She, too, was relaxed in her apparel, sporting a lavender blouse over a pair of fashionable white slacks. As they hurried side-by-side toward their departure gate, his long strides made Nikki speed-walk like an Olympian just to keep up with him. Once aboard the plane, being the gentleman that he was, Tony offered her the window seat, but, being the apprehensive flier that she was, Nikki declined with thanks and was perfectly content to share an armrest with him from the middle spot.

Upon landing in Atlanta, their hotel supplied a shuttle van from the airport, which was the main factor in Tony's selection of these particular accommodations. Likewise, the hotel also provided free transportation to the convention center, where most events of the Southern Regional Banking Conference would be held. Still, Tony thought it wise to hire a rental car as well, for those additional excursions they might wish to take during hours when there were no mandatory SRBC sessions to attend. He did all of the driving, so Nikki was at his mercy in terms of which leisure activities they would pursue. Then again, they could simply remain at the hotel for much of the time. This was understood by both of them but never explicitly stated.

Tuesday afternoon was allocated mostly to late registration—for those folks who, whatever the cause, had not already declared themselves as conference attendees and were compelled to do so in person rather than online. It was also possible to pick up copies of the conference schedule of sessions, as well as such peripherals as personal nametags and the current design of superbly crafted SRBC pins. The latter were highly prized items, much in demand and restricted to one per registered banker. The previous year's version was commanding a price of $250 apiece on the open market. Other than signing in and securing their printed schedules, nametags, and SRBC pins, Nikki and Tony were free to do as they chose on this opening day of the conference.

"Care to go to the Braves game tonight?" Tony asked.

"Sure!" Nikki said. "I've always been a baseball fan ... ever since Daddy took me to my first Tacoma Tigers game at Cheney Stadium."

"So, it's a date."

"But aren't the tickets awfully expensive?"

Tony grinned. "They're not expensive when GoldSpire is buying. It's sort of a fringe benefit for volunteering to endure this conference."

That came as a surprise to Nikki. "Did you volunteer *me* too?"

"How did you guess?"

For the first time, she began to feel uneasy about this Atlanta adventure of hers. Before now, she had assumed that Tony Zeigen would keep his mind almost exclusively on business, but that certainty was fading away.

The Braves were playing the Pittsburgh Pirates at 7:20 PM in the rubber match of a three-game series. Their seats at the ballpark were rather good—in Section 320, on the third deck behind the first-base dugout. Although Atlanta ended up losing, it was a fun game to watch, with plenty of offense for both teams, and the Braves fan directly in front of them barehanded a foul ball for a souvenir.

It was about 11:25 PM when Tony parked the rental car in one of the very few remaining spaces at the hotel, and then he and Nikki rode the elevator up to the fourth floor. Their rooms, numbers 422 and 424, were located right next to each other. In fact, the doors came within six feet of touching. Because the hallway was otherwise deserted, Nikki and Tony stood outside her door, quietly chatting for several minutes. Tomorrow morning at 9:00 would be the opening session of the Southern Regional Banking Conference, and all nine hundred attendees were expected to be there en masse.

"The shuttle van runs every half-hour, so let's catch it at eight thirty," Tony said. "It's only a ten-minute drive to the convention center."

"Okay. What time do you want to meet for breakfast?"

"I'll knock at seven o'clock, and we can go down together. Is that too early for you?"

"Sounds about right. They have those famous cinnamon rolls here, you know."

Tony smiled down at her. "How well I know!"

And Nikki smiled right back. "Yum ... I'll try to limit myself to two of them. They go great with coffee."

Neither of them said anything for almost five full seconds. They simply stared at each other, wondering what should come next. Finally, Tony leaned forward and kissed Nikki gently on the lips. It was just the briefest of kisses, as if wishing her "Good night" instead of something deeper from the heart. But Nikki took the memory of it to bed with her.

•   •   •

Jon always felt disoriented when his wife was not around to manage the household. He and Lauren ate carry-out pizza on Tuesday night and then went to Cheddar's for their evening meal on Wednesday. Thursday was typically leftover night at the Swensons, so father and daughter made do with the remains of Monday's dinner—baked chicken with green beans and fried potatoes.

Lauren spent the evenings keeping up with homework assignments but also found time to practice the violin for at least a half-hour per night. At present, her solo projects were *Hungarian Dance No. 5* by Johannes Brahms and "Solvejg's Song" from the incidental music to *Peer Gynt* by Edvard Grieg. As was Lauren's custom on Wednesday afternoons at 5:00, she and her collaborator—a CD anthology of piano accompaniment—performed these current pieces for the approval of a private instructor. Rarely did three weeks go by before the teacher declared her ready for the next challenges. Consequently, the repertoire in Lauren's fingers was expanding at a rapid clip, and she was even deliberating about the possibility of becoming a music major in college. That would have to wait for some scholarship offers to come her way.

Jon was very diligent to check his cellphone regularly, but no text messages arrived from Nikki for the first two evenings. Not until Thursday did she finally send belated greetings from Atlanta. She wrote that her session as a presenter had gone very well that afternoon, and she was now much less stressed by her workload.

> It feels nice to relax for a change. Today's 1:15 session belonged to me and Sheila Drake, who is from Little Rock. We split the duties, taking lots of questions from the audience, which numbered about 75. There will be more sessions all day tomorrow and until noon on Saturday. I guess Tony and I will do some sight-seeing on Sunday. I've never been to Atlanta before, but

he's visited here a couple of times, so he'll be
my guide. I hope you and L are having fun as a
father/daughter combo.
Love, N

Jon texted her back within five minutes.

Hiya, Nix.
Glad your presentation went so well today.
Did you already know Sheila Drake, or did
you just meet her for this occasion? Everything
is fine at the homestead. L has a date with
someone named Gareth Belew tomorrow night.
(Whatever happened to regular names, like Bill
and Bob?) We'll be eating leftovers tonight, but
I think L wants to go out for dinner from now
on. Can't say as I blame her! If I call or text you,
I'll try to remember that you are now one hour
later than here.
Bye for now, J

Fridays at the radio station were more laid back than the
other six days. For instance, the office workers would often break
away an hour early to beat the rush-hour traffic and try to get a
head start on the weekend. And the administrative personnel—
from president to general manager and on down the supervisory
roster—were even less visible than that. Seldom were they to be
seen past high noon on that day of the week.

Announcer Ronnie Delaney came into the control room at
9:45 AM, carrying the stack of papers that represented his 10:00
newscast. He was reporting a bit early in order to say something
to Jon Swenson before they went their separate ways at the
change of shifts. A double play of oldies was about to begin—
"Western Union" by The Five Americans and "When the Snow
Is on the Roses" by Ed Ames—so Jon would have five minutes to
talk with him.

"Well, old buddy, you've got the green light," Ronnie said.

Jon had a bewildered look. "And what's that supposed to mean?"

"Our California cutie is back in circulation."

"Abby's getting divorced?"

Ronnie laughed. "No. She and Brent are still going strong ... or as strong as they ever were, that is." Smiling, he pointed an index finger at Jon. "Abby is back from Hawaii and wants you to email her as soon as you can. She says you'll need to be the one who restarts the correspondence." Ronnie assumed an expression of smugness—melodramatic, for effect. "Otherwise, my friend, it looks like I'm her sole contact in this part of the country, and if she ever returns here in person, it'll be to see me and 'renew acquaintances,' if you know what I mean."

Jon ignored his friend's quip. "She wants me to use email, rather than text?"

"Yep. She was very specific about what you should do. I guess she's afraid that Nikki might intercept a phone text, whereas your email is more secure and for your eyes only. She said to use 'arph-arph,' and you'd know what she meant."

Jon grinned. "That's a reference to D. W. Griffith and C. B. DeMille, her two schnauzers."

Ronnie had no clue. "Whatever ..." he said. "Just shoot her an email fairly soon if you plan to correspond with Abby again. If you don't, she'll know you've lost all interest in her ... sort of an electronic slap in the face."

"No way! I'm still kind of hypnotized by Abby Harker, like most men who've ever met her. Just don't tell Abby I said that, or her head will get even bigger than it already is." Jon pretended to kick Ronnie's leg cast. "By the way, did Abby say why she sent you the email instead of writing directly to me?"

"After these weeks away, she couldn't remember exactly where she stood with you ... and whether Nikki was still suspicious about a long-distance romance. She figured it would be safer to use her 'go-between' ... me ... until you checked in again with arph-arph."

The Ed Ames song was coming to a close, and that would be followed by four recorded commercials and then another double play—"Don't It Make You Want to Go Home Again?" by Joe South and "The Air That I Breathe" by The Hollies. At 10:00, straight up, Ronnie Delaney would transform into a newsman for five minutes, after which the oldies would resume.

As had become the norm lately, MacKenzie Bastrop was waiting for Jon in the staff lounge when he went off the air. Jon realized this, so he made it a point to drop into that room each day, at least for a short while.

"Any rapport yet between you and F. Scott Fitzgerald?" MacKenzie asked.

Jon shook his head. "I'm afraid not, Mack. My wife went out of town earlier this week, and things have been topsy-turvy at home."

"And you're 'baching' it?"

"Nothing as simple as that. We have a sixteen-year-old daughter, and teenagers' lives can get pretty crazy."

MacKenzie was visibly disappointed in her friend's lack of progress with *The Great Gatsby*, but Jon offered some cheerier news on the classical music front. "By the way, I've listened to Radio Swiss Classic several times."

"Good for you!" she said. "What did you like?"

"One of my favorites was Rimsky-Korsakov's *Russian Easter Overture*."

"Which recording ... if you don't mind my asking?"

"As best I could tell ... from the German announcer ... the conductor was Leopold Stokowski. I remember his name from Walt Disney's *Fantasia*."

"Stokowski is super. His performance of *Scheherazade* is fabulous, too, and the Decca acoustics are amazing for 1965."

MacKenzie succeeded Ronnie Delaney on the air at 2:00 PM, and the first thing Ronnie did, upon being relieved of duty, was hurry directly to Jon Swenson in his radio-sales cubicle. Grinning with anticipation, Ronnie came right to the point. "Well, have you emailed Abby?"

Jon was miffed by the question. "Good golly, Miss Molly ... give me a little time! I'll probably do it tonight."

"We write to each other at least twice a day," Ronnie said. "All she talks about now is her acting job."

That took Jon by surprise. "An acting job? In a movie?"

"Just a series of commercials, but at least it's a start."

"Well, it's about time someone in La-La Land noticed and appreciated her beauty," Jon said. That night, he sat down at his computer and sent her an email.

> Hello, Abby.
> Glad you're back from that "tough" assignment to Hawaii! I spoke to Ronnie Delaney earlier today, and he told me that you have a recurring role in a series of commercials. Way to go! :-) Do you know if we can see them in this part of the country? I really think you should try for an acting career. You certainly do have the photogenic looks to qualify. It could be that Arr-Tee Studios has just the right property for you, and I'm sure Brent would notify you if and when the casting department begins its search. Please reply to this email as soon as you can, and stay in touch!
> All my best,
> Jon

Whatever else might be said of her, predictability was not one of Abby's more distinctive attributes. Despite Jon's encouragement, she delayed for two full days—until Sunday afternoon—before finally writing back to him. Her email was quite newsy but devoid of any attempts at humor, those little witticisms that made her so enjoyable to count as a friend.

> Hi, Jon.
> Thanks a bunch for the kind message that you

sent to me on Friday night. Yes, I have been contracted to play the part of "Meredith" in a series of six commercials. This is an advertising campaign for Howard Klingmann & Son, a financial advisement firm in Los Angeles County. I'm sure that these will not run outside southern California, although it's always possible that someone might put them up on YouTube as a video clip. I have auditioned for roles in three motion pictures, but all I got for my troubles were form letters of rejection. The competition is fierce and cutthroat. Two women actually got into a fist fight before their screen tests to play a nun! Neither got the part. I don't know where we stand on "Kiss Me Where It Hurts" because Brent has not mentioned it to me since you were here for that script consultation. Please tell Nikki that we enjoyed seeing her.
Abby

Jon digested her words several times before moving the email to an archival folder for storage. He had every intention of responding to the message in a timely fashion, but another task took precedence. Tonight he would be going to the airport to take his wife home after her sojourn in Atlanta. For some unstated reason, Tony Zeigen was unable to bring her back to where he had picked her up six days earlier.

•   •   •

All throughout their quarrelsome trip home in the Ford F-150, Jon demanded to hear some credible reason why Tony declined to bring her back from the local airport, but Nikki remained tight-lipped about it.

Even when they went inside the house, and she greeted Lauren with a hug and kiss, the best Nikki could offer was, "I think Allison's parents had popped in for a visit, so Tony was hoping you could pick me up."

Jon was not buying that. "It just seems kind of juvenile for him to skip the last part of his job."

"My gosh! It wasn't his job." Nikki said. "Tony wasn't being paid to be my chauffeur. Sometimes things come up unexpectedly, and this was one of those times. He apologized to me and felt terrible about having to ask you to step in for him. I swore that you wouldn't mind helping, but it looks like I was wrong."

Jon glared at her. "As I told you on the phone, Lauren wanted me to watch a movie with her ... one of her favorites that she's always wanted me to see ... and we were nearly finished with it when you called. All Tony had to do was drop you off. I would have gotten your luggage together and brought it inside."

Now it was Nikki's turn to glare. "Don't be so hateful about this. Like always, you're embellishing things beyond all reason. As you well know, Tony was not refusing to roll my luggage inside for me. That's just plain ridiculous."

This was not the way Jon had expected Nikki's homecoming to be. He paused for a second, wondering whether to continue his tirade. "Okay, okay," he finally said. "You're home safely, and that's the important thing."

"Is it? I get the impression that you wished I'd stayed away longer."

Jon had thought the argument was over, thanks to his feeble attempt at conciliation, but apparently he was wrong. Nikki's unwillingness to let it die a natural death caused him to barge ahead. "You're being very defensive about this whole affair," he said. "And now I'm beginning to wonder what might have gone on between the two of you in Atlanta."

Nikki proceeded to do what she always did in such tense moments. She cried. This was her last-ditch reserve to salvage a partial victory from sure defeat. Nikki was not adept at hiding her feelings, and any suggestion of impropriety with

Tony Zeigen would be handled poorly. Deep down, she was too honest to live a lie of the heart. Before long, Nikki's untruths would become tangled, reducing her to an oracle of true confessions. It was far better to end the argument with a cry and leave the room.

Needless to say, Monday mornings are difficult for any working man or woman, but this particular Monday was off the charts for Jon Swenson. He had not been able to drift into a restless slumber until about 2:00 AM, so when his alarm notified him that 4:30 had been reached, that rude noise cut his sleep short at just two and a half hours. In times past, Nikki would often roll over to give him a loving pat on the back as he began to rise from bed. Not so on this morning. She lay as still and silent as a mannequin, and Jon knew that he was really going to pay for it today. Already he dreaded coming home in the afternoon.

He had just finished announcing the news and weather at 7:00 AM and then introducing a double-play set—"Those Were the Days" by Mary Hopkin and "When I Fall in Love" by The Lettermen—when the control room's hotline rang. He could hardly believe what he saw on the caller ID. In addition to a vaguely familiar cellphone number, the listed name was HARKER, BRENT. He answered the telephone in a professional manner, even stating the radio station's call letters, just as if he did not already know who was calling.

"Jon? This is Abby." He had not heard her sweet voice in almost two months, and instantly its sound raised his lowly spirits. She had that power over him.

"Hi, Abby. Wow, isn't it kind of early for you to be up and around?" He glanced at the clock on his console. "It's only a little after five out there."

"Six minutes past that ungodly hour, to be exact."

Abby added nothing more, and Jon felt obliged to fill the silence. "So, what gives?" He realized that this was a pretty weak attempt at conversation, but it was better than nothing.

She giggled at his discomfort, which was plainly audible. "I was feeling lonely, so I thought I'd give you a call."

"Where's Brent?"

"Still in bed. I'm calling from our car, which is parked in the garage. It's the only private place I can find." There was a delay, and Abby could hear some well-known music playing. "Isn't that 'Those Were the Days'? It was one of my favorite songs from the Dark Ages."

"Right you are! Very good."

"And I think Paul McCartney produced it, if I'm not mistaken," she said.

"I do believe you're right. Maybe you should be hosting this oldies show instead of me."

"Sorry, but I only do financial-services commercials ... under the sexy name of Meredith."

Jon chuckled. "Oh, sure. How could I forget the world-famous Meredith?" He had no choice but to interrupt himself. "Look ... don't take this wrong, Abby, but could you call me back at eight fifteen, your time? I'm on the air right now, and The Lettermen's song only lasts for two and a half minutes."

"No. I won't bother you any more. I was just feeling lonesome and wanted to hear your voice again. Brent and I seem to be on different planets these days."

"Same here with Nikki and me, as a matter of fact. I doubt if we'll be speaking to each other today. We both went to bed in a snit, and she was still asleep when I left for work."

Abby ignored his current plight and expressed no sympathy for it. "Well, I enjoyed shooting the breeze with you, as they say ... even if it was only for the length of one song."

"And part of a second." His hope for a laugh was not met.

"'Bye, Jon," was all she said.

Suddenly, he had a sinking sensation and needed to be pepped up by something positive. "Please call me back at eight fifteen, Abby, on my personal cellphone. I want to talk some more, and I can't do it from home."

"My goodness, okay ... if it's really that important to you."

"It is," Jon said. "I guess I'm feeling a little lonely right now too."

• • •

If there was one thing you could count on from Abby, it was that you could not count on her for anything. When 10:15 AM rolled around, Jon was in the radio-sales cubicle with his cellphone on the desk in front of him. He felt sure that the wait would not be long, but 11:00 came and went without hearing from her. Naturally, he had been unable to make any sales calls at all, so even his job was suffering because of her. It seemed that Abby was always in control of the situation, and this was just another example. Now he would have to select her name from his contact file, and she would enjoy the satisfaction of being in the driver's seat once again.

Swallowing his pride, Jon touched the number, and Abby answered on the first ring. "Hi, Jon. Sorry about not calling at eight fifteen, but Brent was hovering around, and I can't very well talk to you in front of him."

"I wasn't sure whether you'd answer or Brent, but I went ahead and tried."

"No problem. This is my private line, although it's listed in Brent's name. If you call this number ... which I hope you'll feel free to do at any time ... you can bet that I'll be at the other end."

"Can you talk for long, or is he still around?"

"We're fine. Brent went to the studio for a while."

"Are you getting a lot of nibbles for jobs?" Jon asked.

"Two or three a day, but most of them go nowhere. I feel like I'm working full-time by just going to screen tests."

"Are they mostly for movies or TV commercials?"

"Neither. Most of my gigs are for photographic shoots. Apparently, I'm becoming quite popular as a so-called 'fashion model.' But that's just a fancy-schmancy way of saying that some local photographers like to see me in a two-piece swimsuit or a tank top."

"I don't blame them." Jon regretted the remark, but Abby did not seem to mind.

"Two of the photo shoots have been outdoors ... at the beach," she said.

"I know. Ronnie Delaney showed me a few of the pictures."

Abby laughed. "I'm just glad he didn't show you all of them."

"Well, they must really be something. Ronnie told me he was holding a few back for extortion purposes."

"That does sound like something he'd do."

"In the meantime, I'll just have to use my imagination."

"Mmm ... maybe so." Suddenly, Abby became rather serious again. "Are you still feeling down in the dumps, like you were when I called earlier?"

"Not so much anymore. You caught me at a bad time, that's all. Nikki and I had a spat."

"What about?"

"She went to Atlanta for six days with a co-worker from the bank. But then I had to pick her up from the airport when this guy decided that he couldn't drop her off at home." There was a pause. "The problem is, he's about six-foot-three and pretty good looking, so I don't know what to think."

"Did they stay in the same hotel?"

"Yes, but they booked two separate rooms."

Abby giggled. "So did we in Los Angeles, and nothing happened between us. Maybe you're getting all worked up over nothing."

"But Nikki and Tony know each other a lot better than we did at the time."

"We're much more deeply acquainted now," she said.

Jon was not sure what Abby was insinuating, but she had a flair for being suggestive in a playful manner. He thought it wise to go elsewhere with the discussion. "You told me that you and Brent were on different planets these days. What went wrong?"

"That's pretty much where we live our lives ... on different planets ... and we always have."

"Right from the start?"

"Except for about two weeks of preliminary dating," Abby said. "We joke about that being our engagement period, but the truth is we jumped into marriage head first, without even thinking it through."

"When did it start to go downhill?"

"Way less than a year. Being in the film industry, Brent has always been surrounded by beautiful girls ... starlets and such ... and he doesn't try very hard to fight them off. He has no defense against temptation."

Jon gave that some thought. "A while back, you were saying it was like a second honeymoon between the two of you."

"What do you expect? That was when Brent came home after being stuck in rural Montana for several weeks. I think he got tired of that continuity girl up there and needed a change of pace."

"A slower pace?"

"Just the opposite! Remember ... I hadn't been with him in a long time either, and I made up for lost time."

"Lucky guy," Jon said.

She chuckled. "Hey, maybe we should get Brent and Nikki together, so you and I can live happily ever after."

Only Abby Pierce Harker could say something like that and get away with it.

· · ·

Two fruitless sales calls brought the morning to a close for Jon Swenson, and this was one workday that he wished would never end. The dispute with Nikki was still fresh in his mind, and no doubt in hers too. Jon had left his house in such a rush that morning that he did not have a brown-bag meal with him. Consequently, he decided to go to lunch with someone at the radio station, and announcer MacKenzie Bastrop seemed to be the best option.

MacKenzie always ate alone in the staff lounge because that was how she preferred to spend the noon hour—with a literary classic propped open beside her meager repast of sandwich, chips, and apple. In view of his present circumstances, Jon's reasoning made very good sense. How risky could it possibly be to dine with her? She was the very last person who might be accused of inspiring a romantic liaison with a male colleague, so there would be no lasting effects if the two of them were seen together at a restaurant.

Jon drove them to the local McAlister's for combo meals of soup and sandwich. Standing shoulder-to-shoulder at the cash register up front, he insisted on paying for both of their tabs.

"No way," MacKenzie said. "Why should you buy my food?"

"Because I dragged you away from the station against your will. You'd be having a pleasant lunch hour in the company of some dearly departed author right now ... instead of having to entertain me because I didn't bring anything to eat from home."

That brought a rather cute smile from her, and Jon was surprised by how moderately attractive—though not quite pretty—MacKenzie might be if she only made the slightest effort on her own behalf. Removing those ungainly eyeglasses would be a big help, he surmised, though he was not a close enough friend of hers to make such a personal suggestion. They went to a table.

"Well, Mack, what are you reading these days?" That was always Jon's first topic of conversation with MacKenzie because nothing else came so straight from her heart.

"*Anna Karenina*," she said.

Jon nodded his head. "Dostoyevsky?"

"No, but that's the right nationality. It's by Leo Tolstoy, who also wrote *War and Peace*. The heroine ... if you could call her that ... is involved in an extramarital affair."

That terminology was more than Jon's guilt allowed him to hear without plaguing his conscience, so he evaded any further mention of the story line. "Is it a long book?"

MacKenzie smiled at the lowbrow naïveté of his question. "Tolstoy was a wonderful writer, but nobody could ever claim that he was concise. *Anna Karenina* is more than eight hundred pages long ... and even that's much shorter than *War and Peace*."

"And here I thought *The Great Gatsby* was long."

"Hardly! That's more like a novella in length, which is partly why I recommended it as your maiden voyage." She stirred her soup. "Incidentally, how are you coming with it?"

"Not too bad, by my modest standards. I'm on page eighty."

"Is it holding your interest?"

"Sure. It's easy to read, with modern language and characters ... a lot closer to today's world than anything by Tolstoy, I'd venture to guess." He broke into a grin. "Besides, I have an advantage."

"Oh? What's that?"

"I've already seen the movie, so I know how it ends." He waited for his friend's reaction, and it came just as expected.

"Don't be so certain," she said. "Some movies butcher the novels that they're based on ... sometimes even tacking on sappy endings, Hollywood style. It's a travesty."

"That's probably true, but you'll be pleased to hear that the Robert Redford movie does not end happily. Gatsby is shot to death in his swimming pool."

"But how do you know the book ends that way? It could be that Gatsby fires back and kills the service-station owner instead."

"Not likely. I doubt that Jay Gatsby would carry a sidearm while swimming."

MacKenzie had to concede that point, but she was not surrendering quite yet. "Or maybe George Wilson ... despondent over Myrtle's death ... commits suicide before he has a chance to confront Gatsby. There are lots of ways this story could go, and Fitzgerald was an innovative writer. Don't trust Tinsel Town to be faithful to any author."

The two announcers were almost finished with their meals when MacKenzie posed the other question that both knew was sure to come. "What about your classical music listening?"

"I'm actually enjoying it," Jon said. "Whenever I'm sitting in my study, killing time on Twitter, I turn on Radio Swiss Classic and just let it play ... sometimes for a couple of hours or more." MacKenzie seemed happy to hear that, so Jon continued. "And my command of the German language is an added bonus because that's how I listen for the details of what's playing."

"What are some of your favorites?"

Jon curled his lips. "That's hard to say. Let me think." He tried to recall a few of the more monumental pieces of music from the past week or so. "Beethoven's *Egmont Overture* comes to mind because the finish is so ... electrifying." MacKenzie nodded her head. "And all four movements of Dvořák's *'New World' Symphony*." Jon stopped to think. "Then there's Piano Concerto No. 1 by Saint-Saëns. And Howard Hanson's *'Romantic' Symphony*. And a short piece called *Spring Song* by Sibelius. Off-hand, those are probably my favorites, so far."

"That's quite a list," MacKenzie said. "Consider me to be very impressed."

"But I still like the pop oldies as much as ever. That'll never change."

"Nor should it. There's nothing mutually exclusive about those two styles of music. Despite my seemingly snooty attitude, I'm a big fan of both. Lennon and McCartney were great composers ... as was John Barry in your world of the movies."

The rest of the afternoon dragged on at the radio station, with Jon glancing toward the clock from time to time, counting the minutes down to when he would have to leave for home. He wondered whether Nikki felt the same—and for roughly the same reasons.

A short visit with Ronnie Delaney was the only bright spot to enliven Jon's gloom, and even this ended on a downbeat. Their conversation occurred during the first few minutes of the 2:00 hour. Still on crutches, Ronnie encountered Jon in the hallway and informed him—literally in passing—that Abby Harker had sent him a text message that might be of interest.

Jon stopped in his tracks and turned around. "Hold on, Ronnie. Wait up."

Ronnie did so and tried to wipe the grin off his face.

"When did you get the text?" Jon asked.

"Just a few minutes ago."

"Did Abby mention me in it?"

"She did indeed." Ronnie started to move away until Jon grabbed him by the arm.

"Hey, let me see what she wrote. Abby and I talked for quite a while on the phone this morning, and I'm getting hooked all over again," Jon said. "It's not very healthy for my marriage." There was a look of desperation in his eyes.

Ronnie's smile was almost gleeful, as if his friend's quandary was ever so amusing. "I can see that it wouldn't bring you and Nikki closer together." He started to crutch away again, finding this all to be great fun. "I'll show it to you tomorrow."

Jon ran in front of him. "Now! Or, so help me ..."

"Hey, you've really got it bad, haven't you?" Ronnie began to laugh.

"Just let me see what she wrote about me. I'm not fooling around with you. If Abby wrote something about me, I have a right to see it."

That raised Ronnie's ire. "Actually, Jon, you don't have any right to see my text messages. Let's get that straight."

Jon nodded his head. "I'm sorry. I didn't mean that the way it sounded. I'm asking you, please let me see what she wrote about me ... just out of the goodness of your heart."

"That's better. Whatever's on my cellphone is strictly my property."

"Look. I said I'm sorry, and I meant it."

Ronnie's face softened. "All right ... no hard feelings. I'm just giving you a hard time. Anyway, I'm as hooked on Abby as you are ... maybe more so. I'm just a single guy on the prowl, and I think she can see that and appreciates it. Her feelings for you are more complex because of the legality involved."

Jon looked down at the floor. "Just so you know, I've never done anything illegal with Abby ... and probably never will. She's only a distant memory of my past, a high school heartthrob who came back to life. Can I help it if she's also a tease?"

"Speaking of Abby the Tease, I was almost tempted to show you her photos. But now I don't think I should. It wouldn't be fair to you, Jon-Boy. You wouldn't stand a chance."

"What about the text that you just got?"

"I didn't get a text from her. I just wanted to see how you'd react." He grinned at his friend. "Like I said before, you've really got it bad."

Jon could only shake his head in frustration. Now all he had to look forward to was an icy reception at home.

• • •

Monday began no more smoothly for Nikki Swenson. She realized that her squabble with Jon was at least half her fault. The way Nikki saw it, when Tony Zeigen balked at delivering her home from the airport, she had projected her defensive attitude onto Jon, who naturally reacted more forcefully than he otherwise would have. One comment led to another until they were not even speaking when bedtime arrived.

Although Nikki and Tony had done nothing they regretted in Atlanta—except perhaps for that brief kiss outside her hotel room following the Braves-Pirates game—both of them were extremely self-conscious throughout their first morning back at work. Tony went into Nikki's office shortly after 8:00 AM and staged a good act of nonchalance, but neither of them could be comfortable in the other's presence. Every discussion dealt entirely with banking matters, with no allowance for personal small talk.

By mid-morning, Nikki was determined to calm the waters between them, and she did so with an abrupt question—seemingly from out of the blue. "Remember the tomahawk chop that we did on Tuesday night?" Tony stopped walking and turned toward her. He had retrieved some paperwork from Nikki's delinquent-account files and was about to depart silently from her office.

Instead, he gave her a broad smile. "And we were pretty good at it, too, I must say. Everyone around us probably thought we were Braves fans from the Bobby Cox era."

That was all it took to set things straight. A chance meeting later in the morning was more relaxed yet, and the afternoon promised to return them to their normal workplace harmony.

"Care to have lunch together?" Nikki asked. "I don't think anyone would start gossiping about us if we were seen together in broad daylight. Eating at some fast-food joint is not like a secret rendezvous."

"I'd enjoy that very much, but today is out. Allison is meeting me at Fuddruckers for sort of a 'welcome home' meal. I certainly can't ask you to join us."

"No, that might be a little awkward." A grin crept across Nikki's face. "Maybe we can double date one of these days."

Tony squinted at her. "You've got to be kidding!"

"Yes. Of course I'm only kidding. I may be foolhardy at times, but I'm not stupid."

"Is Jon still mad at me for abandoning you at the airport?" Tony asked.

"I'm not sure, but probably. I haven't talked to him since last night."

"You're not on speaking terms?"

"Not as of this morning, when he left for work at five thirty."

"Sorry about that. *Mea culpa.*"

"He'll get over it. He always does ... and pretty quickly too."

For Tony, it was all downhill from there. Something he blurted to his wife at lunch rekindled Allison's well-developed sense of jealousy. The remark was innocent—at least Tony thought so—but his mere mention of "Nikki Swenson" caused Allison to probe more deeply.

"Did you two stay at the same hotel in Atlanta?" she asked.

"Yes ... a Holiday Inn Express near Hartsfield-Jackson Airport. We both loved those great cinnamon rolls for breakfast."

"So, you and Nikki ate breakfast together?"

"Sure. Why wouldn't we?"

"Just a matter of propriety, I suppose."

That observation seemed unjust, and it rankled Tony. "Please tell me why it would be improper for two business associates to eat breakfast together before their SRBC sessions. It was the most natural thing in the world."

"Maybe to you, yes, but not to others who are watching."

"My gosh! All we did was sit at a table and eat."

Allison frowned. "Do you think Nikki Swenson is pretty?"

"Not bad, but nothing special ... not up to your caliber."

"Oh, please! Don't try that on me. Flattery doesn't have much of an effect during an argument."

"Is that what we're having?"

"Can't you tell?"

"All I did was mention Nikki's name, and you grabbed me by the throat," Tony said. "I see her every day at the bank, and we're good friends. But there's nothing more to it than that."

Allison became quite subdued, her voice barely audible. "Did you and Nikki ever kiss?"

Tony turned bright red, and he had no choice but to lie. "Of course not. Like I said, we're just good friends."

"Then why are you blushing? You look very guilty."

"That's just because your line of questioning took me by surprise. I can't believe you would ask your own husband such a thing."

Allison studied Tony's face. "Maybe we should get together with the Swensons one of these weekends," she said. "We haven't socialized with them in a long time."

Tony shook his head. "It's probably not a good idea to mix business with pleasure. Nikki and I get along fine at work, but that doesn't mean I want to carry that over into our leisure hours."

"Like when you two were sightseeing in Atlanta?"

"Almost all of that trip was business ... and you know it."

"Do I? I'm not sure exactly what happened between you and Nikki Swenson. As I recall, she is rather attractive."

"Let's just drop it, shall we?" Tony said. "Even if something happened ... which it didn't ... I sure wouldn't confess my sins to you. What it all comes down to is that you don't seem to trust me anymore. What have I done to deserve this?"

"For one thing, you seem to pay more attention to this banking acquaintance than you do to me."

"During this past week, obviously yes. We were away at a regional conference."

"And you only called me once during that whole time away."

"I was busy. I'm responsible for every loan contract that our branch of GoldSpire issues."

"Even if Nikki writes it?"

Tony glared at her. "Yes, as a matter of fact. I'm ultimately responsible for everything that any of our loan officers do ... and that includes Nikki Swenson. I could lose my job if the loan department becomes a trainwreck. That's why this Southern Regional Banking Conference was so important ... to you and to me."

"Oh, I see. So, now I'm supposed to feel grateful that you and Nikki were able to enjoy a long weekend together."

That was going too far, and Tony brought their 'welcome home' meal to a bitter conclusion. "Have you finished eating?" he asked.

"Yes, thank you. Be sure to say hello to Nikki for me." Allison stood up and stomped away to the parking lot, where each of them had their respective cars. Tony paid the bill, wishing that he had taken his business associate to lunch instead of his wife. At least that would not have felt like he was running through a minefield.

A half-hour later, after Tony drove back to the bank, Nikki went into his office. "How'd it go?" she asked.

He was sitting at his desk, trying to act busy, but there were more urgent things on his mind than banking loans—how he could save his marriage, for instance. "Disastrous. You told me that you and Jon are not speaking ... and now it's the same for Allison and me."

"What went wrong?"

"For some reason, she suspects that there was hanky-panky between you and me in Atlanta."

Nikki's jaw dropped. "What could have made her think that? We didn't do anything physical ... unless you count that one innocent kiss."

"Unfortunately, that itsy-bitsy kiss probably makes me act guilty when I'm talking to Allison, and she figures that I'm trying to hide something that was more intimate."

Nikki gave that some thought. "Maybe you should confess that kiss and be done with it. At least you would be starting with a clean slate."

"You don't know Allison very well, do you? She would never forgive me for kissing someone other than her, and whatever trust we've had would be out the window."

"No, I don't know Allison very well, but certainly she wouldn't equate a single harmless kiss with spending the night together."

Tony shook his head. "That's where you're wrong. I really think they're roughly equal in her mind." He inhaled deeply and sighed. "What it boils down to is that I betrayed her trust, and that is an unforgivable sin."

"I can't believe that anyone would be so judgmental about one tiny mistake."

"But it wasn't a mistake, Nikki," Tony said. "I wanted very badly to kiss you ... and I still do."

Nikki could hardly believe her ears. She hesitated slightly before asking the Big Question. "Do you wish that more had happened between us in Atlanta?"

Tony raised his eyebrows. "To be honest with you ..." He stopped before it was too late. "I'll have to plead the Fifth Amendment on that ... in particular, its clause against self-incrimination."

Nikki pursed her lips, deep in thought. "I suppose that tells me what I should know, going forward."

Tony stared at her. "Sorry."

"Don't apologize." She glanced all around the office. "I sure do hope this conversation is not being recorded. We could both lose our jobs ... not to mention our marriages."

• • •

All too soon, it was time for Jon to leave from work. He had no idea what awaited him at home. Either Nikki would be cheerful and loquacious—her normal self—or she would be as welcoming as a rattlesnake and with just as much to say. Jon resolved to behave like nothing had ever happened to cause a riff between them. He had learned, from eighteen years in the marital trenches, that sometimes such denial was all that was needed to put their relationship back on an even keel. Jon had also discovered that he would know right where he stood within the first three seconds, give or take a second. There would be no prolonged wondering about it.

He switched off his truck's ignition, closed the overhead garage door, and marched stoically into the house. A wonderful fragrance greeted him there. It was fried potatoes, breaded, with sliced okra and onions, and already he knew that all was well.

"Hi, Sweetie," Nikki said. "Is it all right if we eat a little early tonight? Lauren has to babysit at five."

Jon switched into friendly mode, one of the two mental settings that he had prepared for this occasion. "Sure thing, Honey. At whose house?"

"The Kerns'. Tanya's little sister is only six years old, and Doug and Maria need to go to a memorial service and visitation."

"Oh, too bad. Anyone we know?" Jon kissed Nikki hello.

"No. I've never heard of her. She was ninety-three, though, so it was a nice long life."

How odd it was that even the biggest, most scathing argument could be so seamlessly forgotten with the passage of a little time. That is what nearly two decades of commitment had achieved, Jon deduced, and he thanked his lucky stars that life could now return to normal. What had they been quarreling about anyway? Something to do with Abby Harker, he was sure, and maybe even

Tony Zeigen too. Both subjects were hot buttons that should be avoided in the future, if at all possible. And, by extension, the cities of Los Angeles and Atlanta would also fall into that dicey category of topics that should never come up in discussion. That would not be easy to manage.

Jon went directly to the computer in his study to see if any emails had arrived since he last checked his inbox at the radio station. There was nothing of importance, so he hit the DELETE button for all six of them. He wondered whether Abby and Brent ever flew into fits of jealousy over each other. That seemed doubtful, for both Harkers enjoyed what Abby called "an open marriage," wherein most of the traditional ground rules were swept aside in favor of whatever transient gratification was handy.

Nikki was her old self at the dinner table that evening, even teasing Jon about his pronunciation of the word "err."

"Everyone I know pronounces it the same as 'error' ... that is, rhyming with 'hair'," she said.

"Maybe so, but what you hear from others doesn't alter the correct pronunciation. The verb spelled 'e-r-r' should be pronounced as 'UR' ... which rhymes with 'fur'."

Nikki leaned forward, one index finger in the air. "But it could be that both of them are right. Have you ever considered that possibility?"

"I'll give you that much ... grudgingly ... but I know for a fact that 'UR' is preferred."

"Well, you're the radio announcer, so I'll concede defeat ... grudgingly."

Lauren chose that moment to chime in with her own thoughts on the matter. "I've always heard that the verb 'e-r-r' should be pronounced like 'AIR-or', the same as when a baseball player flubs a grounder."

"Go ahead and say it like that," her father said, "and no one will think any less of you. But be aware that the official way to pronounce it is 'UR'." He put both hands onto the table, palms down. "I rest my case."

Quite often, the best part of patching up a smoldering conflict is the reconciliation period that follows, and that was most certainly the case when daughter Lauren Swenson was away at the Kern house, where she was babysitting Tanya's little sister, Frieda. Seldom were Jon and Nikki alone for an extended period of time these days, what with Lauren's homework and violin practice, so this felicitous confluence of events led to an evening of revitalized love that culminated in the bedroom. For the time being, all extraneous thoughts—those visions of Abby Harker and Tony Zeigen—were shunted to the background, where they surely belonged but refused to stay.

The problem was, Tony crossed paths with Nikki countless times every weekday, as a natural routine of his business, and Abby began emailing Jon almost daily, on whatever pretext she could devise at the moment. That left five spouses—Jon, Nikki, Abby, Tony, and Allison—vying with divided loyalties in the home. The sixth spouse of this triumvirate, filmmaker Brent Harker, was perfectly happy with maintaining the present state of affairs.

One interested observer who had no marital stake in the thorny proceedings was from a slightly later generation, twenty-five-year-old bachelor Ronnie Delaney. Abby Harker had caught his eye several weeks ago, when she was in town to make her husband jealous, and Ronnie was not able to rid his thoughts of this lovely creature. Abby, of course, was no help in that respect, for she persisted in teasing the young announcer with her specialties—titillating photographs and sensual innuendos. The poor boy had swallowed her fishing hook, and he was not shy about flaunting his weakness to anyone who would listen.

On Wednesday, during Jon's morning drive-time shift, Ronnie peeked into the control room to tell him something. "Hey, Jon-Boy, drop by during 'Behind the Hits.' That'll give me about eight minutes to show you what our California seductress sent to me overnight. I had trouble sleeping after I read it."

For some reason, puzzling even to himself, Jon was a bit chagrined to hear this. Why was it that Ronnie seemed to receive all of Abby's juiciest correspondence, while his own could be described as newsy and forthright? And yet, perhaps this was just as well, in view of how unsteady his marriage had become—from two opposite directions. Still, it was futile to pretend that Ronnie's preferred status did not chafe him, and Jon was not very anxious to see what latest communication had been received from their lively vixen on the West Coast.

The five-minute feature called "Behind the Hits" continued to be quite popular with Ronnie Delaney's audience. Each weekday morning in the 11:00 hour, he presented another recorded installment from the series, and his scrupulous research was much appreciated by oldies connoisseurs. Jon happened to be loitering in the hallway at 11:23 when he heard the intro for Wednesday's "Behind the Hits." He had promised to join Ronnie in the control room when the nostalgic package began to air, so he went directly inside. Ronnie motioned for him to sit down in a visitor's chair near the control board.

For this day, the subject matter on "Behind the Hits" was John Denver's "Leaving on a Jet Plane" from 1966. Denver wrote the song during a layover at Washington (D.C.) Airport and submitted it as a demo disc under the title of "Babe, I Hate to Go." It was his producer, Milt Okun, who convinced him to change the name to "Leaving on a Jet Plane," and that was how it was marketed on Denver's debut studio album for RCA, *Rhymes and Reasons*, in 1969. The single did not place highly on the charts, but a simultaneous RCA release by Denver's friends, Peter, Paul and Mary—who were also produced by Milt Okun—became the final major hit for that folk-pop trio. Presumably dissatisfied with his earlier versions of "Leaving on a Jet Plane," Denver re-recorded the song in 1973 for the compilation album *John Denver's Greatest Hits*.

While this information was being broadcast—followed, of course, by John Denver's three-and-a-half-minute song itself—Ronnie located his most recent text from California and showed it to Jon. Abby's message was rather short, by her standards, but very much to the point.

Hiya, Ronnie. I haven't written to you in a few days, and my hunger has been building all the while. Maybe yours is on the rise too. ☺ I modeled for a bra advertisement on Friday, and it was interesting to see how much care the photographer suddenly took in making things exactly right for the camera. He had me try on about a dozen undergarments while he made sure that the lighting was just right -- not to mention the fit. I enjoyed this shoot quite a lot, and I'm pretty sure he did too. Sorry I can't attach a photo from the session, but all images are copyrighted and not for distribution. I think you would have liked them!

Ronnie was gleeful as he watched Jon read the text. "Well, what do you think?"

Jon took a deep breath, and his eyes bulged. "Wow! She never sends me tangy stuff like that. What are you doing right?"

"Like I told you a long time ago, maybe she's a cougar."

"I don't think so," Jon said. "From what I can tell, any male from his late teens to middle fifties is fair game for her."

"How old is Brent?"

"I'm not sure, but I'd guess about forty-five." Jon winked. "Ages don't seem to mean very much to him either."

"But he's in showbiz ... so anything goes, and nobody even notices."

"Same with Abby then, I guess. You know, she's landed a couple of minor roles in B movies. Maybe she thinks that entitles her to become promiscuous."

Ronnie grinned. "As if she wasn't already."

• • •

On Friday of the following week, Abby was across town for yet another advertising gig, this one in Culver City. The photographer, whom Abby had not met before, was named Jenö Halász, and he was smitten at once by his new model. Jenö was born in the United States, but his parents were Hungarian refugees from the 1956 uprising. The instant that Jenö first laid eyes upon Abby Harker, he was at a loss for words and could not wipe the silly grin off his face. Fortunately for him, the product to be promoted was nothing more provocative than a thick-crust pizza cutter, and all his model had to do was hold the metallic device just so and smile at the camera.

Jenö Halász's wife of twenty-six years had died nineteen months earlier, after a lengthy struggle with emphysema. The couple had been heavy smokers until her diagnosis. Jenö immediately swore off cigarettes, but Gabrielle was unable to overcome her nicotine dependence and paid the ultimate price. Even now, Jenö's fingers continued to show the signs of his past addiction, and he was self-conscious of these ugly stains to the point of hiding his hands from Abby's view. (Alas, he had been an ambidextrous smoker!) Funny, he thought, but never before had he bothered to conceal his former cigarette habit from anyone. This woman was different from all the others.

About a half-hour into the photo shoot, Jenö had gotten the lighting and positioning precisely the way he wanted it, and he began to be more concerned with his model's appearance. "Are you married, Ms. Harker?" he asked.

Abby rolled her eyes. "Yes ... I suppose you could call it that."

"Excuse me for being so personal. It's just that you have a wedding ring on your left hand, and I wonder if the client will want that to be seen. You know, we need to target the broadest possible audience, and I'm ..."

Already, Abby had removed the ring and tucked it into her back pocket. "Done," she said.

"Thank you, Mrs. Harker. Yes, that's more appropriate for our purposes, I'm sure."

"No problem. I'm not particularly fond of it these days." She gave the photographer a coquettish grin. "And please call me 'Abby.' That 'Mrs. Harker' business sounds so old-fashioned and subservient."

"I meant no disrespect ... Abby. I like that better anyway. It's a pretty name."

"I see that you have a wedding ring on your left hand too," Abby said. "What is your wife's name?"

"Gabrielle ... but she passed away about a year and a half ago." Automatically, he tried to hide his stained fingers from view.

"Oh, I'm so sorry to hear that. I didn't know."

"Of course not. There was no way you could have known."

"How long were you and Gabrielle married?"

"For more than twenty-five years. We met at college ... Pepperdine University in Malibu." Jenö smiled. "I thought she was the most beautiful coed on campus."

"Do you have any kids?"

"Yes, a son and a daughter. Both of them are married and moved away ... one in each of the Carolinas. How about you?"

"I have a daughter by a previous marriage. She's a college student in Ohio." Abby glared at the table in front of her. "But there are absolutely no children in the Harker household. Brent was always much too busy with his film career to be tied down by anything as frivolous as fatherhood."

"Have you ever wanted to have more children?"

Abby was about to tell Jenö what he no doubt expected to hear, but then she decided to come clean and tell him the truth instead. "To be perfectly honest, no ... and I really can't blame that on my job because I never worked for a paycheck until recently." She sighed. "Actually, I was too selfish for motherhood. I didn't want any additional children to change the course of my life."

"Do you regret that now?"

"Not if the father would be Brent Harker. He would have made a lousy, negligent dad ... and his kids would have turned out just like him." Tears began to form in her eyes. "And, to be fair, I would have made a lousy, negligent mother."

Jenö stepped back from the set and its culinary props. "Maybe we should take a break. Is that all right with you?"

"Sorry." Abby wiped her eyes, smearing the liner and shadow, which made further makeup a necessity. She gave a shamefaced look. "Please excuse me."

Jenö shook his head. "Don't apologize for being human."

Abby stared with admiration at the forty-seven-year-old photographer, and she wondered why she felt so safe here, so protected from the brashness of modern life. Perhaps it was Jenö's old-world bearing or his *echt*-polite way of speaking. Now that she thought of it, he was also quite handsome in an urbane sort of way, with elegant, neatly cropped hair that was turning mostly gray—and all the better for it. In contrast, her husband's longish hair was coal black, although Abby suspected that he had colored it for years, probably to intermingle more easily with the younger crowd of starlet hopefuls.

Smeared makeup or not, this Abby Harker was perfectly delightful in Jenö Halász's eyes. Every suggestion that she had, every pose that she struck, every facial expression that she assumed was fine with him. Of course, he well knew that any consummate professional would distance himself from such idealized thoughts, but Jenö felt entirely helpless when she was standing just a few feet away. Then his mind drifted to Gabrielle. How she would laugh at his middle-aged antics, his schoolboy crush on somebody else's wife.

"Give me a smile, please" Jenö said. "That's it ... as pretty as a picture!" Abby did just as he requested, over and over again. Two hundred photographic images were captured by the time this session ended, even though only four or five would eventually qualify as "finalists" in the process of elimination. Jenö would present these few to the advertising agency, whose reps would then choose the winning entry.

Regardless of which image made the final cut, Jenö had a treasure trove that he would file under "Abby Harker Gallery" for occasional viewing on his own. Never would he forget this model who stole his heart—not only because of her classic beauty, but also because of her repressed sentimental side, which she herself did not even realize she had.

"If ever you're feeling lonely, I hope you'll give me a call, and we can talk," Jenö said.

This time Abby smiled directly at him, rather than at the camera lens, and Jenö accepted it like a warm embrace. She turned to leave but stopped. "Don't be surprised if I take you up on that offer. I'm pretty sure that Brent is planning to travel to another location set, and he's usually gone for a month or two. All I'm good for is making sure the dogs are fed."

Jenö's frown was equal parts of sadness and confusion. "I can't understand that. If I were your husband, I would never leave town. I would always be there for you."

"He's not completely at fault, Mr. Halász. I'm probably just as bad, in my own way. I'm pretty self-centered ... and spoiled."

"I don't believe that. By the way, please feel free to call me Jenö. I would like it very much."

"What nationality is that?"

"Hungarian ... although over there my name would be Halász Jenö, instead of the other way around."

"Well, thank you for everything ... Jenö. I've enjoyed this photo session and hope that I gave you what you needed."

"You have no idea." Now tears were gathering in his eyes as well. "Do me one favor, Abby. Telephone me if Brent goes away for this location shooting of his. No one like you should ever be left alone for such a long time."

She did not know quite what to say in response.

"Just think of me as someone you can talk to whenever you're lonely," Jenö said. "I'm lonely, too, now that Gabrielle is no longer here. You and I can support each other emotionally."

Abby nodded. "Okay, I promise ... just as good friends."

"Of course. That's all I meant."

She shook hands with him and turned to walk away.

"One other thing," Jenö said. "I think you are about the most beautiful girl ... inside and out ... that I have ever met in my life. I'll never forget today for as long as I live."

Hearing this profession of chaste love made Abby's face feel hot, which was an unusual sensation for her. She did not blush very often.

•   •   •

"Tennessee Williams wrote, in his memoirs, that he regarded the movie version ... directed by Jack Clayton ... to be superior to the novel." Jon spoke while seated across from MacKenzie Bastrop at a table in the radio station's staff lounge.

"Even so," MacKenzie said, "you'll never convince me that any movie could surpass the excellence of the written word. After all, that's probably why somebody wanted to make the movie to begin with ... because the novel was so good."

Jon had just finished reading *The Great Gatsby* by F. Scott Fitzgerald, and this discussion amounted to a book report for his teacher. "With due respect," he said, "in this particular case, I don't think you can make an informed comparison between the book and the film."

"Okay, you've got me there. I've never seen the Robert Redford movie. All I have to go on is my certitude that a film cannot possibly present as much worthy material as the original novel upon which it was based. Something valuable will be missing."

Jon shook his head. "Still, I maintain that a story's flow can actually be improved by tightening it."

"Possibly ... but I'm sure you'll agree that some screen adaptations are more successful than others."

And so it went, a typical exchange between Jon and MacKenzie during the final hours of a weekday morning. But then, at 11:13 AM, everything stopped. A familiar sound had begun coming from the staff lounge's four overhead speakers—the intro to that day's "Behind the Hits" episode. Nearly everyone at the station made it a daily habit to cease whatever they were doing and listen to the latest installment. As always, the program featured Ronnie Delaney as its producer, editor, and euphonious narrator.

"North to Alaska" was the final hit by country vocalist Johnny Horton. It was recorded in 1960 to be heard over the opening titles of *North to Alaska*, a film starring John Wayne and Stewart Grainger. Mike Phillips wrote the music and lyrics for this song, which tells the back story of the film's main characters—Sam McCord and brothers George Pratt and Billy Pratt—who travel north to Alaska to try their luck at striking it rich during the Nome gold rush of the 1890s. Tragically, singer Johnny Horton was killed in the early morning of November 5, 1960, just two days before the movie's release. The fatal collision occurred at the Little River Bridge on Highway 79 in Milano, Texas, when Horton's white Cadillac sedan was struck head-on by an out-of-control pickup truck. Horton, who was just thirty-five years old at the time, died on the way to a hospital, and his two band members were seriously injured but survived. The intoxicated driver of the truck, nineteen-year-old James Evans Davis, was later convicted of murder without malice and given a two-year probated sentence in a no-jury trial.

Shortly after "Behind the Hits" ended, Jon poked his head into the control room and gave Ronnie a thumbs-up sign to show his approval of the Johnny Horton episode. Ronnie waved for him to come inside. Jon did so but remained silent because Ronnie had two announcements to make, followed by his introduction to a double-play set of "Best of Both Worlds" by Lulu and "Tuesday Afternoon" by The Moody Blues.

When the songs began, Jon hit Ronnie with a piece of minutia. What did the legendary singers Johnny Horton and Hank Williams have in common? Ronnie could give no answer.

"Billie Jean Jones was married to them both."

"One at a time, I hope."

"Yep. Johnny Horton's second wife, singer Billie Jean Jones, was also the widow of Hank Williams."

"I'll try to remember that," Ronnie said. "You never know when her name might turn up on a trivia contest."

"Billie Jean Jones was nineteen when she married Hank Williams," Jon said, "and Williams died two and a half months later. Nine months after that, she married Johnny Horton, whose wife she remained for seven years before he was killed." Jon removed the chewing gum from his mouth and swished it, free-throw style, into the waste basket. "I just thought you might enjoy hearing that useless factoid."

"Thanks. Trivia can't get too useless for me." Ronnie glanced at the play list, noting that he still had over five minutes before his next announcement. "Hey, Jon-Boy, have you heard from Abby Harker recently?" That, of course, was the enamored announcer's usual topic of conversation.

"Not for a few days. Why?"

"I usually get at least one text from her every day, but I haven't received anything since last Friday ... and that was six days ago."

"I got an email from her over the weekend, but it didn't amount to anything special," Jon said. "I wouldn't worry about Abby too much. She's busy with her modeling, so she says."

Ronnie was not so sure. "Just the same, I'm going to write to her tonight, to make sure she's all right. I don't trust that Los Angeles area. Anything could happen out there."

"She's a big girl. She can take care of herself."

"And I also don't trust that husband of hers. Brent doesn't seem to take their wedding vows very seriously, to say the least."

"Obviously not," Jon said, "but Abby doesn't wear a halo and wings either. Who knows what she might have done with me if I didn't tap the brakes?"

"When you were in California?"

Jon nodded his head.

"Do you wish you'd seen how far she would go?" Ronnie asked.

"Part of me does, yes."

Ronnie laughed. "Which part?"

The Moody Blues' song had begun, so Jon figured it was time to let the announcer get back to work. "I'll contact her, too, and tomorrow we can compare notes on what she says to us ... if anything."

Jon's tiny cubicle was the quietest spot for him to make commercial sales calls on the radio station's landline. Although both of his attempts that day were to no avail, at least he made a solid effort, and the rest of the time would be his own. That was a good thing, too, because laboriously composing text messages on his cellphone—as he attempted to do now—seemed to take him forever. Despite his best efforts, ever since the turn of the century, he had never quite mastered the two-thumb method of typing.

> Hi, Abby.
> I have not heard from you in nearly a week, so I am anxious to know if everything is all right with you. Hopefully, you have just been very busy with your modeling/acting career, leaving you no time for correspondence. All is well here, and I am trying to come up with an innovative idea for my next screenplay, which I think will be a psychological drama (a là "The Twilight Zone"). Oh, before I forget to ask, have you ever visited the Music Box steps in the Silver Lake District? They were used in the Laurel and Hardy short "The Music Box" from 1932. I did not see them while I was in SoCal recently, but I intend to do so the next time I'm there. Maybe you can be my tour guide and show these 133 steps to me, one at a time! The GPS address is 923 Vendome Street, Los Angeles, California.
> Love, Jon

What emboldened him to sign the text "Love, Jon" was his fond recollection of an email that Abby had sent to him long ago. She ended it "Love, Abby," and that show of affection warmed his heart. But did he dare to do the same in a message to her? The physical act of typing of "Love, Jon" was easy, but actually dispatching these words to Abby would require all of his fortitude. Jon delayed for almost a half-hour before ultimately touching the SEND arrow. Instantly, the message became irretrievable, and he could only trust that this chancy move would be placed in the proper perspective.

When his cellphone *dinged* about twenty minutes later, Jon naturally wondered whether it might be Abby texting him a reply. But no, the message came from Nikki, who simply wanted to inform him that she would be working late at the office.

> Hi, J.
> Just a quick note to tell you that all seven of our loan officers will be having a refresher course tonight. It should only last about an hour, according to Tony, but I wanted to let you know that we'll be eating a little late. I have already told L about this, so she's planning to not get home until around five.
> Luv, N

A text response from Abby finally came while the Swensons were seated at the dinner table. Jon did not hear the notification alert because his cellphone was lying far out of earshot, next to the computer in his study. And certainly that was just as well, for he did not wish to open the new message in front of Nikki— especially when its sender was a beautiful tease by the name of Abby Harker.

•　•　•

Routines at the radio station were distinctly relaxed on Fridays, when the concept of TGIF pervaded the minds of everyone on the payroll after four straight days of work. This phenomenon was already noticeable to Jon Swenson at 8:00 AM. He saw it in the bright smiles and bouncy steps of most employees, as they walked past the control room's soundproof window on the way to their offices. Several nodded or waved to him, and that was not always the case at this early hour, which many considered to be the last vestige of daybreak. Even Ronnie Delaney, who was still on crutches, displayed an extra spring in his step.

Jon was anxious to show Ronnie what Abby Harker texted to him in response to his own message, and he also wondered if his fellow announcer had received anything from her. Although he was married, Jon saw nothing immoral in continuing to correspond with his former high school classmate, especially since he had so dramatically proven his willpower in dismissing every blatant advance. To his way of thinking, he had earned the privilege to playfully dally with this infatuation—and Abby's unrivaled good looks never failed to make it fun.

Ronnie hobbled directly to the control room instead of stopping at the recording studio. This was a detour that he rarely took, for his first order of business was nearly always to complete the editing process for that day's edition of "Behind the Hits." When Jon's microphone was no longer on, Ronnie pushed open the control-room door and entered with a broad smile. "Well, what's your story?" he asked.

Jon smiled back. "Only that Abby's her normal self again." What about yours?"

Both announcers would have to agree that it was remarkable how one woman could manage to keep two men securely hooked from a distance of fourteen hundred miles. If nothing else, this vividly demonstrated the flirty cleverness that she had at her disposal. Was this a natural instinct or something she learned as a young teenager and then perfected into a science as the years went by? Whatever the case, Abby Harker certainly had "it."

"See what follows 'Behind the Hits' today," Ronnie said. "We can exchange our messages then ... because I don't want to wait until after my whole shift." That day's list of titles, which Jon brought up on the computer screen, showed a double-play set at 11:21 that would last six minutes. When added to BTH and the featured song itself, that should be plenty of time for both announcers to satisfy their curiosities.

As usual, MacKenzie Bastrop was waiting for Jon in the staff lounge at 10:00 AM. By now, she expected his daily visits, for they had become as punctual as clockwork. And yet, MacKenzie always managed to affect a slight surprise when Jon sat down across from her. The very last thing she wanted was for him to feel taken for granted. She had no spare friends to lose.

What really did surprise MacKenzie was Jon's list of books that he planned to read. His newly minted system was to tackle works of literature that spawned some favorite movies he had seen. "You claimed that novels would always be superior to their filmed versions," he said, "so this will be a good chance to see if your theory is correct."

To Jon's amazement, MacKenzie actually seemed supportive of his book list, even though only a handful of the writings could truly be described as classic. "This seems like an interesting approach. Reading any novel will be better than mindlessly watching a movie. At least your efforts will be active rather than passive."

The computer-printed list that Jon showed to her was neatly arranged in two columns, covering a wide assortment of cinematic genres. But one thing remained consistent throughout. In keeping with his own personality, all fifteen of these works of fiction pre-dated the twentieth-first century.

MOVIE TITLE	BOOK TITLE (AUTHOR)
A Clockwork Orange	A Clockwork Orange (Anthony Burgess)
Paper Moon	Addie Pray (Joe David Brown)
An Angel for May	An Angel for May (Melvin Burgess)
Somewhere in Time	Bid Time Return (Richard Matheson)
Enter Laughing	Enter Laughing (Carl Reiner)
Fahrenheit 451	Fahrenheit 451 (Ray Bradbury)
Gone With the Wind	Gone With the Wind (Margaret Mitchell)
Land Girls	Land Girls (Angela Huth)
Lonesome Dove	Lonesome Dove (Larry McMurtry)
Summer of '42	Summer of '42 (Herman Raucher)
Summer of My German Soldier	Summer of My German Soldier (Bette Greene)

The Chisholms	The Chisholms (Evan Hunter)
The Last Picture Show	The Last Picture Show (Larry McMurtry)
Village of the Damned	The Midwich Cuckoos (John Wyndham)
Whistle Down the Wind	Whistle Down the Wind (Mary Hayley Bell)

"I'll probably start with *Gone With the Wind*," Jon said, "because it's the longest ... even longer than *Lonesome Dove*."

"That's a good place to begin. You'll love it ... very witty and historically accurate."

"What are you reading now ... still *Anna Karenina*?"

"Yes. I'm only about two thirds of the way through it, so I still have a pretty hefty chunk to go."

An hour later, Jon waited in the hallway until he heard the intro to "Behind the Hits." This familiar jingle alerted him that it was safe to enter the control room. Ronnie Delaney grinned and motioned for Jon to sit in the folding chair.

Friday's edition of "Behind the Hits" chronicled the story of "Happy Together" by The Turtles. This pop song was written by two members of a New York band called The Magicians—drummer Alan Gordon and vocalist Garry Bonner. They produced a primitive-sounding demo and offered the song to such groups as The Happenings, The Vogues, and The Tokens. No one expressed any interest until a moderately successful California band, The Turtles, thought they heard something marketable in the rudimentary tune. The Turtles devoted some eight months to expanding and perfecting their arrangement before venturing into the Sunset Sound Studio in Hollywood during the first few days of 1967. "Happy Together" was released by White Whale Records later that same month, and it shot to the very top of the American charts, replacing The Beatles' "Penny Lane" at number one. The song features a brilliant vocal by Howard Kaylan and strong guitar work and backing vocals by another founding member of the group, Mark Volman. So popular was "Happy Together" that The Turtles were invited to perform it nationally on "The Smothers Brothers Comedy Hour" in February and then on "The Ed Sullivan Show" in May.

Following BTH and its highlighted song, a double play commenced: "Eres tu" by the Spanish vocal group, Modedades, and then film composer John Barry's "Born Free," as sung by English vocalist Matt Monro.

During this long span of time when a live announcer was not needed at the microphone, Ronnie Delaney and Jon Swenson were able to allow each other to read, in full, the text messages that Abby Harker had sent to them the day before.

> Hi, Ronnie.
> Thanks for your text. I've been unbelievably busy for the past three weeks, but I'm sure not complaining about it. My modeling career seems to have taken off, both fully clothed and otherwise. Don't get too excited -- all I mean is swimsuits or underwear. I have not jumped into the X-rated stuff quite yet. ☺ Sorry to say that my husband, Brent, has run off again, this time to play around with a couple of topless showgirls in Las Vegas. Arr-Tee Studios is shooting a movie there, and Brent insists that the film editor is needed on set. Not so, of course, and he is fooling nobody. Please continue to write to me as often as possible, and I'll try to do the same to you.
> Love, Abby.
>
> Hello, Jon.
> I have finally found a few minutes to text you after receiving your nice message earlier today. No acting gigs to report, but I am becoming a fairly successful model on the L.A. scene. It seems that my name is spreading among some of the top photographers in the apparel, travel, and cooking lines of commercial advertising. There is a chance that I may be flying to the

Greek Isles for a photo shoot to promote some international hotel there. I'll be playing the "role" of a wealthy wife (no relation to Meredith) who accompanies her husband to the world's most glamorous resorts. That is ironic because I can't seem to maintain my own marriage. Yes, Brent has flown the coop again -- this time to Las Vegas, where Arr-Tee Studios is shooting a movie. Actually, of course, he's only there to chase after a couple of showgirls who see him as their own personal ATM. Please send me a text or email whenever you can!

Love, Abby

Ronnie shook his head. "I don't understand that husband of hers. He's going to lose her for good if he doesn't straighten up."

"Brent doesn't know when he's well off," Jon said. "I could sense that when I saw them together. He treats her like the hired help."

The song by Matt Monro was in its final minute, so Ronnie swiveled his seat toward the microphone. "I can tell you one thing for sure. If I lived with Abby, my eyes wouldn't be wandering. They'd be locked on her."

Jon turned to leave the control room. "In my opinion, one big problem is that they're both heavy drinkers, and that doesn't help the relationship any." He stopped walking long enough to add a final thought. "Come to think of it, Brent is probably the reason Abby feels the need to drink so much. She's not a very happy person."

•   •   •

Tony Zeigen had just purchased a new pickup truck, a silver Nissan Frontier, and he was anxious to show it off for his business colleague, Nikki Swenson. He had already done so for his wife, Allison, who gave the vehicle her blessing but told Tony that she was unwilling to drive it. "I can't see behind me well enough to back up without hitting something," she said. "That flatbed ... or whatever they call it ... throws off my judgment about how much space I have."

The lunch hour would be a perfect time for Tony to give Nikki a ride across town. He always enjoyed treating her to a meal whenever their schedules coincided–amounting to five or six times in the past four months–and this Wednesday was shaping up to be another occasion that might work.

"Let me take you to lunch today," he told Nikki. "I want to get your opinion on my new truck."

"How long have you had it?"

"I bought it on Monday, and it's got exactly forty-six miles on the odometer."

Nikki consulted the schedule on her cellphone. "I guess lunch would be okay. My next appointment isn't until two."

"Then it's a date. How about Fazoli's or Taco Cabana?"

"We just had Mexican food last night."

"So ... Fazoli's?"

"Sounds fine. What time?"

Tony glanced at his wristwatch. "I'll come by at a quarter to twelve, so maybe we can beat the crowd."

They finished eating their Italian food at 12:40, which left them more than an hour before Nikki's next client would arrive to sign some loan papers. "Are you in a hurry to get back?" she asked.

"Not really. Two o'clock will be fine. I have to show Lupe Álvarez how to handle a defaulted contract, but she'll be available all afternoon."

There was a protracted silence, as neither quite knew what to suggest. Finally, Nikki gave voice to her thoughts. "Want to drop by the house for a while? We've got a ready-to-eat pie in the freezer ... coconut cream."

"Say no more! I can't resist any kind of cream pie. It's one of my weak points."

"One of them?" Nikki smiled. "What are the others?"

"That's for you to find out." They both laughed at his giddy remark, but there was a definite tension in the air.

Nikki was well aware that inviting Tony Zeigen home with her would lead to disastrous consequences if either Jon or Lauren happened to leave early from work or school. Sure, Nikki could explain that they were just killing an hour before returning to their bank duties, but who would believe that story when told by someone who looked so guilty? She did not possess a convincing poker face.

Dessert was indeed waiting for them in the freezer. Nikki removed the coconut cream pie and placed two generous slices onto paper plates. "Coffee?" she asked.

Tony winked. "Of course. That's the only proper way to eat a piece of pie."

"You take it black, don't you?"

"Bingo! How did you know?"

"I remember our meeting, when you brought those chocolate doughnuts."

Whatever furtive deeds might have happened between Nikki and Tony after dessert were quashed beyond recovery when the doorbell rang at 1:20. They looked at each other with alarm, for getting caught alone together would be difficult to justify.

"Maybe it's just the UPS man," Nikki said. "Sometimes they ring the bell." She began walking toward the front door.

Tony managed to chuckle at the situation. "Should I go hide under your bed? That's what secret lovers do in the movies."

Nikki turned around with a grin. "Is that how you picture yourself?"

"Nope. My love today is strictly for coconut cream pie," Tony said. He stepped back, out of sight.

What Nikki Swenson encountered on the front porch was so startling to her that she nearly fainted. Standing alongside a large piece of luggage was a very pretty woman who closely resembled someone she had met in California—Jon's former high school classmate.

"Hello, Nikki," the woman said.

Nikki was at a loss for words, so she decided to play it safe by acting befuddled. "Hello, miss. May I help you?"

The stranger smiled. "Don't you recognize me?"

"No. I don't think so."

That fib appeared to hurt the visitor's self-esteem. "I'm Abby ... Abby Harker."

Nikki pretended to study the face, as if trying to retrieve it from her memory. "Oh, yes. I remember now. Hello, Mrs. Harker."

This was the wrong choice of greeting, which Abby let her know in forceful terms. "Just call me Abby," she said. "Or, if you insist on using an antiquated title, I'll settle for 'Miss Pierce'."

"Sorry ... Abby." Aware that it would be inexcusable to leave a visitor standing on the front porch, Nikki proceeded to do the only acceptable thing. She asked her to come inside.

"Thank you very much." Abby wheeled her luggage into the entryway and noticed a tall, rather nice-looking man peeking around the corner from the living room. "So, Jon's not here, I take it."

"No, he's not home yet," Nikki said. Embarrassed, she motioned toward the man. "This is a co-worker from the bank where I'm employed. His name is Tony Zeigen."

Tony walked forward, using his innate bashfulness to hide whatever guilt he may have felt.

Abby smiled up at him with mirth in her eyes. "Hello, Tony." He was instantly under her spell, powerless to do anything but smile back.

Nikki stepped between them. "I'm curious about one thing, Abby. How did you know somebody was home? There's usually no one around at this hour."

"I saw a truck in the driveway, and I knew this was Jon's house. I've been here before, you know."

Suddenly, it dawned on Nikki that this was the same mysterious visitor who left a copy of her husband's screenplay on the front porch and then sped away in a shiny blue sports car. No wonder Jon seemed so elusive about who delivered the package. It was almost as if he were leading a double life, with this California girlfriend on the side.

"I'm sorry, Abby, but I can't offer to let you stay with us," Nikki said. "Tony and I need to return to the bank right away, and there won't be anyone here to make sure you're comfortable. I certainly don't mean to show a lack of hospitality."

"Oh, no, of course not. Actually, I already have a hotel room booked. I'll be going over there after check-in time at three."

Nikki was relieved to hear that. Hosting Jon's heartthrob would be out of the question, like inviting a fox to stay overnight in the henhouse. "Pardon me for asking, but why have you come here in the middle of the afternoon, when you know very well that both of us work? That seems a little odd."

The remark caused Abby to scowl. "What's so odd about it? I wanted to see Jon as soon as possible ... about something very important. I wasn't sure what time he got off work, and I thought that might be his truck parked in the driveway."

Sensing trouble between the two women, Tony tried to defuse the conversation. "That's my new truck ... just two days old. Do you like it?"

Abby ignored the question and continued to frown at Nikki. "What time do you expect your husband to be here?"

"Probably not until four thirty. Why?"

"I need to talk with him, that's all. I can either do it here or in my hotel room, whichever he prefers."

Nikki gave a cynical laugh. "I'm sure he'd prefer the hotel."

"Okay, fine. I'll call him at the radio station and invite him over. It won't take long ... maybe an hour." Abby thought for a moment and giggled. "Then I'll give him back to you in the same condition that I found him ... unmolested."

"Do you want to call him from here?" Nikki asked. "He'll recognize our landline number better than your cellphone."

"No, thanks. I've phoned him before at the station ... to his direct line ... and he's always answered when he saw my last name."

Now the scowl belonged to Nikki. "You must feel very special about that." She expected no response and received none.

"Well, nice to meet you, Tony," Abby said. She turned to leave. "And it was so good to see you again, Nikki."

"Oh, sure. Same here."

•   •   •

Shortly after 3:30, when Jon's landline extension showed an incoming call from HARKER, BRENT, he threw aside his sales list as if it were a venomous snake. "Hi, Abby ... or is this really Meredith, impersonating you?"

"It's the actual me. The 'Meredith' campaign was just for six ads, and they're all in the can."

"How are things in Cali these days? Still getting some gigs?"

"My career is going fine," Abby said, "but I can't say the same about my marriage."

"So I gathered from your text message."

"That's why I'm here. I need your help ... or at least your advice."

There was a pause on the line. "What do you mean ... 'here'?"

"I'm calling from the La Quinta ... out by your airport."

Suddenly, Jon felt out of breath, and he could hardly speak. "You're here in town again?"

"That's what I've been trying to tell you."

"Does Brent know you're here?"

"Who?" Abby said. "I don't know anyone by that name."

"So, it's that bad, huh?"

"It's that bad."

"Sorry to hear it. But I can't say that I'm very surprised ... not after reading your latest text."

"Listen, Jon. Can you come to my hotel?" she asked. "I need for someone to be my sounding board ... and you're the only person I can trust."

"There's no one close to you in L. A.?"

"Why else do you think I'd fly halfway across the country to see you?"

"I'm honored that you feel that way about me ... but couldn't we have just talked over the phone and saved you hundreds of dollars?"

"My current mental state won't allow a cheap compromise," she said. "I need human contact, so please say you'll discuss this with me in person."

Not knowing what Abby had in mind, Jon was doubtful that this visit was a good idea. But she sounded desperate for peer support, and that counted for something. "I'll have to make up an excuse for Nikki. She wouldn't be amused that I'm seeing a California model in her hotel room."

"She already knows," Abby said. "I dropped by your house this afternoon."

Jon wondered how that could possibly be. "What time was it?"

"About one thirty or so."

"And Nikki was at home?"

"Yes. We chatted for a few minutes, and then I left."

"Was she ... alone?" Jon asked.

"Let's talk about that when you get here ... room 322. And bring up a couple of free coffees from the lobby."

Nikki's hotel room was on the third floor of a four-story facility. Jon was holding two cups of hot coffee in the hallway, so he gently kicked at the base of her door to let Abby know he was there. For such intimate friends, their greeting seemed rather formal and stilted. The cups had lids, so he and Abby could easily have kissed each other hello with no spillage. Instead, with an almost businesslike tone of voice, she simply invited him to come inside and have a seat. As Jon passed near the window, he noticed a panorama of modern aviation, with airline flights arriving and departing every few seconds. This magical sight always fascinated him, but he realized that his former classmate was terribly upset about something, so he cut the viewing short.

Coffee cup in hand, Abby sat at the writing desk, her chair turned toward the middle of the room. Jon seated himself about fifteen feet away, on one of the double beds, using the end table as a coffee stand. From where he was positioned, he could not see that an opened book lay on the desk behind her.

"Before we start, I need to answer your question about Nikki," Abby said. "You wondered if she was alone when I dropped by today."

"That did cross my mind."

"I'd by lying if my answer was yes. There was a rather tall man with her, but I don't think any hanky-panky was going on." She winked. "Anyway, they were both fully dressed."

"Did he have a mustache?"

"Yes, and it looked very nice on him."

"That sounds like Tony Zeigen. Did Nikki say who it was?"

"Probably so, but I'm not very good at remembering names. She said they worked together at the bank."

"Yep, that's Tony." Jon had a worried look on his face, but he saved that particular burden for later.

Preliminaries complete, Abby took a sip of coffee and launched straightway into her story. "I'm sorry to show up unannounced in town and spring this on you, but I can't delay any longer before making some monumental decisions."

She looked at Jon for a response, but he said nothing and only motioned for her to continue.

"As you know, my husband of twelve years ... whom we shall call Brent, in lieu of some ugly pejorative ... has dropped out of my life once again. This time, to his credit, he is hiding nothing from me. He admits that he's just tired of marriage and would rather chase after a couple of Vegas showgirls for the time being. He estimates that their ages are eighteen and twenty, but that's beside the point. Brent never has worried much about statistics."

Jon smiled at her wit but then shook his head. "He must be nuts to leave you."

"Even adding their ages together, those girls are younger than I am," Abby said.

Jon recalled something that Abby had mentioned to him at Darnell High School's Silver Jubilee Reunion. "How old is your daughter ... the one you had with your first husband?"

"Tamara is twenty, so I guess she was eight when Brent and I got married. He helped me raise her part-time, but of course he was usually away from home. Tammy's real father, Rickie, died when she was three."

"Where is Tamara now?"

Abby's face brightened. "She's a college girl, studying Theater at Oberlin."

"I'll bet she's beautiful."

"I think she is ... and so do her professors. They believe she has a real future on the stage."

"I'll keep an eye out for her," Jon said.

"She prefers to be known as 'Tamara Hutchins'."

"How come?"

"That was her birth name, and she's decided to go back to it. I'm not sure why."

Something occurred to Jon that he had never thought about before. "What did you do to earn a living for all these years ... until you started modeling?"

"I shopped."

"Nothing else?"

"That's about it. Brent didn't want me to get a job, and he was making plenty of money to support us both."

"Didn't you get bored with it all?"

Abby grinned. "Absolutely not. I was a born shopper ... and never tired of it." She drank another mouthful of coffee, which by now was the perfect temperature to swallow. "But enough of my past. The reason I wanted to see you is about my future. I'm at a fork in the road, and I can't afford to make a wrong turn. When Brent jumped overboard this time ... for good ... I became depressed, almost to the point of doing away with myself."

Jon leveled an accusing finger at her. "Don't even think about that. You've got everything to live for. Most girls would give their right arms to be you."

"Hah! And they'd be bitterly disappointed with what they got in the bargain. I try to put up a happy front, but I'm usually miserable inside."

"Even now ... with your modeling and acting career?"

"Especially now." She bit her lower lip, but only for an instant. "You know, I've always had those dreams and aspirations to look forward to in reserve, but now I realize there's nothing more out there for me to fall back on. It sounds trite to say, but the only thing that really matters in life is ... relationships." In spite of herself, she giggled at the hackneyed expression. "Cue the Mantovani violins."

Jon felt like leaping to his feet. "Hey, I didn't know anyone else under seventy had heard of Annunzio Mantovani. That's amazing!"

"My parents had dozens of his records," Abby said. "My two sisters and I grew up on a steady diet of Mantovani and His Orchestra. I still enjoy his recordings ... though of course they're on CD."

"I didn't see them in your collection."

"No. I keep my 'old fogey' CDs in a shoebox ... but I listen to them more often than I care to admit." She chuckled. "I can't stand today's hits, which don't even sound like music to me."

Jon nodded in agreement but then, after sipping his coffee, noted that their conversation had drifted. "Sorry for throwing you off track. I always seem to be doing that to you."

"No problem," Abby said. She gave a deep sigh, her face becoming deadly serious again. "As I mentioned earlier, I've reached a fork in the road, and a wrong turn will probably destroy me."

Jon put down his cup and looked her directly in the eye. "Are you going to call it quits with Brent?"

"Too late for that tiny source of satisfaction. He's already left me."

"Legally?"

"Not yet, but that's in the works ... from his end."

"He must be nuts to leave you," Jon repeated.

Abby cleared her throat, as if about to declaim something very significant, but first she paused to think it over. "I've met somebody who is very special to me," she finally said. "He's not involved in the film industry, but he does work on the outskirts of show business ... as a commercial photographer. He hardly even knows I exist. We did one brief photo shoot together, and every single word he said to me rang a bell inside my conscience." Her eyes were watering. "The whole time I was with him, I felt ... I don't know ... so clean!" She wiped the tears from her cheeks. "Isn't that a silly thing to say? It sounds so sickening sweet, but it's really true." She could go no further.

Jon waited. "What's this photographer's name?" he asked.

"Jenö Halász." The name rolled off Abby's tongue, indicating that she had pronounced it aloud to herself many times over—perhaps to preserve it in her memory.

"That's very foreign sounding to my ear," Jon said. "Where is he from?"

"He's American, but his parents were born in Hungary."

Jon hesitated for a moment, dreading the next answer. "Is he married?"

"He's a widower. His wife died a year and a half ago ... of emphysema."

"Did they have any kids?"

"A son and a daughter, but both of them are grown and moved away." Abby looked down at the floor. "Jenö seems to be a very lonely man. I feel sorry for him, but he would be crushed to hear me say that. He takes great personal pride in himself and his profession."

Although Jon knew exactly what kind of reception awaited him at home—his wife, with daggers in her eyes—there was no escaping the fact that it was time to go. Nikki always kept him on a tight leash, but her profound love for him was never in doubt. "Where do you think all of this is leading?" Jon asked.

Abby laid her empty coffee cup on the desk. Then she leaned forward to articulate her deepest concerns. "Here's what it boils down to." She paused for the right words. "Do you think I should take the initiative to contact Jenö Halász again ... even though we no longer have any professional affiliation? He might consider it to be awfully cheeky to push myself on him."

"Maybe not. Does he seem interested in you?"

Abby laughed out loud. "He nearly fell all over himself during the whole shoot. It seemed like he pictured me as an angel from heaven."

Jon grinned. "And how did that make you feel?"

"Like the Queen of Sheba, to tell you the truth. It's been a long time since anyone worshiped me like that."

"What are your options ... if any?"

"Assuming that Brent files for divorce, and the court grants it ... a slam dunk in California ... I would become a free agent, so to speak. Then, if I could establish a personal connection with Jenö ... and he would have me, despite my checkered past ... I would consider becoming his wife. That would be my third husband, I'm ashamed to say."

"Who's counting? Just so you've ultimately found the perfect person to spend the rest of your life with. Don't take this wrong, but I feel positive that God has a plan for you, if you'll accept it."

Slowly and thoughtfully, Abby nodded her head. "For the first time ever, I do feel that God is leading me." Then, with the back of her hand, she wiped away a tear. "I can't begin to tell you how much I appreciate your encouragement."

Jon rose to his feet, about to leave, but Abby felt compelled to add one further thing. Gesturing for him to wait, she stood up and reached behind her for a book that lay on the desk.

"Do you know what this is?" she asked.

Jon shrugged his shoulders. "It looks like a Gideon Bible."

"It's open to a passage that Jenö recited to me before I left his photography studio. He felt a little embarrassed, I think ... afraid that I would brand him as a screwball or some sort of religious kook ... but I told him not to worry. 'Just promise to give it some thought,' he told me. 'We may never see each other again after today's shoot, but this strange story from the Old Testament might help get you through your present difficulties.'

That took me by surprise because I never came right out and told him about my marital problems ... let alone my drinking binges. But I guess they were apparent to him."

Abby stopped talking and pointed to the passage that Jenö had urged her to decipher for him. The Bible was a King James Version, and 2 Kings 6:6b presented a single baffling sentence: "And he cut down a stick, and cast it in thither; and the iron did swim." Jon read it silently to himself, but the passage was incomprehensible to him—at least when removed from the proper context.

Still, just as Abby had promised Jenö several days ago, so did Jon now promise Abby. Both would try to unlock the mystery— even if it required the assistance of multiple translations and Biblical commentaries.

• • •

Early the next morning, Jon telephoned La Quinta's airport location and asked to speak with guest Abby Harker. The desk clerk reported that Ms. Harker had already checked out from room 322. Alarmed by this disturbing news, Jon called Abby's direct cellphone number, but there was no answer, nor did leaving a message after the *beep* bring any response. For all he knew, she was flying west at 35,000 feet with her phone switched to airplane mode.

Jon felt terrible about not giving Abby a decent farewell, especially since she had traveled halfway across the country to consult with him in person. There was nothing to do but wait until he could talk with her again, whether still in town or far away in California. Even Nikki empathized with his frustration and could not understand why "Mrs. Harker" would disappear so abruptly, without revealing her whereabouts to anyone.

"She seemed a little unstable, if you ask me," Nikki said. "Was she always like that, even way back in high school?"

"I didn't know her in high school, but she certainly seems stable enough to me. There's just a lot on her plate right now." He thought of something and grinned, hoping that some levity might be in order. "Wouldn't you be acting a little deranged if I ran off with a couple of Vegas showgirls?"

"That's hard to say, Honey, because I can't even imagine such an unlikely scenario."

"Don't be so sure. Twenty-somethings really go for men with a little gray at the temples."

Nikki smiled at him. "Mmm. So do forty-somethings."

Jon was pleased to see that matters on the home front had returned to normal. So, this would be a bad time to bring up the issue of Tony Zeigen and why he was at home with Nikki when Abby paid her improvised visit. Jon reasoned that his wife—if she and Tony were indeed attracted to one another—surely would not choose her very own home to take such a foolish chance. That is one site that would never appear on their list of suitable places to tryst.

Not much time elapsed before Jon again gazed upon some words from Abby Harker. On Friday morning, as he was in the midst of shaving, his cellphone indicated that a text message from her had arrived. The bathroom door was closed to their bedroom, so Nikki could not have heard the *ding*. Procrastinating was out of the question in this case, so Jon immediately tapped on the link and viewed Abby's latest message.

> Hello, Jon.
> I cannot adequately express to you how much I appreciate your sage advice about the crucial decisions I needed to make. As you could tell in the hotel room, I was very conflicted about what direction my future needed to go. Only one thing was certain: Brent has dropped out of the picture entirely. He does not want me, and the feeling is mutual. I have become sick and tired of his jumping into bed with whichever

nubile female hops down his bunny trail. But here is my biggest news. With Jenö Halász's counsel, I have committed my soul to Jesus Christ! I am now a Child of God, and the Holy Spirit dwells within me. This just goes to show that nobody (including yours truly, with all my shameful past) is beyond redemption. By the way, have you solved that passage from the Book of Second Kings yet? Jenö helped me, or I never could have done it. Please continue to write to me as often as you can.

Love, Abby

Jon was elated as he finished his shave. Although he himself was a born-again Christian, as was Nikki, neither of them was strong enough in the faith to publicly express their beliefs to others. And yet, here was Abby, a brand-new believer, willing and eager to proclaim the Good News to others. Had that photographer come into her life by accident? Jon was certain that no one could ever convince Abby of that.

At the Swenson household, there was an inviolable rule that Jon would not awaken Nikki before he left for work. This meant that Ronnie Delaney figured to be the second person who would lay eyes upon Abby's life-changing text message. Jon was not at all sure how Ronnie would react to what he read. Although several years Ronnie's senior, lovely Abby Harker was his ultimate dream girl, and no one his own age could hold a candle to her. Beyond Abby's physical appeal, perhaps it was her abundance of streetwise experience that captured Ronnie's devotion—to the exclusion of the many other attractive females in his diverse circle of friends and lovers. For him, Abby stood alone at the top.

When Ronnie came walking by the control-room window shortly before 8:00 AM, he waved at Jon Swenson, but Jon did not respond in kind because he was in the process of reading a live, thirty-second commercial and could not be distracted from the copy. As was his usual practice these days, Ronnie went directly to the recording studio to sharpen the production on that morning's edition of "Behind the Hits." He had a standing reservation in the studio, each weekday morning from 8:00 until 9:00, and he could not afford to squander that invaluable hour.

The Friday installment of BTH was "Abraham, Martin and John" by Dion, a recording on the Laurie label that was released in August of 1968. The song's writer was Dick Holler, who two years earlier had scored a major hit with his novelty tune "Snoopy vs. the Red Baron," as performed by The Royal Guardsmen. "Abraham, Martin and John" was entirely different, a poignant tribute to four assassinated Americans—Abraham Lincoln, Martin Luther King, Jr., John F. Kennedy, and Robert Kennedy. In late 1968, the song peaked at number four on the Hot 100 chart and was awarded a gold record by the Record Industry Association of America (RIAA) for selling a million copies. Singer Dion DiMucci had gained early fame in the 1950s as lead singer of Dion and the Belmonts. Then, with "Runaround Sue" in 1961, he won big as a solo artist. In the 1980s, he recorded several Christian albums and even won a Dove Award in 1984. But Dion continues to be best known for his memorable "Abraham, Martin and John," which in 2001 would be ranked at number 248 (of 365) on the RIAA's prestigious Songs of the Century list. Dion DiMucci was inducted into the Rock and Roll Hall of Fame in 1989.

After "Behind the Hits" began airing at 11:33 AM, Jon Swenson entered the control room and allowed Ronnie to read the latest message from Abby Harker. He expected Ronnie to gloss over her profession of faith, and that is precisely what he did. Probably disappointed that his carnal image of Abby as a "wild child" was dashed by her own words, he nonetheless restrained himself from outright criticism of her sincere beliefs. All he would say is, "She's going to look mighty pretty in Christian movies."

In the days to come, Abby wrote several times to Ronnie Delaney—both in text messages and emails—and she never failed to sign them "Love, Abby." Ronnie accepted them with his enthusiasm of old, but never again did he view himself as a realistic contender for her charms. Now Abby became the unattainable ideal—much too beautiful to be true.

• • •

Even in the freewheeling state of California, it takes a considerable amount of time for a divorce action to wind its way through the court system. Brent Franklin Harker filed his intent for divorce and submitted the required fee of $450. Then the court served papers on his spouse, Abigail Renée Pierce Harker, and the six-month waiting period commenced. Just happy to be free again, Brent remained courteous throughout the process, agreeing to divide the Harker holdings into two equal parts, except that David Wark Griffith and Cecil Blount DeMille—legal names of the miniature schnauzers—both became the exclusive property of Abby.

Brent's presence at the filming site in Las Vegas lasted for two months, during which Abby lived in the California house that they once shared. Brent rented an apartment in Los Feliz for the balance of the waiting period, though he spent much of it in Colorado and Louisiana, on the location sets of Arr-Tee Studios. According to provisions of the court, he would be granted possession of the house when the six months ended, with fifty percent of the current market value being paid to Abby.

So it was that legal proceedings occupied the passage of a half-year's time. Then, one month thereafter, Jon and Nikki Swenson received in the mail an invitation to attend the wedding ceremony in Culver City of Abby Pierce and Jenö Halász. It goes without saying that Jon would move mountains to be there, but Nikki's attitude toward Abby was more ambivalent. There was a certain amount of natural jealousy to overcome, for it was no secret to anyone that Jon had always been—and no doubt continued to be—badly smitten by the pretty Californian.

Jon hesitated for a moment but then posed the question. "Can you get off work?"

"I'm not sure," Nikki said. "When exactly is the wedding?"

"Two weeks from Saturday."

"First I'll need to check with Tony Zeigen because that's right in the teeth of our busy season."

Hearing her co-worker's name caused Jon to cast a suspicious eye, even though there was no hard evidence that Nikki and Tony were anything but good friends and banking colleagues.

"Could you run that by him tomorrow?" Jon asked.

"I'll try ... but sometimes I don't even see him for most of the day."

"Well, please try."

Nikki glared. "I said I would try, didn't I?"

Jon noticed that his wife would always become testy whenever the subject of Tony Zeigen reared its ugly head. Could that be the outer manifestation of a guilty conscience?

"We would need to be gone for three days," Jon said, "from Friday through Sunday. Even though both people have been married before ... Abby twice ... this will be a church wedding because that is what Jenö demands. He is very adamant about it."

Nikki curled her lips. "What kind of name is 'Jenö' anyway? I've never heard that before."

"Evidently, it's a common name in eastern Europe. Abby tells me that it means 'Eugene' in Hungarian."

"Why doesn't he just go by 'Gene'?"

Jon grinned. "I'm sure it's good business for any photographer to use a foreign-sounding name ... very sophisticated, you know."

"Hmm, that's probably true." Nikki quickly pondered the immediate future, and a practical concern sprang to mind. "Where would Lauren stay while we're in California? She can't be left alone here for three whole days."

"Can't she stay with the Lippmanns? She and Valery could practice their music together, and Walter's wife ..."

"Jessica."

"... Jessica has invited her over several times."

The trip west was simply meant to be—or at least that is how it seemed. All of the plans fell right into place, including the purchase of two airline tickets on relatively short notice. Jon would drive Lauren over to the Lippmann house on Thursday night, so he and Nikki could make an early departure to Los Angeles International Airport in the morning.

Chief Loan Officer Tony Zeigen was very understandable about his colleague's absence, even going so far as to cover for her at GoldSpire's tri-state meeting. Meanwhile, Allison Zeigen had brought to a screeching halt her husband's mid-life dalliance. Never again did he go so far as to brush against Nikki's hand, let alone venture a brotherly kiss on the cheek or a goodbye kiss on the lips. Their working relationship suffered not at all in the wake, but Tony grumbled to himself that the days had become unbearably long.

Passing through the TSA screening went smoothly, as did the Friday flight to Los Angeles, and Nikki even overcame her visceral fear of a window seat. LAX offered numerous car-rental agencies, but this convenience came at a price. Jon bit the bullet and used his credit card to pay for three days of transportation. Their hotel of choice, the Courtyard Los Angeles Westside by Marriott, was a very nice facility and just a four-mile drive from the airport. But that seemed much simpler than it really was, for the snarling L. A. traffic lived up to its ghastly reputation.

After finally checking in to the hotel, the Swensons took the elevator up to room 809 and unpacked their belongings, which included formalwear for Saturday night's nuptials. But the first event would take place in the morning, when they and other guests would be hosted by the imminent bride and groom at a 10:30 brunch. Jon could hardly wait to see the happy couple, but Nikki was less than thrilled at the prospect.

"Give Abby a chance," Jon said. "I think she's changed quite a bit since you saw her in California."

"That remains to be seen. I didn't care for her then, and my opinion of her probably hasn't improved any."

This was Jon's opportunity to catch her off-guard. "How about when Abby visited you at our house?"

"What do you mean ... at our house?" As always, Nikki's poker face was ineffective and almost instantly deserted her.

"That afternoon when you and Tony Zeigen were there by yourselves until Abby spoiled the party."

Nikki shook her head, but it was clear that Jon had the goods on her. "We were just killing time before my meeting. There was no funny business between us, I can assure you of that."

"I guess I'll just have to take your word for it."

"That's right, you will," Nikki said. She tried to turn the tables on him. "Listen, Jon, I think we've been married long enough for you to trust me with other men."

"Even the good-looking ones ... like Tony?"

"Of course. Tony and I are just co-workers who happen to also be friends. And what's wrong with that? I'll bet you have some women friends at the radio station."

"Sure, but none that I've taken home with me when no one else was around."

Nikki's face turned red. "Oh, please! Don't give me that holier-than-thou routine. You've had plenty of close contact with Abby Harker, and you can't deny it." She thought for a moment before proceeding. "Maybe not in a physical sense ... but who knows?"

This was not an argument that Jon could win with much integrity, so he backed off, marveling at how fluently Nikki had reversed the field from defense to offense. "Let's just try to be civil tomorrow ... with each other and, most of all, with Abby on the day of her wedding. Can we at least do that?"

Nikki calmed down and even managed a weak smile. "Okay, I promise. I'll be the very epitome of sisterly love."

•　•　•

Saturday morning's brunch drew a crowd of nearly three hundred to the Los Angeles hotel's sumptuous dining room, and they were about evenly divided in support of the two honorees. The vast majority hailed from southern California, of course, but a good number attended from out of state, including a group of theatrical types—denizens of the Broadway scene—who had come all the way from the East Coast. These may have been acquaintances of Jenö, for he held ancillary connections to show business, or perhaps they had been friends of both Harkers before the divorce.

Abby Pierce and Jenö Halász were seated alongside various members of their families. This was far across the room from where Jon and Nikki were randomly placed, which made it inexpedient for the Swensons to meet Jenö and offer best wishes to the future couple. Even from such a distance, Jon could see that Abby looked radiant in her glittering, royal blue gown. As he recalled from the Darnell High School reunion, this was her favorite color, and it suited her lovely eyes to perfection. Now that he thought about it, this was probably the very same dress that he had seen several months earlier. No wonder she chose to wear such a stunning outfit again on this auspicious occasion.

"We'll go say hello to them after we finish eating," Jon said. "There are lots of people here who know Abby much better than I do ... forty percent of them, I'd wager."

"Did that friend of yours from the radio station show up?" Nikki asked. She poured syrup over her French toast.

"Ronnie Delaney? No. He told me that he wants to remember Abby as a 'wild child' ... not as a 'matron caught in the undertow.' That's how he put it." Jon grinned, staring at the table of honor. "She sure doesn't look like a matron to me."

Nikki shrugged her shoulders. "Some lucky people just never seem to grow old. I envy someone like that ... who's pretty enough to be in the movies and hardly needs any makeup at all. And then there are the rest of us, fighting a daily, losing battle against the calendar."

"You still look great to me," Jon said.

She squeezed his arm. "What you need is a good optometrist."

Jon chuckled at the comment and turned his attention to the ham-and-cheese omelet.

Nikki, though, was still entranced by Abby, and there was a dreamy, faraway look in her eyes. "Honestly," she said, "I wonder how she does it. I'd give anything to be that beautiful."

Jon began skating on thin ice. "I happen to know that Abby maintains her muscle tone by working out three times a week at a gym. Her good looks are not just by accident." He gambled that his wife would accept this explanation with the proper, clinical attitude, and fortunately she did so.

"But what about her face?" Nikki asked. "That sure didn't come from any weight machines at a gymnasium."

"Just what you'd call fortuitous heredity, I suppose."

Thirty-five minutes into the brunch, Abby and Jenö ascended a slightly raised platform and switched on the microphone that rested atop the stand in front of them. "Ladies and gentlemen, thank you very much for being with us this morning," Jenö said, "and for helping to make this such a wonderful day for Abby and me. We invite you all to be with us again tonight, as we join our lives together in marriage." He smiled at his wife-to-be. "Abby?"

Abby stepped forward to the microphone, lowering it to accommodate her five-foot-six height, and spoke in a charming voice. "Yes, both Jenö and I hope you'll plan to be with us in the church's sanctuary this evening at seven o'clock. We look forward to talking with each and every one of you at the reception, which will follow right after our wedding ceremony. Please excuse us now, as we go next door for a photo opportunity." She giggled. "This is one picture session that Jenö can enjoy from the lens side of the camera instead of the viewfinder." The crowd joined her in laughter. "God bless you all, and we'll see you again tonight."

A warm round of applause concluded the pair's remarks, and then a half-dozen smiling ushers escorted Abby and Jenö through the throng of well-wishers to an open doorway. There was absolutely no chance for Jon and Nikki to so much as wave to Abby before she departed from the dining room. And so, their sole opportunity to talk with the new couple would be at the wedding reception.

The church, quite modern and yet majestic, was located on a busy boulevard in the Los Angeles suburb of Culver City. People began arriving for the Halász-Pierce wedding at 5:00 PM, and the commodious parking lot appeared to be fully occupied by 6:15. Those driving up later than that had no alternative but to use the unpaved vacant lot that stood at the extreme rear.

Abby was exquisite in her aqua-green gown. Even though she had worn white for neither of her two civil weddings—and thus might be justified in doing so now in a church setting—she again chose to evade this sensitive issue by opting for a more neutral color. This time around, there were no wedding parties for bride or groom, so Abby and Jenö shared the altar with only a rather youthful Baptist preacher. The ceremony itself was simple but eloquent, abounding in Christian doctrine—this, despite the fact that Abby had been married twice before, and one of her ex-husbands was still very much alive. She was not the least bit apologetic, for Abby was a recently converted believer whose faith outweighed any petty concerns about what some gossipmonger might say.

Jon recognized several pieces among the musical selections that were heard. Besides "Amazing Grace," there were Bach's "Jesu, Joy of Man's Desiring," "Pie Jesu" from Fauré's *Requiem*, and Pachelbel's ubiquitous *Canon in D major*. It crossed Jon's mind that listening to Radio Swiss Classic, as advocated by MacKenzie Bastrop, was already paying dividends after just a few short weeks. He was not sure who chose the wedding celebration's music, but chances were strong that Jenö was responsible. People of eastern European stock, especially those with an artistic bent, were just naturally predisposed toward music history and literature.

Jon and Nikki sat in a pew on the bride's side of the church, a scant three rows from the front, so this gave them a good view of the ceremony. However, because the sanctuary's five hundred celebrants all vacated together toward its rear exit, the Swensons' favorable vantage point relegated them to the tail end of the single-file line that led to the reception. This was shaping up to be a long wait to greet the newlyweds, and Jon realized that it could very well be the last time he would ever see his former high school classmate.

Their place in line proceeded ever so slowly forward. Never did movement actually stop for more than a minute or so, but neither did it ever accelerate beyond what a lethargic sloth might consider to be optimum speed. The queue wound its circuitous way out of the sanctuary, across a corridor, through an anteroom, and then finally into the side entrance of the fellowship hall. On the opposite side of this hall was the receiving line, at the head of which stood Jenö and Abby Halász, as well as members of their immediate families.

No doubt Abby was exhausted by the time Jon came within shouting distance of her and Jenö. How much bubbly small talk could one person manage with a steady stream of unknown, hardly known, or conveniently forgotten acquaintances? Even among the blood relatives, statistically half were probably from her new husband's side of the genealogical tree. Abby stole a glance at Jon and smiled, but as invariably happened, the people in front of the Swensons were perhaps the most voluble chatterboxes in all the line.

At last, it was time for Jon and Nikki to step forward and try to come up with something original to say to the betrothed couple. But before even a single word could leave Jon's mouth, Abby raised herself on tiptoes and kissed him on the cheek. Blushing, he turned to Nikki, who did not appear to have noticed.

"Best wishes to both of you," he finally said. So much for originality.

"Thank you for traveling so far to help us celebrate, Jon. That means the world to me." She squeezed his hand and turned. "You, too, Nikki." This was clearly an afterthought, but Nikki accepted it with good grace. She well knew that a receiving line was the very worst place to think on one's feet.

"Congratulations, Abby," Nikki said. "I'm sure you two will be very happy."

Abby gave the briefest of smiles, a product of overused facial muscles. "Jon and Nikki Swenson, I would like to introduce to you my husband, Jenö Halász."

Jenö extended his right hand and clicked heels in European fashion. "I'm so very pleased to meet you." Without question, he was unduly formal with strangers, but at least he did not insult them, as some people might, by promptly looking away.

"Is your daughter here?" Jon asked Abby. He scanned the remaining faces in line but saw no one who fit the description.

Abby's sad expression made him regret the question. "Tamara was unable to come," she said.

"Oh, that's a shame. I was very much looking forward to meeting her."

"We had an argument," was all Abby would say, except to add, "It's a long story."

Jon felt timid about monopolizing the newly married couple for any longer than his allotted time, so he gently nudged Nikki forward. But Abby would have none of that, and she persisted in gazing directly at him. "When does your plane leave for home?"

"Four thirty. We both have to work on Monday morning, and that was the earliest flight we could get."

"Come see us in Jenö's photo studio at ten," Abby said, "and please bring Nikki with you."

The invitation took Jon by surprise, but he was flooded with delight. "Okay, but where is it?"

"I'll send you a text in the morning." Then, tired muscles or not, Abby flashed him a glowing smile. "We'll be quite busy tonight, you know."

• • •

A text message *dinged* for Jon's attention after he was back in the hotel room and had switched his cellphone from SILENT to RING mode. He was surprised to see that this new communication came from the radio station's midday announcer.

> Hey, Jon-Boy!
> I never did have a chance to answer Abby's RSVP request, so please give her my regrets and explain that I was tied up here with my announcing shift and recording "Behind the Hits." Also, my cast doesn't come off for another three days, and the leg room on planes is skimpy. As before, Irv Koslov sat in for you yesterday. I haven't heard any complaints, so he must have done all right. Does Abby's new husband seem to be a better match for her than Brent Harker? That brainless film editor didn't appreciate what he had in her, so I say good riddance to him. Do me a favor and give Abby a big, wet kiss -- and tell her it was from me!
> See ya Monday.
> RBD

Most of Ronnie Delaney's text was rhetorical in substance, so Jon did not bother to send a reply. Besides, Monday morning was plenty soon for Jon to describe the Halász-Pierce marriage ceremony and—all Ronnie really wanted to know anyway—how gorgeous the bride was in her wedding gown.

Jenö Halász's place of business had no curb appeal whatsoever—just an orange-on-black sign proclaiming THE HALÁSZ PHOTOGRAPHIC STUDIO atop a fifty-foot-wide leased property within a strip mall. Available parking spaces were plentiful on a Sunday morning, so Jon edged the rental vehicle forward to a concrete car stop that was not even three long strides away from the glass entrance door. In the next slot over was a very respectable Mercedes-Benz, which presumably belonged to Jenö.

Inasmuch as the front door was locked, Jon knocked on it, very politely at first but then with more insistence when there was no response. It was Abby who finally came to the front, keys in hand. Her lovely smile could be seen through the glass, and the first words she spoke were, "Hi, Jon. A little ahead of time, you obedient boy!"

Jon retorted with a quip of his own. "I know when it's dangerous to ignore strict orders."

"And hello to you, Nikki," Abby said. Her smile remained as before, which put Jon's wife at ease and caused her to prefer, even such an early stage, this "new" Abby to the one who had gone by the surname of Harker.

Right after Abby invited the Swensons into the building, photographer Jenö Halász came in from a room at the rear. Like Abby, he appeared to be younger than his years. Jenö's bearing, as at the reception, was excessively formal for this occasion, but he soon relaxed enough to begin calling the visitors by their first names. "Thank you so much for coming to our wedding last night," he said, "and from such a long distance. That was beyond the call of duty." His gaze went from Jon to Nikki and back, indicating that both of them were included in the expression of gratitude.

When preliminary greetings had run their course, Jenö suggested that everyone follow him to what he called the "prep room," which is where he routinely interviewed prospective models and also readied his contracted subjects for their photo shoots. Its elegant *fin de siècle* furniture included four padded armchairs surrounding an ornately carved giltwood table, upon which lay some movie fan magazines and a stack of large-format photography books.

Abby took the lead, as she invariably did in groups with mixed company. "Jon," she said, "I want to tell you, right up front, that I think God brought you and me together at the DHS reunion. I made a fool of myself in front of everybody ... drinking enough to float the *Queen Mary* ... and you, being a gallant rescuer, dragged me away from becoming the laughing stock of our whole senior class."

Caught flat-footed by this acclaim, Jon glanced at Nikki, who nodded her support. "Colby Reed helped at least as much as I did," he said. "Probably a whole lot more."

"But you stayed in contact with me from then on, and I never heard from Colby again. With my former husband away for months at a time, you filled a crucial void in my life. I was so lonesome and depressed. It's very possible that you saved my life."

"I'm just glad I could help," Jon said, "but I don't know what I did that was so magnanimous. To be perfectly honest, my interest in you was anything but angelic." He glanced again at Nikki, fearing what she must think of him. "It was more like a schoolboy crush. I thought you were one of the most beautiful girls I had ever seen ... prettier than most movie stars."

Abby, being Abby, was narcissistic enough to accept the compliment without protest. In fact, she luxuriated in it, while at the same time making a halfhearted attempt to feign humility.

At this point in the conversation, Abby's new husband took control, and it quickly became evident that he was not as meek and unassuming as first impressions might have suggested. "My wife's outward beauty is obvious to everyone, and I wholeheartedly agree," he said. "But what most people don't know about her is that Abby is even more beautiful on the inside. I could sense that with my very first sight of her ..." Jenö motioned toward the adjacent room. "... right there in my photo studio." Pensive by nature, he paused to stroke his chin. "Abby and I had much in common, of course. I was a widower, and her marriage was as good as dead. She was lonely for trustworthy male companionship, and I dearly missed my Gabrielle."

Abby gave a polite cough, and all eyes turned her way. Jon could not help smiling at how deftly she retook the stage, but Abby was, after all, a part-time actress. "Those things that Jenö mentioned were definitely parallels in our lives," she said, "but they alone could never have brought us together. I think it was God's will that Jenö should lead me to Jesus Christ."

Abby's husband countered with a touch of modesty. "My amateurish sermonizing was nothing new," he said. "I always make it a rule to speak about my Savior with everyone who comes into this studio. Most people brush it off as the ramblings of an eccentric, and I don't force my beliefs on any of them. But others, including a few internationally famous models, have been very receptive to the Word. There are lots of devout Christians in Hollywood ... and even the film industry has more than its fair share, though most of these folks are afraid to go public with their religious or political convictions. There exists an unstated blacklist in America today ... but it's an almost exact antithesis of what we had in the early 1950s."

"The colleges are full of it too," Abby said. "As of last week, my own daughter won't speak to me anymore. When I invited her to the wedding and told her about my salvation, we had a huge quarrel over the phone. Before she hung up, Tamara labeled me a 'Christian conservative' and refused to come. It makes me wonder what she's being taught up there in Ohio. Or maybe she just figures that a leftist attitude will expedite her career."

"Unfortunately, she's probably right," Jenö said.

For the first time, Nikki joined the discussion. "What are your plans for the future, Abby? Will you continue with your modeling and acting?"

"Oh, yes! More than ever before. Jenö wants to use me in several advertising campaigns, and I've hired an agent for whatever film and television work is out there ... plus the few odd chances for appearing in local theater. I'm under no illusion that producers will be breaking the door down for someone in her lower forties, but I hope to have a few good years left before I'm labeled by casting directors as 'grandmother type'."

Jenö shook his head. "She looks more like 'beach bunny type' to me."

All four of them laughed, and it was plain to see that Abby was pleased to hear her husband's flattery.

Jon peeked at his wristwatch, but that did not go unnoticed. "By the way," Jenö asked him, "have you solved that riddle from Second Kings?"

"Maybe so," Jon said. "Anyway, I've located some explanations in a couple of commentaries. Does that count?"

"Sure it does, and I applaud you for being so conscientious. Most people just give it one shot and give up."

It occurred to Jenö that Jon's wife did not have the faintest idea what they were talking about, so he provided her with the basics. "There's a baffling passage from the sixth chapter of Second Kings that reads like this in the King James Version: 'And he cut down a stick, and cast it in thither; and the iron did swim.' Any ideas?" He giggled at Nikki, who could only gaze at him with bewilderment.

"Here, let me take a stab at it," Jon said. "From what I can gather, the sons of the prophets had borrowed some axes to chop down nearby trees for building a new place to live. But the iron head on one of the loaned axes slipped off and fell to the bottom of the Jordan River. When this man who was using it told Elisha what had happened, Elisha ... the man of God ... asked him to indicate precisely where the axe head had disappeared into the water. Elisha then cut a stick of wood and tossed it upon the river at that same spot. Immediately, the iron head floated up to the surface, and the axe was restored."

"So, what does it all mean?" Jenö asked. He grinned, reasonably certain that Jon had invested the necessary research.

"Well, first of all, I'm no theologian."

"That's fine. Just trust in the Holy Spirit for wisdom."

Jon forged ahead. "The most amazing thing about this passage ... to me anyway ... is that it was written almost six hundred years before the birth of Christ. And yet, it still makes reference to the Crucifixion."

"Correct."

"As best I can tell, the wooden stick that Elisha cast upon the Jordan River represents the Cross of Calvary, and the floating iron is a graphic illustration of the miracle that occurs when eternal salvation is secured through a belief in Jesus Christ."

"Precisely," Jenö said. "This is just one of many Old Testament prophecies that foretell the coming of Christ." He glanced at the two women. "To my way of thinking ... strictly that of a layman ... these are vivid confirmations of the Bible's inerrancy."

Jon nodded at the Halász couple and slowly began rising to his feet. "We really should be going. Nikki and I haven't repacked yet ... and my guess is that our plane won't wait for us to show up at the gate."

The others stood, too, and Jenö shook Jon's hand. "Many thanks to both of you for being here. Fourteen hundred miles is a long way to travel. Please do keep in touch."

"Yes, please do," Abby said.

"Where are you going on your honeymoon?" Nikki asked. "Or is that a state secret?"

Abby put a finger to her lips. "Shhh, don't tell anyone until at least Tuesday ... but we'll soon be basking in the sun at Waikiki."

"Nice!" Jon said.

Jenö agreed. "She'll put her bikinis to good use, and I won't be complaining one little bit." He winked at his wife, who beamed with pride. Photogenic models and actresses are like that.

As the Swensons were departing from the prep room to return up front, Abby took Jon by the arm and spoke to him in a soft voice. "Come with me for just a minute. There's something I want to give you."

Jon motioned for Nikki to go on ahead, "I'll be right there, Honey. Talk with Jenö for a few seconds."

When the door between the entry room and the prep room clicked shut, Abby placed both of her hands on Jon's cheeks and kissed him on the lips. He could see that her eyes were watery. "Jonathan Swenson, I will never forget you," she said.

Surprised at this show of emotion, Jon felt his own eyes beginning to moisten. "I'll never forget you either. One of the best decisions I ever made was to attend that Darnell High reunion."

Abby smiled through her tears. "Here, you'd better take this." She handed him one of Jenö's studio brochures. "Nikki heard me say I wanted to give you something. I really meant our goodbye kiss, but she doesn't have to know that."

Jon grinned at her. "Better that she doesn't." He flipped through the colorful publication, which, at sixteen pages, was the size of a small booklet. "Are you in any of these pictures?"

"Not yet, but I have a feeling that Jenö plans to design a new edition after we get back to the mainland."

"I'd say that's very likely."

The couples said their goodbyes just outside the building. Then, through the rental car's windshield, Jon concentrated hard to capture the last glimpse of his high school heartthrob. He did not know whether he would ever view her again in person. Jon's mind took him back to that night, many months ago, when Abby arrived at his hotel room—hair piled high, dressed in a sparkly blue gown, and giving him no choice but to escort her to the Silver Jubilee Dance.

Although Jon Swenson's nostalgic side would always recall Abby Pierce as the prettiest girl in his graduating class, she was now a transformed person, much more joyful and fulfilled, firmly committed to a marital relationship that was free from the human bondages of verbal abuse, loneliness, and depression. Above all else—and despite everything that life threw at her—Abby had become a Child of God.

Later that day, Jon and Nikki flew home to their daughter, Lauren, who immediately informed them that the internet was on the blink again, the refrigerator was making a funny noise, there was a large wasps' nest above the back door, and the neighbor's dog was running wild after digging a hole under their fence.

"Let me out of here!" Jon said. "I wonder if Abby and Jenö would mind if we joined them in Honolulu."

Nikki punched him gently on the arm. "Sorry, but no beach bunny for you. And wipe that innocent look off your face."

Lauren could only shake her head. "I have no idea what you two are even talking about."

"Just as well," Jon said. He hugged Nikki and gave her a big kiss. "Anyway, we're still on an extended honeymoon of our own, right?"

Nikki chuckled at him. "Close enough."

• • •

In the morning, life returned to normal at the radio station, but with one very noticeable difference. Announcer Ronnie Delaney had lost all interest in Abby, whom he once regarded as his ultimate dreamgirl. No longer was she the principal topic in his daily chats with Jon. That honor now devolved either to the Swedish pop group ABBA, the discographic legacies of The Beatles and The Beach Boys, reruns of vintage television shows like "Seinfeld" and "The Twilight Zone," or—closest to Ronnie's heart—the brainstorming of future "Behind the Hits" episodes.

Another colleague at work, fellow announcer MacKenzie Bastrop, pressed forward in her quest to scale the pinnacles of classic literature. After mastering Tolstoy's *Anna Karenina*, she plunged directly into *Middlemarch*, a sprawling portrait of Victorian provincial society by George Eliot (Mary Ann Evans). Content in her own skin, MacKenzie held no desire to prime Sunny Shade for promotion to a larger broadcasting market.

Only twice would Jon Swenson ever again hear from the former Abby Pierce. The first time was almost exactly a year after the wedding, when he and Nikki received a birth announcement from Mr. and Mrs. Jenö Halász of Culver City, California. An eight-pound, six-ounce boy had been born to the couple, who were naming their infant son Eugene Jonathan Halász.

The second time was about six months later, when the Swensons received a family portrait from the Jenö Halász Photographic Studio. The copyrighted 8x10 color glossy print showed baby Gene between his beaming parents at the child's christening, inside the same church sanctuary where Jenö and Abby were pronounced husband and wife.

To Jon's eyes, Abby looked every bit as beautiful as before— still the homecoming queen of Darnell High School. However many years might pass by, that is how he would always see her.